A CONVERSATION ON THE QUAI VOLTAIRE

LEE LANGLEY

A Conversation on the Quai Voltaire

Chatto & Windus

LONDON

Published by Chatto & Windus 2006

2 4 6 8 10 9 7 5 3

Copyright © Lee Langley 2006

Lee Langley has asserted her right under the Copyright, Designs
and Patents Act 1988 to be identified as the author of this work

First published in Great Britain in 2006 by
Chatto & Windus
Random House, 20 Vauxhall Bridge Road,
London SW1V 2SA

Random House Australia (Pty) Limited
20 Alfred Street, Milsons Point, Sydney,
New South Wales 2061, Australia

Random House New Zealand Limited
18 Poland Road, Glenfield,
Auckland 10, New Zealand

Random House (Pty) Limited
Isle of Houghton, Corner of Boundary Road & Carse O'Gowrie,
Houghton 2198, South Africa

Random House Publishers India Private Limited
301 World Trade Tower, Hotel Intercontinental Grand Complex,
Barakhamba Lane, New Delhi 110 001, India

The Random House Group Limited Reg. No. 954009
www.randomhouse.co.uk

A CIP catalogue record for this book
is available from the British Library

ISBN 9780701179120 (from January 2007)
ISBN 0701179120

Papers used by Random House are natural,
recyclable products made from wood grown in sustainable forests;
the manufacturing processes conform to the environmental
regulations of the country of origin

Printed and bound in Great Britain by
Mackays of Chatham plc, Chatham, Kent.

Contents

In Memory of
Colin McEvedy

A Conversation on the
Quai Voltaire

In his memory, places claim their own colours. Paris was red, the red of revolution and of blood, though it had been silver once, a glitter compounded of frosted brocade, the blades of ceremonial swords, bright buttons and decorations on uniformed chests.

The palaces of St Petersburg were washed in faded yellow; he saw Naples as coral and jet and the deep lapis blue of the bay. Sicily was the pale stone of a ruined Greek temple, the grey of duck shit melting in puddles.

Egypt had brought him a new palette: a panorama of emptiness, the gold of the blazing sun, the blinding white of the midday sand, a landscape that hurt the eyes.

Venice alone defied category: it shifted, fluid, melting, now jade and pink, now a soft purple, as when the setting sun was veiled in clouds. Venice was the blue of a Tintoretto Virgin's robe, the brown wood of the Cross in a Carpaccio; Venice was the darkness of Isabella's eyes, the rose pink of her mouth, the black of gondolas and grief.

Nostalgia is a function of age; he accepts that, but it pains him that only in his mind does he now touch life's rainbow. Today, all that splendour, the vividness of lips and eyes and landscape has shrunk and dimmed into the gloom of a Parisian room on a rainy evening. And he an old man.

It is hard to accept that life has grown less colourful. In the dim room, where everything is drained of brightness, shades of grey prevail. Even the Watteau, in its heavy frame on the opposite wall, seems to have lost its glow. Were it not for this feverish chill he would climb out of bed and cross the room to peer more closely at the painting that above all others touches his heart: a moon-faced boy, standing awkwardly, arms at his sides, sleeves wrinkled. A look of − what? Bewilderment? Trust betrayed?

From below he hears a sound, possibly a knocking at the front door. Whatever is happening downstairs he is not part of it. Here he is, trapped in the absurdity of confinement when he should have been preparing to dine out. In a nightshirt, when he should have been choosing the perfect waistcoat. He rests his eyes for a moment on a portrait he did of Isabella: had he been a painter he would have reached for oils to feed back the richness of her colouring on to the canvas, but he was restricted by his medium: pen, pencil or chalk; engraved, printed. His best work sparkles in monotone. Perhaps his life, too, is entering its monotone phase. He pauses: he realises that, as always, he is running ahead of himself.

He has always believed in looking forward, to the next room of life to be explored. Bonaparte once asked his opinion of a painting in the Louvre and he gave his view that it was priceless; carried away, he airily pronounced it immortal.

'How long will it *actually* last?'

Oh, he had replied, without thinking, hundreds of years. The dark gaze swivelled towards him.

'Some immortality!'

He was fifty-something then. Now, eighty beckons and there seem fewer new rooms to explore. Instead, he finds himself drifting back, into a Neapolitan sunset or trapped in deceptively smooth Egyptian sand. He recalls the way winter light shone on Russian cobblestones. Surely he is not ready to relive his past? Not yet.

A young woman crosses the Seine and turns on to the Quai Voltaire. The river is a shiny grey, like gathered rain, the water running fast, slapping against the stone of the bridge. The air is full of the sound and smell of the river. She looks up at the tall houses, counting the numbers.

It is 26 April 1825; a blustery day. She shivers, although she is wearing a fur hat and her coat is warm. Outside number 5 she stops. There is a bell pull and an iron door knocker in the shape of a ram's head. She reaches for the heavy knocker and lets it fall. Waits. On her face, a look of concentration; a wary intentness that seems more like anxiety: she is thinking what to say.

The door swings open.

An orchard, a hot summer day. A child of seven plays in a sunlit garden with another boy about the same age. They fight lazily, like puppies, their loose cotton shirts stained and dusty, sweat darkening their hair at temples and nape.

The orchard is filled with half-heard sounds: the humming of bees; birds twitching in the branches; the myriad sighs and creaks of plants nudged and nibbled by insects and small animals. The plum trees drip syrup from overripe fruit and the children yell and tumble in the long grass. They do not see the gypsy woman until one of them, flinging himself to one side, is caught up in her bunched skirts.

They get to their feet, staring up at her.

She studies them both for a moment, then bends to the shorter, sturdier child, a boy with curly hair and round, bright eyes.

'Are you afraid of me?'

He shakes his head and asks, formally: 'Would you like some fruit?'

From the house a voice drifts through the orchard: a maid, summoning the boys.

The gypsy reaches for the child's hand and studies the palm.

She traces the lines criss-crossing the soft skin, predicts a future involving the company of kings, fame, achievements honoured, desires fulfilled.

'A lucky hand.'

The concept of luck, good or bad, is not something he has thought about, but somehow he knows she expects him to be pleased. The child's lips curl into a smile. She reaches out and touches the dimple in his cheek. She murmurs to herself, 'Many women will love this one.'

He notes that her eyes are the colour of plums; her teeth, when she smiles, gleam with an amber sheen. Her finger on his cheek feels rough and he sees that the tips are so deeply scarred they have a look of burned pastry. Round her dark throat she wears a necklace of tangled glass beads, blue shading into green, like the summer sea when he saw it for the first time with his parents.

Had she asked his name, he would have replied, 'Dominique-Vivant De Non.' These are his orchards, or will be one day. As will the château, the land, the Burgundy vineyards marching to the horizon. A life of plenty, it would seem, lies ahead. Success. The love of women. He will be happy, she promises.

The fortune-teller could perhaps have told him more: she could have extended her prophetic telescope to reveal regicide, chaos, mass murder, flight. But why frighten a child? A wise woman knows when to keep her mouth shut.

The future seems settled and secure then – except that the boy (and the man he will become) eludes a defining category. Who is he behind the dimple and the bright eyes? Even the name will alter with time and circumstance, he himself wavering like an image seen through flawed glass or the heat of flames, and there will be flames. To his family he is Dominique, a prodigy; later, friends will call him Vivant, but they will know only a part of him; this will be a man of many coats: Dominique will be left behind in childhood,

4

De Non dressing down to become Denon in deference to a new, egalitarian order, until the next new order signals another change . . . One of his names at least captures the essence of him: Vivant. A word that means not only 'living', but 'alive', 'lively' and 'full of life'. All those he is. But also ambiguous, concealed. Mutable as mist. Why not give him room to breathe, to shift his shape? Let's call him V.

The second boy, whose future remains unpredicted, watches and listens; a bystander. He will grow accustomed to this role. He sees the gypsy turn, kiss her fingers and wave, disappear round the side of the stables. Much later he will recall this day and become aware that he was present at the moment V won over his first woman.

'She said you would get everything you want.'

The smaller boy chews a blade of meadow grass, sucking moisture from the green sludge through his teeth.

'This is all I want.'

He flings himself on to a shady patch of ground, breathing in the fragrance of the grass, a smell like unbaked bread. His companion frowns down at his own palm, stroking his unread lifelines. 'But what about me?'

'You'll be with me, Baptiste. You'll be happy too.'

When the maid calls again from the house, the boys get to their feet and wander towards her, brushing grass from breeches and shirts. They reach the house and separate, the smaller climbing the steps to a terrace that leads to a long, many-windowed room, the taller child absorbed into the gloom of the kitchen.

The door to the house on the Quai Voltaire swings open; the man in the doorway looks questioningly at the young woman, at her *démodé* fur hat and cloth coat. The wind blowing off the Seine is heavy with rain. It gusts, catching at the door. He holds it steady.

She says, 'Monsieur Denon –'

'The Baron is unable to see callers today.'

'The Baron!' She sounds disconcerted.

'I regret . . . He is unavailable.'

'I have travelled a great distance.'

'People frequently travel great distances to see him.'

She nods.

'I can wait.'

The man in the doorway, his pallor accentuated by his dark clothes, frowns. She realises she must retreat or say more.

'I am Zenobia.'

She enjoys his movement of surprise: the way he steps back a pace, out of reach. She is not aware of the panic in his eyes as she adds:

'And you must be Baptiste.'

A Burgundy orchard in high summer. Two boys, life ahead of them: this could be a way to start. But . . . here is a tall house overlooking the Seine on a raw April day, some seventy years later. A visitor from far away appearing unexpectedly.

Could this be the way to deal with the pattern of a life? Pluck the thread at its end and follow the clue through the labyrinth.

Outside the house on the Quai Voltaire, the weather has deteriorated, flocculence giving way to drizzle; raindrops sparkle on the fur hat, and on the olive-bronze cheeks of the visitor. And Baptiste has drawn the door wide open and is stepping to one side as Zenobia enters.

He ushers her through the hall towards a salon. She is aware of a trace of something in the air, an acrid hint she can't place: the after-sense of an extinguished candle perhaps. She has been trained to analyse, draw conclusions. She watches him wiping his hands on a handkerchief, rubbing his fingers. He continues to dab absently at his hands, the gesture mechanical.

'Baptiste,' she says, but he walks ahead of her, leading the way, his narrow back a closed door, and although deferential, he remains silent, formal, as he ushers her into a salon, indicating where she should sit. Zenobia takes in the room and the furniture; on every side are objects she is familiar with, though she has never seen them: paintings, *objets de vertu*, hangings. Ink and paper have fed her a version of their outlines. Now she can know them at first hand. On the walls she glimpses more engravings, watercolours, a carving, a delicate ornamental shelf. His things.

There are yellow flowers on a side table, filling the room with a smell like honey. The house is dark on this dull day, the Seine a murky mirror, reflecting no brightness from an overcast sky.

From somewhere above them there is the slightest of sounds. Baptiste excuses himself and goes to the door, hesitates. She is aware that he is not happy to leave her but she looks away, out to the Seine, as though already alone, and reluctantly, he leaves the room. She feels feverish: beneath her flesh her body seethes; she clasps and unclasps her hands, sits up straighter, looks this way and that, and finally, unable to remain motionless, she rises and begins to pace the room.

In the salon the light is wavering, almost aqueous, reflected from the river outside; she seems to be suspended, drifting through water, and when Baptiste reappears, pale in his black clothes, he hovers in the doorway peering in warily, like a long, dark fish. His eyes do not meet hers.

'The Baron is resting. Not to be disturbed.' He gives an apologetic shrug. 'I regret . . . You should have given us warning.' He adds, 'We could have arranged matters.'

There is something about the tense he uses that puts the notion of a meeting into the realm of might-have-been; of the not-now-possible.

She is aware that he wants to get her out of the house. 'Another time,' he says, 'it would have been easier to arrange —'

'Easier?' She sounds astonished; there is an edge of anger. '*Easier*? I have waited all my life for this. Can you wave me aside as though I were an inconvenient casual visitor?'

They are watching each other, the tension almost palpable.

'What if I were to say I shall remain until I am seen; demand —' She breaks off. Then: 'I have to ask. Why did he abandon me?'

'You were not abandoned — you must know that —'

'I *know* nothing.'

Before Baptiste can reply, she has noticed an object on a rosewood chiffonier; her fingertips touch a piece of marble: a fragment incised with a bee. Her expression changes.

'I have seen this before! Perhaps in a sketch —'

'It belonged to Madame de Pompadour.'

'Surely he cannot have met her —'

'Just before she died. He was about sixteen.'

'When I was about sixteen he sent me a ring.'

Baptiste glances at her naked fingers. 'Turquoise set in silver. For your saint's day.'

'Too small for me now; I keep it in an alabaster box.'

'Ah yes, the box.' He adds, 'A ring can be enlarged.'

'Yes, but when I work I prefer my hands to be bare.'

A slight pause. She says, 'I have been rereading his letters. I brought them with me.' She holds out her bag. 'I'm sure you know about the letters.'

He is aware she is trapping him with questions and assumptions. He should show her the door but he hesitates. Perhaps this could be a way of dealing with the problem: directing her into the distant past. A place of safety.

The silence of the room is broken by the sound of a wall clock telling the hour, signalling an afternoon turning point. Before it stops another has begun to chime, and then, from beyond the room, other timepieces are striking, or chiming, or booming softly. She listens, following the counterpoint of many clocks, her head turning this way and that. Then, her fingers tapping the bag:

'One of the first letters I remember – there were others, but I was very young –'

'Perhaps for a child they were too difficult.'

'No, no. I learned to read them. They were my education. There was one, with a little drawing: the crowning of Napoleon . . . I thought he looked very short.'

'No one would have observed that at the time.'

Baptiste remembers a day, forgotten until this moment: V hurrying back to the house, eyes bright with amusement, gleefully carrying home the latest gossip about the Emperor – 'Emperor! How odd that sounds, but it will soon slip off our tongues with ease.'

But before Napoleon crowned himself Emperor, before Joséphine met the young general, and long before V met Joséphine, he encountered La Pompadour, preceded by the fragrance she wore, as she swept into the studio of her own preferred artist, still beautiful, though the glow of her cheeks came from a porcelain pot rather than from within, the glitter of jewels replacing the sparkle that once brightened her eyes.

In his room on the upper floor of the house on the Quai Voltaire, the Baron – unavailable to visitors today – watches the light as it changes. Baptiste has brought him a cup of bitter tisane and it sits, cooling, beside the bed. Once it would have been a glass of Burgundy, drained as he headed for the door. Like the etching he did of himself, a young traveller in a hurry, the coach waiting nearby as he pissed against the wall of an inn, one hand controlling his aim, the other reaching out to grab a tankard of ale from a serving wench: life at a gulp.

Nowadays he has learned to sip and measure out his pleasures. Who was it, long ago, who talked to him of the passing of pleasure . . .? He sifts the sand of memory and brings up the rouged and powdered features of La Pompadour. Fretting over the loss of unthinking gratification, she had talked of the sad moderation that old age imposes. And she had added that of course none of this would make sense to him, child that he still was. And he had smiled, knowing that he was immortal.

L'Après-midi d'un Faune

Self-portrait by Dominique Vivant Denon (*Musée Denon, Chalon-sur-Saône*)

V was almost seventeen, working on a sketch in Boucher's studio, when La Pompadour paid her visit. The rustle of her silks, her perfume – the surge of deference surrounded her like the wash following the progress of a boat. La Pompadour in the studio!

She paused by the door, unaware that a sharp pair of eyes was studying her from across the room.

She was not yet gracing the students' canvases with her attention: she had paused to look for a moment at a small stone bust of a girl, standing in a niche. Somebody had twisted a strand of ivy into a wreath and stuck it atop the marble head.

The King's mistress had other interests besides politics and the bedroom preferences of Louis XV: she collected paintings and porcelain. And marble. An impressive quantity of marble. Some she acquired deliberately, more had been thrust upon her by admirers. She possessed medals and dishes, busts, statues – some modelled on her own figure – fragments from old columns, engraved pieces from distant lands; stelae, plaques . . . a jumble of picturesque stone, forgotten for much of the time, though occasionally the Marquise made a note to do something about it all – usually when a new gift arrived.

She drifted through the studio, pausing here and there while Boucher offered a word or two on the various young men.

'A nephew of mine, Jacques-Louis David . . .' The rest a murmur . . . 'The young De Non . . .' Another murmur.

'What did he say about me?' V hissed to David, at the next easel.

'A talent for something – I couldn't hear.'

The sixteen-year-old with a talent for something unheard, examined the jewel-decked presence more closely, noting the contrast in texture between her pale silk slippers and the paint-splattered floorboards, observing the shadow beneath her lovely eyes. He liked the way the light fell on the wisp of pink chiffon draped over the ample curve of her bosom to lend a glow to flesh grown dull. He would remember the way light behaved with chiffon; it pleased him. He smiled appreciatively.

Turning away, she murmured to herself: 'Charming . . .'

Boucher caught the word and glanced about to discover what had prompted it. He noticed the small marble bust. He recalled La Pompadour's interest in such things.

'Would the Marquise be gracious enough to accept . . .'

Now he needed to delegate the task of delivering the marble to La Pompadour's Versailles retreat. His questioning eye noted a fugitive smile.

'Ah! De Non . . .'

Time passed. La Pompadour sickened, grew frail. She found summer uncomfortably hot and she no longer took delight in *fêtes champêtres* or boat trips.

She recalled how once, for a celebration, some of her artist friends had created a blazing sun of brass that moved across the ballroom sky as the guests danced on. The room, filled with light, held back the night. Now, the dark came early. Those past days seemed longer, filled with gaiety, amusement. Boucher would have been painting her portrait – he was always painting her portrait – she in one of her thousand gowns, ivory or pink or that green silk with the flower garlands he captured so well, her hair upswept; he was particularly good at her hair. Today it looked dry, and by the time she had been laced and stiffened and powdered and painted and pushed into this and pulled into that, she felt ready for bed. Alone, as had been the case for quite some time.

The King and court were busy, as always, filling the days with pleasure. Once, La Pompadour would have been at the centre, glittering. But as the sickness ate into her, she no longer radiated *joie de vivre*. Boucher's portraits charted her decline: the tender curve of cheek and throat thickening; the famous hair veiled. The King's personal needs had long since been gratified elsewhere. She took up gardening, needle-work, tried her hand at engraving. Her marble collection gathered dust. Chips and damage could be observed here and there, where servants proved clumsy. From time to time she reminded herself she needed someone to look after it all, sort and catalogue the pieces, protect them from casual harm. Someone congenial, someone amusing.

A beautiful woman in the public eye, a figure usually glimpsed behind a barrier of jewels and furs, at the centre of an exclusive group, or on the arm of a powerful man, surely she could never find herself without admirers, friends, acolytes. Who would have imagined La Pompadour alone? Lonely? One of a sad line – mistresses, divas, actresses – goddesses spinning into mortal despair at the end, with no one to fend off the darkness.

Now she scanned the horizon of the past for memories of *jouissance*; those unregarded days of easeful pleasure; the delights of a summer night, a phrase of music heard from afar, the vulnerable sweetness of a young man's neck before the flesh roughened into maturity. That boy she saw in Boucher's studio when she paid an informal visit – her last excursion before the sickbed trapped her – a provincial dandy, eyes as ingenuous as a puppy's, touching in his flamboyant lace and close-cut breeches, attempts at courtly gravity undermined by the dimple in his left cheek. He had brought her a little stone head, a gift from Boucher, and she had pressed some trinket on him, in thanks. She remembered the innocent boldness of his smile.

As so often lately, she found her thoughts wandering . . . increasingly she felt tiredness sweeping over her. She drooped at her roll-top desk; there were letters she should write . . . She must speak to Louis about the marble collection.

In the upper room of the house on the Quai Voltaire the tisane remains untouched. Baptiste persists in bringing him these vile drinks in the belief they do him good. In fact, V usually tips the liquid into a plant holder or pisspot and thus, since he remains alive, maintains the fiction that lime flowers must be beneficial. The truth is that he cannot hurt Baptiste's feelings. Last time he was unwell he submitted to some foul-smelling unguent being rubbed on his wrinkled chest. Another triumph for the valet's pharmacopoeia.

When he was young these absurd indignities would have been unthinkable. There was always fun, *jouissance*, the laughter of the King; a time when he did as he wished and waited for no man. Then he thinks again and sees he is falling into the error of the recalled perspective. For as he well knows, a life at court was precisely a life spent in waiting.

At Versailles, Louis had become aware of a young man standing to one side of the spacious corridor leading from the King's apartments, his back to the wall. Each day, when His Majesty passed, there was the boy again, gazing with unusual intensity into the King's face, as though fixing it in his mind.

A cat may look at a king. But a courtier at a monarch? Permissible? How often? And for how long?

Had it not been for the expression of almost idiotic cheerfulness bordering on rapture that the youth displayed, the monarch might have felt a twinge of unease: such close attention was not always benign: there were ill-wishers around, but there was about this youth an absolute lack of menace, an air of such open delight, that Louis felt no qualm. Still, when day after day the boy continued to fix him with those wide, enquiring eyes, as though drawing nourishment from the royal presence, His Majesty decided enough was enough. In mid-stride, he came to an abrupt halt. Ahead and to the rear, others skidded to a stop, seeking a cause.

Louis confronted his unknown admirer, face grim. 'What is it you want?'

'To be permitted to gaze upon you, sire, and fix in my mind the admirable features of Your Majesty.'

'And?'

'And what, Majesty?'

'Nothing you *want*? Nothing to request?'

'Only that I may be permitted to pass beyond the bayonets and rifles of those that prevent me from approaching Your Majesty more closely.'

Louis maintained the appropriate monarchal impassivity. He was accustomed to flattery delivered by the carriage-load, but this youth avoided the usual spangled words, his very *gaucherie de style* was engaging.

'Who *are* you?'

'Your Majesty's devoted servant: Dominique-Vivant De Non.'

Louis studied him for a moment. The youth was absurd: he smiled before the monarch had said anything amusing; he stared, he had no discretion. His eyes were – impossibly – at the same time knowing and innocent. Beguiled, the King gave orders: the young man could go wherever he wished, gardens, rooms, galleries . . . The procession moved on.

Behind Louis' back, behind lace handkerchiefs, fans and

fingertips, the smiles were less kind: the court had plentiful experience of a newcomer keenly polishing the King's posterior with obsequious tongue. Just another *arriviste*.

When Louis asked, 'Who are you?' V could have mentioned the Burgundy wine connection – ('My grandfather did some small service to Your Majesty's grandfather . . .') or used Boucher's name as a link . . . But a monarch is a busy man. Keep it short: name, pledge of loyalty. '*Your Majesty's devoted servant . . .*'

V was aware, as he begged permission simply to look at the King, that the words sounded inexcusably sycophantic, but in truth, it was not entirely an obsequious response. He needed to gaze upon the King's countenance, to learn it, as it were, by heart, for a practical purpose. In fact he did want something: he wanted to capture the King's image, but a king is not available as a sitter to an unknown artist. The lowliest courtier had easier daily access to the monarch than some obscure pencil-wielder could hope for.

So V wandered the court, studying the ormolu, the tapestries, the glassy surface of walnut and mahogany; the imperfect surface of the human countenance. He breathed in the rich perfumes of sandalwood and amber, examined the lustre of silk. By no means overwhelmed (occasionally he came upon a piece which ranked lower in his estimation than something similar at home in Burgundy, though he kept that opinion to himself), he looked at detail, at what was new and what enduring, at how this went with that, deciphering the code of art and fashion; noting, classifying.

But who could classify what he in turn brought to the court? In some cabinet, in some bureau drawer, there must be a scroll, a parchment: *Dominique-Vivant De Non, created Gentleman of the King's Chamber for services rendered.*

Services rendered?

★

'He catalogued La Pompadour's collection of marble after she died,' Baptiste tells Zenobia. He clings to the safety of those early memories. 'This' – he picks up the fragment of stone, its surface delicately scored with the outline of a bee, and weighs it in his palm – 'was a gesture of thanks from the King. That was how it began. Later of course, he drew Louis' portrait.'

He should get rid of the girl, not feed her information. But the words have awakened dormant feelings. Opened doors into places he had forgotten.

At the young cavalier's modest lodgings, Baptiste brushed the nap of his master's velour hat. He sponged and hung up his jacket; prepared shaving materials. As always, they talked. Or rather, V talked. Baptiste had never seen Versailles, but he could itemise the treasures, conjure up the soft bloom on damask walls, the predominating colours of Sèvres and Meissen. Because what V saw, his valet, too, saw, through his master's eyes. Together they shared the day, V carrying Baptiste along, describing it all, every shade and contour, while he was shaved and bathed and powdered and dressed. And in the retelling, Baptiste liked to think, he could be useful: through the valet's questions, V might be made aware of some quality he had originally overlooked; take note of an additional detail – detail was all-important: 'Look closely, approach the heart of it.' Art was mysterious, it must be examined, questioned, to be understood.

And Baptiste would nod, and go on listening.

He was aware that he was living V's life at one remove. His were the first eyes on a new work; his the admiring reaction to an account of a social triumph, an amorous conquest. If he occasionally yearned to live life for himself he put aside the disloyal wish. The master's life was full enough for two.

Meanwhile, V, at a desk by the window, sketched, studied, erased, began again, getting the King's features to his

19

satisfaction. Here, in one face, he saw the contradictions of nobility: the force and vigour that formed part of the trappings of power; the droop of a muscle that signalled a weakness; the signs of good living visible in a blurring of jawline, a pouchiness where there should have been taut flesh and bone. The this-and-that a portraitist must note – and sometimes, discreetly, disguise . . .

And V, lost in his work, was vulnerable too. Not yet formed, feeling his way.

Who first spoke of the marble? It could have been the King, vexed over La Pompadour's legacy, a chore that he must deal with as she had requested. Did she mention the boy's name to him? It might have been V who raised the subject, intrigued by the idea of the unseen collection, asking artless questions, longing to learn what it contained, where the pieces came from; classification led to knowledge, to answers – the route to solving mysteries.

He had a way of asking questions that avoided giving offence. Women told him things only their maids would normally have known; the maids, too, found they could talk to him. He listened intently, head cocked, occasionally nodding. Secrets were safe with him. Perhaps it helped that the young man was not handsome: with his round face, upturned nose and short stature he offered no threat to husbands, who also confided their thoughts. Even the monarch felt safe with him.

What does a man have to do to be honoured by the King? V could amuse him, lift his spirits. A long-serving courtier trundling his way through an anecdote one evening was stopped in mid-sentence by a royal hand. The King turned away and beckoned impatiently: 'De Non! Why don't *you* tell us the story?'

Here was a problem: he could make the story more entertaining and create an enemy for life. On the other hand, the King's command hung in the air.

'Sire, the fault lies not in the teller but the tale. To retell it could inflict on Your Majesty twice the boredom – surely a punishable offence!' Instead, he offered a fresh nugget of gossip not yet heard at court . . .

Already his presence had lightened the mood. The King's irritation melted, *joie de vivre* absorbed like a barely heard melody. Someone did a drawing of V once, *Portrait of a Young Man Dancing*. Even when he stood waiting for the King to pass, body curved into the question mark of a courtly bow, V was dancing.

Later, he took over La Pompadour's jumble of stone and put it in order, properly catalogued, separating Greek from Roman, European from Oriental; but his real job was to amuse Louis, talking nonsense when nonsense was required; demonstrating a knowledge of wine when asked ('You will recall, Majesty, your grandfather had a particular liking for our family's Burgundy . . .'). How pleasant it all was! How comfortable. How right the gypsy had been.

He was occupying his ideal environment: the King had given him a commission in a congenial regiment; his duties at court were undemanding; he was often to be found at the Comédie-Française, seeing the play or entertaining the little actresses backstage. On other evenings he attended the opera, the favoured companion of a mature beauty, a comtesse with a complaisant husband. But in the early hours he would carry a glass of wine to his work table and return to what increasingly engaged him: the mastery of the steel plate, lines engraved with his favourite cutting tool, the plate inked and wiped clean, leaving just the right quantity of liquid gleaming darkly in the incised lines. The pleasure involved in the delicate transformation of a blank sheet of copper into a complex design that would come to life on paper.

He was twenty. Life was kind. He walked on air. And one evening he met Angélique.

★

He is tempted for a moment to sample Baptiste's disgusting tisane to slake his thirst, but to his surprise the effort of sitting up, reaching out and picking up the cup proves too demanding. He slumps back on his pillows. When one is old, he acknowledges, one no longer walks on air. One no longer lives without taking thought for the morrow. But in truth, old age is no time to be prudent. This is when – with so little left to lose – one should be daring. But hasn't he always been so, a gymnast of a sort, throwing himself on the mercy of life's bosom? It must have been the memory of Angélique that brought bosoms to mind. His mouth curves into a ghost of his wry smile: had Angélique's bosom, like Cleopatra's nose, been fractionally less perfect, perhaps the whole history of his life might have been different. A frivolous thought. But then, he has always taken frivolity seriously.

Ambiguous Liaisons

They met at the opera – before the opera, to be precise, V waiting for his Comtesse to arrive, scanning the audience, speculating on the evening ahead. The Comtesse would arrive late, probably tiring of the music by the end of the first act. She would turn to him, the pressure of her cool fingers on his wrist indicating that it was time to leave. Then, with a rustle of silk, she would be ahead of him in the corridor, and into her carriage. A slam of the carriage door, the opera left behind. Supper ready for them in her salon, candles lit, tall in their silver holders, the servants waiting to pour and serve and retire.

At their first meeting the Comtesse had glanced up at the young courtier and gestured to the empty chair next to hers.

She murmured, 'Monsieur . . . De Non? Tell me all about yourself,' and smiled encouragingly.

He began to tell her about Burgundy with its orchards and vineyards, his own passion for engraving – intaglio – the way the depth and thickness of a line could be altered by the slightest pressure of the hand . . . When he spoke the word 'passion' she smiled again, but when at a certain point he asked a question, a question that invited a response, she failed to reply, and he became aware that the Comtesse had not been listening to him. Her eyes were on his mouth, her mind elsewhere.

Ah. V paused. He modulated the key, he changed the subject: he offered flattering comments on the Comtesse's coiffure, her eyes, her lips, her shoulders – he thought possibly he might be moving towards impertinence but her smile intensified: now she was listening.

Later that night he passed on to Baptiste a fundamental discovery he had made about life: 'People do not really want to hear what you have to say. What they want is for you to echo what they are thinking.'

Baptiste nodded, listening, eyebrows raised.

V gave him a sideways look. 'I suppose you knew that already.'

'Yes, sir.'

They broke into laughter together.

'Baptiste, Baptiste, what would I do without you?' He yawned and lifted his arms to slip into the nightshirt Baptiste held out. He sank into the soft bed. Yes, life was kind.

And then he met Angélique.

At the Opéra, the flash of jewels, the buzz of conversation, the heat from the lamps created a closed world of warmth and animation. Backstage, music was rehearsed, scales practised, scenery readied, but for the audience what mattered was the meeting of glances, the exchange of confidences and laughter; the pulse of life.

As usual, V was waiting for the Comtesse. As usual she was late, and after a while he became aware of a woman in the next box whose smile seemed directed towards him even when she addressed her companions, whose eyes – mocking yet kindly – had a way of meeting his. She beckoned.

He joined her, bowed, kissed the air above her perfumed fingertips and stepped back, dazzled, like a man who has glanced at the sun.

Angélique gleamed like a burnished statuette: her eyes, like her gown, were golden, her ivory skin reflecting the glow. He had seen her before at some soirée or other; they had been introduced, and she had moved on. Now he heard her voice, so soft and low that he was compelled to bend close to her to catch the words, look into her eyes.

She was studying his face with a calm curiosity and he felt for a moment like a butterfly, caught in a glittering net by a goddess playing naturalist, examining the latest specimen before consigning him to the killing jar. She smiled, her teeth small and even.

She was commiserating with him, sympathetic: 'The Comtesse keeps you waiting so often.'

There was no way he could reply to that: to agree would be disloyal. To disagree, impolite.

The lights dimmed. The overture began. The adjoining box remained empty. Angélique turned towards him and murmured a phrase or two: he moved closer, straining to catch her words; her warm breath filled his nostrils. Her perfume seemed stronger, her eyes dreamy, gazing into his. When he mumbled something about returning to the comtesse's box, she shook her head, still smiling.

'I cannot permit you to languish alone, the embarrassment would be shaming. Stay with me. See: I've come to your rescue.' V was astonished: the goddess was interested in the poor specimen! She put her hand on his, almost maternally, and turned towards the stage, allowing him to admire her profile.

When Act One came to an end, she leaned towards him questioningly.

'Do you have plans for this evening? I trust not.' And when he hesitated, she added, seeming a little flustered, how kind it would be if just tonight he could accompany her, dine with her, adding, before he could voice the possibility, 'The Comtesse will not be here tonight, I assure you.'

How could he refuse? 'If I can be of service –'

She became all at once quite brisk: 'Come!' and she was on her feet, pausing for him to open the door of the box. A brief whisper to the servant waiting outside then, beckoning with a mischievous finger, she was rustling ahead of him, down the marble stairs and out to where her coach – how fortunate! – already waited.

Later, when he tried to pin down the events, to distance himself from the scalding shame and anger, he tried to think back to a point where he might have picked up clues. But thinking was impossible. All he could do was to try and feel: feel his way back to the beginning. When he tried to recall the night in detail, he found himself swimming through fog, like a drugged man attempting to hold a grip on surroundings that shift and melt.

Was it in the carriage that he touched – by accident – her breast? Or was that later? And when her yielding body was flung against his, that must surely have been caused by the wheels bouncing over rough ground, so they were out of Paris by then, driving through the night.

He did manage to enquire, above the noise of the wheels and the cracking of the coach-driver's whip, 'Where are we going?'

'To see my husband.'

'But surely –'

'We've been estranged for some while, but certain tedious official matters have been settled . . .' She smoothed the silk of her bodice. 'This will be an evening of reconciliation.'

V's gloom deepened. 'But why am *I* here?'

'I simply could not endure the boredom of a tête-à-tête with my dear husband.'

He searched for tactful words: to choose the day of their reconciliation to introduce another man to her husband struck him as bizarre.

'Reconciliation has nothing to do with pleasure. Your presence will give me pleasure.'

'I feel awkward.' Tentatively: 'I can see no merit in this threesome.'

A creasing of the smooth brow, almost a frown. 'You have missed the point. You are here to amuse me, not to lecture me!'

He had been aware there was a difference in their ages, but surely not many years; she gleamed with youth, no sign of lines around eyes or mouth, but suddenly she seemed imperious, commanding. She began to laugh. 'How stern you look! Not amusing at all.' He tried to smile, surrendered to the moment and her laughter.

She invited him to admire the countryside bathed in bright moonlight; to gaze up at the stars. Her cheek was pressed to his – unavoidably, as she insisted they share the same coach window. The perfume from her powdered hair clogged his brain. The stars spun.

At last, greeted by voices, lights, the barking of dogs, they drew up at the *porte cochère* of a château. Servants hurried to open the coach door, to place steps for them. V saw a tall man emerge from the house and stand, motionless, at the top of the steps, radiating an air of lassitude bordering on malaise.

'My husband,' Angélique murmured to V, somewhat unnecessarily. Raising her voice, she introduced 'a young friend from Paris'. The young friend was acknowledged with a sort of exhausted courtesy before her husband led the way through the house.

Embarrassed, uncertain what note to strike, V fell back on compliments, fervently professing himself astonished at the treasures on every side. The exclamations were sincere – the château was a shrine to the finest taste – but to his own ears he sounded false. His words festooned with exclamation marks, he felt like a character by Molière.

In any case Angélique waved away his compliments: 'This is nothing. You should see my dear husband's art collection in Paris –'

The 'dear husband' turned an ironical eye on her: 'My *dear* madame, I got rid of it two years ago.'

'Oh! Really?' She shrugged prettily. 'Ah well.'

When they moved to the dining room Angélique was the concerned hostess, ordering the choicest cut of veal to be offered to the master of the house. Again the ironical glance as he pointed out that he had been on a meatless diet for quite some time.

'Oh?'

'For my health.'

'Really!' A tiny shrug and sideways nod. 'Ah! Well . . .' V watched her, filled with admiration for the way she managed to lend the gesture a blend of compassion, rueful sympathy and generalised charm. He noted the angle of the head: in a portrait that tilt would show a long neck to advantage, improve the jawline.

Only the clink of wine glass on table top, fork on plate could be heard. Between these small noises the silence rang like a bell at a pitch too high for the human ear. V studied the fine chasing on the silver centrepiece, the crystal of the decanter, the flower arrangement, the candlesticks. He took morsels of food and chewed slowly. The servants removed dishes. The master of the house took a sip of water and put down his glass with some care.

'Now I think I shall retire. I hope my dear wife will forgive me.' Turning to V, he added (perhaps, again, a trace of irony?), 'Monsieur, too, I hope will forgive me . . .'

He drifted from the room. The door had barely closed behind him when Angélique was on her feet, drawing V towards the tall windows leading to the terrace.

'Come! You must see the gardens! I can't breathe in here . . .'

The path wound through the grounds, between trees and shrubs, past stone statues ghostly in the moonlight. The warm air was perfumed with lilies. V saw that in her narrow silk shoes Angélique found the gravel path difficult to walk on; she stumbled, and he offered his arm, maintaining a proper distance, but she put her arm through his and drew him closer, to prevent herself falling. They had, she murmured, so much to say to one another. In the dimness her mouth was sharply etched against the pallor of her skin. When she spoke it opened, gleaming, like a sea anemone in search of food.

'I feel I can confide in you . . .'

He was astonished by the intimacy into which they were so quickly drifting. She was speaking of a man who had been her lover for a while, a marquis, encountered by V once or twice at soirées. She mentioned his comtesse, questioningly, encouragingly, but V never discussed one woman with another and the conversation dwindled.

Quite soon Angélique announced she was tired of walking and sank to the ground with her arm still in his, so that V found himself stretched out beside her on the grassy bank above the river, her warm body disturbingly close. The dark ribbon of the river slipped past them, an occasional ripple catching the light of the moon. Head lowered, Angélique gave him a questioning upward glance, her eyes troubled.

'I fear the encounter with my husband has upset you. You're displeased.'

'Not at all!'

But she clearly needed reassurance; some gesture of conciliation, of affection . . . She raised her face to his in a wordless invitation. He felt giddy. His lips touched her cheek. One touch led on to others, to kisses on eyelids, throat, mouth, all offering the reassurance she sought.

Aware of a husband, of servants not far off, V drew back, suggesting that perhaps this was unwise.

She frowned. 'You think we should go back to the house.'

He protested, she insisted: yes, yes, they must go in at once; the night air was humid, unhealthy. He had thought himself a practised cavalier but Angélique confused him. She was like a ringmaster at the circus, in control, cracking a whip. Her confidence undermined his own.

They began to walk back, though he had the feeling neither wished to do so. Her arm rested on his, but she no longer drew him close, no sweet-breathed words drifted his way; they seemed to be disconcertingly at odds, all ease evaporated. In the silence the crunch of the gravel was loud beneath his feet. Angélique's silk shoes moved as soundlessly as moths over the crushed stone.

They were almost at the door of the house when she paused, and said petulantly, 'I am not at all pleased with you. Usually people enjoy talking about someone they are in love with. But you have told me nothing about the Comtesse!'

Helplessness swept over V: this whole encounter was beyond his control. He said stiffly, 'I find it puzzling –'

She stopped his mouth with two white fingers laid across his lips. All she wanted, she murmured, was to talk about *him*.

She said warmly, 'Does she make you happy? I fear not, and that saddens me. Tell me, don't you feel sometimes that you're the victim?'

Through the windows he could see into the house; the damask walls, the glowing lamps, a tapestry. A cool breeze wafted across the terrace, smelling of the river.

V no longer knew how to respond.

'Madame,' he found himself stammering, 'I thought you wanted to go in . . . the humid air –'

'It has changed,' she said briskly, and took his arm.

She led the way through the moonlit garden, V in such a state of distraction that he had no idea in which direction they were now walking. She was speaking again of her friend, the Comtesse.

'Such an exquisite creature! So graceful! A falsehood on her lips becomes a witticism; an infidelity somehow the right thing to do. She's amusing, clever, coquettish . . .' A pause. 'Such a dear.' The tone remained admiring, affectionate. Then a change of tone. 'I sometimes feel she lacks tenderness – perhaps you've found that?' She gave him no chance to protest, but went straight on: 'Just between ourselves, Paris is full of those she has duped. She's been making a fool of that dear husband of hers, *and* of that Austrian prince who's been her lover for a while.'

The existence of the Austrian prince was an unwelcome surprise to V.

'When she turned to you, I suspect it was to distract two rivals who had both become too jealous of each other and were on the point of creating a fuss, possibly a scandal. She brought you on to the scene, and that kept everyone busy. What a hold a clever woman has over you men!' Her tone had changed; now she sounded flustered, uncertain. 'Lucky woman, she can pretend whatever she likes, she doesn't have to *feel* anything.'

She shook her head and gave a long sigh that seemed drawn from her inmost being. Clearly, Angélique could feel, deeply.

V was astonished: it was as though a blindfold had been lifted from his eyes, his mistress revealed as the most false of women. He too sighed, shakily. And now, it seemed, Angélique really did wish to return to the house.

'It's so long since I was here. Now that my dear husband and I are friends again I'll come more often. There's a little boudoir, a temple of love, next to my bedroom. He designed it years ago, when such things mattered.'

Another of her deep sighs. 'That little secret chamber . . . Just to think of it makes my heart beat faster.' She smiled, and he saw her lips part, the gleam of her teeth, the dark cavity of her mouth. 'If I could be sure you would behave, I might show you my little jewel box.'

The air was undoubtedly cool, yet Angélique's hand on V's wrist felt hot, moist. He himself was by now in a fever, and not only of curiosity, and was searching for the right words when he found that they were back at the house with Angélique preceding him through the door. The lamps were out and they felt their way slowly through the maze of rooms in darkness. Angélique guided his steps, drew him on, her hands by chance touching him in thrillingly unexpected places. She stifled her laughter as they bumped into a table, an escritoire, V convinced that at any moment he would knock over a priceless porcelain vase, which would shatter noisily and bring servants running, to be followed no doubt, by Monsieur.

After a few minutes they came to a door which opened on to a corridor lit by a flickering lamp. For V, at that moment, reality ceased: he had the feeling of being part of a dream, a drifting journey through a chimerical landscape. Along the corridor, to another door, an ante-room. In one corner, an elderly servant woman, curled up asleep like a pet dog, stirred as they approached, then quickly got to her feet, curtseying to her mistress.

Angélique whispered a few words to the woman, who appeared to vanish through the wall: V saw that part of the carved panelling was a door. Angélique had loosened her golden hair, and now she whispered to V to help her unfasten her tightly corseted gown. His fingers felt huge, clumsy, his hands shaking. But he was astonished at how easily everything fell into place – or rather, fell away: it seemed that with no more than a twitch of this and a stepping out of that, she was now clad only in a chemise of some floating cloth that veiled her without quite concealing her body. The secret door opened, Angélique took V's hand and the door silently closed behind them. They seemed to be at the centre of a floating world, a delicate cage of mirrors painted with flowers, fruit, birds, endlessly, dizzyingly reflected around them.

Between the mirrors was a flower-decked trellis, with bowers, one holding a statue of Eros; there were cherubs holding garlands, and a canopy above a pile of silken cushions piled on to a carpet as green and velvety as the softest grass.

And V was lost. The close observer who noted detail, who knew what people did with their faces, their hands, their eyes, was like a blind man falling through space as Angélique sank

34

back on to the cushions and drew him into her arms. There were sighs and gasps, groans and exclamations. She tore at his clothes; they fought, with fierce pleasure.

Pinned beneath him, she writhed, apparently helpless, trapped. When, after a while, V flagged she found new strength, astride him now, provoking, arousing, burning with infectious heat.

At last, exhausted, the silken cushions beneath their bodies damp with sweat, they lay as though dead. After a while Angélique murmured, teasingly, 'Will you ever love your comtesse the way you love me?'

Before V could reply, the secret door opened noiselessly and the maid slipped into the room. Once again, events moved too fast for him as the servant gathered his scattered garments, helping him to his feet. She shepherded him towards the door with some urgency. 'It's already morning.'

Angélique lay without moving, eyes closed, while the maid, elderly, but surprisingly strong, steered him out of the chamber before he could collect his wits. The door closed and everything dissolved with the speed of a dream on waking. He found himself alone in the antechamber, holding his clothes, the sweat drying clammily on his skin. He should go to his room – he assumed a room must have been prepared for him – but where was it? This was hardly the time to ask. Any questions of that sort would certainly lead to embarrassment and possibly disaster. As would the sight of an unclothed man attempting to navigate the unknown territory of the château.

The best thing would be to find his way to the garden, and remain out of sight for a while, then return as though from an early-morning stroll. He began, clumsily, to dress.

Once again he found himself crossing the terrace beneath the trees. He reached the river bank, the air chill against his skin, and looked down at the water. In the early light it looked like beaten steel. He had barely eaten the night before and became aware that he was both hungry and thirsty. His mouth was dry, his tongue as rough as a lump of chewed fur in his mouth. Trying to clear his head, he reviewed the situation: should he now consider himself to be the lover of the woman he had just left, lying like a marble statue on her couch of cushions?

She who just yesterday – how long ago that seemed! – spoke frankly of the Marquis who had been her lover; and he himself, who just yesterday would have considered it unthinkable that he could be unfaithful to the Comtesse; were they now, swept away by a nocturnal tempest, a new mathematical unit: a clandestine pair?

And had he replaced the Marquis in Angélique's affections and, so to speak, her bed? Or had he been selected as an instrument of punishment, to teach an unwanted lover a lesson? Whichever it would prove to be, his head still spun from the dreamlike night. He paused to adjust his clothing, tighten his cravat: he should at least look presentable when he returned to the château.

He was engaged in straightening his wrinkled stockings when he became aware of footsteps on the gravel path, a figure approaching. Walking towards him was Angélique's erstwhile lover, the Marquis, who seemed very much at home; genial, amused.

He raised his eyebrows enquiringly. 'How did it go?'

How did it go?

'You knew I was here?'

'She sent me word by her servant when you left the opera. So: did you play your part well? How was the husband?' He moved on without waiting for a reply. 'One of Angélique's coachmen will take you home. You really did her a favour, livening up the supper as well as making that dull journey more enjoyable. I'm most grateful –'

I'm most grateful?

Hastily V broke in, choosing his words carefully: 'No, no:

on the contrary, it was my pleasure . . .' He was rather proud of that phrase: he felt he and the Marquis, in the most civilised fashion, were fencing to secure the best position. So far, in his view, he was winning. He ventured a question:

'But why are you here so early? Isn't that rather unwise?'

The Marquis said cheerfully, 'Oh, it's all going according to plan: I'm supposed to be on my way back to Paris – the story is, I've been staying with some people who have a place nearby –' He saw V's expression and said, contrite, 'She didn't tell you? I'll have to reprimand her, after all you've done for us.'

All you've done for us?

V began to sense the ground shifting beneath his feet; unease growing in the pit of his stomach. Where was his normal social poise? He felt increasingly helpless.

He said, feeling his way, 'Perhaps if she had told me everything, I wouldn't have played my part so well.'

'So you enjoyed yourself? Good! Tell me about it – I want all the details.'

V gave a polite smile: 'I had not realised that we were play-acting, that I was one of the cast.'

'I'm afraid you didn't have a very good part.'

'Oh,' V said reassuringly, 'There are no bad parts for good actors.'

'I know what you mean. And you handled it well?'

'I think I carried it off adequately.'

'I'm sure you're being too modest! And Angélique?'

'She was sublime.'

The Marquis took V's arm in the friendliest manner and they began to walk back towards the house.

'She dotes on me, you know. But, between ourselves, she does have one failing. She feels nothing. She's as cold as marble.'

For a moment V saw Angélique, curled up on the silken cushions, looking indeed like marble, a classic reclining nude, but hers had been the stillness of exhausted passion, of the warrior drained after battle. He refrained from smiling.

'Well, I'll have to take your word for that, you know her almost like a husband –'

'– And on that point: how was Monsieur, at supper?'

'Very much the husband.'

The Marquis laughed delightedly. 'What a game it all is! Though, to my mind, you don't seem to be finding it as amusing as you should. The theatre of life really does offer us some treats! Now: I should pay my respects to the husband. Come with me, I want to tidy myself, my wig needs fresh powder, one doesn't want to look dishevelled . . .'

V caught an eloquent sideways glance: clearly in the eyes of the Marquis it was V's appearance that required attention.

'So you think he took it on trust you're her lover?'

V shrugged. 'You must judge that by the way he greets me, perhaps.'

It was not an entirely comfortable meeting: Monsieur made an enormous fuss of the new arrival; there were exclamations of welcome: the Marquis must stay a few days. As for V, Monsieur made no such suggestion, saying only that by the look of their visitor from Paris, the country air had been far from beneficial. He recommended that V should return to town without delay.

'The reconciliation seems to have gone off well, thank heavens,' the Marquis murmured. He glanced about approvingly. 'This house is going to be an excellent base for the future.'

They found Angélique seated at her dressing table while a maid attended to her hair. She turned to V: 'I was afraid you might have left before I was up.'

She looked closely at the two men. To V it seemed as though she was searching their faces for clues. Was she wondering how much the Marquis knew? How much *he* knew? The new arrival embarked on a sprightly description of their encounter with her husband, and how well V had played his part – 'We have a friend here, Madame,' he exclaimed, 'we should be grateful –'

'Yes,' said Angélique, cutting in, 'we are.' She put out her hand to V. 'Shall we just say I know how much I owe you?' He bowed over her fingertips.

At which point her husband sauntered through the door.

V glanced from one to the other. What a quartet: the Marquis was tricking the husband and saw V as part of the stratagem – his accomplice. The husband regarded V with contemptuous hostility: an outsider and a threat who could damage the delicate fabric of a precarious marital set-up, to be got out of the way without delay. V himself, on the evidence of his night of passion, was deceiving both the husband and the lover. As for Angélique, what was her role? He felt once again that he had stumbled into a Molière farce, though he was still unsure who exactly was deceiving whom.

Meanwhile, the 'dear husband' gazed out of the window with an abstracted, mild curiosity as though counting the trees in the parkland. An awkward silence grew in the room like a thickening in the air, until V remarked that it was time he left. Nobody disagreed. Angélique followed him out to the *porte cochère*, under the pretext of asking him to do her a small favour when he got back to Paris. As soon as they were out of earshot she leaned closer and murmured, 'I wanted to thank you . . .' Her scented breath drifted across his face like gauze. 'Wasn't last night a beautiful dream?' She had found his hand and was holding it intimately close against her warm body, pressed among the folds of her flimsy robe. 'Goodbye again.' And then she was gone. As the footman closed the carriage door, and the coachman cracked his whip, it seemed to V that Angélique was with him, being carried rapidly away from the house, but then he realised that it was only her perfume, still clinging to his clothes.

★

It was a long and wretched drive home. With no moonlight to lend it mystery or sunlight to gild it, the countryside looked ugly, a place of mud and desolate fields. The seat of the carriage was hard and the wheels juddered on every bump in the road. It seemed to V that while he and Angélique had floated to the château on a magic carpet, he was now being subjected to some kind of punishment designed to bruise his body and lower his spirits. By the time the carriage drew up outside his door he was ready to weep with gratitude.

'Baptiste!'

No further words were necessary. Stale, crumpled clothes were removed, water heated, the tub filled. A glass of wine, a plate of fruit and favourite cheese. V sank into the water and as Baptiste, ever the good listener, scrubbed his back and washed and rinsed his hair, V went over at least some of the night's adventure. And as he began to describe the mysterious, baffling events V saw how different it all looked, in daylight. Was it indeed an affair of ecstasy and over-whelming passion, with two people swept away in the torrent? Or was it a calculated exercise, planned and carried out with the skill of a chess gambit, a game. He saw it all differently now: the callow youth called on, groomed for a role which he would play but once; presented to a husband who needed to be put off the scent of his true rival. And with the manoeuvre completed, the redundant actor, nothing more than a figure of fun, a clown, was bundled offstage without delay.

He groaned aloud, berating himself for his naiveté, his lack of perception – he who prided himself on observing, analysing! There was, after all, no mystery to be solved.

He pictured Angélique, her marble limbs melting as she writhed in passion, her skin sheened with sweat; surely when she covered him with her searching mouth, when she mounted him so urgently –

The water in the bathtub was still warm, yet V found himself shivering, as though chilled or in the grip of a fever. He shook his head, trying to blank out image after image of the night before when he had played the part not of lover but fool.

In the salon of the house on the Quai Voltaire, the valet has discovered an unsuspected gift for necromancy: he has conjured pictures from the past to keep Zenobia engaged. She who had dangerous questions to ask has been fed more answers than she needs: the court, the king, the sweet life before the deluge.

He waves at the shelves of books lining the wall next to her, and she leans closer, examining the spines: works on Sicily, on Italy . . . parcels of a man's life bound by leather covers.

Her eye is caught by a book that looks different from the others. Tucked into a corner of the shelf is a small volume, no thicker than a finger.

The book sits comfortably in the palm of her hand, its cover soft as silk. She reads aloud the title:

'*Point de Lendemain.*'

She leafs through it, puzzled. Nothing here of art and archaeology, or travel. This tiny volume seems out of place, with its feverish talk of a moonlit journey to a distant château, its bewildered young narrator.

'What is this book?'

Baptiste says smoothly that it is not something she would find of interest. He takes the little book from her and replaces it on the shelf.

'It is a novel.'

'He wrote a novel!'

'His name was not on the cover when it came out, just initials. People thought one of his friends had written it.'

'That must have upset him.'

'Not really. It was only a novel. Nothing important.'

Pawn's Move

The opera had lost its appeal. The boxes that held fragrant ladies of fashion, an occasional marquis or prince, those elegant little corners were less welcoming than before. Smooth, smiling faces took on the appearance of masks. Behind them lay guile and trickery. V remembered Montaigne's advice and went back to his books: Virgil could still touch his heart and fire his spirit, though now, when he read of the way wily Venus got through male defences, 'caressing here and there, delighted with her own cleverness', the lines struck home with painful force. Goddesses had a way of getting what they wanted, the man – even a god – merely the means to an end. He still occasionally groaned aloud at the memory of a certain night, a clever game in which he had played the pawn.

He spent more time with pencil and etching tool; he felt safer pinning down beauty on the page than exposing himself to the lure of the killing jar. But he was, after all, not yet twenty-one, so there were nights when he took himself off to the Comédie-Française, sometimes in the auditorium, more often backstage, surrounded by the young actresses and those aspiring to be actresses, girls who clustered in the wings; who chirped and giggled; an unchoreographed corps de ballet to his prince. They flattered him sweetly, repowdered his wig, admired his choice of waistcoat and shoe buckle. He presented them with flowers, compliments. He sketched them. No doubt there were more intimate moments between the sketch and finished drawing, but it was an intimacy everyone enjoyed. There were no uncertainties here. He was gentle with the dewy, pink-and-white girls, and they in turn were blooms without thorns, no hurt or pain in the games they all played. The young actresses were grateful for the attentions of a young man who not only admired them, but listened to them as though he really cared what they said. And such a witty young man, with such an understanding of human nature.

'You should write a play, Vivant, everyone would come.'

'Yes, you should certainly write a play, why don't you?'

The King was intrigued. 'Ah, De Non! We hear you've written a play! We shall be seeing it at the Comédie, I suppose?'

Diffidence was something V did rather well, partly because he was sincere. He genuinely doubted there would be a production.

'Sire, the work may not merit . . .' But the monarch's interest, and words dropped in various ears by influential friends, proved helpful.

'Have you heard? Vivant's play is opening at the Comédie. Shall we all go?'

Julie or the Good Father opened. And everyone went.

First-night applause covered a combination of despair (the author's friends) and discretion (an audience reluctant to displease the King: De Non was, after all, a favourite). Above all, they were surprised that a man whose conversation sparkled, whose presence brightened a room, should produce such a play. How *conventional* it was; how *traditional* . . .

'What do the critics say?' one pink-and-white girl called to another, after the first night.

'None of them like it.'

She flapped a page, reading aloud: ' "The piece is mediocre. The young author, far from possessing a talent that should be encouraged, demonstrates a mania for creation that must be stifled at birth".'

'Beast.'

Friends consoled him; at the Comédie, the girls made cheering comments:

'I *really* enjoyed it . . .'

'We all did . . .' The failure of a play is a very public event: a book can sink quietly into oblivion; an unsuccessful painting can be ignored. But a play signals its defeat all over town: posters and reviews catch the eye; disappointed theatregoers explode irritably at parties – 'The poor actors! One feels for them: bad enough to have to *listen* to those wretched lines; imagine having to repeat them!'

'Not for long, I imagine.'

For a dramatist a flop is a public execution, and V rose each day of the run to be cut down afresh. The play struggled through a few performances, then died, trapped in the unkind lights of the proscenium arch.

And the young playwright, also trapped, bruised in places invisible to the eye, felt death might have been a kindness. Sleepless and smarting he vowed never to write again. The etching needle, the crayon – even the less controllable brush – would be his tools. Words were for bandying lightly among friends. Leave the written stuff to the masters.

It took courage to appear in public, smile held in place, a rueful witticism to cover the pain. But once again there was a sense of knife-blow between the shoulder blades.

The court came to the rescue: a modest diplomatic appointment, though to a far from modest posting: Russia! V had not, previously, thought of himself as a diplomat, but the idea was appealing. Surely it could not be difficult to represent the King, mingle in the highest circles of gossip and conspiracy, personify Gallic charm. In addition (there are always unwritten instructions) he might cast an eye on any suspicious naval or military movements, en passant.

More enticing still: the appointment would give him the opportunity to travel – his first foray into the unknown, the great waiting world. The experience of an outlandish court would be a challenge. And he would be saved from the sharp tongues and lances of theatre critics, amateur and professional; the painful sympathy of friends. Never had the far away been more tempting.

'Baptiste!'

'Sir?'

'We are ordered to St Petersburg! Start packing.'

V looked up to find the valet still standing by the desk, as though waiting for further instruction.

'Well?'

'St Petersburg, sir. That's Russia, isn't it? I can't speak Russian.'

'It won't matter, they all speak French.'

'The servants too?' A pause. 'May I know how long we'll be staying?'

'I'm not sure. Why do you ask?'

'Your wardrobe. We shall need to pack suitably for a cold climate, but if we are there for the summer I'm told –'

V cut him short. 'Baptiste, I'm busy. Surely you can look after the details?'

'Yes, sir.'

V noted his grim expression. 'A wise Italian playwright once said he who never leaves his own country is full of prejudices.'

'Yes, sir. But when *he* travelled, he left Italy behind. We, on the other hand, will be leaving France. And for Russia. It's not the same.'

'You've never even *seen* Russia; how can you have a view?'

'I've never stuck my hand in a fire. But I have a view of what it would be like.'

'Baptiste, the more you know about something,' V said,

'the more interesting it becomes. The thing about Russia . . .'

This was the way it had always been, since they were boys: a Latin lesson passed on with Julius Caesar's murder; history translated to him via wooden swords and shields as two boys played on the banks of the stream:

'We'll do Castillon. The last great battle. You can be the English. I'll win.'

Now he would learn about Russia.

As Baptiste was leaving the room some time later, head spinning, V called after him, 'And before St Petersburg, we'll be calling in at Potsdam.'

'Potsdam. Yes, sir. For how long?'

'Oh, not long.' Pause. 'Cordial greetings from Majesty to Majesty.' Pause. Baptiste waited.

'The Emperor has an interesting collection.'

Ah. The diplomatic call on Frederick II, in fact, was a chance for the master to examine some paintings.

The young French courtier bowed and presented appropriately cordial greetings from the King. He studied the Emperor. He noted that Frederick looked bored; the long face with its soft folds of skin curving like parentheses either side of his mouth was grim. Moreover, he had a cold and was sniffing, which added to the effect of disdain.

V curtailed the ritualised cordiality and ventured a personal question:

'I hear Your Majesty has an unrivalled collection of works by Watteau . . .'

'We have a few.' He blew his nose with some thoroughness, eyes screwed shut.

Not encouraging. V sought a way through the royal barrier:

'Envy is not the most attractive of sins, but I confess that where Watteau is concerned . . .'

Frederick was surprised by the Frenchman's interest. 'Isn't

it all Boucher and Fragonard for you people these days, hmm?' A sniff.

Here was one of those tricky moments that V had to deal with from time to time: to agree meant that he might be deprived of Watteau. To disagree meant that he was denigrating court artists, and word could get back to Paris. An ambiguous smile usually worked. It did now.

Never one to prolong formalities, Frederick got to his feet and led the way, complaining of his arthritis, dropping a word or two about a new species of grape he was experimenting with at Sans Souci, 'an exceptionally successful grafting'. And then they arrived at the pictures and V stopped listening. The Emperor fell silent. For a while they studied the canvases.

V said, at last, 'Why does a Watteau *fête galante* carry a sadness that sharpens the pleasure of the moment; you observe a scene full of sunlight and laughter, and you sense the transience of youth and beauty . . . time blowing a cold wind through the trees . . . and those beautiful people in their shimmering summer silks, just for a moment feel the chill –'

'As do we,' Frederick murmured.

'Ah yes, wrapped in our silk and velvet, we feel the shiver of mortality . . . That sensual melancholy, that ache. *Sunt lacrimae rerum et mentem mortalia tangunt.*'

Frederick put his hand on V's velvet sleeve. 'Virgil and Watteau; I had not considered the connection!' He himself had no love of silk or velvet: plain cloth was the thing; a sensible man had no need of a multitude of suits. But he sensed a kindred spirit.

'You must come to one of our concerts before you leave. There's one in the music room tomorrow; a little thing of my own, a *concertante* I composed last week. I shall be playing the flute.'

'Ah!' V did his best to sound delighted, but clearly he failed to achieve the necessary fervour because Frederick remarked distantly as they paused for a moment before another picture,

'Voltaire always enjoyed my playing when he was here.'

V realised he had been insufficiently diplomatic and quickly added how much he looked forward to –

But, blowing his nose loudly, Frederick had already moved on.

Queen's Gambit

Zenobia reaches into her bag and shuffles a bundle of letters, searching. She unfolds one, the fragile paper split across the creases, the ink faded to a pale brown. She reads aloud:

'"When you are a grown woman, Zenobia my dear, I hope you will wear fur. It can be flattering as well as comforting. It is one of the consolations of a severe climate. When I went to Petersburg many years ago, I was aware immediately of beautiful women in fur hats . . . The smoothness of skin against fur . . ."'

She stops reading and looks up at Baptiste. 'He sent me a fur tippet –'

'Silver grey, I seem to recall.'

'He said it was like a Russian birch forest on a frosty day. Such a beautiful gift, my most treasured possession. It has remained with me always though the weather was never cold enough for me to wear it. Till now.' Her fingertips touch the rim of her hat. 'I had it refashioned.'

Baptiste, looking more closely, sees now that what he had dismissed as *démodé* is in fact an object of sentimental value: a silver-grey fur hat.

She says, 'I could show him the hat – he might be amused to see how the fur has changed its form and function –'

'All this was a long time ago.'

'Yes.' Her expression hardens: 'It has taken me a long time to find him.'

He knows she is watching him from across the room. Her

dark skin and thick curly hair give her the look of a small, purposeful predator; he can picture her searching, sniffing the air intently as she follows the trail across borders and years.

Baptiste knew V's opinion of women in fur; he was at his master's side as they drove into St Petersburg that chill, wintry day, V exclaiming at every turn. Dazzled by the splendour, the egg-yolk stucco of the palatial façades, the onion domes; the wide opal sheen of the Neva, the narrow canals spanned by bridges. But it was the women he noticed first, faces glowing under romantic brims of sable and ermine. He took in the detail, the look of the women as though memorising it all, murmuring the words to himself as much as Baptiste.

'Pale skin, nacreous against fur; the salon and the forest, the rough and the smooth; intriguing contrast.'

But St Petersburg was not a success.

Baptiste always thought of it as a place of darkness and mystery: velvet curtains swaying, candles guttering, doors quietly closing, carriages waiting at wrought-iron gates while assignations of one sort and another took place. Pretty women turning to glance back with knowing smiles. Treachery.

He experienced none of this at first hand, of course: but he remembered it all, as he heard it from V, returning from the latest encounter –

'Baptiste, you should have seen her!'

And in his mind, Baptiste did. He saw everything.

He had never been optimistic about his young master's suitability for the post of a secretary at the embassy. This was a diplomat who was inept when he should have been devious; impetuous where he should have been oblique; trusting when he should have been watchful. So he was not surprised by the way the St Petersburg affair ended.

There was a strangeness, an exotic quality to life in the city. Those Russians who had travelled called it a northern Venice. The canals, the hypnotic glimmer of liquid light created an erotic miasma in which V found himself drowning before he realised he was out of his depth.

He had been warned that Catherine possessed a formidable mind and a sharp wit. But he assumed that lurking within her, there must be an enlightened soul – which was, perhaps, an assumption too many.

It had sounded quite agreeable, in Paris: De Non, while representing His Majesty, would mix with the embassy people, be affable, keep his eyes open for unusual naval or military activities. And chatting to ladies at court he could extract from their gossip nuggets of information of value to France.

But in St Petersburg, finding his way about the court was like walking on ice: Catherine herself proved glacial, her pale face expressionless – 'She could cut bread with a glance,' V remarked ruefully. He had swirled his charm before her like a courtier offering his cloak for a stepping stone but the Empress had declined to thaw. He found her unfathomable.

'She gets up early and lights her own bedroom fire,' Baptiste remarked.

'What on earth for?'

'She likes to start the day with a glass of tea; makes it herself, in a sort of copper kettle.'

'Clearly our Empress has more facets than a well-cut diamond.'

V was a Burgundian: he held on to optimism; and it was too soon to lose heart.

'It should be amusing here, don't you think, Baptiste?' He sounded in need of encouragement.

This was not, the valet felt, the right time to remind the master that Catherine had almost certainly had her own husband murdered. Nor to mention the floggings and executions. He wound the selected cravat round V's neck and concentrated on the intricacies of the latest fashion in fastenings. He was concerned to demonstrate to these barbarians how a true gentleman wore his clothes: the wig curled above the ear and powdered to a silken finish, the ensemble *comme il faut*. He finalised the knot with a gentle tug and stepped back. He nodded his approval.

'Yes,' he murmured. 'Perfect.'

'The cravat or Petersburg?'

Baptiste's eloquent eyebrows rose. 'I'm an expert on cravats, not Petersburg.'

'Well, I am an expert on neither, so that gives me equal licence to express my views.'

He paused while the valet helped him into his flared brocade coat.

'Anyway.' He studied his reflection in the mirror. 'I could hardly have refused an official suggestion from Versailles. Even if it was made unofficially. Do you suppose the Russians think I'm a spy?'

'Quite possibly. You must be aware, sir, that we already have a whole cadre of people who might be considered spies, working in Moscow.'

'We? You mean France? We have a cadre? Baptiste, where do you get these words from? *Cadre*! It's not the sort of word that comes up in normal conversation. And I suppose you also know what these people are engaged on?'

But before Baptiste could reply, V's coach was announced, to carry him off to supper with the Empress. He was aware that once again he would be feeling his way in the dark.

Baptiste collected his master's discarded clothes and set aside the linen to be washed. He brushed and hung the rest in the wardrobe, swept away all signs of hair powder. Then he poured a glass of wine and allowed himself the luxury of a few minutes spent in thought, thought tinged with anxiety, about his young master – V was in fact slightly older than his valet but Baptiste always thought of him as younger: too trusting, too impressionable – in a word, guileless. Already Baptiste knew a good deal about the Empress, possibly more than the French agents in Moscow: the servants' network frequently surpassed the spy-cell for intimate information. He had discovered that, of course, the servants spoke French.

He was asleep in his chair when the coach drew up outside the house, but when V came through the door, Baptiste was on his feet, ready to take his hat, remove his shoes and hear an account of the evening. Her Majesty, it seemed, had been more gracious this time; almost warm.

'We did have quite a dose of Voltaire. She refers to him as the Master. Sickeningly obsequious . . .'

And V was not the only Frenchman being entertained.

'Diderot was there. He gave me a nod. Twisted his face into a smirky sort of smile. I remarked – in a casual way – that he once reviewed a play I wrote for the Comédie. He said, "It's difficult to remember them all; I saw so many plays." Yes, I felt like saying, but I wrote just the one, so it's easier for me to remember. Particularly as he was vicious about it. He was barely aware of my existence; I felt invisible.'

'Ah,' Baptiste said, 'I know how that can feel –'

But he was attending to the fire at the time and V – already half asleep and murmuring drowsily – did not hear him.

'He taps her on the arm if he wants to contradict her. Bangs his fist on her knee to emphasise a point. When I left they were settling down to a game of chess.'

It was possible, he thought, that for an empress, the rare luxury of being disagreed with disagreeably might have the exquisite pleasure of a good scratch at a scab: temporary bliss, though ultimately damaging. But Diderot, a difficult old man, brought out the best in Catherine. V noted her kindness – 'to buy the man's entire library and put him in charge of it for life – an act of true delicacy!' He was lulled: that evening, her face gentled by the candlelight, she had talked to him of painting, invited him to look at her collection. He decided she was a woman of discernment, a lover of the arts.

On balance, V thought, it had gone well.

'She said she enjoys the company of intelligent diplomats. She appreciates logical thinking.'

'She's a Prussian, after all.'

'At one point she said, "A youthful mind offers a refreshing perspective."'

'So she likes young men,'

'She's observant: she noticed the cut of my breeches.'

'Or what's inside them.'

Yes, it all seemed to be going well. He yawned.

An old man in an overheated room – how assiduous Baptiste is at keeping out draughts! – V pulls at his nightshift collar and recalls the airlessness of those Petersburg chambers; the sweat that trickled from wig to collar, from armpit to groin. The ladies-in-waiting were more comfortable in their low-cut gowns, with skirts that stood away from thigh and hip.

Petersburg, a city he found enigmatic, swirls now in his old head like the water that surged against the grey stone embankments. He sees himself stepping out of a coach, through the doors of a palace, a curly-haired courtier, touchingly confident, young enough to think himself clever, to imagine he could outmanoeuvre the barbaric *arrivistes* on the outer edges of the civilised world. Only as he grew older did he appreciate how much they had known all along.

The city was a contradictory blend of icy streets and warm-fleshed women. For the newly arrived young Frenchman it was a dream of sensuality and *luxe*. There would be an intimate tête-à-tête with one or two of the ladies, and if the performance pleased them and the gentleman proved to be discreet he could safely be handed on and up to the Empress.

He happily submitted to the test and the ladies too were

delighted. For the moment he put aside the question of his vaguely defined assignment, the unspoken orders concerning naval details; the sketching of a map or two that might prove more informative than those available to foreigners. Social life here was exacting.

But when winter came, there was a slowing, then a suspension of normal activity: everything at the mercy of the thermometer. This was a land where a man hesitated to put his head outside, the air so cold it froze his eyelashes. When the temperature fell below seventeen degrees social life ceased – dinners cancelled, visits abandoned. With the creaking of ice, and the muffling of city noises by a carpet of snow, this northern world seemed wrapped in sleep.

Until the temperature rose, and the court came to life again.

One of Catherine's ladies led V through the palace, expressing her sympathy for the unfortunate people of France. 'Our houses are so warm! Only when I went to Paris did I actually *feel* the cold. At home, we simply see it through the windows.' She paused at a pair of carved double doors. 'The Empress is expecting you.'

Catherine in a good mood could be deceptively gentle, like this mild winter day.

'Monsieur De Non,' she purred, 'We hear pleasing accounts of you.' She knew how to listen but she could also be direct: 'Tell me: what is your first memory of the female breast?'

V blinked. 'I suppose my wet nurse.'

Catherine's brows arched in surprise: this was not what she had expected. 'Really.'

'A large, comfortable woman, with the softest skin in the world. And she cooed like a dove while she rocked me –'

Catherine broke in impatiently, 'We all had our wet nurse. Mine sang me nursery songs. I still remember them.'

She hummed with some vigour a few bars of an old favourite. V listened attentively, an appreciative smile stretching his facial muscles. He decided that Prussian folk songs must be an acquired taste.

Catherine gulped her wine; nostalgia hung in the air: ah, those old nursery songs, and fairy tales . . . She found herself smiling at the boy. He was not handsome, she could see, but he was amusing and bright-eyed, and when he smiled, there was a dimple which did wonders for the round young face. And it was pleasant to speak French; the Russian she had acquired so painfully came naturally now, but she had always admired the elegance of the Gallic tongue. Certainly, he chatted agreeably. He could discuss art and philosophy. Well, of course: he was a Frenchman, like Diderot, like Voltaire, the Master; a representative of the Enlightenment. She decided to be charmed.

Bumping home in his carriage at dawn, V was elated.

'No icy stare tonight,' he told Baptiste.

Unbuttoning his shirt, his hand brushed his small, cold nipple.

'I told her about your mother.' He dropped his shirt to the floor. 'I trust she's well?'

'Much as usual.' The master had forgotten, if he ever knew, that servants did not receive news from home; Baptiste wrote to his mother from time to time, and his letters were read aloud to her by one of the De Non personal maids. Once a year he reminded V to send her greetings, which she kept in a trunk under her bed. The master's relationship with her had always been closer, his mouth had first call on her milk; she was wet nurse first, mother second. Baptiste had waited his turn.

Who was to blame? And who betrayed whom? Later, thinking back on it all, V felt that shifting of the ground underfoot, a hollow in the pit of his stomach that reminded him of a certain velvet night; a distant château and a woman

62

whose eyes were like stars. No one would have described Catherine as beautiful; when she beckoned him to her side and leaned close with a question, she was not always fragrant, her breath redolent of rich meats and pungent seasonings. She told him once that her white fur mantle had been made from the skins of four thousand ermines, and as she spoke he seemed to hear the screams of small living creatures, sacrificed for a decorative cloak.

And when her pale eyes fastened on his, he felt again the velvet-gloved power of a female predator, and found it difficult for a moment to breathe easily.

To get away from the stifling rooms and the cramped formalities of the court he took to riding out of the city on horseback to sketch the countryside, the waterways, the vast Russian skies above the endless horizon of the sea. The Russians said that the return of migrating birds heralded the beginning of spring, and one day he watched as distant specks, a pattern like ink spots against the sky, became birds that settled noisily in the trees. His pencil moved across the pad; he was at ease; in a bleak Russian landscape he felt at home, doing what he most enjoyed.

Catherine was warming to the young diplomat, though she received reports that he was often away from the city, engaged in sketching the countryside. It all seemed innocuous, but his drawings had occasionally included the coming and going of the Russian fleet; some of his landscapes could even be said to resemble a map of sorts.

She paced the council chamber, brooding: a man who manages to indicate how many ships lie in which bay, and in what direction they are heading, may perhaps be suspected of putting information before art. 'Is this pretty cavalier more interested than he should be in our political affairs?'

Certain orders were given, certain arrangements put in hand.

Baptiste, returning from a marketing expedition one morning, noted a drawer not quite closed in one of the chests; his master's documents arranged more tidily than was usual; a letter thrust back into its envelope too roughly, the edge torn. He became aware that the apartment had been searched.

While Catherine was being fed fresh reports on her dubious cavalier, Chevalier Langeac, of the French 'cell' in Moscow, invited V to dinner – 'Try the sturgeon, it's rather fine' – and over the brandy asked his guest's help with what he described as a daring and gallant coup. There was, it seemed, a small problem with one of his people – a Mlle Dorseville – 'Charming girl, quite useful in a minor way, but the Russians have suddenly become suspicious and locked her up. She's being held under lock and key in the ballet wing of the theatre in St Petersburg. We'd like to whisk her quietly away; let the whole thing die down . . .'

The room was swathed in rich velvet drapery; shadows moved on the walls, wine in fat decanters glowed in the candlelight. V's head was swimming with the excitement of it all. If Langeac wanted to rescue the young woman of course he must help.

Baptiste, undressing him later, felt a sense of unease as he heard what lay ahead – in fact he already knew: a good servant could hardly avoid overhearing and observing. He had the strongest sensation of something about to go wrong.

'It sounds too simple, sir. The young lady may be working for the French court as the chevalier says. But then again, there's the possibility –'

But who listens to a valet?

A sparkling May night. Some of the town clocks were striking twelve. Messages had been delivered – notes slipped under plates, tucked between the leaves of books – and the date and time for the rescue had arrived. The moon was obscured by fast-moving clouds as two young men waited below a shuttered window in the dark courtyard of the ballet school.

The window was cautiously opened, a whispered password exchanged and the young woman stood wobbling on the sill, and jumped, arms flung up, wide skirts fluttering, billowing in the air so that for a moment she appeared to be floating on an invisible swing. Then she was safe in their arms.

A moment to recover, and they hurried her away from the building – 'Your carriage is waiting.' Supported by her intrepid rescuers, Mlle Dorseville skimmed the cobblestones, gasping, breathless, and allowed herself to be lifted into the first carriage. The door slammed shut, but before the coachman could crack his whip, before the horses could lift a hoof, there was a shout from behind them; a soldier cried, 'Halt!'

Afterwards V found it hard to recall exactly what happened next: the alarm was raised and guards came running, it seemed from all directions. The two young men, taken by surprise, leapt into the second coach and urged the drivers on towards a narrow alleyway. Flaring torches, the clatter of spurs, shouted instructions, chaos and confusion. The coaches rattled on, to be blocked by another line of guards. The drivers wrenched on reins, horses reared and snorted in panic, the two young Frenchmen sweating with apprehension, as the carriages turned this way and that, trying to find a way out of the ballet school square, down another alley – this time to find two rows of guards lined up, firearms cocked and ready. The coaches stopped. The guards moved in and the young woman was carried back to her little room at the ballet school. The two gentlemen were escorted politely but firmly from the scene. It almost seemed they had been expected.

While Catherine was enjoying a leisurely game of chess with Diderot, it was officially made clear that Monsieur De Non and Chevalier Langeac were required to leave without delay.

Russian nesting dolls, so popular as gifts, so intriguing to visitors, each brightly painted babushka figure opening to reveal another, and another; V had bought a set to take home for his sister. But in St Petersburg, puzzles were not confined to wooden dolls, as V found when he attempted to deliver a farewell message of commiseration to Mlle Dorseville, at the ballet school. His letter was handed back to him: the elderly porter assured him there had never been such a person as Mlle Dorseville listed among the performers, and the porter prided himself on knowing all the names. There was, he added helpfully, a young French dancer who had been with the corps for quite some time – a *Monsieur* Dorseville, but obviously this could not be the same person . . .

Almost half a century later, when V, moving home, was sifting through his papers, he said to Baptiste, 'I was never any good as a diplomat, was I?'

'No,' said Baptiste, 'and how fortunate that was. If you had proved successful as a diplomat you would never have done anything else.'

'Still, when I look back, my failures –'

And Baptiste, without irony, broke in, 'Most people have one life to live; you have managed half a dozen. Did you expect to do well in all of them?'

He was standing on a library stepladder, reaching to the back of a high shelf for the last of many small objects that, forgotten, had nested invisibly for years. He pulled out a dusty wig whose once-white powder had aged into an appropriate grey, and held it out for V to see.

'I wonder when you last wore one of those.'

'Before the Revolution, for sure.' V wrinkled his nose at the disintegrating wig. 'It wasn't all *douceur de vivre* whatever Talleyrand might have thought. A lot of it was nothing more than a pretty dance. And sometimes not so pretty. Marionettes obeying the strings.'

'But you enjoyed the dance.'

'Oh, when you're young, you always enjoy the dance, don't you?'

Baptiste dropped the wig into a basket and brushed the powder off his hands.

'I suppose you do.'

When you're young . . . He had been young, once, but a valet has no time for dancing; lucky if he can seize a few precious moments between duties. Baptiste recalled a night in Venice, a girl with black hair: she stepped from the gondola and looked up at him, her face as pale and delicate as a mask, sweetly thin arms reaching forward, dark eyes full of tears . . . his own, now, to his surprise, grew moist and he sniffed, pushing away memory. Dust composed of the past and the present filled his nostrils and Baptiste sneezed, almost losing his balance.

He was reaching for something to hold on to, to steady himself, when V stretched up and gripped his hand, to help him down. Two old men, one small and round, the other tall and thin, but here the cadaverous one was the faithful servant, the rotund one the chivalrous dreamer, and dreams notwithstanding he had fought real giants of one sort and another, and on one occasion, in a distant country, he had saved a maiden in real distress.

When Baptiste was safely down from his step-ladder, V gently patted the back of his valet's hand where liver spots glowed against the pallor of old skin; a gesture of affection and of rueful acknowledgement that he was aware not everyone had shared the dance, not everyone had spun the hours of sunshine into a magical veil, wearing silk and a powdered wig.

'Thank God you were always there when I got home,' he said. 'Appearing to listen to everything I said.'

'Oh, I was listening,' Baptiste said.

A Change of Key

Ambassador Vergennes was amused and indulgent when the new recruit presented himself at the French Embassy in Stockholm. 'Are you usually as foolish as you were in Petersburg?'

V looked embarrassed. 'I didn't think I *was* being foolish at the time – that's what is so worrying.'

'We all need our baptism of humiliation.'

Stockholm should have provided a breathing space, a chance to allow St Petersburg to fade, but V found the city unpleasing.

'What's wrong with it?' Baptiste asked.

'Too many herrings. Too much water.'

'But you're always saying you want to see Venice, and Venice is full of water, isn't it?'

'Don't be absurd. Venice is Titian, Bellini, Canaletto; Venice is Raphael. That special, Venetian light –'

'The light that reflects the water.'

'What do you know about light reflecting water?'

'You explained it to me once.' Yes, V had explained it, in one of his didactic, late-night moods.

Still smarting from St Petersburg, V found it hard to believe the Duc de Vergennes could ever find himself in similar humiliating circumstances: the ambassador had substance, dignity, while he himself was closer to a clown; not for the first time, a figure of fun. *A certain château . . . the moonlight* . . . Well, at least here he had a kindly, experienced mentor.

'Try not to put indiscretions in writing,' Vergennes advised. 'Spoken words drift away, they can never be pinned down with certainty. Pen and paper have a way of surviving fire and flood to betray you.'

'Who could betray me here? The herrings? And if you're writing to someone you trust –'

'Can you be sure no one else will see what you write? And can anyone be trusted?'

'So in fact,' V said, 'diplomacy means clinking glasses with betrayal.'

'Only if you fuel the winds of rumour. Be discreet.'

'Discreet! Me?' V looked dismayed. 'But indiscretion is the breath of life!'

When Vergennes was beckoned back to Paris to take charge of Foreign Affairs, V followed him home with some relief. But Paris was not the place he remembered. Kindly Louis, who had demanded of an unknown youth at Versailles, 'Who *are* you?', who had laughed at the boy's silly jokes and discussed the family vineyards in Burgundy, had joined his forefathers. A new Louis with a new number – XVl – was in charge of the royal shop; a quieter, more sober Louis who put a quieter, duller stamp on the public face of the court, while his consort played games – 'cavorted' was a popular word – with her cronies.

Scope for gossip there was, in plenty, but somehow Marie-Antoinette failed to inspire V and, spirits lowered, he found the scene as remote as a distant planet.

'The Season is not what it was.' Bored with suppers and balls he thought this might be the time to get some serious work done.

He stood, arms raised like a conductor poised for the opening downward beat, while Baptiste, his mouth full of pins, fitted and remodelled a brocade jacket to the new, slimmer line. The valet mumbled an encouraging 'Mmm', and slid the pins, one by one, into a repositioned side seam.

'Is this going to take much longer?' V asked. 'You're interrupting my reading.'

Baptiste had become aware that where other young masters might splash too much of their allowance on new shirts, embroidered surcoats, jewelled pins and buttons, for V, these days, the most unpromising items – an old book, a faded drawing, a battered curio picked up in a dusty shop filled with bric-a-brac – were what brightened his eyes and lightened his purse. The allowance from Burgundy had never been intended to fund a collecting mania and the valet grew skilled at maintaining V's existing wardrobe in immaculate condition. Black velvet breeches could look elegant worn with coats of different colours; last season's braided trim could be adapted. Only when fashion was undeniably calling a new tune – when, say, a full-skirted frock coat would have stood out embarrassingly among this season's narrower models - were new clothes purchased – and even then, not always, thanks to Baptiste's skills.

Immobilised while Baptiste folded and pinned, V stared across the room at the work in progress on his desk. The drawing needed refining; his engraving technique called for attention. It was seductive, the process; the incising, the steady driving of burin and etching blade into the yielding copper; his fingers itched. If he had learned anything, it was that while conversation might last an evening and amorous dalliance a night, art was for ever; art did not deceive, did not sigh fragrantly and smile and betray. You could count on art.

His condition was one of yearning, but what he yearned for was not the pale hand discreetly leading him into a sensual maze but, rather, the road to the horizon; or the boat, the mule track that led to an unknown world. There had been glimpses, here and there: a church, a ruined temple, a canvas on the wall of a foreign monarch, all of which had whetted his appetite. To travel and observe; to unlock mysteries, to acquire objects of beauty, to learn – this was what he craved, when he allowed himself to admit it.

He abandoned his waistcoat to Baptiste, and went to dinner with an old friend, Jacques-Louis David, home on a brief visit from Rome.

'Why don't you come to Italy?' David enthused. 'For an artist, Italy has everything. Florence, Bologna, Venice . . . you could spend a lifetime there.'

V felt a lowering of the spirits as the evening wore on: Paris had always been the centre of everything for him, and his place was at court, but for an artist . . . He drank a lot of wine; they toasted Raphael, Cimabue, Giotto . . .

When David had gone back to Rome, the worm of dissatisfaction continued to nag and there were nights when V declined an invitation so that he could stay at his desk and work, or he might snatch up his hat and go out into the older, winding streets where cramped shops were filled with old books. He bought as many as he could afford, piling them up on every surface of his cramped quarters, to be arranged on ever more crowded shelves later.

Italy would have to wait, while he spent his time looking at paintings closer to home. He would stand before one canvas for half an afternoon, his eyes slowly exploring its brushwork landscape. There were messages in these strokes of paint, coded messages that a *cognoscente* could read. Like a man following a faint but insistent scent, he was charting the world of the antique, or at least, as much of that world as he could reach. He had been lucky: St Petersburg, Potsdam, but there was so much more and his means were modest. He had said as much, despairingly, to David: 'Italy, the Orient . . . How am I ever to explore their treasures?'

'Well, if you chain yourself to the absurdity of the royal

circus, what can you expect?' David had shrugged. 'You're mingling with mediocrities!'

The stately royal minuet plodded on at court, but V was not part of the pattern: the new King mistrusted this young charmer whose lack of discretion had caused the court some small embarrassment at Petersburg, while the Queen found his priorities baffling: art before everything? What could that mean?

Her gambling and fancy-dress *soirées*, her bedroom games with dubious confidants and camp followers were equally baffling to V.

'When I try to explain something quite simple, she doesn't seem to understand what I'm talking about,' he muttered, returning from a particularly difficult evening.

'She's Austrian, remember.'

Baptiste removed his master's cravat, noting sweat, grime and a smudge of something greasy, all needing attention.

Fingers burned in Russia, V now kept away from politics. Lost in his own world he could disregard the simmering resentment building up against England, the cautious signals being exchanged with America, the underground rumblings of the domestic disaffected. But the frowning concentration on a page, the close study of painted detail and brush stroke were occasionally abandoned – he was only twenty-eight, after all – and then he was to be found in society, eyes sparkling, the dimple signalling the sighting of a pretty woman.

Welcomed with delight at the best salons, he enjoyed the champagne glow and watched with glee the rise and fall of coiffures that towered like birdcages, the sudden popularity of diamonds as big as military buttons – indeed of diamonds used as buttons; of fragile silk gauze that would not survive a single wash; gold lace that lost its appeal when it tarnished . . . the excess of it all!

Thanks to Baptiste, he himself was wearing the latest subtle shade in stockings and the narrowest of coats. He was a man of fashion and he relished the red-heeled, bag-wigged, flaring display. But when he reeled home at dawn, kicking off his fancy shoes with their buckles and glowing heels, ribboned wig flung in a corner, clothes abandoned in a heap for Baptiste to deal with, he went to his desk, picked up pencil or etching scalper, and the true pleasure began. The quiet delight of the work.

The little actresses welcomed him backstage at the Comédie, though there were to be no more plays by Monsieur De Non. There were more ways than one for fingers to be burned.

He was glimpsed at a fashionable *vernissage*, a concert. He was seen at the Opéra, and there was the occasional, civilised *amitié-amoureuse*. At the best salons, beautiful women relished his sense of fun, and were gratified that, unlike most men, he listened to them. How intently he listened to them! They failed to notice that behind the smile and the good humour the door to the inner sanctum was shut tight.

Undiplomatic Exchanges

'Le Déjeuner de Ferney'. Denon's etching of Voltaire in his night-cap, July 1775. (*Bibliothèque nationale de France, département des Estampes et de la Photographie, Paris*)

'What can I *possibly* say that will interest a man who's rejected the world?'

The Duc de Vergennes, in his new role as Minister for Foreign Affairs, had thought up a little job for his young protégé: a tour of the Swiss Cantons.

'Any spying mentioned?' Baptiste asked. 'Any suggestions of maps you might sketch, or young women needing to be rescued?'

V decided to ignore the tone of voice. Switzerland was bound to be less exciting than Petersburg. But just as Baptiste was silently giving thanks for what sounded like a satisfyingly dull trip, his master recalled that not far from Geneva, on the very edge of the border, was a small town called Ferney, and in Ferney a once-dangerous philosopher was hibernating.

'Voltaire always enjoyed my flute playing,' Frederick had remarked to V in Potsdam, and in St Petersburg, the Empress had talked much of the Master, 'the man I most admire', though that admiration might have been tempered had she actually spent much time in the same room with him. Voltaire, as many – including Frederick – could testify, reserved his sharpest bite for those that fed him. But at eighty-one he was comfortably tucked away, largely keeping his mischief to himself.

'We'll go to Ferney. Everyone's waiting for him to die. It's my chance to meet him before he does. The greatest living

Frenchman!' He caught the valet's eye. 'Except for His Majesty, obviously.'

The journey had something to offer after all.

Now V, squatting in his Swiss bathtub, sifted his available options. He knew Voltaire doted on Catherine, so he could dangle the conversational lure of Petersburg before the recluse. Hint intriguingly at some duality of purpose to his present trip. Flattery never went amiss, he had learned that at Versailles, but Voltaire, unlike the monarch, would never take it straight: V planned to interweave humility with cocky confidence, and lay it on so thick that it startled, make it so sycophantic that it achieved irony. Bait to tempt an old fish.

Baptiste held out a large towel that he had warmed at the coal fire and V stepped into its comforting embrace, rubbed himself dry and read through his letter. He felt he had achieved a nice balance:

Geneva, 3rd July 1775

Monsieur,

I have an overwhelming desire to pay my homage to a great man. My fear is that you may be unwell – or may decide to be - but I trust not.

I am a Gentleman of the King's Chamber, and you know better than anyone that if we present ourselves at the King's door – or anywhere else – we are never turned away. I claim my privilege, therefore, for your door to be opened to me!

Recently I spent some time at the court in St Petersburg. I normally live in Paris, but have been criss-crossing the thirteen Cantons on official duties . . . If you think that I might merit the sacrifice of a few minutes of your time, which is all I crave of you, my pleasure would be unalloyed.

I won't presume to pay you compliments. You have no need of my humble words of praise . . . I can only hope that writing this letter may prove a way to effect a comradely meeting. There is no one more devoted than your very humble and very obedient servant, De Non.

Voltaire replied the same day.

Ferney, 3rd July
Monsieur, and much respected comrade,
Not only *might* I be unwell, I am, and have been for the last eighty-one years.
But dead or alive, I have to say your letter fills me with a desire to take advantage of your generosity. I never dine; I take a little supper. I therefore shall await you at supper-time. My niece, Madame Denis, will look after the details.
Your very humble and very obedient servant, Voltaire.

V at twenty-eight still had the bright, enquiring eyes, the smile that had charmed La Pompadour. The old philosopher took his time studying the picture of youth and outrageous confidence poised in the doorway. He noted the low and elegant bow, accepted the well-honed words of homage. Voltaire was indeed dying, as he often claimed, but he had a while yet to live. Was this boy as innocent as he looked? Certainly he had the gift of likeability. Perhaps he should be given a chance. The old man straightened his nightcap and made a gesture of welcome.

Voltaire has turned to dust, but the letters that flew between Geneva and Ferney, between an old master and a young tyro, lie intact. Fifty years after they were written Baptiste has brought them out and laid them on a table in the salon of the house on the Quai Voltaire, for a young woman to study; part of a paperchase, to lead her away into a more distant landscape.

Zenobia opens a thick leather folder, its crimson cover faded and cracked. The letters are filed in order, and she bends closer to study the first, the faded words hard to decipher.

'. . . *your very humble and very obedient servant, De Non . . .*'

She turns a page, reads a line and stops.

'He *met* Voltaire!' she looks up from the crimson folder.

Baptiste leans forward to straighten one of the letters that has slipped out of alignment with the rest.

'It was . . . a complicated encounter,' he says, choosing words that are imprecise, that do not pin him down to an opinion. It was probably the only time he withdrew his approbation from the man he served.

He turns his head slightly, listening: he has picked up an almost inaudible sound, something which might be the trace of a cough. It comes again and he moves towards the door. She gets up, as if to follow him.

'Will you tell him I'm here?'

'You will find the letters of interest,' he says, waving at the red leather folder, leaving the room, putting off again the danger of more questions, questions he dreads.

In his heyday Voltaire wrote some harsh words about his monarch, and the King threw him in jail for his presumption, but time has a way of changing things, and three years after V's little visit to Ferney, the old troublemaker was back in Paris, his bust crowned with a laurel wreath, his carriage cheered by the crowds who lined the streets as he drove past. And shortly afterwards he died in a high-ceilinged room by the Seine – on a *quai* renamed Voltaire, where nearly fifty years later, in a similar room in a neighbouring house, a young woman sits, head bent over the pages of letters that passed so long ago between two disingenuous wordsmiths.

★

Again, it all began so well. The visit must have seemed a perfect meeting of minds: the deferential young admirer on the threshold of life; the revered old philosopher in his retirement. The encounter went splendidly despite Voltaire's opening words:

'So, young man: you want to hasten my death, do you?'

But V was not to be intimidated: the smile remained in place, he gazed about him with those watchful young eyes. They talked of politics, of mutual friends in Paris, and Frederick of Prussia:

'Quite a reasonable flute player,' Voltaire murmured, perfectly aware he sounded patronising. 'He writes his tunes after breakfast, sits there while his hair's being curled and does his composing.'

'He showed me his paintings —'

'Did you talk about literature?' Voltaire clucked impatiently. 'He's a decent writer, but can't take the slightest criticism. Excessive sensitivity . . . Now Catherine, *she* could take criticism. She sent me one of her plays, demanded severe assessment. Wonderful woman!'

'In some ways.' V decided to be provocative. 'But if one stripped the Empress of the pomp and ceremony that surrounds her I wonder whether she might not emerge as quite . . . ordinary.' He was aware that Voltaire was beginning to seethe with irritation. 'Forgive me, but I cannot help thinking that you are speaking of the public figure, while I can only describe her as I saw her.'

And V was indeed thinking of the Catherine he saw: the pale eyes, the ruthless composure. The tuneless voice singing Prussian nursery songs. The power.

Voltaire, glancing up at a portrait of Catherine on the wall above his desk, seemed not to have heard.

'A woman of vision —'

'Vision, yes' — V's shrug was barely perceptible — 'but I found perhaps her heart lacked sensitivity.' The quality Voltaire had found too plentiful in Frederick.

Voltaire ordered his muscles into a thin smile. They agreed to disagree about Catherine, but V felt it was time for a compliment: 'She always refers to you as her Master.'

The hours spun by but Voltaire made no move to end the audience. The chevalier De Non brought a breath of something rarer than fresh air into the room: the optimism that comes from inexperience.

Supper had been taken between six and seven, but when the devoted Mme Denis, in her ambiguous incarnation of niece and mistress, suggested, some time after midnight, that it might be time for V to leave, Voltaire waved her away: he was enjoying himself. The visitor stayed on.

The thank-you letter was a *mille-feuille* of praise layered with extravagance. V flung himself into full hyperbole:

You are eternal, not subject to the laws of nature. No longer earthbound; you are equipped for immortality.

I have just one regret about our meeting: before I left Paris, my old friend Laborde asked me to bring him back a picture of you, and I am mortified at having failed to ask if I could draw your portrait while I was with you.

Voltaire's reply was warm: he felt V's youth had proved indulgent to his own 'decrepitude'. He no longer had a portrait in his possession, but he would send V a good likeness in Sèvres porcelain that was even then being prepared. 'Thank you for all the kindness you have shown an old comrade quite unworthy of the honour.'

Two foxes, one old, one young, and youth had the advantage of speed. Before the Sèvres porcelain portrait could reach him, V had finished several drawings.

'Have a look, Baptiste.'

Baptiste studied the picture. It captured a vivid domestic moment: the old philosopher tucked up in bed in his nightcap, a tray of coffee by his side, the famous features in sharp profile. The devoted Mme Denis close by, flanked by a young serving girl . . . Off to one side, looking on, in the manner of a Renaissance painting, two curious outsiders: a visiting Jesuit priest and a French nobleman.

'Well: what do you think?'

'He looks frail.'

'He has a mind as sharp as an eagle's beak.'

In Paris, V's portraits of Voltaire began to circulate – sketches, drawings – one in particular, printed by Mssrs Née & Masquelier, signed, like the rest, De Non and dated 4 July 1775. *Déjeuner de Ferney* revealed the celebrated philosopher in a moment of touching, if slightly absurd, domestic intimacy. It became an instant best-seller.

At Ferney, Mme Denis unpacked a package from Paris: an engraving, 'from Monsieur De Non'. A small head and shoulders portrait in an oval frame; a suitable offering to a sitter. With it a letter, another of V's blithe confections, the sentences gilded with disarming flattery: he dwelt on the joy of being at the side of the master, the privilege of listening to him talk . . . Mme Denis read aloud: ' "Drawing your portrait afterwards was an attempt to prolong the experience, to preserve your features, which might otherwise have been lost with the passage of time . . ." ' There was talk of 'homage', mention of 'confraternity'. Alas, the reverential tone was undermined by the fact that Voltaire was already aware of the brisk French trade being enjoyed by a rather different portrait, the *Déjeuner de Ferney*. He was, not surprisingly, enraged.

An image can appropriate the real person more effectively than any journalistic assassination. As image-conscious as La Pompadour, Voltaire – like the King's favourite – relied on artists to provide the iconography, the visible proof of what a hero looked like. Now, the man who had spent his life lampooning kings and court favourites with a lethal pen thought he had been made to look ridiculous. He was not one to shrug off offence . . .

'I must thank the young man for taking so much trouble.' He cast about for an appropriately stinging comment, something to wound a young artist. He might say he had not realised his guest was a cartoonist; that would have a certain edge . . . The malicious smile came and went.

A note arrived in Paris, the letter preceded by a few sardonic lines of verse:

Ferney, 20th December 1775

From Callot the droll you've borrowed a quill;
Your writing is charming, your drawings burlesques.
With Apollo to guide both your hand and your will
Do you need to invent such grotesques?

The little poem seemed light-hearted, but the attached letter carried a sting:

Why [Voltaire enquired] have you drawn me looking like a crippled monkey, with a twisted head and one shoulder four times higher than the other? I am sending you a small box made by craftsmen in the village here, on the lid of which is an honest and true likeness. It is a misfortune to seek the extraordinary and flee from what is natural.
    Your very humble and very obedient servant, Voltaire.

Touché?
The parry was swift and cutting:

I must thank you for the little box and I admire the zeal of your village craftsmen in their effort to please you . . .

V was, he assured his revered comrade, desolated by the impression his work appeared to have given –

my aim was to do honour to its subject. In Paris it is recognised and applauded as a true representation by those who know you. It is a great misfortune, in painting as in anything else, to see objects other than as they are. Forgive me, monsieur, but I felt I must tell you, not only how I feel for having upset you with the portrait, but also, in contrast, to allay your fears by telling you what a success the print has had here.

The print had indeed enjoyed public acclaim; V would be able to buy some rare books with the proceeds. But there was a sour aftertaste to the success.

The letter from Ferney was read and cast aside. Picked up and reread, a wine stain in one corner indicating that it had been studied over a glass or two. The dutiful valet reached for the crimson leather folder in which earlier letters from Ferney were kept safe. He picked up the latest, but paused before putting it away, reading it slowly, his lips moving. V called irritably across the room, 'Why does he bring Callot into it? A *cartoonist*! I don't draw cartoons! He obviously hasn't seen my work!'

'Or he has and is giving an opinion.'

'Perhaps I should write back and say: "Surely, Monsieur, while you disapprove of what I have drawn, you would defend to the death my right to draw it"!'

'That's very good.'

'I took it from something he said. You could call it an *hommage*. To him.'

'Like the portrait.'

There was a flatness in Baptiste's tone.

'What?'

Baptiste tidied the table, straightening papers, moving an inkwell, placing the letter from Voltaire in the red leather folder while his master watched him. V put down his pen and leaned back in the chair.

'What's the matter?'

A busy silence, Baptiste occupied in fastening the leather folder with a clasp of engraved brass.

'What's the matter?' V repeated.

'It's not my place –'

'A pox on that! What do you mean, your "place"? We're hardly talking about *droit de seigneur* here. What are you thinking?'

'I don't think you should have done it. I don't mean you shouldn't have done the picture, if that's how you saw him. I mean selling the prints.'

'I'm an *artist*, Baptiste. I make pictures.'

'So you're an artist. I thought you were a diplomat.'

'My skills as a diplomat are limited, but I'm a rather good artist. On occasion I earn money by selling my work. That's satisfying. It's what artists do.'

Baptiste nodded, and replaced the leather folder on the shelf. 'So when you first wrote to Monsieur Voltaire, you described yourself as an artist.'

Pause. 'Not exactly.'

'What exactly *did* you say?'

'I said I was a Gentleman of the King's Chamber. Which I am.'

Baptiste had now picked up one of V's silk waistcoats and appeared to be deeply engaged in removing a small stain from one of its lapels. 'I hope this isn't juice from one of those Italian peaches –'

V said irritably, addressing the ceiling, 'That's the trouble with the lower classes: they are so insufferably self-righteous. Of course, they can *afford* to have high principles, it's one of the advantages of being at the bottom of the heap.'

'It was you who taught me about principles. Must I now forget all that?'

'No. And don't let *me* forget either. Just don't look so bloody sour-faced while you lecture me.'

He picked up an uncompleted sketch of a Swiss landscape, studied it for a moment, frowning. Then he crumpled it in his hand.

'Not good enough.' He threw the crumpled paper into a corner of the room. 'I'll do better, next time.' It was an acknowledgement; an olive branch.

And Baptiste now thought he might be able to save the waistcoat: 'You can hardly see the stain at all.'

Some time later, a salon acquaintance asked V to tell him about the visit to Ferney. V dealt briefly with the episode: 'We should all remember that Voltaire said the way to be a bore is to say everything . . .'

Strolling home, he thought again about the visit to Ferney. Was it a betrayal? he asked himself. On one level, it might seem so. How uncomfortable some questions could be. Up the steps and through the front door, he tapped the thermometer hanging in its case. Oh, to have a moral compass one could tap and watch to see if it trembled.

The salon of the house on the Quai Voltaire is darkening, as the light thickens and a blanket of low cloud spreads across the afternoon sky. The two people immobile in their carved and padded chairs are blurred, like rough pencil sketches for an interior still to be completed.

Zenobia studies a print of a frail old man in bed, Voltaire peering out from beneath his nightcap.

'He does look like a wizened old monkey.'

Baptiste considers the consequences of the act of image-making: truth may be in the eye of the beholder, but what if the sitter sees nothing of himself in the portrait unveiled before him? Whose truth has the final word?

'Surely an artist must be true to what he sees,' Zenobia says. 'Truth must be served.

The room is dark, though a milky stripe lingers low in the sky. Baptiste rises, moving from lamp to lamp like an alchemist, creating globes of light, pushing the shadows away, so that they lurk, wavering, against the walls. He wishes she had not mentioned truth.

'I should tell you the Baron is unwell,' he says.

'Why did you not say –'

'It's just a chill. He returned in good spirits yesterday from a private show; he was his usual self. In the night I heard him coughing. I thought he should rest today.'

'Have you told him I'm here?'

He stares at her, helpless, unable to order her to leave, which is what he most (and least) wants to do; unable to tell her what might pass for the truth, unable to extricate himself from the man-trap of his own devising.

He gets up. 'You must excuse me for a moment . . . The household does not run itself.'

He leaves the room, closing the door. She begins to sift again through the letters in her lap, the ink faded, the paper fragile from much folding and unfolding. She pauses at one to read it yet again:

My dear Zenobia,

Paris is cold and grey today and I find myself thinking of the sun, the heat, the sharp, bright light that dazzles the eye. You would find the sun easier to live with than I do; its rays warmed your infant years, and your first steps were taken on earth dried hard by the fierceness of the sun.

You were so tiny, and so frail. We watched over your small body, willing you to live.

She folds the letter and replaces it among the others. Beyond the window, lamps now glow. Somewhere in the house, above her head, there are small noises, muffled, barely audible.

How long this journey has been, and how tortuous, searching for a man about whom she knew so much, yet at the same time so little – not even, at the beginning, his name. But she learned early to be tenacious.

Baptiste comes into the stuffy bedroom and notes the untouched tisane. He moves it and picks up a bottle of dark liquid from the table.

V, sunk in his pillows, looks up at his servant, poised over him with a bottle of tincture. Obediently he opens his mouth and swallows the spoonful of liquid. He licks his lips, amused by the fact that the hint of alcohol in the solution is giving him a moment of pleasure. He says, 'It falls somewhat short of the best cognac,' or rather, he intends to make that comment, but finds that a hoarse croak is all he can manage. Baptiste straightens the bedclothes, pulling up the covers V has pushed away, and says severely, 'You must keep warm . . .'

The tincture has a curious aftertaste, like sulphur. It may also be a sedative, for V feels his head swimming unpleasantly. Sulphurous fumes could signal the arrival of an underworld figure, come to drag him down to Hades. Is it time to account for his sins? Will he be lifted to safety or cast into the pit?

His soul is hardly spotless: he may have killed a man, yes, but in the heat of battle. He has been unfaithful more than once, but never unkind. Still, the whiff of sulphur reminds him of something . . .

Pluto's Kingdom

After the embarrassment of Petersburg and the uneasy business with Voltaire, Baptiste had hoped for some peace in Paris, but V fretted. He wearied himself searching the pages of books for passing references to lost works of art, an intriguing altarpiece, an unexplored ruin.

The world held its treasures in tantalisingly faraway places: Spain, Italy, the Orient – he itched to catch an afterglow of long-gone glories, breathe the dank air of the dead past, sift through tombs, dig up urns and fragments of terracotta vivid with decoration. Drown in antiquity. Ovid and Poussin opened inviting windows on Arcadian scenes. But where was Arcadia to be found? Hardly in the Paris of Louis and Marie-Antoinette.

It was the court that once again directed his steps, this time to Italy, but not to the north he had dreamed of exploring, with its art, its architecture, its cathedrals and cloisters. He was ordered to the south: secretary to the embassy at Naples.

'I gather there won't be much for me to do.'

Baptiste did not feel optimistic. Experience told him his young master had a way of creating activity where others might have rested. And experience, as usual, proved accurate.

The master, never one with the good sense to stay happily in one place, was joining a gentlemanly expedition to Sicily. For Baptiste this was entirely bad news: it was well known that Sicily was a land of bandits and barbarians, and moreover the food was terrible. In the kitchen of some embassy or other he had once been served what was described as a Sicilian speciality: a vile dish composed of sardines, chopped up and stirred into pasta and decorated with pine kernels and raisins. He had no desire to learn more about Sicily.

'I think most of us would benefit more from going about the world less and spending more time at home,' Baptiste said grimly.

'I didn't know you had read Voltaire.'

'I haven't.'

'Well you seem to think alike.'

Baptiste reflected for a moment. 'Which is more odd: that I should think like him, or that he should think like me?'

'I'm not sure. That's a nice philosophical point. Now. You'll be packing; here's a list of the books I'll need.'

Of course, the master knew nothing of the thousand and one jobs involved in setting up the expedition: the assembling of everything needed for a trip into the wilderness: the purchasing of provisions and items of robust clothing, the means to keep the precious books dry, safe passage for drawing materials. All that was mere detail. And a valet took care of the details.

In later years Baptiste recalled the adventure with mixed feelings. Now and then he would take a book off the shelf and study the ivory vellum cover: *Voyage en Sicile par M. De Non Gentilhomme Ordinaire du Roi et de l'Académie royale de peinture et sculpture, Paris,* and think back to one of the strangest episodes of his long term of service. A season in Sicily, a savage island across the sea.

V's notebook recorded the departure to Messina from Reggio at noon . . . *A little rough weather . . .*

Below decks, Baptiste lay, flattened by seasickness. But despite the discomfort, he would later think of the crossing as the comfortable part. Nothing came easily here, in this

96

bleached, sad place of penury and exhaustion. He compared the inertia of the Sicilian peasants with the sturdy independence of their French counterparts. At odds with his surroundings, he viewed the island with a hostile eye.

V was happy in Sicily as he was in every foreign place. When he set off on a journey he sprouted wings; he felt himself fly free of the earth. In a new land, though not part of it, he was a blank canvas: he could paint himself into the picture in whatever colours and whatever style he chose. In this temporary limbo he left behind his quotidian problems and his established identity. Landscape and classical ruins, glowing mosaics and keyhole arches, Norman churches and palaces, he celebrated them all on paper. They became a part of him.

Heading for the sun he was no longer the maladroit diplomat, the undervalued courtier, the bemused lover, the fool. Ah, to keep travelling for ever!

As the expedition toiled its way across the interior, ruined Greek temples emerged from folds of hillside or rose from the rocky seashore. And if in a sunlit grove he caught a murmur of *Et in Arcadia ego* he was young enough to shrug it off. If a man travels light enough, he can outstrip thoughts of Death. Here it was not the grinning skull he confronted but the enduring bones of an ancient culture.

For Baptiste, travelling meant trouble. Others might gaze at wonders; he was in charge of the small necessities of life: while V examined the intricacies of a Moorish column, Baptiste worked out where the master would sleep and wash, what he would eat. When they got to Taormina the Greek amphitheatre was pronounced a jewel by the gentlemen. The sun beat down; the master stood in the centre of the stage and murmured, 'I'm parched, dying of thirst,' the words clearly audible to Baptiste, hovering by the last row of stone seats. In Paris, V had once beckoned the valet into his box at the opera, and Baptiste, standing behind V's chair, had watched and listened, so he was aware that the clarity of the Greek amphitheatre was not to be found in an opera house. On the other hand, audibility was of no great comfort. Today it simply meant that he had to clamber, legs aching, over row upon row of stone seats to where his master stood and hand him a flask of drinking water.

It was an unwieldy party and not always in accord: arguments about when to stop, and for how long, gradually grew sharper. It was clear to Baptiste that the master could teach the rest of the party a good deal about the antiquities around them, but the abbé who led the group held the purse strings. Uneasily yoked together, they travelled on, by donkey and mule, or on foot.

When they urged their horses up the slopes of Mount Etna, through flower-filled meadows and then, the air growing colder, through the grey cinders of old eruptions, V was up front, urging his mount forward, leaping to the ground to crouch and examine some fragment that had caught his attention. Baptiste, freezing in a wind so cold his cheeks stung as though rubbed by ice, hung back at the rear, teeth clenched against the glacial air. This was worse than Petersburg: at least there people had the sense to stay indoors in cold weather.

He was pierced by a longing for an old familiar place; not Paris, but the Burgundy he was beginning to fear he would never see again, with its vineyards, the grapes growing plump and bronze in the calm sunny autumn; the stream where two boys had caught fish in their bare hands; the scrubbed kitchen table, the yellow dishes piled with beef and chicken, golden pastry, fruit from the château orchards. All bound for the dining room upstairs, where the food would be presented on fine porcelain. But with the masters satisfied, what was left for the servants was still a feast compared with the uncivilised offerings of these grim parts.

As the horses stumbled higher up the slope, sinking deep

into cinders, breathing became difficult. Baptiste felt a sharp ache, like the burning of ice, behind his eyes, and held his hand over his nose and mouth, using the warmth of his fingers to try and filter out the cold. And there ahead was the master, flinging himself full-length to peer down into the crater, waggling his feet like a boy confronted by wonders, venturing perilously close to the edge.

Master and servant both recorded their impressions of the trip. For V, myth was never far off: capricious gods and unlucky victims hovered at the edge of vision. The travellers moved through history like visitors to a cyclorama. In Palermo V noted the Arab and Christian architecture; at Mont-Reale the slender columns glittering with Moorish jewelled mosaic.

Baptiste wrote in the small ledger he kept for accounts and expenditure: 'At the inn last night we slept on tables to escape the bed bugs.'

V scribbled: 'A girl with yellow eyes smiled at me. Dark red lips. I would have asked her name, but they speak a language of their own on this island. She waved at me and laughed and ran off.' Baptiste recorded: 'Mosquitoes. Sour cheese.'

It took a day and a night to reach Sciacca, where they turned their back on the sea and headed inland. At noon they found a shady place to rest. While the rest of the party stretched out like dead men in the heat, V unwrapped the parcel of books and pocketed his copy of Ovid. In the late afternoon they reached a small hill town poised on a high plateau, with a natural balcony overlooking the deep valley. At sunset, the light fell like dusty gold on the huddled village clinging to the next peak, and the scene glowed as though painted by an old master's brush. V leaned on the stone balustrade, trying to catch in his sketchpad an idea of the fugitive light as it touched the rooftops.

Glancing behind him, he saw a small girl in a sun-bleached

dress engaged in some private game. Humming to herself, she circled the stone fountain, trailing a leafy twig pulled from one of the trees, her pale frock growing luminous as the light faded. For an instant, watching as the child skipped and sang to herself, V was pierced with a new awareness of fleeting time: he and she were being drawn along in the same stream, but for him, already the current was pulling more strongly, while the child was barely – as yet – aware of the movement; the child was still immortal, as he had once felt himself to be.

Renewal was a form of immortality. Passing Sciacca's hot springs on the way out of town they had smelled sulphur from the healing springs; for Baptiste it had the foulness of bad eggs, though V called them emanations of Hades. Nearby lay the shady lake where, according to Ovid, Persephone was snatched by Pluto. V gazed down on the water through the cobweb fine branches of the trees and wondered out loud: 'Ah, but *was* she snatched?'

No tubs in this remote town for visiting gentlemen to bathe in, but Baptiste managed to find a vast preserving pan in which V could at least soak his feet while he turned the pages of his book. 'A domineering mother. Lonely days spent in the dimness of the wood, gathering violets and so forth; was she really so unhappy about being carried off by Pluto? What do you think, Baptiste: does the story ring true? Might she not have given an interested sideways glance to a tall, dark, confident stranger? It's ambiguous, wouldn't you say: was it a violation or a proposal?'

Baptiste knew questions of this sort required no answer from him; as with the Romans or the Hundred Years War, he would be hearing more of Persephone shortly. And indeed V was not waiting for a reply. He turned another page.

'Ovid describes her here, wandering in the "well-tended" gardens of Hades, which doesn't sound too bad, apart from the smell of sulphur.'

Baptiste poured a jug of water over his master's head while

V held the book at arm's length and shook water from his curls like a dog after swimming.

'I can almost see them through those trees down there: pale Persephone cradled in Pluto's dark limbs, six months of passion. At the end of winter he delivers her back to her mother for the long summer visit. Which leaves the two of them free to get on with their lives. Perhaps all marriages should be arranged on a seasonal basis!'

Baptiste pictured himself for a moment as Pluto, dark and confident – at least he was tall enough for the role. He would ask her name, and she would smile. Persephone, with lilies in her hair. He breathed in the fragrance (using the smell of V's Paris soap to conjure up the flowers). Then, like Pluto, he would wrap her in his arms and –

'Towel, Baptiste!'

V was becoming an expert on volcanoes: he had glimpsed Vesuvius from afar, he had looked into the hot heart of Etna. But Sicily had more to offer: a secret valley strange enough to pull him off the known track.

'We should see the Malacubes.'

They were already in the neighbourhood. Such a phenomenon, V suggested, was surely worth a detour?

Baptiste was ordered to guard the equipment so he saw the Malacubes only from the distance. He recalled something the master had said earlier about volcanic eruption; that one of his old writers had called it *cacafuego* – fire-shit. It certainly looked like that from where he stood: boiling hot gobbets of wet clay shooting into the air to descend on anyone unlucky enough to be close. He stared down at the party picking their way into a valley of clay where nothing grew except cone-shaped chimneys, and gave thanks that he was not required to share in these pleasures. But crossing a ditch that afternoon, V stumbled and ripped his hand on a bush with thorns as sharp as stiletto blades.

'Tonight, Baptiste, you will take notes for me; if I attempt to write I shall bleed all over the book.'

Baptiste stared down at a blank page and realised he felt unwell.

'I can't do this.'

'Don't be absurd. Of course you can. You can write –'

'Not quickly. And there will be words I've never heard of.'

'I shall spell them out.'

'Surely one of the gentlemen could do it for you?'

'The "gentlemen", Baptiste, can be less than gentlemanly sometimes. It grieves me to say this, but I would prefer my ideas not to be picked up like fallen fruit in an orchard and then offered around as someone else's.'

He could have given an order; Baptiste would have obeyed. But that was not his style. The smile that had won over so many women hovered. 'I really need your help.'

And of course he got what he wanted.

'Right: take this down. "The intriguing question is: are the Malacubes actually volcanic? They might well be – Etna is visible not far away, but this site is like no other: sixty small craters scattered across a barren plain of grey, spongy clay popping and bubbling quietly –" Are you getting this down, Baptiste? Good.' He continued: '"As we watched, one of the cones went into effusive mode and sent a plume of liquid clay shooting sixty feet into the air, to spread out like a mushroom and fall to earth. Before us lay the flat valley of cones, their mouths gushing liquid clay. Within the cones the surface of the remaining liquid rose and fell, bubbling, like coffee when it comes to the boil in a pot."'

Baptiste paused in his scribbling and looked up. 'That's good, bubbling like coffee.'

'Thank you. Don't stop, note this: "As hot air breaks through from below, a multitude of tiny new craters forms. As I went closer to one of these, my foot broke through the crust and I stumbled, almost falling into the crack –"'

'You should take more care!' Baptiste exclaimed.

'After that I did. Carry on writing: "I flung myself down full-length so that my weight was more evenly distributed. I put my ear to one of the orifices –"'

'What? What's that word?'

'Orifices, it means holes.'

'Spell it, please.'

And a few lines on: '"I heard a sort of susurration –"'

'Sus *what*? Spell it!'

'"– susurration like the rustle of thistles brushing together, and I realised that this was caused by bursting bubbles, releasing air. I stuck my tongue into the flowing liquid, and it tasted of sea salt, bitter. And then I realised that beneath me the ground was dissolving into a quagmire into which I would soon be sucked down – a particularly nasty way to die. I believe the eruptions are indeed volcanic. One thinks of Aristotle's theory of wind –'

Baptiste paused. 'Whose theory?'

'Aristotle.'

V leaned over and studied the page. 'A few spelling mistakes, but I can make it all out. Good.'

'Tell me which words are wrong. I'll correct them.'

'It's not important, I don't care –'

'*I* care. Tell me the words.'

Somewhere within Baptiste's body – he could not have pinned down the exact place – he felt a growing pressure that made breathing oddly difficult: his hand shook as he wrote, so that he could barely set down the words; it was as though he himself was recording the strange sight below them; that the words bringing it all to life on the page, were his.

That night he decided to spend his spare minutes reading his way through at least some of the master's travelling library. He soon found an author who made sense: the old monkey in Ferney: '*Il faut cultiver notre jardin.*' Well, obviously.

Not that Baptiste particularly desired to cultivate anything:

there were gardeners for that sort of thing, but the idea was sound. The way clever people often failed to grasp quite simple notions always astonished him. As now, with this trip. Bad food, filthy accommodation and extra work.

One book took him by surprise: slowly, reluctantly, he found there was something to be said for the hitherto resented Ovid. For the first time he saw the possibility of transformation.

As the gentlemen conferred, Baptiste shifted his load from one shoulder to the other, waiting to move on, to the next awe-inspiring lump of rock, the next wonder. Weighed down with baskets of food, bottles of water and wine and drawing materials, he trudged through the maze of streets in yet another old town, following V, who was by this time plentifully decorated with cuts, scratches, abrasions, and rashes caused by poisonous plants, but was, as usual, in a state of elation. Baptiste was of the opinion that only someone born into the certainty of ease and privilege could so cheerfully – indeed eagerly – embrace discomfort.

'Where to this time?' he called, the sweat gathering in armpits and groin, sliding between his buttocks.

'The fountain of Arethusa. On Ortygia. The only place apart from the banks of the Nile where papyrus is known to grow. There's a story of a nymph –'

'Yes,' said Baptiste, 'I've read the story. Artemis changed her into a fountain, to keep her safe from –' He paused. 'From – the river god who was pursuing her.'

'From Alpheus, yes. Very good!' Sometimes Baptiste surprised him. 'But Alpheus turned himself into an underground river, flowing beneath the sea, and the waters of the river mingled with the fountain of Arethusa.'

He strode on ahead. The gods were perverse, ruthless, inexcusably malevolent at times, but just occasionally, Ovid caught a note that struck to the heart: to flow as one stream, to merge yourself with the beloved was surely an entrancing way to be reunited. He himself had never felt that overwhelming sensation: wary of humiliation he hugged the emotional coast, not venturing out too far. But sometimes he felt a questioning pang, a longing for deep water.

The route to the fountain, along the shore, delighted him. The narrow sea walk ran between the parapet wall and the sea. Sheltered from the wind, filled with the warmth of the sun, the little ledge clung to the rocky shore, a place of lapis and gold; the blue of sea and sky filling the eye, while the stone reflected the rays of the sun.

And then he reached the fountain and the romantic note was shattered. 'A malodorous drain,' he scribbled in his notebook, 'among a few wilting papyrus reeds. A wretched thing, trickling between two crumbling walls, *not* ancient, where filthy linen is washed by weary local women almost naked, skirts hitched up to their thighs.' And around them, he noted, shabby ducks shitting plentifully into the greasy puddles. The smell worse than sulphur.

But despite all that, the power of the myth could not be completely destroyed. He pictured Alpheus, melting like an ice sculpture, his limbs dissolving, spinning into a whirlpool, driving like a liquid drill through the earth beneath the sea, surfacing to swirl the object of his desire into a watery embrace – not altogether fanciful: rivers can run underground, waters can merge. But V could see the woman's view of events, her appalling helplessness, and he challenged the gods: what gave Alpheus the right? Why could he not take no for an answer? Was Arethusa the object of an obsessive love, or the victim of a rape?

By the time the expedition trundled into Messina for the return voyage, V's portfolios were bulging with drawings and sketches and his luggage was the heavier for a number of ancient terracotta vases. For Baptiste, the little ship riding at anchor in the harbour was a sight of rare beauty, the calm blue sea a magic carpet that would carry them back to the real world. And was there not also something magical about the woman making her way through the crowd towards them, slipping through the dockside throng like a cat, a now-you-see-her-now-you-don't figure, weaving deftly where others might have bumped and stumbled against jostling strangers and their awkwardly piled baggage. The woman was tall, her face dark, her eyes the colour of amber; barefooted, she wore strings of some turquoise stone around her wrinkled throat, the colours bright against skin burned to mahogany. There were two broad streaks of white in her black hair, sweeping back from her temples like the folded wings of a bird. Baptiste watched her with interest, but her eyes were on his master, intent as a hawk on a sparrow. Then, one more sinuous evasion of a passing body, and she was upon them. She came to a stop at V's side and smiled, her teeth a row of broken amber beads that matched her eyes.

'And how are you, young master!' The greeting was respectful enough, but the tone was familiar, verging on the brazen. Was there mockery in the smile?

V returned the greeting, but absently: they would be boarding soon and it was not the time for a quayside conversation with a gypsy. He turned away towards the boat.

'Well, was I right?'

Baptiste saw the frown of incomprehension that creased his master's brow; the shoulders lifting in a puzzled shrug. The gypsy's thick brows drew together.

'You don't recognise me, then.'

Baptiste bent his mouth close to V's ear.

'You will recall the lady, sir, in your father's orchard. She told your fortune —'

It was all V needed; he swung round, arms flung wide. The gypsy received the noonday strength of his smile, his sparkling eyes engaged hers.

'Of course! That day in the orchard!'

'And? Are you acquainted with kings as I foretold? And loved by the ladies?'

V's smile broadened. 'Your gift is powerful. I fear to ask you what lies ahead.'

She took his hand, studying the palm, as she had so long ago.

There is a particular skill to the language of soothsaying as the gypsy knew: too specific and the oracle can be boxed into an awkward corner. Too generalised and the words will fail to impress.

She traced a line across V's palm with her scarred fingertip. 'A long lifeline . . . much travel . . .'

Baptiste groaned silently. More travel when he was hoping for less. He wondered about his own lifeline: would he drop by the wayside to be buried in some wretched foreign hole while the master strode on to further inconvenient destinations? Would he be loved at all? *What about me?*

The shape of his existence was dictated by that of the man he served, but his yearnings, his despair, his secret vices, remained his own. *What about me?* He was an unread book, an unheard melody, as far as the world was concerned. He could be writing his own story, composing his own song, with every breath. But who would hear it?

The gypsy droned on: ' . . . beautiful women, one who will cause you trouble. And I see blood spilt. I see a child –'

'And will I be happy?'

'You will have what you most desire.' To Baptiste's eyes her smile was now definitely mocking.

I see a child – She had been about to say more, but V had cut in with his question. Baptiste, listening as usual, wondered about the child: did that indicate marriage, a family, a settled future, a fortunate destiny that he might share? A child.

The sailors were shouting, the crowd jostling, pushing them towards the gangplank. V pressed the gypsy's hand in thanks; silver passed between them. He raised his hat courteously and stepped on board.

For a while the sea remained calm. The ship swung gently, like a rocked cradle as she moved through the waves. Somewhere a man strummed a guitar; a baby cried and his mother guided the hungry mouth to her nipple. The boat was crowded, and people made themselves comfortable where they could, the wealthy in cabins or comfortable seats, the less privileged bedding down on deck, on bundles and sacks.

They were well into open sea when, sweeping from the horizon, dark, scudding clouds blotted out the blue sky and rising waves sent the craft pitching heavily in the wind that came down on the strait like a wolf clawing at the sails while rain hammered the decks. Passengers ran for shelter, tottering like drunkards, and cargo incompetently stacked broke loose as waves the height of a house crashed over the bows. And Baptiste came close to death. How they laughed, the gentlemen passengers, when the sailors came upon him, half drowned, gasping for air, pinned down by a huge plank with the water up to his ears and rising, only his nose still above the surface, while the storm flung the boat about like a piece of flotsam. He had never regarded the sea as a friend; thereafter it was his enemy.

V found him huddled in a bunk, eyes closed, his face a greenish white.

'Baptiste? Do you need something? Food, wine –'

'Nothing, thank you.' He did not open his eyes.

'It smells awful down here.'

It seemed to Baptiste that V's voice came from far off, and since he was stating the obvious, required no reply. Then, to his dismay, he found himself hauled out of the relative comfort of the bunk by his master and marched off, unsteadily, up to the deck. The storm had moved on, leaving the boat battered but whole. From somewhere V had conjured a cloak which he was now attempting to wrap round Baptiste's hunched form. Since the valet was several inches taller than his master, and V was unused to adjusting garments other than his own, the operation became increasingly laborious, until Baptiste, losing patience, seized the cloak and, turning his back on the wind, swirled it expertly round his shoulders as tightly furled as a parasol.

Zenobia turns away from the window, from the dark and gleams of light. She is gripped by a wild notion: she will tiptoe through the house, listen for voices, and burst into the Baron's room. 'I am Zenobia!' she will cry, and watch his face grow – what? Dismayed? Ashamed?

But thinking has taken too long, and as she strides across the room, Baptiste is back, blocking the door with his deferential presence. Books, engravings, prints litter the table; she realises he has been using information as a way of keeping her at a distance. She pushes one of the books away from her angrily.

'I am not one of his admiring visitors, Baptiste. Why are you treating me like a child?'

'As I said, today is not the best of times.'

As though talking to a child herself she says carefully, 'I want to see him. Despite everything, I love him.'

His laugh is deliberately unkind: 'You are not the first.'

'But perhaps I am different: I owe him my life.'

One of the yellow flowers on the table has crinkled and turned brown. Baptiste removes it from the vase and turns to drop it in the fireplace. He considers the small heap of black ashes and fragments of browned and curling paper in the grate, and on the floor nearby a box crammed with folded flimsy sheets. He turns back, the dead bloom in his hands.

'I have sent for the doctor.'

'You said it was just a chill!'

'Indeed, but he is no longer a young man –'

'I am medically trained, I could offer a diagnosis –'

'I don't think –'

'You don't think a *woman* could be of help?'

Her words have astonished him: *medically trained* . . . He is still holding the long-stemmed, crinkled flower, cupped in his hands, as though waiting to present it to her, an elderly cavalier, a withered bloom.

As they stand frozen there comes a knock at the front door; the sound of light footsteps, voices and a maid ushers a visitor into the hall.

She glances towards the door. 'I think the doctor is waiting for you.' Her voice is calm: 'I am not leaving, Baptiste. Not until my questions are answered.'

An Encounter at Pompeii

The court at Naples was, in V's opinion, a very odd affair. He watched the scene with incredulity and a lowering of spirits.

'Did you and I ever enjoy court life?' he enquired of his reflection in the mirror as Baptiste attended to an errant wisp of wig. 'Did a royal Entertainment ever prove entertaining? I'm dying of boredom here.'

While Marie-Caroline ordered gold-encrusted gowns and took lovers, the King went fishing. Ferdinand had the Bourbon nose but nothing more. The royal presence, the will, the nobility, in V's opinion, all were lacking.

'Gross manners, half asleep, talks with a local accent and wants nothing more than to be left in peace to catch fish!'

Afterwards the monarch would set up a stall in the harbour and sell off his haul to apparently eager courtiers. They might roll their eyes in private, but many a fine calfskin boot was baptised in mud and fishguts.

'And moreover,' V remarked in a letter to Paris, 'the poor sot is completely under Madame Ferdinand's thumb.'

Marie-Caroline was a queen in the Marie-Antoinette mould – unsurprisingly, as they were sisters. And like her older sister, she had a vigorous sense of pleasure. If V had bothered to flatter her, matters might have taken a different turn, but she was uneasy with his waspish humour and ambiguous smile. When he complimented her on her coiffure, her jewels, her new gown, his choice of adjectives was cryptic; she found herself looking questioningly in the mirror afterwards.

For V the lacklustre royal receptions and dinners were punishing, but there were consolations: a congenial *principessa* or *baronessa*, invited to inspect his garden, would be led along shadowy paths bordered by pale, fragrant flowers. V and the ladies understood each other perfectly: they might share *un'avventura*, or, if the stars were kind, move on to *una relazione amorosa*. The Frenchman was discreet – at least where passion was involved.

Visitors from home were always welcome. Jacques-Louis David arrived, rather full of himself, flourishing his Prix de Rome, and his contempt for monarchy in general.

He strode about V's terrace vehemently forecasting doom for the ruling class and was crisply snubbed by the court. The two had kept loosely in touch and V sensed a fragility beneath the present confidence and bravado. He recalled rumours of Jacques-Louis' threatening to take his own life by starving himself to death in stoic style if – yet again – he failed to win a Prix de Rome. He had found himself defending David's work in the past. So now, V welcomed and fed the prizewinner, and soon had him laughing at the latest royal scandal. From that point the Queen's view of the new embassy secretary and his friends shifted from suspicious puzzlement to mistrust. Naturally she had him watched.

'How can you stand this place?' David enquired irritably.

'It can be amusing. A local poet said to me, "Naples is a theoretical city, a state of mind, a dimension of the soul." I said: in other words, the laundry gets lost.'

'It's intolerably provincial!'

'Of course. It's *rus in suburbe*. But there are consolations.'

David had noted the pleasing, dark-eyed girls the region produced so plentifully, even the barefoot ones flaunting their red, white and black Neapolitan coral at throat and wrist; lace shawls draped low over their breasts. He studied the portraits on V's desk. 'I imagine you've claimed a few local trophies.'

'You make it sound like bird-catching or hunting deer.'

'So what's the secret?'

'Well . . . I *like* them, for a start.' That helped. 'And I listen to them.' Women, he had long ago realised, did not get much chance to say what they thought, what they felt. So when a man listened, not only simple village girls, but clever women too, found it appealing.

'And the grand ones? The ladies of the court?'

'Perhaps one or two. I'll say no more . . .' A grin. 'My ellipses are sealed.'

V picked up a drawing, a portrait of a young woman seated by a window. He touched her cheek with a fingertip. 'Something happens to a woman's skin in the warmth of the sun; one warmth becomes another . . . And, thank God, Naples is not Paris, the women are less devious – or so they have led me to believe!'

'What do you do with yourself here?' David asked, 'It's a desert!' He would have been surprised to hear that his old friend often passed the day wandering in a landscape that was, indeed, desert-like with its dry, barren soil, searching for signs of long-buried life.

Courtesy restrained V from letting his guest know that he was interrupting anything, but as soon as David had left, he penned a message to the British Embassy: 'My dear William, I shall be with you at Pompeii tomorrow.'

Crouching alongside the archeologists, clearing mulberries and vineyards, William Hamilton spent as much time in the field as on his ambassadorial duties. They worked together, scraping and digging out layers of volcanic ash and the accumulated soil of seventeen centuries to reveal, little by little, a buried Roman world. When possible, V joined him, watchful as a surgeon, questioning, his sketch-pad pages filling.

Hamilton in his English hat and V in his French brim, picked their way over the exposed stone tracks, through the streets and shops and villas of Pompeii. They encountered its citizens, transformed into statuary, trapped for ever in the moment, that August day, when Vesuvius sent its ominous smoke signal towering into the sky, to rain down on the town in a storm of lethal debris, blurring the buildings into a dirty snow scene.

Hamilton, as assiduous with his note-taking as V, reconstructed the scene as they walked. 'When the crater split, a boiling wall of rock ash roared down that hillside at the speed of an avalanche. Those who could, ran from it. Some paused, to look back – there will always be some who look back . . . Then it engulfed everything – the houses, the people, the cups, the coins, the helpless gods in their niches, while the glowing ash continued to fall from the sky.' He walked on ahead, moving among the loose stones with care.

' "Dust hath closed Helen's eye," ' he called back to V. 'How differently one reads that line after seeing this.'

V had pulled a muscle attempting to move a piece of inscribed Pompeii stone. Baptiste's fingers moved across the aching shoulder, tracing the muscle route, rubbing ointment into his master's pale skin. The valet breathed in the pungent herbal paste; it might help a damaged muscle, certainly it cleared the nasal passage, though his master protested that it smelled like an apothecary's dust hole.

'It's made by the medical school up the coast at Salerno.' The King's valet had informed him it could cure a stomach disorder or an ache within the night. He continued massaging the shoulder.

Next day V was back in Pompeii, his sketch pad capturing fragments of an apocalyptic vision; a day of terror: vessels that survived, still holding honey or the residuum of wine; a couple entwined in a last, desperate embrace, overcome by deadly fumes, sealed for ever where they lay.

He scribbled disjointed phrases . . . *think on these four last things: death, judgement, heaven, hell.* Then scored them out. Echoes of anxiety persisted. A sense of disaster lying in wait. There were biblical precedents, but a modern man could hardly go by such a book. Why should he even be pondering the question: how much future do we have?

He walked carefully among the excavated ruins, as one might walk on eggshells, or the bones of those long dead.

Further off, a moving figure caught his eye: in the distance a girl was walking slowly through the ruins, pausing now and then to stoop, to study something more closely. At a certain moment he saw her head lift and turn this way and that, warily, almost like an animal sniffing the wind: that gesture of a woman who suspects she may be observed. Then, locating the distant watcher, she surprised him. What he expected was an abashed withdrawal, possibly flight. Instead, the girl made her way directly to where he stood, before what had once been a temple, now roofless, with a flight of crumbling steps leading to a ruined courtyard above.

She came to the foot of the steps. V removed his hat, sweeping low in a bow worthy of Versailles.

'*Signorina . . .*'

The girl was pretty and well-spoken, her voice melodious, and instinctively V moved into his charming mode, engaging her and – he hoped – attracting her, perhaps. But she surprised him by the turn their conversation took: she told him she was to be a nun.

Entertaining a healthy mistrust of religious hierarchy, V greeted the news with disappointment:

'Why would a young woman like you, with all of life ahead of you, with all the possibilities of love, laughter, family life, shut yourself away in useless seclusion? No more alive than these Pompeian bodies!'

She was severe but gentle, like one chastising an ignorant child:

'Sir, laughter and love are for *men* to enjoy.'

A girl's expectations were an arranged marriage, servitude, and long, exhausting years of childbearing.

'I shall study, help the sick, console the dying. I shall enjoy peace. I do not find the choice difficult.'

He listened, touched. The convent, he told her sincerely, was lucky to have her.

'And I, to have the convent, where no man can force himself on me.'

'But a *dying* man could claim a portion of your time. Even an undeserving one. Would you pray for me?' he asked.

'You are not dying, sir.'

'But one day death will come to me, as to all men. *Then* you might pray for me.'

Her face was pale, the skin fair and velvety, and across her cheeks was the finest sprinkling of freckles like dark gold dust. For a moment he imagined her with the long hair masked by a nun's coif, her slender body hidden by black garb, and felt a pang of regret. She smiled at him, shyness forgotten, and said, 'Shall I pray for your sins to be forgiven?'

'Indeed. And you must give me the name of this convent you plan to enter. Perhaps one day, near my end, we may meet again. I shall remind you of our conversation at the temple of Isis.'

'Is this the temple, then?'

'Yes, these steps would have led up to a marble courtyard framed by four fine columns – so,' he showed her the sketch he had begun, 'beneath a pediment – so,' swiftly drawing in the shallow triangle, 'and worshippers would have brought offerings. There would have been a statue of the goddess. You could make an offering to Isis even now. She is, after all, a healer, a giver of life. She taught her women followers how to spin flax and weave, and cure sickness. And,' he added with a grin, 'how to control unruly men.'

'A useful goddess, then!'

They talked on, as he drew the delicate carvings that had survived the eruption and, separately, the goddess herself, a sketch which he offered to the girl as a little gift.

That evening, he sat at his desk reading the younger Pliny's description of the eruption. From the window he could see the volcano in the distance. Lit by the setting sun Vesuvius sat quietly, like a coiled cat, apparently asleep, but occasionally it could growl a warning.

He thought of the older Pliny, the boy's uncle, incorrigibly curious, putting out to sea, sailing towards the falling rocks. Was there a moment when Pliny knew curiosity could be more than dangerous? Could be fatal?

Hot ash and burning rocks fell on to the deck as the small boat sailed in close to the mountain ships; the shallow sea grew warm as bathwater –

'They should have turned back,' V remarked as Baptiste set down a tray of wine and olives on the desk. 'But Pliny said, "Fortune favours the brave."' His fingers traced the words on the page.

' "The heat came off the mountain like the blast from an oven . . ." The old man called out for water, and while he was drinking it – while he was swallowing – the sulphur filled his lungs . . .' V took a gulp of cool white wine and held it in his mouth, his eyes on the volcano. His face was burned unfashionably brown by the sun that he ignored while he sketched and studied. Baptiste, pale from hours spent working in dim rooms, hovered ghostlike behind his burnished master, waiting.

The taste of sulphur on an old man's tongue. He remembers a burning city, a girl by the temple steps. Life and death, the two mixed up together in an upstairs room on the Quai Voltaire. With the curtains drawn he has no way of knowing whether the sky outside is light or dark. Swaddled as he is, he lies in a sort of limbo.

V's tongue explores his dry, cracked lips. The Greeks believed we move into death backwards; what lies before us is our past. And we are all moving towards death. The ghosts of his past jostle for space. He stares across the room at his beloved *Gilles*, Watteau's gawky Pierrot. He and Pierrot are divided by a vast humming silence: in that shadowy grove the boy waits to be touched into life, while here, *he* waits to be drawn into the inevitable alternative. Not yet, of course. This chill, this fever will pass, as have others. Yesterday he was offering advice to a young artist. Next week's diary is full. He is, *après tout*, a survivor. Fever is just another obstacle, another adversary, to be outrun or outwitted; he's never been beaten yet.

In that long-ago Naples, in a room he recalls dimly, like a faded illustration in an old book, two young men are busy with the present they occupy. He watches them, watches that other him dance across the surface of his life, fragile as a mayfly, with no way of knowing the world is due for a change; a punishment perhaps. Speeding away from that darkening room at the speed of a star he, now, cannot tell its occupants what lies ahead. Nor do they know to ask how disaster will announce itself. How will the walls be breached? The cities burn? Knowledge comes with the moment. Lot's wife looked back, wanting to know more. Then, overcome by fumes, she was trapped, her body stiffening in the salt-filled air. Did the Roman matron or young blood of that great empire feel the balance of the world shift, as Decline tilted into Fall? He cannot protect his younger self, only follow in his footsteps, towards the moment when his world is blasted in its turn, when the blade falls, and falls again, when dust and cries fill the air, and the balance wavers.

In the Neapolitan salon, V followed Pliny through that burning night, the marble floor cool beneath his bare feet, while nearby Baptiste went through the sketches of Pompeii, wiping the dusty pages, filing them in leather folders. Among them the valet found some sketches of a girl next to a ruined temple which seemed not to belong with the rest.

V looked up from his book. 'Pliny writes that when Vesuvius erupted it looked as though a pine tree was growing out of the top of the mountain, a tree of smoke that grew while you watched.' His hand stroked the page. 'The darkness lasted for two days.'

There was in V's voice that familiar note of regret for something missed: the distant treasury of experiences he could never possess. Life flowed on, inexorable as lava. There was no way to catch up with the past.

Baptiste, who recognised the tone and what lay behind it, and who occasionally noticed a plume of smoke rising lazily from the cone of the volcano, prayed with some vigour that they would not have the luck to witness a fresh eruption. He could live happily without the excitement of nature's fireworks.

Social fireworks were harder to avoid: a new arrival? He must be welcomed!

Over dinner V might talk of the moonscapes of Calabria; or Puglia with its baroque extravaganzas and mysterious stone huts. But there were places as yet unexplored. There was always the unseen landscape on the other side of the mountain, on the other shore, beyond the horizon.

Usually restlessness set in when the ground beneath V's feet grew too familiar. And Naples had grown familiar, but to Baptiste the master today seemed more preoccupied than rest-less, turned in on himself. Perhaps the Pompeii exploration was going too slowly? Or Caroline had thrown another tantrum?

'I hear Her Majesty threw a porcelain vase at her maid. It shattered –'

'One should be grateful: she has no taste.'

As Baptiste set down the shaving brush his hand nudged a package newly arrived from France. A small, elegantly bound book lay on the table beneath the window.

'Anything new from Paris?'

A flinch. A frown. Ah!

V grabbed a face towel, wiped the remaining lather from his cheeks and sprang out of his chair.

'It seems a small, unimportant book is enough to set the Paris gossips grubbing about like pigs after truffles.'

Gossips? Baptiste was put in mind of the pot calling the kettle black-arse, but decided against voicing the thought. That night, when he had completed his duties, he took the 'small, unimportant book' to his room and began to read it, while outside his window the moon moved across the sky. The scent of jasmine drifting through the open window melted for a moment into the fragrance of the cool and confident Madame de T, plucking a wide-eyed young man from his box at the Opéra and – and what? Playing with him? Using him? Perhaps falling a little in love with him? Heat rose from the printed page: a château in the moonlight, passion; velvet cushions damp with sweat . . . Not for the first time Baptiste's loins ached in proxy lust: a servant's bodily needs were not easily accommodated in a life shaped to others' ease.

He recalled, now, a night in Paris when the master had set out for the Opéra, had returned at dawn in a mood veering between elation and gloom. He had scribbled for some time in his personal journal. Baptiste never read journal entries: they were private and should remain so (letters were different, being destined for another's eyes in any case, or so he had decided). He never learned the full story of what went on that night after the opera, but now, it seemed, the world had shared the adventure: the little book described an episode of wild excess, an elegant seduction, a game of trust and double bluff. In Paris the anonymous novella had become the object of conjecture.

Given the watchful eye of Madame Ferdinand in Naples, it was perhaps as well that the identity of the author was shrouded in mystery, a set of (not unfathomable) initials providing the only clue.

Along with the book, the package had contained pages from French newspapers. Now, with his personal knowledge of the work being assessed, Baptiste read the critics' words:

'A jewel of indiscretion, an erotic *jeu d'esprit* . . .' 'An adventure – in effect a rite of passage – experienced by an ingenuous young man in the course of one summer night . . .' 'Is *Point de Lendemain* a romance? A memoir? An exercise in cynicism?'

For Parisian society, further questions hung in the air: in his elegant little book was the author reliving the passion of a moonlit night or seeking catharsis for the mortification of the morning after? Who *was* the author? And what really happened that night in the château on the bank of the river?

V at almost eighty knows what he knows, but no one is privy to the whole truth. The man who made the real journey to the real château is not the same man who pulled on his breeches in the clammy dawn on the page of a small novella. The V who stole treasure for Napoleon is not the V who wept for a lost love in a curtained Venetian gondola. And none of them is the restless, sweating occupant of a sickbed on the Quai Voltaire.

Those who know him as a friend, a lover, a colleague, would not think of V as a man given to dwelling on thoughts of disaster. This is the man to liven up a salon by his arrival; laughter and pleasure his stock-in-trade. But the face a man reveals when he shuts his own door to the outside world might surprise even the closest of friends. And as the man ages, as the curls thin and the waistline thickens, the laughter itself changes its nature. 'I would call it a sceptical smile,' someone says who knows him in his later years. 'Gently malicious. Reminds me of Voltaire.'

And V himself?

When the blood was hot and choice not an option, he surrendered like a swimmer to a tide. But now, when the heat in his body comes from an ague that pierces his old bones, he can choose, he can recall the past more calmly.

How sweetly the words had slipped off his pen, how easy he found the writing of that *jeu d'esprit*, the polished complicity; the manipulation of an innocent youth trapped in an erotic cat's cradle of deception . . . Was there, between the lines, an unconscious revulsion from the silvery decadence of the aristocratic world, though the author was himself part of it? Was this little book the literary equivalent of a Watteau: a group of privileged, silk-clad aristocrats going through an elegant *pas de quatre* where beneath the knowing smiles and the laughter there is tragedy – heartbreak for some? And, though no one knew it, waiting in the wings, a flashing blade, a Tree of Liberty, the deluge.

In Paris, the initials of authorship – M.D.G.O.D.R. – had swiftly yielded up their secret: *Monsieur De Non, Gentilhomme Ordinaire du Roi.*

Society concluded that the young man could not only draw, he could write – against all the evidence of that early fiasco at the Comédie-Française. And as for the rumour that the story was based on fact . . . The men were amused; the women intrigued. Whose were the pearly breasts?

They were given no answers. But in Naples, the Embassy Secretary, forgetting his old mentor's cautions about putting things in writing, yet again forgot to be discreet:

Shall we consider who is in bed with whom . . . which unfortunate nobleman has been caught cheating at cards . . . whose hand has found its way up which welcoming skirt . . . and which member of the court – dead drunk – fell flat on his face in an upper corridor of the Palazzo Reale last week? One of the royals, following in his footsteps, was himself so drunk that he walked over the prostrate figure remarking that the palace carpets really were remarkably lumpy these days . . .

The gaffes, the feuds, the lapses at the court of Naples went winging to Paris, surfacing (in gleeful parentheses) in V's official dispatches from the embassy. Without delay, the stories found their way to Marie-Antoinette, who was not amused by her sister's *modus vivendi* being held up to ridicule. She made her feelings plain.

In Naples, the Queen was having a bad morning: the little French shit had been amusing himself at her expense:

'Once again Paris has been privileged to hear about our lapses of etiquette, our sartorial shortcomings and –' she consulted the letter from Versailles – 'the "quite remarkable lack of intellectual rigour at court".' She screwed up the letter, removed the lid from her porcelain coffee pot and with some violence forced the letter into the pot, coffee overflowing and flooding the painted tray.

'I think we can forget to inform Monsieur De Non of our next reception. In any case,' she stabbed at the sodden letter viciously with a silver spoon, 'I'm sure he must have far more important, more *intellectual* activities to occupy himself with.'

Dropped from the guest list, V paced his terrace, aware of laughter in the next room – not literally, and not even figuratively, because he suspected the royal reception would be short on fun. Still, one would like to have been there to observe, to be privately amused.

From his garden high above the port he looked down at the Palazzo Reale, the pattern of trees and walks, the vast piazza. Was tonight's guest of honour yawning into his wine? Was Ferdinand giving him fishing tips? The Queen cheating at cards?

Baptiste heard the news first, from the ambassador's valet. He carried V's breakfast tray into the bedroom and drew back the long curtains. The sun was already high, and golden Neapolitan light flooded the room. V opened his eyes, flinched and felt his way blindly into the silk robe Baptiste held out for him.

'Monsieur Voltaire is dead.'

An old philosopher beckoning a young visitor into his room . . . a night spent talking . . . Baptiste, head bent over a silk waistcoat, rubbing at a stain on the cloth, his face stiff with disapproval. V's mind sheered away from uncomfortable thoughts: a profitable engraving, a correspondence of veiled bitterness and the lingering presence of stains that would not be wiped clean; a painful awareness that he had behaved less than honourably. He tried to banish the ghosts from the feast, knowing life had others lined up, waiting to make their appearance.

And after all, he desired no breakfast that morning; found he had a headache, asked Baptiste to take the tray away.

But Ferney was another time. Naples was the present, not just a new chapter, but a new book, with bright new bindings, fresh hope and sense of fun. Unquenchable élan. And, it seeemed, no lesson learned. Even when he was promoted – *chargé d'affaires* – his letters home were no less colourful:

What we have here is a Goldoni extravaganza, with a stream of grotesque characters popping in and out of Caroline's boudoir, the cast changing between the acts – *voilà* Mr Acton, John, known as Giovanni, *le seigneur*

Irlandais, who has the ear of the Queen – firmly clenched between his teeth.

And who might, as everyone knew, frequently be found in her bed. Mr Acton was, in V's view, *de facto* the monarch.

The acerbic descriptions of Ferdinand and Marie-Caroline presiding over the messy farmyard of their royal household flowed, unchecked, into his dispatches. Discretion was never V's style. What followed had a familiar inevitability:

'Monsieur De Non is recalled.' *Fiat*.

Another diplomatic debacle. Recalled. Nine years in Naples, and nothing to show for it but two slim travel books, a portfolio of drawings and a collection of Greek vases.

After Naples, Paris seemed surprisingly dim, the company less sparkling than he remembered. He put himself forward for appropriate positions and was politely but firmly passed over. He walked the city streets and lingered in antiquarian bookshops, breathing the dust of crumbling pages. Outside, the sun was weak, the air sharp.

What was it about Italian air that had made him feel freer, more in touch with himself? What was it about Italian women that set the spirits dancing and caught at the heart? Here, where he should have felt at home, he was, instead, unsettled, wandering along the Seine, beneath the trees, sketching stray cats and tramps. This unwished leisure gave him time to think, and also to talk to friends who were busier than he was.

Calling in at Prud'hon's studio he found him home on a brief visit from Rome, at work on a small engraving. V watched approvingly as the cutting tool delicately gouged the copper, transforming the blankness into an ordered network.

'Clearly Their Majesties have no need of my presence at court.'

'But do you want that existence?'

'When one thinks how pointless it is . . .'

He fell silent, studying one of his friend's preparatory drawings. He picked up an etching tool, stroked it absently, put it down. Touched a steel plate, straightened a stack of paper. Prud'hon was once more absorbed. Scattered about the workbench were prints of the old masters. V picked one up.

The distant past, wasn't that what had always attracted him? The darkness, the mystery provided a peephole into the lives of others, like Dr Hooke's *camera lucida*. When he looked into the past the view was clear and brilliant; it was the present that offered disappointment. And the future was not encouraging. He found himself wondering aloud what could be achieved in the brief time available.

'What can a man leave behind that will outlive him?'

Some men did it with a dynasty: the Bourbon chain outlived the individual monarch. A child of one's own forged a link with the future –

'You could say art outlives us,' Prud'hon offered, squinting down at the steel plate.

'True.'

If he could join the immortals . . . But he was not Watteau, not Rembrandt. As a writer he was not Racine or Shakespeare; he had already proved that, at the Comédie! An account of some journeys, an elegant novella, were these to be the sum of his offerings to posterity?

'Perhaps I could honour the greatness of others, as Palomino did in Spain –'

'You could do better than Palomino; think of Vasari. You have the taste, the skills – you *are* an artist. And it could be your monument. It's the *Lives* that have made Vasari immortal.'

'I could commemorate –'

'You could be our recording angel!'

They drank to the future: to De Non, the next Giorgio Vasari.

But, for the moment, art was pushed to the background; life intervened, or rather, death, with a letter from his mother: 'Your father is growing weaker.'

Why had he remained away so long? His father had been ill for some time and he had known, but an odd emotional inertia prevented him from doing what should have come naturally. He loved his family, but at one remove; they remained distant, framed by their vineyards like a Burgundy family portrait rather than the real thing.

V went home to a house filled with a sense of mortality. He stood by the window in his father's room and looked out at the gardens. He saw himself sitting on the grass next to his sister, drinking lemonade with his mother's friends, a well-behaved small boy already noting the contrast between linen and silk, the way a woman's body curved into a garden seat, the delicate snail-shell of an ear glimpsed through an elegant coiffure.

From where he stood he watched another boy, his sister's child, tumbling in the grass, life filling him as it drained from the man lying in the bed across the room. He could hear his father's breathing, loud and shallow, each rattling breath fought for. The two had not been close: aspiring to nobility, the family maintained the correct aristocratic distance between the generations. Now, faced with the need to show appropriate emotion, V found himself ill-equipped.

Had it been his wet nurse who was dying, he would have held her in his arms as she had held him, in infancy, her bosom an expanse as comforting as a feather pillow. When he left home he had hugged Baptiste's mother, laughing; he had kissed her hand extravagantly. His father was for greeting respectfully, bowing; his mother was embraced formally on both cheeks at appropriate times. A spontaneous show of affection or the physical manifestation of loss now were beyond him. He suspected that he might weep more easily at the sight of a poignant Watteau group than at the fundamental moment of grief, the death of a parent.

When it came he remained predictably dry-eyed, as would in any case be considered only proper for someone in his position. He received condolences, and in turn consoled his mother. The moment that took him by surprise came when he entered the drawing room late that afternoon and noticed, above the fireplace, lit up by a long beam from the setting sun a self-portrait by a young boy (now a mature man), showing him at work on the bust of a king (now dead). A lively exercise, and remarkably prescient, considering that the young artist would not meet the royal sitter until several years later *'Who* are *you?' Louis had demanded of the provincial newcomer to Versailles. 'What is it you want?'* The painting had been a part of V's childhood, both parents confident that the boy was born to achieve great things, and he remembered gatherings when he would be called in, the prodigy aged ten, to display a new work, and receive the smiling applause of guests. And he recalled now the look on his father's face: not only pride, but delight. Love. And the tears came.

Sorrow surprised him, welling up from somewhere long ago sealed off, so that he walked the grounds overcome by the sense of helplessness, of vulnerability that afflicts the living following a death; the guilt of the survivor.

But sorrow was not to be his only surprise: his sister alerted him to a loss of a different kind.

'If you had been here you would have seen it for yourself. We are short of money, Vivant. I think the worry helped to kill him; the upheavals in Paris . . . our revenues are not what they were.'

Trapped by their very possessions, the land, the production of wine, there seemed no way to improve the situation: it was hardly a case of getting rid of a few servants and eating simpler food. Certainly they would need to modify their needs. V had always taken the future for granted. He would have to reassess his expectations.

Back in Paris he threw himself into work: he drew; he painted, he looked at pictures and began to make notes for his book. He copied a Rembrandt in order to understand it better, and offered it to the Academy as a formal study. Somewhat to his surprise the Academy invited him to be a Member. He was now officially an artist: *Monsieur Dominique-Vivant De Non, Membre de l'Académie.*

This was clearly the time to press on with the serious work, the history of art. Indeed, with his new-found understanding of economic fluctuations, he saw that a substantial publication could provide income. So: work then. Instead he found himself, like a rudderless craft, drifting.

On a walk along the Seine one afternoon he stood watching the brown-green water slap the stone quays, light wavering across the arches of the bridge; walls and trees and the hulls of boats captured in mirror image. Water. Reflection, refraction, antiquity, elegance. History. Above all, art. An idea came to him.

Reflections in a Lagoon

Contessa Isabella Teotochi Marin. By Denon, after Louise-Elisabeth
Vigée-Lebrun

In the salon of the house on the Quai Voltaire, Zenobia feels the cold; the temperature has dropped and she rubs her hands together, adjusts the collar of her jacket. She listens for sounds from another room – the creak of floorboards, the murmur of a voice, footsteps. She hears the soft, heavy thud of the front door closing, and then Baptiste is back in the room, materialising in that fluid, unobtrusive way.

'What does the doctor say?'

'He will return later. The Baron is sleeping.'

On the wall to the left of the window she notices a portrait in oils, a man poised between youth and middle age, elegant, curly-haired, with an ironical half-smile, a look of quizzical amusement. There is a shadowed indentation on the side of his face.

'Is that him?'

Baptiste follows her glance. 'The Baron. Yes.'

She looks more closely: 'He has a scar?' She imagined a glancing bullet, possibly a dagger – a man who travelled in dangerous places –

'A dimple.'

She studies the face, one she has tried to visualise so often, attempting to build from his letters a picture of the man himself. Now with his features before her, she tries to go deeper, to read what lies behind the bright eyes and dimpled cheek.

Baptiste wishes her elsewhere, wishes her gone, but she

seems smaller, less dangerous, as she presses herself against the unwelcoming stiffness of the armchair. He has deliberately refrained from offering her anything to eat or drink; now he relents – to a point.

'A tisane, or a chocolate, something to warm you before you leave,' he says.

She is aware that the offer is a way of reminding her she must go. She looks away from the portrait.

'I would prefer chocolate. Thank you.'

She notices again his movement, an almost balletic turn of the body as he closes the door behind him.

On the mantelpiece are a number of porcelain figures delicately moulded and coloured, and she gets up to look at them more closely. It is then, stepping back from the fireplace, that she sees the box of letters on the floor, and the small heap of ash in the grate. Ash, and some fragments of paper not quite consumed by the flame. When first Baptiste had shown her into the house, she now recalls, she had been aware of a hint of something acrid, a faint smell of burning. Before she can stop herself, censor her own indefensible action, she has plucked an unburned scrap from where it lies, brown with smoke: words, ends of lines, making little sense – *to see you again . . . your laughing mouth . . . and in the gondola . . .* Then, three words and a signature: *all my heart, Isabella.*

Appalled to find herself behaving like a thief, she tucks the scrap of paper into her reticule and returns to her chair. She can feel the unsteady speed of her heartbeat. She rummages in her bulky bag, and brings out some letters.

When Baptiste returns, followed by a maid carrying a pot of hot chocolate on a small silver tray she is studying one of the flimsy sheets.

The chocolate sits untouched as she reads from the page in her hand: ' "My dear Zenobia, for you, born into heat and parched horizons, it would be difficult to picture a city built on water. To think of houses that resemble confectionery;

sugar-pink palaces, rising out of angelica-green canals." ' She says, 'I think Venice was the place he was happiest.'

Without looking up she knows he has glanced quickly towards the fireplace. He remains silent, and when she does look at him she sees he is frowning.

Someone in the coach said it was Venice, but what V saw was a smudge on the horizon, a layer of cloud, perhaps a clump of trees . . . then the road changed direction, the view sank out of sight – Venice swallowed up not by water but by landscape. For the traveller that spring morning in 1788, heading towards the Veneto from Padua, it was too fleeting and too distant to make an impression. The true impact came later, as it did for all new arrivals, when his craft bobbed and surged its way round a curve in the Grand Canal and the incomparable waterfront met his eyes.

Afterwards he was astonished that it could have taken him by surprise. But that day, curving into view for the first time, it robbed him of his breath – *Mozzafiata!* he thought, reaching for his Neapolitan vocabulary.

In retrospect, Venice was a secret room filled with pictures, each of which captured a moment – scenes from a life, vivid, bursting with detail. But in those first days his was still an empty gallery, its works as yet unpainted.

Later, V's chamber of the mind would have its quota of grand canvases: the *ridotto*, where the real games dealt not in cards but seduction . . . the *parlatorio*, with its swirl of conversation, rumour, scandal, puppet shows for children . . . scenes pulsating with life and people, interspersed with the intimate moments: here a portrait of a young woman combing her hair; there a country idyll, sunlight through trees; the same young woman, half turned, looking into the eyes of the artist. Smiling. And the gondola rides, when the boat drifted lazily on the glassy water while its two occupants lost themselves in talking or read aloud from a favourite book – here she was again, the young woman with wanton, curly hair.

Later, there were nocturnes in tones of indigo and ink, when darkness dropped a concealing veil over passion, tears. Grief.

Each of these moments was self-contained, offering glimpses of a particular world at a particular time; they would depict a man finding, and then losing, the love of his life.

In time these scenes, imprinted on his mind, some little more than sketches, others with all the depth and richness of oil, will give an ageing man a fresh perspective on faded highs and lows. Meanwhile, the past still lies ahead, waiting to be explored.

The coach had deposited them at Fusina where the mainland merged into the archipelago, and Baptiste was overseeing the loading of their baggage on to a *gondolone* manned by four oarsmen. Cosy inside the cabin, V surrendered to the rhythm of the water. They drifted through a lagoon pale and milky as moonstone, with black wooden posts rising through the mist, and fishermen poised over nets and lobster pots, so still that they too might have been carved from wood.

Lulled by the motion of the boat, he must have slept, then started awake and opened his eyes to see through the window the subjects of familiar paintings rising from the water, moving past him like canvases being unrolled. The *palazzi* with their faded, flaking stucco, their extravagant chimney pots, one jostling the next, the colours of their flat fronts – coral, ochre and grey, dark red and terracotta – decorated with delicate fretwork and filigree; their Byzantine and Gothic windows arched or pointed, their entrances flanked with shallow steps down to the water. Gondolas lined up, bobbing like ducks, tied to mooring posts striped in green and white, red and yellow, blue and gold. Now and then a shaft of darkness sliced between the buildings when a narrow waterway barely wide enough to let through a gondola slithered its inky way to the canal. In one backwater he glimpsed a boatyard, with craftsmen creating a gondola from its skeleton. A *piazzetta* ran along the quayside, shaded with trees beneath which small children and dogs raced and tumbled, and women carried untidy bundles, fed babies. A man squatted, mending a chair. At the balconied windows washing was hung out to dry. The stuff of everyday life, its domesticity at odds with the turbulent waterfront.

The heavy *gondolone* thrust its way through the choppy water and the setting sun sank lower behind V's back. As he watched, the houses lost their individual colours, turning gradually to gold, then grey, and the water darkened. It seemed that everything was in motion: clouds and shadows and the last, lingering rays of the sun, the boats and people. The special light of this moment, the fading gold, the darkening grey, would stay with him for ever. Humility came upon him then, and an acknowledgement that even the greatest painter, brush in hand, could never match the artist now at work. Something like a sob rose in his chest so that he found himself gasping for breath.

'Baptiste!' he cried out, as though calling for help, but then could think of nothing that needed to be said.

V disliked living in a hotel room. Not that the detail of domestic inconvenience affected him; that was, of course, Baptiste's responsibility. What irritated was the absence of a proper desk and a place for his drawing and etching materials. Somewhere for pacing up and down. Hotels were for sleeping, washing and eating *en voyage*; nobody should be required to live in one for more than a few days. Even a well-placed establishment, close by the Piazza San Marco.

'We really must find somewhere, Baptiste.'

Baptiste, who had spent the early hours making his way up

and down the steep staircase between three floors, unpacking, steaming and pressing the garments V would wear today, and later bringing up breakfast, was now buttoning and lacing his master into shirt, breeches and jacket. He had no argument with the general intention; his only quibble was with the word 'we'. There would be no 'we' involved in finding a place to live: he would find it; 'we' would then occupy it.

'And nothing too extravagant: we must learn to make economies.'

In Baptiste's view the economies were remarkably selective. Only the day before the master had returned home with two engravings, a watercolour and a large book wrapped in silk. Economies?

The search for a place to live provided Baptiste with some bewildering choices: which neighbourhood to choose; north or south . . . part of a large *palazzo* or something smaller that offered privacy . . . In tavern and marketplace he called on the informal freemasonry of those who serve; an invisible, reliable, infinitely flexible network. In the wig shop, at the fruit stall, the wine merchant's, Baptiste found experts who could guide a newcomer's steps.

V, too, was busy: the shape of the social day must be established: which were the fashionable hours to meet? Were certain days of the week set aside for such and such an activity? How much fresh air was considered proper? In Naples, life had been lived much out of doors: on the shady loggias, the terraces poised above the bay, '*Fuori!*' was a familiar royal cry; outside was the place to be, cradled in the blue of sea and sky.

For Baptiste, Venice was difficult at the beginning. With his dislike of water-borne transport, he wore out shoe-leather making circuitous journeys to avoid gondola rides. He had always preferred the efficiency of Paris where shops kept reasonable hours and people arrived at the time agreed. Quick, industrious, impatient, he fretted in this place where *dolce far niente* was the rule.

For V it was different. The gondola carried him from church to church, from altarpiece to frescoed chapel; he lingered over madonnas, each with her halo-ringed and invariably ugly child; he studied every crucifixion and *pietà*, the brush strokes and the fall of light; the positioning of martyrs, the folds of drapery, and in a city where the patron beast was the lion, he looked at the changing face of lions carved and cast and painted over a thousand years. Lions sleeping or rampant; guarding porticoes and gateposts; lions winged or domesticated. Seventy-five of the creatures guarded the entrance to the Doge's palace, and he was made aware of the forty different ways the same beast could be depicted at the feet of St Jerome. He soaked himself in art. What else was life for?

In time, he came to know the city's many moods, its ferocious summer noon, with colours hammered flat by the sun, shadows lying like black velvet alongside the houses . . . the white mists of autumn spreading over a city grown blurred and uncertain, the days when high-tide water rose to engulf even the broad piazzas, gondolas plying from door to door where normally men walked dry-shod. He knew it perhaps best by night, when he wandered in the early hours from one narrow alleyway to another, crossing town, until he came to a particular stone bridge. Here he would stand, gazing up at the green shutters of a certain *palazzo* and picture the woman in the lamplit upper room as she sat reading or sketching, or lying asleep.

St Petersburg had been a place of stuffy rooms and heavy curtains, things half glimpsed: doors closing, skirts whisked out of sight, carriages disappearing round corners, enigmatic, beautiful women in fur hats; a sense of events forming a pattern without his knowledge. It concealed itself, one puzzle inside another, mysterious. He did not look back on it with pleasure.

Venice too had its mysteries; did not open itself readily to strangers; but Venice was all movement and flux, light wavering on water, the dip and sway of a gondola's silver prow seen from the shrouded intimacy of its covered *felze*. Venice floated, languid; its gaiety and movement had a dreamlike rhythm. Venice was music and laughter and passion; it was oil on canvas: Bellini, who brought an incomparable stillness and concentration to his Holy Families, his saints and musicians bent over their instruments; Titian whose brush dripped gleaming flesh and splendour, Veronese with his silvery tones. Venice was a play whose actors were also its audience. But above all and for ever, Venice was Isabella.

He was aware of her presence before he saw her: from across the room, where a knot of male figures clustered; he caught a few words, the tail end of a sentence, the voice soft, low-pitched. There was a ripple of appreciative laughter from the men. Then he was drawn away: someone wanted to meet him; an evening at the *ridotto* was, after all, a social occasion, everyone too busy talking or flirting to actually do any gambling. A little later, again cut off from view by a wall of shoulders, backs, tricorne hats and cloaks, he caught a not-quite-glimpse of a female form, her figure blurred by a cloak of fine black silk; hair and face concealed by a mantilla and half-mask. Surrounded by men. He would grow accustomed to this, to the magnetic quality in Isabella that drew men to her, the way they hovered, poised a little forward as if to catch her every word, mouths sagging open in a vacant half-smile. 'She's the Madame de Staël of Venice,' Byron told V many years later. That first day he did not even know her name, only that her fragrance had drifted his way, had risen into his head and was disturbing his balance. He found himself leaning forward, as though pulled her way. Then she moved away and was lost to view.

The *ridotto* was a place of self-presentation – but at the same time of elegant concealment. The nobility mingled with the card-sharps and professional gamblers, the circling tarts as much at their ease as the gentry. The game of identity was an elaborate one: everyone knew who everyone was, but no one was actually recognised unless he wished to be. A man whispered in the ear of a woman who was not his wife; women exchanged glances with promising strangers. A senator, too, could loosen the confining bonds of office here, shedding his gown, donning a mask and turning to the card table or a woman who had caught his eye. V's host, Hennin, the French consul, murmured helpful, identifying phrases, pointing out agents of the Holy Office, also conveniently masked, wandering through the crowd.

'They have their task made easier here; informed without inconvenience to anyone. After all, what goes on may be illicit, but it causes no public disorder.'

V watched in astonishment a scene as artificial as an opera, played out in everyday life. He bowed at appropriate social moments, smiled at the half-hidden, smiling faces from behind his own mask; joined in occasional card play, the taking of refreshment, and the serious business of gossip, though here – unlike Paris or Naples – he was, unusually, at a disadvantage: he knew no one. Still, like the others he played his part, all of them motes drifting and dancing in a world as bright as a shaft of sunlight.

One exuberant young aristocrat escorted a woman whose oval velvet mask covered her face. V bowed over her hand, complimenting her on the beauty of her city. She inclined her head, unspeaking, enigmatic. She and her escort moved on.

'You have now experienced the phenomenon of the silent woman,' Hennin commented. 'She's wearing the full *moretta* mask. There's a button on the inside of the mask which she grips between her teeth. I find it strangely erotic.'

Looking more closely, V saw how these women clamped

to their masks, became both alluring and anonymous; in one sense helpless, bound into speechlessness, but in their subservience using a potent shrug of a shoulder, turn of the head, discreet pressure of fingers on male wrist, to make their wishes known. *Pale fingers pressed to a hot wrist, pulse racing . . . a night of passion, a cold awakening – how long ago that seemed . . .* V cut into the nostalgic stream: it *was* long ago; the wide-eyed youth had matured; nothing could surprise or humiliate him now, he had been passionately acquainted with a number of beautiful women; he had outgrown the killing jar and was in no danger. He was in Venice to look and learn; to paint, to draw, and begin his history of art. He was here to work, he told himself again. To work.

She caught him unawares. Glancing about, his eyes skimming silk and velvet shoulders, he found his masked lady of the soft, compelling voice close by, almost in touching distance, her back to him, addressing her companions.

'I am uneasy with *Dido and Aeneas*. Composers allow me to listen to the music, which is delightful. The story is a heartless trick played by the gods and as usual, the woman suffers, poor, deceived Dido.'

And V exclaimed, self-mocking, '*Arma virumque cano, Troiae qui primus ab oris Italiam fato profugus Laviniaque venit litora . . .*'

Her head turned, she swung round to identify the unknown voice filled with laughter declaiming Virgil's portentous lines, of Aeneas and his song of war. She remarked, to no one in particular, 'Judging by his accent our visitor comes from Gallic not Trojan shores, from Paris – a Frenchman, perhaps?'

A moment later the introduction had been effected: Monsieur De Non . . . Contessa Teotochi Marin, and she was wondering aloud why a man who smiled so cheerfully could have his mind fixed on ancient tragedy.

'Ah,' he murmured, 'but "Now do I know what love is".'

'More Virgil! Are we to spend the evening waving other men's words at one another like flags?' she asked. 'If so, I might as well have remained in my library.'

'And thereby saved me from eternal wretchedness!'

'And whose words are those?'

'Inadequate, but mine own. Blame Dido, blame Juno, when a man is under a spell and the siren song fills his head, he is lost. The goddess can never be his, hence he is doomed to suffer. And, having lost his wits, talk nonsense.'

Through the half-mask dark eyes gleamed. Beneath the half-mask full lips rewarded him with a smile, above the half-mask her curls tumbled; appalling cliché, he acknowledged, then watched the movement of the dark hair and repeated to himself: her curls tumble . . . if he could just run his fingers through their silken –

Lost for words, he mumbled something unintelligible. His pulse raced, his skin felt hot. He was a youth again, drowning. But this time, it seemed, the goddess was not bent on killing the poor specimen. Later, pacing his small room, flinging open the shutters although the night was chilly, he explained to Baptiste that the lady was beautiful but also witty, beautiful but also kind; beautiful but also gentle.

'The locals say *la donna è bella da impazzire*,' Baptiste offered drily, since his master indeed appeared to have lost his mind for the moment.

' "Bewitchingly beautiful", that's a neat phrase.' V splashed cold water on his face. 'Where did you hear it?'

'Servants talk.'

'I suppose they must.' V scratched his back thoughtfully. 'But I never see them at it. Do the others talk to you? Do you talk to them?'

'Of course. I am human, after all.'

'I'm not at all sure about that. You have a way of knowing everything, and of knowing what to do about it, that is positively superhuman.'

'If you don't sleep now, you will not be fit for the *parlatorio* tomorrow, sir.'

'You always know what is best for me, Baptiste.'

Zenobia says, studying the fragile sheet of paper, 'He wrote me such beautiful letters about Venice; it was long afterwards, of course, but he made me see it as though for myself. He told me about the little theatres and the music. The covered market with its blue clock by the Rialto, the boats carrying fruit and vegetables, and the months of carnival.' Baptiste has relaxed, nodding. And now she takes the risky step into unknown territory. She adds, carefully casual, 'And of course, he told me about Isabella.'

There is a pause. His stillness is willed, conscious. No sudden movement of hand or head, his skin pale as marble. Then he says, 'Isabella? You must be mistaken. The baron cannot have written to you about —' a hesitation, 'such a person. You are mistaken.'

Zenobia is folding and unfolding the letter. He watches her hands, the unpolished nails and workmanlike, scrubbed fingers. They would probably feel rough to the touch. Women in Venice, he recalled, even servants, had elegant hands. Lucia's fingers touching his, a letter passing from one to the other; the fragrance of violets — was the letter perfumed, or did her flesh smell of flowers? Her hands were all he knew, at first: smooth fingertips, slim wrists. Days passed before he saw her eyes, days more before she smiled.

He says, briskly, 'You really must leave now. Where are you staying? Tomorrow I can send you word —'

'When I arrived, I had to find my way across Paris. I came straight here.' She glances out, into the evening gloom, 'Would it be —' She stops. Then, desperate, astonished by her own daring: 'I am unfamiliar with the city. Could I stay here, tonight?'

Through the thin fabric of her reticule her fingers feel the scraps of paper, the shredded words from someone called Isabella. She waits, watching his face.

The Old Music

Dressed and fortified with coffee, V stepped into the pandemonium of the rowdy, surging street. So many vendors of this and that, baskets on head or slung from shoulders; merchants and artisans crossing town from the Rialto to San Marco, the Arsenale to the Dorsoduro, crowding the tiny streets and the bridges – so frequent, humped and potentially dangerous, especially in the dark, often with no balustrading or handrail to protect the unwary. But once a gondola was hailed, once the step from land to buoyant wood was taken, everything changed: bustle turned to calm; the slap of water against hull blotting out the counterpoint of voice calling to voice. The world was distanced.

He needed to make Venice his own; therefore the *parlatorio* must be attended. He moved from gondola to *palazzo* entrance; from *portego* up a marble staircase to the *piano nobile*. And there, amid the swirling, smiling throng, ringed by what he now realised was her constant escort of admiring males, he saw Isabella, this time without her mask. He heard her speak his name.

'And here we have Monsieur De Non. From Paris. Who loves Virgil. And tragedy.' Then, sweetly mocking: 'Looking as cheerful as ever.'

He was aware, through the roaring in his head, that she was asking a question; jumping prettily through the social hoops she was enquiring what brought him to Venice?

He could have said he was a diplomat, which would have

sounded acceptable, impressive even – *Gentilhomme du Roi*, in this city of extravagant titles and theatrical role-playing, would have a certain appeal. But he was aware that the Contessa's eyes were direct as well as beautiful. She looked at him closely, as though memorising his features, and before he had modified the clumsy words for presentation he said, 'I hope I am an artist.'

'Yes,' she said. 'Let us hope you are.'

She moved away, but not to move on: she glanced sideways, and drew him with her by invisible strings. They walked to the loggia windows. Today, in sunlight, the city had the detailed clarity of a Canaletto. It seemed to V that its artists had appropriated Venice, had removed it from the realm of the everyday world and imprisoned it within the gilded frames of their representations so that 'their' painted Venice had become the reality, the city itself merely the model.

But when he murmured this to Isabella she shook her head. 'There is always something more, something that cannot be pinned down. This is why, for me, the artists come closest who acknowledge that, who leave something for the onlooker to add. Look at Francesco Guardi, at his gondoliers. His waterfronts. Look closely and what do you see?'

'His casual strokes of the brush.'

'Casual, seemingly, but also tremulous, elusive. He has given us the *idea* of the gondolier, the city, not quite finished, so that we can complete it for ourselves. Give us everything and we are left with nothing to do but admire perfection. I admire Canaletto, but I love Guardi.'

'So you find imperfection appealing. Then I am encouraged; I have hope.'

Behind them fine boots and pointed shoes tapped the terrazzo floor, rings flashed from fingers rubbed smooth with oil and sugar, there was the gleam of a necklace, the glow of wine. The room was on the move, figures circling, as if on a dance floor, to the music of words and laughter. Unmoving, like rocks, as the tide swirled past, stood these two: in repose like old friends, who yet were barely acquainted. Between them a sense that they need say nothing further, no words needed, and at the same time that they were embarking on a conversation that would continue until silenced by death.

An odd couple at first sight: a short man in his forties with a round face, unimpressive nose and ambiguous smile; a ridiculously youthful dimple and curly hair turning grey. A woman no more than twenty-eight, with the glow of a ripe peach, her eyes dark; her skin velvety as she stood with the curtain shading her from the sunlight that flooded through the window. He studied her the way he absorbed a work of art. Surely such a woman should be attended by some blade-slim, flashing escort, his face unmarked by life? As a *cavalier-servant* he was hardly a prize.

He was by her side for the rest of the day. With darkness and a dispersal of the gathering, he led her to her waiting gondola, disregarding those who were there to assist her. She, for her part, knew how to disengage gracefully from the lover of the moment; in Venice this was part of the pattern.

'Shall we meet later perhaps? Come to my *casinò*,' she called as the gondola slid away.

He watched it go, the oily wake catching the moonlight, the water heaving like a dark, sleepy snake. This contrast was the essence of the city; the *chiaroscuro*, the sombre and the sparkling.

'I admire Canaletto,' Isabella had said, 'but I love Guardi.' In the church of San Angelo Rafaele he had discovered a cycle of seven paintings sprawled above the baroque organ loft, done by the Guardi brothers, Antonio and Franceso. Episodes from the story of Tobias, they showed the encounter with the angel, the healing of his sick father, his marriage . . . V had returned to study and copy the paintings. Unlikely as it seemed, he found in them something that reminded him of Watteau: the lush sweep of colour and fabric, the delicacy of the landscape; an unexpected tenderness. V borrowed now from those images to create, on the walls of his mind, an instant fresco of a life with Isabella; their meeting, their first parting now, and the years ahead. This imaginary fresco was just beginning; it would spread, like Guardi's, scene after scene unrolling like a great scroll. Surely it would need an entire cloister to contain it, to hold the life he would share with Isabella.

He walked on, into the darkness.

Where the narrow *rio* came to an end, losing itself in the width of the Grand Canal, the houses leaned towards each other across the water, their rooftops almost touching. A little shrine in a niche cast the faint light of its oil lamp on the flagstones. He had found such shrines at every corner of the city, glowing, their lamps reflecting haloes and holy robes, golden points against the black velvet of the night, their lights guiding his steps. He turned and carried on walking. From here he could return to the hotel on foot; it would take longer than a gondola, following the maze of streets now left, now right, along a narrow *fondamenta*, over bridges, under arches, but in this way he built up a picture of the place – more than a picture, a portfolio, a panoply of images as detailed and decorative as an old map. And while he walked, he composed the first of many letters.

Dear Friend,

My man will deliver this to you, I trust no one else. *Mon vieux* is scared of fog, of the sea, of everything, but he is the most dependable man I know . . .

When Baptiste read the letter – a valet had to keep abreast of events – the description irritated him. Yes, he was cautious in fog, any prudent man would be; he had learned to take care in Naples, where unseen potholes and missing cobblestones in ill-lit alleys made for a hazardous cross-town journey. The sea? Well, of course he was afraid of the sea and with good reason, after the voyage from Messina when he almost drowned.

Now, crossing Venice, he asked himself why man would devise so eccentric a method of steering a craft: a boatman balanced precariously at one end of a misshapen canoe, flinging himself and his oar forward almost to toppling point to draw the boat laboriously through the water. Apprehensively he looked about him.

Venetian ladies wore black. In Naples, even quite poor, barefooted women would flaunt coral beads at throat and wrist. Their skirts might be blue or green; their blouses white; their shawls bright with embroidery.

Here, looking across the great piazza, Baptiste felt he was watching an endless funeral procession, the pale Venetian faces luminous against black velvet and silk; black shoes elegant as they stepped into the black-painted gondolas, the cabin like a shrouded coffin amidships. The gentlemen's black breeches and jackets, cut in the latest fashion, were black as ink, as were their cloaks and mantles, powdered wigs white in contrast. It was already evening, and Baptiste saw that some of the women had fixed glow-worms by threads to their hair, the creatures glittering in the darkness like tiny, winking diamonds.

The Republic maintained a sober public façade. Within a fashionable *casinò* or a private *palazzo*, colour leaped from every side: Baptiste had seen walls clad in silk and covered with paintings in gilded frames; cushions and coverings woven from brilliant threads. Gold and ivory plaster putti, painted gods and heroes spread themselves across ceilings. Mirrors from Murano reflected candlelight glowing on jewels which in private could still be flamboyantly displayed. Venetian servants wore extravagant livery.

Now Baptiste stepped out of the gondola and went up the

steps to the Marin *palazzo*. He had a letter to be delivered, as instructed, into the hands of a trusted servant.

'The Contessa's maid,' he requested of the footman who barred his way at the top of the mossy, green steps from the canal. Later he learned her name – Lucia. With time, he became familiar with every part of her: smooth throat and small breasts, black hair scraped into severity that escaped into curls when loosened, the slender arms that wound about him, the strong legs that tapered to fine-boned ankles. But that first night all he saw was the blur of her face, and her hands emerging from the darkness as she took the letter from his master to her mistress.

He said, '*Buona sera, signorina,*' and saw the white of her teeth as she smiled – probably in amusement at his accent. He noted, as their hands touched, that her skin was soft. He was aware of the scent of violets.

Letters to Isabella. So many letters.

Before long 'Dear friend . . .' had become 'My dearest Isabella . . .' and then, '*Ma chère* Bettine . . .'

When did he first call her Bettine? And, bringing the letter to a close, where earlier he had ended with formal expressions of friendship, there came the shift to 'I embrace you with all my heart . . .'

They wrote to each other almost every day – a few lines, a postscript to an interrupted conversation; sometimes pages of thoughts. They revisited Virgil and Dante, compared histories; they looked at paintings . . . for these two, the physical was always intertwined with an intimacy of the mind. They would sift hidden meanings, test accepted truths; debate the ambiguous significance of a painting – 'the expression on the Virgin's face at the moment of Annunciation: how should that be read? Resignation? Exaltation?'

Isabella suggested alarm might be a more appropriate

reaction to hearing you were to be the mother of God.

Their days and nights were taken up in amusement, the ongoing conversation of the fashionable *casinò*, where they could always be seen. There were no witnesses to the hours of tenderness in a curtained gondola, of moans and sighs and secret laughter.

They would set themselves diverting tasks, say, to count and compare the infinite variety of footwear in the paintings of the masters – stout sandals, plaited or fashioned from plain strips; criss-cross or simple thong; knotted or tied, winding round ankles, sometimes no more than a wisp of cloth, at others gilded leather, studded with brass, feathered. And later, in the gondola, V took Isabella's foot and gently removed her pointed, silken shoe, offering instead his hand to cradle and protect her flesh, his lips to trace the line of her high instep; bones that seemed as fragile as a bird's.

Swaying, cushioned in velvet, he felt them whirling through space, brief sparks in the darkness of the universe. Then the smile, a lift of the brows. 'Shall we stop for a while to sip a few drops of bitter liquid made from the ground seeds of the kahavé plant?' He breathed in her scent. 'Florian's does it particularly well.'

He had always believed the seriousness of life demanded to be treated lightly.

At first Isabella's letters were written in Italian; later she charmed him in both tongues. When V took one of his excursions, to Florence or Bologna or Ferrara, to look at this painting or that drawing, searching out material to include in the projected History of Art, his thoughts winged their way back to Venice like homing pigeons with flimsy paper wings.

He drank in the frescos, altarpieces, triptychs, and gave thanks. And missed '*ma chère* Bettine'. Back in Venice he missed her between one meeting and the next. And told her so.

Baptiste marvelled that these two could have so much to say since they met almost every day, at her *casinò*, her salon, in the house with green shutters. Here they would mingle with her guests before discreetly withdrawing from the crowded salon to the private boudoir.

Against the soft buzz of voices and the tinkle of wine glass or porcelain, passion might be sparked by the unlikely tinder of a conversation about antiquity.

'I have something to show you, Vivente, *a proposito* Virgil,' Isabella called to him one evening, moving away from the group. 'There is a place where Venus asks Vulcan to do her a favour. You must give me your opinion . . .' They drifted through the entrance to her dressing room, the painted door swung shut; she took down the book and found the place. He leaned over her shoulder, following the words she read aloud, ' "Venus called Vulcan to their golden bridal chamber . . . and as he hesitated the goddess caressed him in a tender embrace, on this side, and on that, in her snowy arms . . ." '

Isabella caressed him, still holding the book, and on this reading he saw the passage quite differently, no longer a cynical view of female wiles, but a celebration of passion, and now he read aloud, ' "He felt the familiar flame, and that warmth penetrated him to the marrow, and ran through his melting bones . . ." '

And with the softest of thuds the book fell to the carpet, abandoned.

Years later he would write to her, 'Ah, *ma chère* Bettine, how happy we were, and how innocent in our pleasure!' And, echoing Dante, 'how sharp is the pain of past happiness recollected in misery.'

The letter made its usual journey: from V to Baptiste, from his hand to Lucia's. The footman was out of sight, but they kept their voices low.

'How is she today?'

'Much as usual. Two concerts and a private dinner. At the moment she is having her portrait done by some boy who wrote to her from Florence – she'll give him at least an hour.'

Good news. Just as V's intense social life occasionally freed Baptiste, so Isabella's maid sometimes slipped away when not needed, down the wet stone steps and into the gondola, the curtained hideaway for a precious hour, at first for hurried passion, later as often for the luxury of conversation.

At the beginning Lucia spoke little: her experience was to listen – to Isabella, to senior servants, the priest. Prompted by Baptiste, Lucia was learning to speak for herself.

First came the questions. He told her about Burgundy: the vineyards, the orchards where he spent long summer days with the boy who was almost a brother, until the maid called them in, and sheep and goats were divided. Then V dawdled up the steps to the salon while Baptiste, crossing the kitchen threshold, stepped back into the world of servitude. He tried to explain his confusion as he crossed and recrossed this line: fencing lessons and classes in reading, writing and mathematics with the young master. Clothes of fine cotton and wool, as befitted a companion-servant. Sleeping quarters so bleak that the ink froze in the inkwell on winter nights.

In turn she told him about Corfu. Uprooted and transplanted when her mistress the young Contessa married a Venetian nobleman, the maid's willingness to experience exile taken for granted: servants did not have preferences, even the most benign of masters or mistresses could not have stretched their imagination that far.

Haltingly, she began to find the words to tell Baptiste about her island with its wild rocks and hillsides carpeted with a thousand different wild flowers, white, purple, blue, 'each with its own scent – better than a perfumery'. She told him about tiny coves with pebbles as small as beads, a pink castle set high above the sea, and the town with its elegant, arcaded streets and fountains. He told her about Paris, St Petersburg, Naples.

The conversations would end, like their lovemaking, when the trusted gondolier had circled the quiet canals for an hour and brought the boat back to the little *rio* and the imposing entrance. In the gondola, curtains drawn, Lucia could hurriedly do up her buttons and tidy her skirts and whisk discreetly into the *palazzo*.

She was folding her mistress's undergarments, interleaving them with lavender, when Isabella returned to her bedroom and collapsed with theatrical exhaustion on to the daybed.

'The sitting took much longer than I had planned, but he looked desperate.' She smiled, with the amused tenderness she could never withhold from young poets and artists. 'So thin. And nervous: when he began, his hand shook. He had to start again, full of apologies . . .'

Once, the portrait sitting would probably have led to a meeting less confined to art, to several such meetings, where the young poet or artist would for a while occupy the centre of the canvas or the page. But now, V would be waiting, and the young Florentine had used up the time available to him.

She kicked off her silk shoes. Lucia picked them up and stuffed clean rags into the pointed toes. 'I'll prepare your bath.'

'Choose me something cool to wear.'

Isabella knew everyone, resident or passing through. Tonight, as he greeted her, V glanced round her salon enquiringly: 'Someone's missing; I heard Goethe's in Venice.'

She gave him one of her quizzical looks and led him to the window. She pointed across the narrow canal to a house with tiny balconies framed by terracotta balustrades.

'He's staying there. You'll meet him later.'

'Of course. How could I have doubted you!'

'He insists on hearing the gondoliers' songs.'

'While I have ears only for you.'

They teased each other, she mocking his delight in the treasures her town had to offer, he expressing ironic deference to her status as local goddess.

'Half of Venice is in love with you and I am deeply jealous.'

Their faces were quite close, separated only by the wine glasses they held. The fine bubbles rose from the champagne. She laughed, touching her glass gently to his.

'Ah, *mia cara* Isabella,' he murmured, '*ma chère* Bettine, if we could undergo a magical transformation, be changed, intermingling, what would we choose to become?'

'Could the two of us dissolve into a picture by Guardi? You the canvas, I the paint, clinging to you, our surfaces touching, indivisible?'

She drew him closer to the window; the curtain swung between them and the rest of the room and, briefly, their surfaces touched, hers silken and yielding, his 'imperfect, alas!' he remarked wryly. 'Oh, for some Guardi brush strokes to improve me!'

Cut off from the noisy crowd, for a moment they were isolated. Faintly, from another room, came the sound of a musician at a harpsichord playing Scarlatti.

Small wonder that for V, looking back later, Venice and happiness were synonymous: Isabella and art, Isabella and music, Isabella and conversation, laughter; the light-hearted wickedness of carnival with the privacy of the gondola, swirling cloaks and delicately fashioned masks. There was elegance, congenial companions, Monteverdi to listen to, and all bathed in golden Venetian light by day, or the glow of tall candles at night. He was not yet aware that he was being watched.

The Inquisition had begun to look more closely at his affairs, to draw up lists of names, movements, study police reports where each hour of the day and night was detailed.

'The Frenchman often works through the night – apparently on an engraving or a drawing. He sleeps till ten, at which hour three young students arrive at his door . . . At seven in the evening the wig-maker arrives to arrange Monsieur De Non's coiffure. An hour later he leaves the house, usually to visit the Contessa Isabella Teotochi Marin . . .

'He walks a great deal, in various parts of the city, and it has been recorded that he occasionally pauses to speak to French people in the street.' In the margin a question: 'For what purpose? For secret news of his country perhaps?'

The police report ended with a note that it had not been possible to obtain personal information on these conversations. As yet.

Unaware of the monitoring, V was in every sense afloat. As was Baptiste.

There was moonlight, and the wash of water against stone. Lucia had managed to arrange a whole evening off duty and was wearing an old gown of Isabella's, handed down, fine black silk, and a gauzy mantilla in her hair, for once allowed to curl, released from dutiful severity. As she took Baptiste's hand and stepped into the gondola the sleeves of the gown fell away, revealing the slenderness and velvety bloom of her arms.

They spun away from the quay and Baptiste wondered how he could ever have questioned the grace and skill of the Venetian boatmen. They slid beneath an arching bridge and then, quite casually, in that half-voice the opera house calls 'veiled', the boatman began to sing, barely loud enough for the two of them to hear. Nothing grand or celebrated, just an old Veneto ballad.

Baptiste rested his head in her lap, his arms round the softness of her. She stroked his cheek, and they listened to the gondolier.

As with most Venetians, Isabella's delight in the city's water-borne songsters was somewhat modified: the gondoliers, she told V, had become too businesslike, keeping their singing for visitors, who had booked – and paid well – in advance. The romance had gone out of the experience. Nevertheless, she conceded, there was something to be said for their warblings, and she had promised Goethe the experience.

The boatmen ferried them to the Giudecca, moored and leaped ashore, and made off in opposite directions. From the shadows, their voices drifted in unison, chanting verses by Ariosto, and the flight of Erminia from Tasso's *Jerusalem*. The sorrowful lament, fading, growing softer, came to them, wavering, as though floating on the water.

'Poor Goethe is in tears,' Isabella whispered, peering through the darkness to where he sat, in the prow. In the seclusion of the little cabin, V kissed her and she sighed but not with sadness.

Life in Venice for V was happiness at its most intense, but it was also, in its way, a purgatory. He worked relentlessly at his drawing, etching and engraving – 'I'm at my desk, trying out a new engraving tool,' he wrote to Isabella one night. It gave an interesting effect, drier, more blurred, perhaps more subtle. Thinking of her, he added, his hand became less steady, certainly less subtle . . . He insisted on comparing himself with Dürer and in his own eyes could only be found wanting. Recognising genius made it no easier to acknowledge one did not possess it.

He moved among the wealthy but the royal pension Louis had granted him was more token than reality and the revenues from the estate, even bolstered by the Burgundy he imported for sale in Venice, were stretched by a mania for collecting – hardly a day went by without the purchase of another painting, another object, another book. Baptiste, who looked after the household accounts, was aghast as he added up the columns. He tried to talk to his master but V, busy at his desk or studying an old engraving, would wave him away. 'You can look after the details, Baptiste.'

V was at home in his maritime metropolis, but felt a jolt when a visitor brought news of Paris – particularly when the news became less agreeable, when friends wrote of an ugly mood in the city, of almost unthinkable possibilities being whispered, streets and public gardens less safe than they used to be. Paris was a long way off, and in Venice the carnival continued. But the real world continued to exist, and to make itself known now and then, with a rumble like distant thunder. When, as they drifted from *casinò* to ballroom, V would read aloud to Isabella not Virgil, but letters from home where fear lay between the lines, there were descriptions of disturbing episodes – a carriage jostled, windows broken, abuse shouted. A pet dog found dead.

There were other cracks in the flawless surface of life in the Serenissima: he loved and was loved, but he knew that '*ma chère* Bettine' could never be wholly his. There was, after all, her husband, a kindly man, older and patently complaisant, as can be the way with elegant marriages of convenience. But was it enough to be the constant companion of the uncrowned queen of Venice? Was it enough to be her *cavalier-servant*, her confidant? Occasionally he allowed himself the sweet pain of imagining an alternative existence, where he carried her off to a mountain top, where, like a fairy-tale prince and princess, they lived happily ever after. But he knew that Venice was as close to a fairy tale as he could hope for. In fairy tales no princess ran off with a painter.

The very next day he felt the cold fingertips of reality on his shoulder. From her husband Isabella had heard that the Inquisition were having V watched; she was worried. He refused to be.

He held out his hand and touched the blue tracery beneath the skin.

'Once, the Inquisition might have sliced me open to encourage the flow of information,' he said. 'They would have failed to observe that my blood is tainted, ink runs in my veins. An artist is not quite human, *ma chère*, so I'm safe.'

He was sketching her as she sat leafing through a book, capturing her image, pencil flashing across the page. She said thoughtfully, 'If artists are not quite human, does art matter more to you than people?'

'You, *cara mia*, matter more to me than life itself –'

'Here is a question: from a burning building you can save either a person or a painting. Which will it be?'

'Which painting?'

Isabella looked across at him, brows raised. 'I think you've answered my question.'

'You make me sound a monster,' V protested, laughing uncomfortably.

But she pursued the argument: 'Very well: you could save a human life or you could save, say, a Veronese. So . . . ?'

'Well,' V considered the matter: 'a Veronese, if saved, will last virtually for ever, whereas a man's span is unlikely to be more than three score and ten. Think how many people would benefit from the work of art. I would certainly save a Veronese rather than save my own life. I'd like to think I have a sense of proportion!'

Zenobia is waiting. The silence lies between them like a strip of no man's land that neither can enter – she, because she knows words can only weaken her position; he, because he fears the next move could land him in a quagmire from which there is no escape.

She breaks first: 'Baptiste? Will you allow me to stay? – I'll just rest in a chair somewhere. In the morning, when he is feeling better, if he still refuses to see me, I shall leave, immediately. Without a word.'

He knows what her plan is: to be in the house, no matter how awkward her position, to count on the good servant sooner or later passing on the fact that she is here, that she has asked to see him. She has guessed, correctly, that her presence has not been made known to his master, though she could never guess the reason.

'You're a very determined young woman.'

'I learned to be.'

And she has won. Baptiste, too tired, too confused to resist, says, 'It is not for me to put you out of the house. But you will do exactly as I say. And you will ask no more questions.'

She is transformed: she removes the hat with its fur brim, she pushes her fingers through her hair, smoothing the black, wiry curls. She smiles, and he realises it is the first time she has done so since she entered the house. Whether it is the smile, or relief, or something else, he has no way of knowing, but her face is brighter, her eyes shining. Sitting so still and straight in her chair, hands in her lap, she is like a deity seated on a throne, a goddess carved from some dark stone that glows with inner light; her skin – which he had thought of as dusky olive – is golden.

'I've dreamed so often of this; of sitting in his room, hearing him talk –'

'He is not to be disturbed!'

'Of course not.'

He stares at her helplessly, caught in this trap of his own making. He says, 'Your chocolate is cold.'

'Do you imagine my life has been so perfect that a cup of cold chocolate will trouble me?'

Someone is knocking at the front door of the house. She picks up the cup of chocolate and sips it, curving her hands round the cold porcelain. He watches her, unhappily, for a moment or two. Then he leaves the room. She puts down the cup.

She hears the muffled sound of Baptiste's voice explaining that the Baron is indisposed, he regrets visitors cannot be received this evening. She listens as he climbs the stairs. She imagines his progress, to the room, the bedside. Will he now mention the unwelcome visitor, the intruder?

She sits in the armchair, clenched, as though awaiting judgement. She feels the room around her creaking and trembling with information: the books that have come as a surprise – the descriptions of faraway places, the small, elegantly bound novella telling of a night of passion in a mysterious château, they all speak to her. There are pictures – engravings, sketches, watercolours – each of which fills in bits of a story without words. She arrived angry; she is becoming more and more confused. But she has agreed she will ask no questions. This does not mean that she is no longer seeking answers; it means simply that she will find other means to do so.

She looks over to the fireplace, to the small pile of ashes in the grate and the box of letters on the floor. Listening out for a footstep on the stairs she gets to her feet, crosses the room and plucks a letter from the box:

My dearest Vivente . . .

As always, when his day ended and before he could contemplate sleep, he began or finished a letter to Isabella. This particular night was no different:

Ma chère Bettine,

After leaving you I could do nothing . . . I read for a while, then attempted to finish a large engraving, I worked till nine, then gave up. After dinner I walked down to the Regio Canal – as close to you as I could get . . .

Gondoliers, waiting for customers, observed a middle-aged man slightly below average height on the bridge, gazing at the upper floor of a narrow *palazzo*. He swept off his hat to reveal greying curls and bid a silent good evening to the green shutters. Would she hear him, through the walls, were he to shout aloud? If the gondoliers caught him declaiming to a high window he might get a sympathetic look: they knew about frustrated lovers here, there were songs . . .

I looked in on a couple of people . . . had a glass of wine in the café and could then think of no good reason not to go home, so I did, and read for a while and had some soup.

Now it's almost four. It seems like a hundred years since I last saw you.

And, he added, if he were not to see her next day, he would not survive.

Soon after they met, while they were still exploring each other, she asked him, 'Do you like the countryside, Vivente?'

'Of course. I'm a Burgundian, after all.' It was an answer of a sort, but the truth was more complicated.

Long ago, he had thought of himself as a country boy rather lost in the big city, missing his father's orchards, the vineyards that marched across the gentle slopes. In fact, his visits home had been few, and he recognised that he languished in the healthy country air. But occasionally he joined Isabella at the Marin villa on the Brenta – hardly 'countryside' as she called it: a gondola ride to the mainland, a pleasant afternoon drive.

It was time for another visit, she suggested now, 'Come for a week or two. It's a joy to get away from the city heat.'

What she left unsaid was that she felt it was also safer for V to be out of the city for a week or two. The Inquisition had been asking more questions.

Ma chère Bettine,

After our days together by the river, the walks under the trees, I waited at home for a letter. Venice very empty without you. And no letter.

He thought of their brief escapes to the country as holes cut into reality: small patches of heaven. Riding together, their horses reined in to an amble while they talked; the picnic in the long grass – a swaying green stockade that held them in a cup of warmth, shielding them from other eyes; the taste of domesticity: a quiet breakfast, laughter with a midday meal, a childish expedition to an orchard to steal fruit. The comfort of one another's arms in a thunderstorm . . .

Ah! A letter has arrived. A precious little note, it is not always the longest letters that give the most pleasure. Yesterday I saw everything black. Now, tinged with hope, I see life as grey. If I can summon up a little wisdom, with the help of discretion and illusion, perhaps I'll see *la vie en rose* this evening . . .

He took to drawing her portrait, again and again, as though to make up for lost time. And when Elisabeth Vigée-LeBrun arrived on a visit from Paris, V asked her to paint Isabella's portrait. He sketched them both, lamenting that his pencil paid poor tribute to the porcelain prettiness of the Frenchwoman, and the luminous tints of the portrait she was creating of his *chère* Bettine. And during the sitting, Isabella sketched V, with his curls and the curving smile that creased a cheek no longer taut and smooth.

'I'm getting old, Baptiste,' he glanced in the mirror, lifting his chin slightly to improve his jawline.

The valet carefully adjusted the black brocade jacket on V's shoulders, gave the hem a brisk tug. 'A man of forty-five naturally shows evidence of having lived.'

Behind V, he glimpsed himself in the mirror; always thin, he had grown gaunt with the years; his cheeks hollow, the nose more prominent, the mouth drooping. He added, 'Experience and character, rather than age, are what is visible. Youth is a blank.'

'That's well put, Baptiste. Where do you get these ideas from?'

'I listen to you,' the valet said.

He held out his master's cloak. 'Do we go to Bologna next week?'

'Alas, and even worse: Ferrara. Florence. Why do I drive myself to these places when all I want to do is stay here?'

'Could it be because you have now seen all the paintings Venice has to offer?'

'How cold that makes me sound! Is that what I am? A man who loves paintings?'

V was almost at the door when he turned back, weighing his cloak in his hand, swinging it to and fro like a pendulum.

'Baptiste . . .'

The valet looked up, awaiting some order, some request.

V said, 'There used to be more time, in the old days, for conversation. I used to enjoy our talks.'

'Life is busier in Venice.'

'Don't insult me with tactful answers. Your welfare matters to me. Are you happy, here?'

The pale, impassive face was lit with a momentary radiance. Unusually, Baptiste was smiling.

'Yes,' he said. 'I'm happy here.'

Had there been more time, V would have extended the conversation: he was aware that the old closeness had been eroded by the demands of society, of work, of *la bellezza di vita*, of everything concerning Isabella. But he was late and the Venetian clock was ticking, so he nodded, and went out to where the gondola was waiting to take him to San Giorgio Maggiore to look at a favourite Veronese. There would be time for a Turkish coffee at Quadri's then on with Isabella to a concert. Life was good. Had he been a poet, he reflected, had he been Dante, he could have celebrated in lively *terza rima*, but he was a mere sketcher, so he made do with sketching a tender little *veduta* of the Rialto as the gondola floated beneath its arches.

'Ma *chère* Bettine . . .'

Ferarra, he told her, had been appalling: only one painting worth the journey. Bologna was better than Ferrara but nothing was as good as Venice.

'I miss Venice. I miss you. Your letter was the brightest moment of my week.'

He was working like a madman, achieving in ten days what it would normally have taken him three months to do; making notes, drawing, recording, at his desk for six hours a day, and four or more at night – 'which is the only thing that reconciles me to not being in Venice. I am shortly off to Modena. Give my regards to your dear husband, and to my friends, and tell them I miss them, I would be inconsolable if I thought I had been forgotten. Write, tell me what is happening in Venice; anything that has anything to do with you is infinitely interesting to me. I shall soon be with you again. *Adieu*, dearest friend.'

The news from Paris seemed suddenly much worse: letters were couched in guarded language but a picture emerged of a society under siege. There were disquieting hints of menace and unease; clusters of hostile men glimpsed from the windows of the well-to-do – insults, jeering voices, arson. A new mood in the street. Danger. A different sort of dance was under way.

'This is bad.' Baptiste was studying a French newspaper, one already out of date.

'Yes.' V was uncertain whether his next words were to reassure Baptiste, or to lull his own fears. 'But it will pass.'

And the news from Burgundy at least had been reassuring: no peasants chopping down the orchards or burning the barns. V was convinced concessions or brutal reprisals in Paris would soon curtail this rebellion. Still, he was aware of a drumbeat, of . . . *something* in the air. But from afar it all sounded unreal, theatrical; an affair of cheering crowds and singing in the streets.

He worked late into the night, and near to dawn laid down his roulette and flexed stiff shoulders: he had spent too long hunched over the desk. Time to fall into bed.

Clearing away wine glass and bottle, Baptiste picked up the newspaper again. Certain words stood out, once unthinkable, now in print. It will pass, the master said. To be sure. Unless it was time for change.

Baptiste glanced at some sketches as he tidied the desk. He liked the one of San Jerome arriving at his monastery followed by the lion, the monks almost blown off their feet by a hurricane of fright. The master had told him Carpaccio was saying, 'Don't flee from the unknown.'

Baptiste had countered: 'But suppose the lion *had* been looking for a supper of monks. What then?'

'But we know he wasn't. We know how the story ends.'

He opened the shutters and breathed in the cool, pre-dawn air. Across the canal the buildings were ghostly in the darkness, but in the sky there was already a veil of pearl, like the master stirring white into a pot of dark paint. He closed the shutters and slowly began to collect discarded clothes for steaming and pressing. The great virtue of things that went on in the past, he told himself, is that you know how the stories ended.

Even paintings didn't tell you everything. He'd like to ask the master, for example: what about that lion? Sometimes Baptiste thought of himself as filling a similar role: there the valet was, in the picture, but tucked away in a corner while the master occupied the foreground. One painting showed the death of San Jerome, and Baptiste wondered what happened to the lion after Jerome died. About to fall asleep, he thought of an important question: who looked after the poor beast when it grew old and frail? And what would his own end be? How would *his* story conclude?

Outside the windows, on the Quai Voltaire, two men pass by, murmuring, their voices barely audible. It is as though the thickening air of night has muffled the sound, wrapping the house and its occupants in a cocoon of quiet.

Zenobia is crouched by the fireplace, half a dozen letters in her hands, her eyes skimming the faded words, when she hears footsteps in the hall. By the time Baptiste opens the door she is back in her chair, heart thudding, forcing herself into stillness.

He motions in a maid carrying a tray. The girl places it carefully on the table and disappears, and Zenobia watches him as he stands, studying the tray closely, as though making an inventory.

'You should have something to eat.' When she makes no move he adds, encouragingly, 'Please.'

Zenobia sees that he has arranged pieces of white chicken, dark red ribbons of cold beef, bread and pickles, in a manner to make it easy for her to pick at them. There is a glass goblet and a small jug of wine which he moves closer to her. The placing of the objects has the rightness, the satisfying arrangement of a still life. She smiles.

'Thank you.'

As she reaches for a morsel of chicken, her eyes on the food, he allows himself to observe her for a moment without reserve, greedily. He speaks, reciting the words mechanically: 'The wine is Burgundy, from the Baron's vineyards.'

He pours some, and she sips from the glass.

She looks up at him. 'Burgundy! From his vineyards? I think I've tasted this before!'

'Surely not –'

'Yes, yes. I was lying in the shade; there was a blanket beneath me, quite scratchy, and someone wiped my face with a damp cloth. I kept my eyes shut tight. And then someone fed me a spoonful or two of something that burned my throat but felt warm and comforting in my stomach. There was less pain. And then I fell asleep.'

Baptiste feels an ache like hunger spread through his guts, as though her words have passed the pain to him; his eyes prick and he longs to reach out and stroke the wiry curls, as one comforts a child. Instead he says, formally, 'What a good memory you have. Even remembering that it burned your throat.'

'Yes. Just a little.'

'And who fed you the wine?'

'Well, I suppose he did.'

He takes a plate from the tray and holds it out to her.

She is nervous, conscious of the letters hidden in her skirt, unaware that he too has something to conceal.

There was an almost feverish quality to the sweet life as the news from Paris grew more troubling. Venetians told themselves the upheavals were taking place in another country, and had nothing to do with them. True, there were some – radicals and Jews – who felt this intriguing idea of liberty, equality, fraternity might usefully be imported. But like St Augustine with chastity and poverty, not *yet*. Not today.

At first V tried to see the upheaval as a temporary aberration; then as an inevitable historical evolution that would adjust itself, balanced by expediency. The royal family was confined to the Tuileries, but unharmed he reported to Isabella. 'There'll be some sort of compromise. Enlightenment cannot be reversed. Reason will prevail.'

Meanwhile, he went travelling, from one northern city to another, in search of material for the book that was slowly taking shape. He dreamed of a future where libraries would have to possess not only Vasari but also De Non's contribution to the history of art. It would be his gift to posterity, and was, moreover, a way of distracting him from terrible events unfolding across the frontier. He drove himself hard, and he wrote to Isabella every day, counting the hours till he saw her again.

But in the refulgent serenity of the republic of St Mark, French gentlemen now found themselves in insecure circumstances: some – aristocrats fleeing the scything blade – were welcomed by the authorities. Others were tainted with suspicion. Monsieur Hennin, the French consul, for example: as the official representative of an unstable neighbour, where did he now stand? And certain familiar figures, certain social butterflies, literary figures, artists, how free of the Jacobin stain were they? The Inquisition would be interested to know where their funds came from. Who were their intimate friends? Did they have, undeclared, revolutionary sympathies? In short: could they be trusted?

V presented himself confidently for examination; he offered documents that might have a bearing, prudently shaping his statements to make it clear that his allegiances were royal, his interests artistic, his residence of choice Italian:

'Technically, I am a Frenchman. But rather tenuously connected. More than eight years representing His Majesty in Naples, five years here in Venice for research on my History of Art.'

In his view the meeting with the Holy Office was a mere formality; a matter of a signature here, a declaration there, a few financial details to disclose – he was, at heart, sincerely, a Venetian . . . Unaware that he was under surveillance, it never occurred to V that he might be at risk.

In France an ill-considered flight had been organised; the

royal family attempting to escape by night, only to be captured at Varennes, fifteen miles short of the border.

'And isn't it typical of Louis and Marie-Antoinette that they refused to leave until a special carriage, large enough for the whole bloated entourage including the hairdressser, was built for them – delaying the escape by three months!'

But the thought of those frail, pampered creatures, those doll-like children recognised, hauled from their unwieldy carriage and thrust into captivity, appalled him; he wrote home, to family, to friends, tried to learn what hard truths lay behind the shouting.

When the expulsion order arrived, he found it, at first, impossible to take seriously: surely some technicality, some clerical error was to blame. He remained light-hearted, treating the matter almost as a joke between gentlemen. But it was no joke.

The Inquisition remained sceptical, for instance, about his financial arrangements: when they heard that his royal pension had been suspended by the new regime, that revenue from estate rents and the sale of wine had dwindled, they wondered how it was that he did not charge his students for lessons. To live as Monsieur De Non did required funds: he could be working covertly for the new French regime. He could, in short, be a spy.

He appealed again against the expulsion, and began to think seriously about his future.

Returning from the market, Baptiste found him pacing out the room and making calculations on scraps of paper.

'Here, Baptiste; I neeed you to take some measurements and draw a plan of the two rooms –'

'I can't draw.'

'Nonsense, of course you can.' He looked up from his scribbling. 'I've had an extremely practical idea; we can enlarge this place. Extend the room, knock down that wall. We need more space, Baptiste!'

'Yes, sir.' A pause. 'May I ask what for?'

'I've seen a new printing press; if I put one in here, and create a workshop I can do my own printmaking.'

Baptiste had just circled the vegetable market, comparing prices, choosing the cheapest, haggling over a chicken.

'Surely it will cost a lot?'

'Worth it. Dürer made more money out of the prints he sold of one picture than he would have made doing twelve originals! Of course we'll need labourers to knock down the wall and get it all ready –'

'Would it not be cheaper to rent a studio?'

'Far less convenient. Anyway, I'll leave the details to you. You get on with the measuring, I'll order the press.'

But again the outside world intervened: the Inquisition remained unimpressed by V's explanations. 'I'm a Frenchman, so they don't trust me,' he told Isabella. And they noted his loyalty to dubious people – like his old friend, the French consul.

Crossing the piazza, seated at Florian's, V blended into the Venetian crowd, seemingly at ease. But he was watchful now. A survivor needs to be fast on his feet, good at thinking his way out of an error, skirting a trap; quick to make the right choices. Later, his enemies called him a turncoat. So, a portrait of the artist as a chameleon, perhaps?

The Holy Office had once again summoned the Frenchman for an interview. V, shown to a seat in the dark, high-ceilinged room, tried out his smile on the robed men the other side of a wide oak table. They remained impassive. There were papers before them, papers that perhaps related to him. Exchanges were courteous, elegant as ever.

'Monsieur De Non, it is noted that you communicate regularly with a number of people in France –'

'I write a lot of letters, yes. Is that now a crime?'

The response was reassuring: the writing of letters could

not, of course, be considered a crime. The interview continued.

When the door had closed behind the foreigner there was a raising of eyebrows; papers were shuffled: the evidence must be considered.

Newly arrived émigrés were ready to provide information about their fellow Frenchman. Old resentments, given an easy conduit, surfaced. Jealousy fuelled a whispering campaign; calumny and innuendo swirled. The Marquis la Porte dropped a hint here, a murmur there, about V's past: his hostility towards the French court – 'It's a known fact De Non was recalled from Naples for making disloyal reports about the royal family. Everyone knew Marie Antoinette and the monarch loathed him . . .' And, woundingly, it was 'common gossip' that he was snubbed when he applied at court for diplomatic posts.

At first V refused to take the stories seriously; gossip had always been society's stock-in-trade, adding spice to the day, fading with the sunset. Then came something more damaging: another émigré making it known that De Non should be considered a revolutionary, spying for the murderous regime.

V's honour had been put in question; there was only one response.

He called on Isabella, attempting to treat the affair as an embarrassing joke. 'This is quite nonsensical but I thought I should tell you; I am to take part in a duel.'

Isabella, who found it helpful to regard life as a series of elegant charades in which she and her friends, while enhancing the scene, remained inviolable, felt a chill: a cold blast from a harsher world had found its way into their protected space.

'Don't be absurd!'

'Absurd it is, but I have to. This appalling man – I made a joke at his expense once in Paris, describing his crimson heels as paler than his nose, and he has never forgiven me. He's been feeding the Holy Office with exactly the sort of lies they were looking for. I had to challenge him or accept that what he said was true.'

'But you know perfectly well that duelling is against the law.'

'We'll make it an "accidental" encounter.'

'I'll accompany you. I shall bring a doctor –'

'To attend to my adversary?' He refused to treat the duel seriously. 'Dearest Bettine, an accidental encounter will lose a certain degree of credibility if there is a medical practitioner in attendance, don't you think?'

'He could act as a second –'

'Obviously, we will not have seconds. But we can settle the matter honourably.'

'Only a *man* could describe behaviour akin to stags locking antlers in the mating season as "honourable". Childish might be a better word.'

'This is something women don't understand.'

'Whoever "wins" the duel, both will be losers.'

Privately, V agreed with her. He reflected that the so-called honour involved was a foolishness. To defend himself from the lies of a shifty puffball he now had to endanger his own life, or that of the venomous liar, in an exercise as ritualistic and meaningless as a courtly dance. This would not be an experience to recall with pleasure.

Baptiste received the news with alarm: 'Aren't duels against the law?'

'Yes, but this one will be stumbled into, an aristocratic tavern brawl. If only Casanova had thought to use that trick he'd never have found himself in jail!'

Dawn was grey – isn't dawn always grey? V asked himself, but we invest it with a special sombreness when it seems appropriate. He recognised ruefully that there was a banality about the whole idea. Baptiste dressed him, as usual, but their normal conversation was missing, each preoccupied with thoughts.

In V's mind, possibilities jostled one another: he could be killed and never see Bettine again. That prospect was not to be contemplated, too painful, and he shied away. There were other losses to be considered. Never to glide beneath the Rialto past Carpaccio's waterfront, or feel the soft warmth of the Venetian winter sun on his face. As Baptiste reached forward to adjust his master's jacket V saw that the valet's face was drawn, his eyes red. Mortified, and jolted from his dark musings, V flung out his arms and wrapped a surprised Baptiste in a reassuring hug, though – the shorter of the two – he felt for a moment as though he was the one being comforted.

'Baptiste! Such a long face! This will all be over in an hour and then you can give me breakfast.'

'Yes, sir.' For once Baptiste was relieved that a servant did not contradict his betters. But with duels and firearms, with hostility and the tendency of a human hand to shake under stress, could anything be certain?

To make matters worse, the master added, 'And if things go another way, make sure you order a decent coffin – I'm sure you know where to go.'

The rendezvous had been selected carefully: a bleak *campo*, not too remote, to give the notion of a casual encounter some credibility. The weapons were chosen and the paces counted out. Earlier, V had felt an odd lowering of spirits, swept with a tired sorrow, betrayed into regret: how pointless it would all be, if it ended here! Now, with the moment upon him, he was filled with a burst of energy. He would not allow this product of an inbred provincial family, this turd, to ruin his day, especially if it proved to be his last. He gave an exclamation of delight, glancing up at the sky and flung out his arms, pistol dangling from one hand.

'It will be a fine blue day! I shall be able to work until late!'

He saw his adversary flinch, then raise his arm. When the word rang out and the shot flew harmlessly past his shoulder,

V took aim, the metal of the pistol catching the morning light. Then he allowed his arm to dip, before he fired. The yell of pain confirmed that, as intended, he had shot the fool in the foot.

It was indeed a fine blue day. He presented himself at Isabella's *palazzo* filled with exhilaration: 'I never knew a duel could provide such entertainment!'

'And I never saw myself welcoming a victorious hero home from battle!'

Laughing, she allowed him to pull her into his arms. 'Such force, my dear! It will be looting and pillaging next!'

But the silencing of a rumour was not enough: when the day's excitement had subsided, one stark fact remained: the expulsion stood.

It was a time for despair. To put off the evil day he took to his travels again to Bologna, to Florence. As always, when life proved imperfect, art was the consolation.

'My dearest Bettine, I believe above all in the eternal love which we have sworn. The rest – freedom, happiness, et cetera are no more than a dream.'

But in truth, it was love that was the dream.

The letters went back and forth, sometimes no more than a dashed-off note of affection; sometimes pages of anguish, questioning, debate, and more dreams. They analysed the situation in France and sketched out possible paths the revolution could take as preludes to their own reunion:

'It looks hopeful: they tell me the King has been given a comfortable apartment, he's being well cared for.'

Did he believe his own words? Could wishing make it so?

The news, when it came, seemed beyond belief.

An execution order? Regicide?

The previous monarch, who died peacefully in his bed, had always been sanguine about his personal future; there was enough of everything to see him out. '*Après moi le déluge,*' V recalled him saying. And now the floodgates had burst. Destruction, a bloody fever, the downfall of a monarchy – these were the cataclysmic events shaking V's world. But as Louis bowed his head to Mme la Guillotine, and sent a shudder through the crowns still in place, Isabella's latest letter contained a less public piece of news: Francesco Guardi was dying quietly in Venice, without any public demonstrations to mark his passing. And V clutched at this small event, as though to distance himself from the rest.

'A second-rate ambassador to an unimportant country would receive more recognition,' he wrote back. 'Working artists, even those of genius, can leave the world without disturbing the cosmos. But you and I will mourn them.'

He felt a kinship with the undervalued artist; Guardi was a man with a sense of fleeting time. V thought of the heartbreak behind the laughter in a Watteau *fête galante*; the ambiguity of *The Embarkation for Cythera*: an elegant crowd playing at pilgrims, in truth seeking oblivion on the island of love. The painting was enigmatic: no one had ever been sure whether the gilded ladies and gentlemen were arriving or leaving. Now he knew: it was a departure, of course. For those pilgrims, as for him, the dream of love was over.

The gondola slid quietly away from the *palazzo* steps. Two people concealed from view, her cool hands in his.

'I've run out of delaying tactics; I have to leave.'

'Where will you go?'

'I don't know yet. Here and there.'

'Write to me. Wherever you are. When I read your words I hear your voice, and we're together.'

'I will write. I promise.'

Curtains drawn, only her eyes shining in the darkness, the gondola was their hiding place, their temporary confessional. Here they could speak the truth and weep, her face with delicately painted eyes and mouth smeared in grief. He could crumple and sag into ugliness. There was no elegance in their anguish. Then, through the gap in the curtain, lights flickered, voices called. They were arriving at the *ridotto*. When they stepped ashore, Isabella's beauty was safe behind her veil and domino, V – as always – smiling. A redness about the eyes would be ascribed to yet another late night and too much wine. He offered her his arm; they made their entrance. Friends waved from the gaming tables, others clustered, drawing them apart to exchange news. Between them the noise, conversation, laughter, thickened like a wall.

Another gondola rode the dark water, sliding away from the *palazzo* steps. Two people clung together.

'I have to leave you,' Baptiste told Lucia. He stroked her hair.

'Where will you go, what will you do?'

'I have a plan. The revolution has changed everything. Dead masters don't need valets, and in this new "egalitarian" world, milords who survive the guillotine will be leading a different sort of life.'

He too would lead a different life. The talents he possessed would always be in demand, even in a republic. For a quick-thinking man who could read and write, who knew how to order food, care for clothes, deal with tradesmen, there would be opportunities.

'I have some savings; I can open one of these new restaurants I've been hearing about. You can join me. We'll be together.'

'The three of us.'

Baptiste rested his hand on the scarcely perceptible bulge of her belly.

'The three of us.'

The child would be named, if a boy, Dominique, if a girl, Isabella – her mistress would have to be informed of the impending event. Meanwhile, they made plans.

They would live in Paris, or perhaps in Burgundy. His

mother might enjoy looking after a grandchild. It struck him that this could be a more intimate time than his own infancy, when baby Dominique-Vivant took precedence at her nipple, before Baptiste took his turn.

'A wet nurse can't always satisfy her own infant,' he told Lucia.

'Poor baby, perhaps that's why you are so thin.'

'Who knows? Later, there was always food in the kitchens, but I never had a large appetite.'

'I shall learn to cook! They don't let me in the kitchens here. I'll make Venetian specialities for you: polenta with liver, and sweets with almonds. You will grow fat. When we're together.'

The gondola had circled back to the *palazzo*. Their hour was almost over.

'They are to spend all tomorrow together,' Lucia told him.

'Then so will we: I shall wait here for you.'

Baptiste opened the curtains and drew Lucia to her feet. He went ahead, held out his hand to help her on to the quay. She paused before stepping from the gondola and looked up at him, her face as pale and delicate as a mask, her sweetly thin arms reaching forward, dark eyes full of tears. Both were crying as he walked with her to the *palazzo* entrance. Blinded by tears, she stumbled, and he helped her across the threshold to the *portego*. There was no need for concealment: had Isabella's amiable husband the Count happened to cross their path he would have noticed nothing. Servants are invisible.

Zenobia is feeling her way. She picks at the food on her plate. The stolen letters have been thrust out of sight in the folds of her skirt but she can feel them, she can almost hear the rustle of paper when she moves. She burns with curiosity, and takes another sip of wine, as though to relieve both the burning and the curiosity itself. Her hands shake.

Years of convent education weigh on her conscience, make her shamingly aware of her moral position: '*Sister Angelina, I have become a person who can steal . . .*'

Hanging on the wall of the salon on the Quai Voltaire there is an engraving of Venice: the steely glint of the water, the smudged softness of the stonework. Beside the canal people are strolling, she sees their elegant cloaks, their hats. Some wear masks. She expresses astonishment that while the Revolution was taking place in France, Monsieur Denon was apparently content to enjoy life in Venice. And Baptiste tries to explain.

'We heard from Paris that the queen was being cared for in a pleasant apartment; she and her family were comfortable –'

Zenobia says bitterly, 'What you're saying is that he detached himself from the unpleasantness. He has a gift for detachment!'

In her agitation she throws herself back in the chair and the stolen letters slip from their hiding place in a fold of her skirt and cascade to the floor. She stares down at them, hot shame flooding over her, filling her eyes with tears that scald her cheeks. No one has been murdered, she has committed no act of violence, but she has overstepped a mark. The nuns taught her well: on the Day of Judgement she will find no holy hand reaching to save her from the flames, the devils with pitch-forks who will rend her flesh, the agonies of the damned. Stricken, Zenobia forces herself to look up at Baptiste's sorrowful face. Nervously she brushes her hair away from her brow.

On her way to the Quai Voltaire earlier that day, she had become aware, as she tucked a loose strand of hair under the brim of her hat, that her hands carried a hint of something clinical: antiseptic, sharp; a smell that brought to mind sickness and antidote, wound and cure. This was a part of her working life, but it was not a smell, she felt sure, to be found on any of the women she was passing here, in the streets of Paris.

Zenobia has a sense of otherness, of not belonging; it clings to her like an unwanted scent, at first barely perceptible, like a shadow at noon, then growing, a sombre shroud, to darken the scene and isolate her. This dislocation, this sense of displacement, she learned long ago, came from being uprooted from 'your' place and set down somewhere else, screaming like a mandrake, but silently. Left to shrivel on what feels like barren soil, or cling to life, unwelcomed.

As she threaded her way through passers-by she imagined herself at her destination. Ushered into the presence of the man she had waited so long to see, she would hold out her hand; he would bow over her fingertips, and become aware of something alien, not a female fragrance but something whose very emphasis on cleanliness somehow conjured up its antithesis: putrefaction, mortality. He would be repelled.

At the next corner a gypsy woman was accosting people. From a basket over her arm she took tiny bunches of white lavender, exhorting the ladies to buy a good-luck charm that would transform their lives, bring them happiness. The Parisiennes hurried past, spurning the possibility of bliss.

Zenobia would certainly have done the same, but the gypsy blocked her path, and held the lavender beneath her nose.

'Take it! You will have good luck! You will find what you seek.'

Zenobia breathed in the lavender and felt warmth and languor rising from her nostrils to her head. As though following instructions, she took coins from her purse and the gypsy placed the tiny bunch in her palm, folding Zenobia's fingers over it, patting her hand. The dark, wrinkled face glowed like polished wood in the raw morning air. Then she was away, whirling to stop another possible customer.

As Zenobia walked on, she squeezed the greyish-white dried flowers between her fingers, rubbing her hands together, warming them, releasing the perfume into the air.

The lavender had accompanied her along the street.

Crossing Paris she adjusted her rapid pace to the unhurried stroll of others, glancing about: here was the Seine, for so long known to her only on the flimsy pages of the letters. Along the banks were trees like any other trees, a boat or two, moving with or against the current as boats do. This was a city and she had known many cities. But the people strolling past her were different: they belonged here.

Then the crucial moment was upon her: the house was found, the name spoken, the threshold crossed.

And now, as Zenobia brushes her hair away from her face with a gesture she realises has become a mannerism, she also realises, ruefully, that her hands smell like a herb garden: fragrant, yes, but still faintly medicinal. She would never have felt at ease in the house on the Quai Voltaire; she is not 'at home' here, she is not 'at home' anywhere. She watches what others do and does likewise, she behaves 'as though': as though it were natural to her. She is an outsider and this is what outsiders do: they learn to mimic life as it should be lived. Like mermaids who try to live on land, the displaced are negotiating an alien element. The displaced must seem sure-footed when they are feeling their way, reject caution; though, like a blind man running, they can surely never quite banish it.

She is ever the impostor, aping the tones and gestures others use instinctively; dancing, twirling, and how easy it looks. But balanced on a high-wire, it feels far from secure. A wrong move, a wrong step and she's falling – indeed, she has fallen. Disaster: stolen letters, cascading from her skirt. The sadness of disappointment on an old man's face. All she wants now is to escape.

Tears, unstoppable, slide down her cheeks. She stoops and gathers up the letters; crosses to the fireplace. She replaces them in their box, then picks up her bag.

'I'm sorry. Please try and forget I was ever here.'

Baptiste takes her arm and guides her back to the chair by the window. She looks into his face for signs of anger, disgust even, but sees only a tired sadness.

He says, 'Sometimes reading letters that do not belong to you is a way of finding your way through the dark.'

A valet has much to occupy him: his master's linen must be fresh, his boots clean, food and wine at hand, appointments remembered, enemies kept at a distance. A servant must know which way the wind is blowing, everything must be in readiness for the moment the world beckons. And, at the worst of times, a valet has things to do: he must be, as it were, in the picture, though invisible. Read other people's letters. Burn them when ordered to do so. A servant learns how to be helpful.

Voices in the hall, a tap on the door and a maid hovering: 'Monsieur Baptiste, you are needed.'

Homeless, expelled from his Venetian garden of Eden, V was trawling his way across country, Isabella's letters his life-line, forcing him to maintain at least a façade of hopefulness.

'*Ma chère* Bettine . . . The thought of you keeps me sane . . .'

He was travelling light: just the usual chests, trunks, crates, boxes – the everyday requirements of a gentleman *en voyage*. The bulk of his art collection he had left in Isabella's safe keeping – 'One of these days I will be back.' But even on his travels he could not resist the collecting urge, so the chests and boxes proliferated – 'Unexpected treasure: I have seen a Giotto fragment I must have . . .'

And Baptiste, aware that inns were charging them double what he would have spent on food and wine, watched with dismay as yet another canvas was carried in. To the master, the concept of living beyond his means was incomprehensible – 'I am not extravagant, Baptiste!' – he was simply living as he had always lived, without the income to support the style.

Baptiste kept an increasingly careful watch on inn accounts.

'*Ma chère* Bettine, I thought of you last night . . .'

At the theatre he had noticed a young woman a few rows in front of him: the shape of her head, the slender neck, the way she held one of her dark curls in her finger – it was Isabella, surely! Convinced she had taken a carriage and driven across country to surprise him, he was barely able to stay in his seat till the end of the act. 'Then I sprang up and pushed my way forward – and a perfectly charming stranger turned towards me, offended, I'm sure, by my groan of disappointment at the sight of her face. I am becoming a social hazard . . .'

The evening had been tedious; the theatre dull, but just as Isabella was no doubt at the *ridotto*, he attended the local theatre, it was expected; they were both prisoners of their place, and played their parts conscientiously.

'Goodnight, *ma chère* Bettine, when will we talk again, when will I hold you in my arms? When will I die of pleasure?'

They had spent five years together. Would he have found it easier to bear, or harder, had he known their letters would link them for the next thirty years?

Once the call would have rung out gaily, in anticipation of adventures, discoveries, dalliance, but this time V's voice was flat:

'Baptiste.'

'Sir?'

Where to next? Baptiste might once have asked, even if silently. But questions were no longer needed. They had spent long enough dragging themselves round Italian cities, killing time in Switzerland, while V wrote respectful letter after letter, appeal after appeal. The Inquisition remained implacable. It was time to go home.

Words could certainly change their nature, Baptiste

reflected. The word 'home' which once would have put a smile on his face now simply described a country where Lucia was not. If he had said as much to V, master and servant might have wept on each other's shoulders. Instead, Baptiste loped about organising the luggage and V sat writing at his desk, each miserable in his own private way. When it was almost time to leave, Baptiste prepared a tray of wine and cheese and ventured a question.

'Could we go to Burgundy for a while? In Paris, things must be difficult –'

'Difficult? *Difficult!*' V stared up at his servant through narrowed eyes as though trying to assess the features of a stranger. 'Things, as you call it, are atrocious. People can hardly breathe for fear. The guillotine can't keep up with the waiting list. Yes, I would say Things are Difficult in Paris. But we have to go.'

He returned to his writing, the silence in the room broken only by the scratching of his pen. Baptiste checked the position of glass and plate, moved the tray a few inches and began to collect up the last of the books for packing. His face was closed.

V stopped writing. He threw down the pen and put his hand on the valet's arm, shaking it gently to and fro. 'Forgive me, Baptiste. I am not myself. And I am being thoughtless. *I* have to go to Paris. They're about to sequester the estate. I'll be penniless.'

Baptiste was aware that V's last formal appeal to the Inquisition to reconsider his expulsion had received a stony response: there could be no return to Venice. And he knew now that protests to the Tribunal in Paris had failed to get V's name removed from the émigré list. The master was like a climber trapped on a ledge between two rock faces, able to reach neither. If he returned to Venice he faced imprisonment. In France it could be the guillotine, his carriage the tumbril.

V drained his wine glass and stood up. 'So I have to risk it. But you don't.' His hand rested briefly on Baptiste's shoulder. 'Of course you can go to Burgundy. See your family.'

This was the moment. Words raced through Baptiste's head in a chattering jumble: give up the job, leave now, begin a new life. A life with Lucia. He took a breath.

V said, 'Yes. Go to Burgundy.' He looked up and smiled sheepishly: 'But not for too long. I wouldn't know how to look after myself.'

'You could learn, you're not a child!' The words, too loud, were out before Baptiste could stop himself. He stepped back a pace, mouth dry, and braced himself: he had crossed the line between informality and insolence. Servants had been whipped for less.

There was a silence, V's face blank with shock. Then he said, 'You've always been there. Remember when I was frightened of the shadows on the staircase at home? The devils? When my father sent me to bed in disgrace, saying a boy of eight should not be afraid of shadows! And your mother smuggled you up to my room to sleep outside my door and keep the devils away.'

He frowned and sat back in his chair. 'It only occurs to me now, how bizarre that was: that you should have slept on a mat on the floor while I occupied a feather bed. Well, some things have changed, for the better thank God.

Baptiste remembered the shadows on the staircase. And he remembered the gypsy woman in the orchard reading V's palm; that must have been earlier, they would have been about seven. When she told the curly-haired boy he would enjoy success and have a happy life. Baptiste had said, 'What about me? What shall I do?' And the boy who would one day own the orchards said, 'You'll be with me of course. You'll be happy too.' The first part of the statement had proved to be accurate. But the second . . .

Baptiste picked up the tray with the empty glass and plate

and carried it into the kitchen. He put the plate into the stone sink and tears ran down his face and dripped off his chin on to the dirty plate. After a while he wiped his face and told himself there would be another time.

He supervised the loading of the coach and thought how he would explain things to Lucia and they would make new plans. Meanwhile, life was receding like the dwindling Swiss skyline behind them.

Melody in a Phrygian Mode

Paris seen through the eyes of the returning travellers was shocking. The city seethed with fear and anger; people screamed curses, fights broke out in the street. Everywhere filth lay unswept.

'Fraternity has clearly been the first casualty of the Revolution,' V commented to Baptiste, 'closely followed by cleanliness.'

Decapitated bodies filled tumbrils, bleeding heads stuck on pikes were carried through the streets to encourage the stragglers. Luckily the weather was freezing, which moderated the smell of putrefaction. Snatches of Rouget de Lisle's new battle song were heard here and there; the people still sang as they marched through the streets celebrating the dawn of liberty, equality and brotherhood, but 'La Marseillaise' had changed key: there was a less elated ring to it now. The Tree of Liberty was proving a heavier burden than expected. At what point did they refashion it into a scaffold? And when did the brotherhood of man succumb to the Terror? For now, indeed, terror reigned. The streets, Chateaubriand commented, were full of Terrorists.

V wore his sombre Venetian garb, and when he stepped into the street he realised that he looked like a foreigner - or an aristo inexplicably still at large: clean linen and expensive velvet, albeit subfusc, was not the fashion of the time; he cut a suspiciously conspicuous figure. He made good use of the foreign possibility, avoiding elegant gestures - no bows or waves of the hand here, nor any consciously graceful opening of doors or twirling of heels. In anonymity lay safety.

When he heard himself being hailed in the street he thought, for a moment, of walking on, casually quickening his pace. Reluctantly he turned, to see a shabby individual crossing the road towards him, waving a manicured hand rather cleaner than his clothes.

'De Non, isn't it? You don't recognise me: William Beckford, we met in Venice. Or was it Naples? Or both?'

V was amused to see the exquisite and fastidious Englishman attempting the disguise of a proletarian Parisian; a disguise hardly assisted by his penetrating, high-pitched voice.

Beckford glanced up and down the street. 'Quite a scene, what?'

'We've improved on Dante: it's a new circle of hell.'

The Englishman looked about cheerfully. 'You must be wondering why I'm here.'

'Well, judging by the interesting ensemble, possibly you have been invited to a fancy-dress ball.'

'Quite! *Cette tenue farouche!*' Flicking at a speck of dust on his grubby sleeve. 'I find it convenient not to stand out in the crowd.'

'In which case you might consider washing less frequently.'

'Oh, now that would be going too far! I came over to buy a few things at auction – the owners have little use for their possessions, having lost their heads. And judging by the amount of money I've been spending, I must have lost mine too! I'm stuck here for the moment. I assume you've just returned?'

'Still sore from the coach.'

'You will find Paris is not what it was,' Beckford said, somewhat superfluously. 'Last week a perfectly respectable *citoyenne* of mature years almost had the coat torn off her back because someone in the street thought her white hair was powdered – hard to believe, isn't it?'

'Where are you staying? Do you need a bed?'

'Thank you, no. I am being looked after: a picture-framer I've used in the past is putting me up. I sleep in the workshop – the apprentices are the sweetest boys you can imagine, it's quite amusing. One doesn't want to attract the attention of the mob, not the sort of people one would have to dinner, on the whole. When I think of Lisbon! Fifty servants waiting at table, a swarm of musicians hovering like bees round a honeypot . . . Well!'

Another wave of a pale hand and shabby sleeve, and V saw him disappear into a side street. Englishmen of a certain class would always find an exercise of this sort 'amusing'. His own situation was rather less so.

Letters to the Tribunal had been written. And ignored. V tried again: 'I enclose for your attention . . .' this time with some artful shaping of past events, offering documentation to prove he was no émigré, having travelled abroad long before the upheaval in France. He brought in Russia, Switzerland. Italy. He made mention of the years in Naples where – as he pointed out with some care – 'my reports to Paris displeased not only Queen Marie-Caroline, but her sister Marie-Antoinette, whose hostility cost me my job'. (*That* would impress them, surely?)

He begged leave to remind the Tribunal that his passport would show he had left in 1788, *before* the revolution. And moreover he had now been expelled from the most serene republic of St Mark as a suspected Jacobin sympathiser, 'to which my papers, stamped by citizen Hennin, the French consul, testify'. He looked forward to hearing, etc., etc. He almost signed himself 'Your Humble Servant', but thought the concept of humble servant might be politically suspect, even dangerous. However, the signature was discreetly modified: Chevalier De Non consigned to history, V had prudently reverted to the original family name. He signed the letter, respectfully, 'Denon'.

Silence.

That night the terror seeped under the door of V's room and crept across the floor like rising flood water. He leaped from the bed and inexpertly lit one of the lamps, the flame smoking, acrid, as he turned the wick too high. The shadows danced. He had lived through danger in the past and emerged with no cause for shame; he was not, he hoped, a coward. But it was difficult to keep up his spirits when he breathed in the stench of death and in the distance heard the shrieks of the condemned.

For a moment he contemplated calling Baptiste, requesting a drink of water or change of pisspot. But he held back. He knew that what he would really have been asking for was someone to guard the threshold and keep the devils at bay.

Wasn't there a philosopher who claimed that if a man danced fast enough he could skim over waves without sinking? That was the trick of it: to move on. To keep dancing.

From his room above the Quai Voltaire V hears the faint sounds of doors opening and closing. The pillows, the sheets, are hot and moist and he waits for Baptiste to appear, as he always does, when needed. But when the valet comes into the room he is not alone.

Through half-closed eyes V observes a grey-haired man carrying a large leather bag which he places on a side table. It occurs to V that he has not invited this person to enter his room, and he feels a mild but growing irritation that Baptiste has neglected to ask permission before ushering the creature into his presence.

'*Monsieur le baron* . . .'

Doctors, in V's experience, are never good news. No one ever said, 'Look, the sun's shining, let's send for the doctor and open some champagne.' True, he has reason to be grateful for one or two. In Egypt there was an army doctor who, unusually for one in his profession, had feelings. V recalls him weeping. Tears were surely not a normal part of a doctor's equipment. He could ask this greybeard now: tell me, doctor: when did you last weep? Professionally? He opens his mouth to put the question. His voice creaks like a rusty door.

The doctor is murmuring, 'If the Baron will permit . . .' and a bitter liquid trickles between V's lips. He coughs. No one asked him if he wished to swallow this unpleasant concoction. Nor if he wished to see the doctor. He must remember to reprimand Baptiste: the man is clearly getting old and forgetting his place.

He mistrusts the medical profession. With one exception, doctors do not excite his gratitude. That doctor in Egypt was a skilled surgeon. They were all skilled men, the scientists, the engineers, his own contingent, all of them scribbling away. Was it young Redouté who called on him one day in Paris before they sailed and asked, 'Do you suppose there will be flowers in colours we have never seen? For which we have no equivalent in paint? How shall we capture them? We don't even know where we're going! What lies ahead, Vivant?'

And V, the dimple darkening a cheek whose flabbiness could no longer be ignored, had opened his arms in an embracing gesture: 'Adventure, *mon cher* Henri-Joseph! On with the dance!'

Zenobia sits crouched in her chair, wrapped in mortification. The letters are back in their box but the life in those pages cannot be locked away, packed out of sight like a genie put back in a bottle. The long-ago love affair, the elegant Frenchman and the woman with the smiling mouth live on in a Venice unaltered by time and turmoil. The city and the people have changed. But the faded ink brought to life a brighter, older world, one that she has penetrated, an interloper.

Baptiste stands over her, abstractedly washing dry, restless hands.

'The doctor gave him something to soothe his throat and help him sleep,'

She nods. Shame has robbed her of speech, even breathing is difficult. That she is still here in this room astonishes her. The man upstairs has eluded her for too many years; she had dreamed of the sweet vengeance of a reunion and she has wrecked everything.

'I'll go now.'

Baptiste notes that Zenobia's face is grey with fatigue, the golden radiance drained away. 'You could —' words unfamiliar, words he forces, as though pushing a door unwilling to be opened — 'Perhaps you could keep me company for a while.'

Lights glimmer on the dark slick of the Seine beyond the window. In the houses, chandeliers sparkle and the sounds of conviviality filter through velvet-curtained windows. The spartan rigours of the Revolution have receded into history: was there really a time when women feared to go out dressed in silk? When a powdered wig signalled the status of the wearer as forcefully as a leper's bell? Thirty years have spun by and the world no longer rocks on its axis. People live in the here and now.

In the house on the Quai Voltaire, however, the past hangs like a pall, darkening the present as the night swings by, and they sit across the table from each other and for a moment he succumbs to the hallucination that she is part of him and they are sharing a domestic moment.

A Dangerous Vagabond

What does a man do when he is faced with disaster? Sooner or later he talks to a friend. V saw that personal intervention was all that could save him. He prudently left his wig at home and called on Jacques-Louis David.

The vulnerable, prickly youth was long gone. This was the artist as revolutionary, and glorying in the role. He welcomed V warmly, the embrace almost tearful – 'The only one who believed in me! And said so. I'll never forget that.' He laughed: 'Look at us, Vivant, I'm losing my hair. You too.'

He poured wine for them both. 'Well! This is better than Naples. All that royal shit.'

Better than Naples? V could hear the screams and yelling from the streets even in this curtained room. Yesterday he put his nose out of the window and came face to face with a severed head on a passing pike, teeth bared in a grin of agony, an eyeball spilling from its socket. Everywhere he could smell blood in the air and it sickened him. David was a Deputy, a member of the Committee for Public Safety, but V had hoped to hear some private reservations, regrets, an awareness that things had got out of hand. Instead, he was told to make himself comfortable for a few minutes while his host finished signing a few papers:

'So many signatures, two hundred so far, and more every day.' He flexed his fingers and looked up, 'I hope they keep the blade sharp, I don't want anyone to suffer unduly.'

'You're signing *death warrants*?'

'Yes.' David raised his eyebrows enquiringly.

V remained silent. To say that he would be unable to send men to their death sounded both pompous and accusatory, particularly as David had voted for the execution of the King. The Queen too, poor gilded butterfly languishing, her wings growing ragged, losing their brilliance. On the desk lay a sketch David did on the day of her execution: there she sat with downturned mouth, grey dress, grey hair, grey skin. Captive but quiescent, on a wooden chair.

But it was not the moment to question death warrants: he needed his friend's help. So: a change of subject; something an artist would want to talk about, before the visitor brought the conversation round to the reason for his visit. The new portrait of Marat was propped against the wall: that would do. V put down his wine glass and crouched low to examine the painting, a suitable compliment at the ready. But he saw that the compliment was not, after all, suitable: this was not the expected portrait.

'It's a *pietà* . . .'

'That's sharp of you.'

David, still busy consigning citizens to the guillotine, paused in his signing. 'They wanted the assassin with raised knife, the stabbing. I wouldn't have that. This is how he should be remembered. Forget the diseased skin, the pustules, the medicated water. Give them the stillness of death. The martyrdom.'

'How did you capture the dead flesh tone —?'

'There wasn't much time, he was decomposing before my eyes. I was in tears before the end.'

'And the way you have everything at the bottom of the picture; that's daring: it draws us to the body, and then the arm dangling, the earth reclaiming him. Genius.'

'Yes, I thought so.' David absently picked up V's glass and drained it.

★

V is awake, his skin itching, burning. All those years ago, David talked about Marat's ravaged flesh, the disease the revolutionary leader had picked up when he hid in the sewers, a fugitive, on the run . . . Now V knows what it feels like, to have skin that torments its owner. Surely it was just a few minutes ago that Baptiste smoothed the bedclothes, wiped his brow and melted into the shadow of the door, but already V feels the heat returning to his body. His skin crawls, as though a thousand insects are feeding on him at every pore, piercing, sucking his blood. He holds up a hand and studies the puckered, vein-laced surface: old flesh. It looks ugly. Didn't it always – except when David was wielding the brush.

Now he hears his old friend is sick, close to death, and who will capture *his* last moments? Their lives have run in parallel: both caught up in the tempest that was called Napoleon . . . But they differed over Robespierre . . . The thought drifts across his mind almost absently, and he is aware that his thoughts are rambling. Death. Marat. The pale, almost colourless flesh, the greenish tinge, how did the artist get that tone? It was unmarked flesh from which the life had been drained; an ideal rather than the blotchy imperfect stuff of reality.

'Do they really like it?' David had wondered, after he presented his portrait of the martyr to the Convention. V recalls now with sudden clarity that they did not. Too daring after all. But V remembers the way the portrait glowed, livid against the studio wall. The dead man would live for ever. He himself had no such legacy to provide him with immortality. Nor had he created a masterpiece by which he would be remembered.

At the place of execution heads were falling. From the street another burst of jeering rattled the windows as the passing voice of the people made itself heard in David's studio. V's collar suddenly felt tight as a noose around his neck and he eased it gently with his fingertips. His guts churned, liquid.

When a man's name appeared on the blacklist of émigrés, two simple actions followed: his estate was confiscated. Then he was added to the condemned register. How would his head look on a pike? He nerved himself to ask for help. Meanwhile David was still talking:

'They think I can turn out a masterpiece every few days; I tried to tell them: it's not like making a chair! The old masters had assistants to fill in the background, do the clothes . . .' He looked up at V consideringly: 'Now there's a thought: *you* could help me. You could do the uniforms! All those bloody uniforms! And they keep asking me to design new ones! Everything – collars, sashes, cloaks – every detail needs attention . . .' He made a decision: 'Vivant, if you want to, you can take care of all that.' He put down his brush. 'I here and now declare citizen Denon to be ordained Official Artist in charge of Revolutionary Uniforms!' V was relieved to see that David had regained his ability to laugh. Though it turned out that he was being completely serious.

Palais des Tuileries. In what had been the Pavillon of Flora, now renamed the Pavillon of Equality, V waited. Summoned by Robespierre. An unusual hour for an appointment: midnight, and it was now 2 a.m. but in the offices of the Committee for Public Safety the members worked a long day. He glanced about, trying to recognise the palace he knew in earlier days.

The once elegant rooms now had an institutionalised, underlit harshness. The outer chambers and corridors were filled with republican officers and bureaucrats trying to look busy, but V had been shown into an ante-room, a large empty chamber. With only one small lamp on the mantelpiece it lay in almost total darkness. He walked around, trying to distinguish detail in the dim light from the open door, trying to work out where he was.

Years later, he recreated the scene in a well-polished anecdote for the benefit of his dearest friends: the salon hung on every word as he described his late-night rendezvous with a monster, his mounting fears, the inappropriateness of the setting, as it was borne in on him that this place of dark silence was once the setting for laughter and frivolity: that he was standing in what had been the apartment of Marie-Antoinette, where once the Queen and her intimates played fatuous card games, extravagant skirts billowing around them, faces masked by paint and powder, hair hidden beneath confections as white and frothy as whipped cream. There would have been whispered indiscretions, musicians, flunkeys. Twenty years before that, another monarch had occupied the room, his own Louis, the King who always enjoyed V's jokes, laughing in that way he had, heavy shoulders shaking. The gusto of the King's laughter had set the candles wavering as though blown by a wind.

That was how V recalled it, but those gloomy rooms were not always the scene of past laughter and gaiety. 'Everything here is ugly,' the Dauphin had whispered to his mother when they were led in by the guards. The apartments had been shuttered and empty for years, forgotten and falling into disrepair until they proved an all too suitable setting for a wretched royal incarceration.

Small wonder that as V waited for Robespierre, the rooms gave off an aura of midnight despair. But when V, elderly and balding and surrounded by *le tout* Paris, conjured up the scene in an anecdotal trifle, decades more had passed and he was recalling events through the unreliable prism of nostalgia. He chose to recall what he remembered best: the laughter, the *jouissance*.

And unexpectedly, laughter broke into the grim scene: from beyond double doors to an inner room, V heard muffled voices, and a rumble of masculine mirth, a banging on a table to call the meeting to order. Then one of the doors opened and a figure slipped out, closing the door behind him. He was crossing the dark room when he became aware of V's shadowy outline a few yards away and cried out in alarm. It was Robespierre.

For a moment the two blinked at one another uncertainly. Then V saw Robespierre's hand moving towards an inner pocket. It struck him that it would be the ultimate irony to be shot dead by the man whose command had brought him here.

V backed away cautiously, bowing (though not elegantly; revolutionaries, he imagined, did not appreciate elegance). He was at the door when Robespierre barked,

'Who are you?'

A rush of *déjà entendu* to the head; a royal palace, a querulous monarch: '*Who are you?*' The King, puzzled, piqued by the continuing presence of a gauche young courtier in the corridor, the brusque question; the eighteen-year-old's fawning reply, and then, later, the hours – days – spent capturing the royal features on paper, the years of conversation, the jokes, the laughter, the affection, the snows of yesteryear –

'Denon, Citizen Robespierre. You sent for me.'

A pause. A recollection. 'Of course.' He beckoned. 'Come in, come in.'

The room seemed brighter now. Robespierre greeted V with elaborate politesse, as though he had just arrived: the visitor was assisting Citizen David with an important work, was he not?

'The *Jeu de Paume* engraving, yes.'

(In the privacy of the studio Jacques-Louis tearing his hair: thirty-five foreground figures, not to mention all those in the background, and a dozen or more up at the windows – a nightmare of a composition that needed someone with a facility for drawing, for capturing the moment in all its vividness –)

'Citizen David was kind enough to suggest we should work together.'

Uniforms. V had groaned inwardly, in dismay, when he realised David was not joking: was this a proper occupation for an artist? For a man – ah, hubris! – trying to follow Dürer?

David's hero prowled the dim room giving out appropriate phrases: France needed its artists to remind the world of the great events they were living through. 'This may not be an opinion that is generally shared,' he added. He made a movement of his head, a small shrug, dismissing the occupants of the room behind him, beyond its closed doors. He himself, he pointed out, had always been aware of the importance of the artist. Indeed, in more leisurely times he attended many a *vernissage* of those he admired –

'Really! And who did you admire, citizen?' V realised at once that the question had been ill-chosen: the pinched features almost disappeared; the mouth a downward arc. The room was suddenly chilly. V continued his sentence as though he had been merely pausing. 'Fortunately, our great country has been blessed with many artists worthy of attention. Citizen David is certainly at the pinnacle.'

An easing of rigid muscles. The grim countenance relaxed. 'Indeed.'

The night spun on, dreamlike, the room expanding and contracting, Robespierre a shadow with a voice. V felt giddy, faint from hunger and sweating with anxiety. His legs ached: he nodded and smiled and gave polite responses. Far from safe, he could still be fighting for his life. Tomorrow, or the next day, his name could be added to the list of the doomed – David might even have to sign the papers.

Robespierre talked on, moving restlessly round the room. There came a moment shortly before dawn, when the light from the corridor fell on him as he paused, and V could see for the first time what the great man looked like. He was prepared for the sallow skin, the clenched, skeletal body. The clothes took him by surprise: the cravat was sparkling, the jacket had a suspiciously high collar, and from beneath the jacket peeped a delicately embroidered muslin waistcoat bordered with rose-pink silk. Robespierre, it seemed, was a dandy. Ah.

As dawn was breaking V staggered home. He had been on his feet all night, without so much as a glass of wine on offer.

Baptiste brought in refreshment, helped him undress, listened.

'He's terrifying. And tireless. He gave me his views on Nature, Portraiture, and the decadence of certain court artists who made their worthless reputations depicting the frivolous activities of the nobility. I kept my mouth shut.' But V thought about the pink silk waistcoat, and felt reassured. He was smiling as he fell asleep.

The sky was already growing light; Baptiste drew the curtains to darken the room and poured himself a goblet of wine. He thought about the plans he and Lucia had discussed on their last night together, a place of their own, a small inn perhaps, with the child. A life.

What held him back, what stopped him from demanding his release? Loyalty? An odd sense of companionship? That was certainly part of it, but also, perhaps, a passivity that came from a life in servitude. The Revolution freed those who had the strength to seize their freedom.

V snored gently. For the first time Baptiste looked at the man he served without the blurred vision of an affectionate eye.

How pliable the master had grown. The Gentleman of the King's Chamber, who danced at Versailles, who discussed wet nurses with Empress Catherine and French art with Frederick at Potsdam, was now hobnobbing with the devil responsible for chopping off the royal heads.

The man whose faithful companion he had been since they

were boys, whose secrets he was privy to, whose fears only he knew, had always been at the centre of Baptiste's life. Now that place was occupied by a woman whose tearful eyes and soft mouth he was permitted to see only in his dreams.

Day and night a servant remained a servant, despite the Revolution. His master might be citizen Denon, man of the People, donning a new coat, adjusting himself to the cut. But he still needed his valet to help him get dressed.

'*Ma chère* Bettine, I've become a member of my neighbourhood *comité* and take my turn at standing guard . . .' He got on well with the men, performed his share of duties. 'Of course there are the uniforms, everlastingly the uniforms.' But to his surprise, he was rather enjoying it, he said. And he was, it seems, in part at least, sincere.

He approved of turning palaces into museums: 'Rather than pleasing one patron, artists must answer to 'a nation'. And now that the nation has released my belongings and my estate from its grasp, I have no complaint!'

He corrected himself: oh, he had complaints: he missed his *chère* Bettine. The situation with Austria exposed Italy to danger and he missed his *chère* Bettine. On Venetian walls were those great works that he had grown to love: he missed them. 'And every moment of the waking day I miss *ma chère* Bettine.'

And while V busied himself working with David, old friends were dying, one after the other, on the guillotine, or scattering in exile – Madame de Staël and Elisabeth Vigée-Le Brun, who painted Isabella's portrait, had fled – and those graceful houses and châteaux where V once dined were burned down or looted, the topiary scythed to the ground, the tapestries carried off for bed-coverings . . . His own château in Burgundy had been spared; his family was safe, though their revenues were dwindling. He could leave the running of what remained of the estate to his sister and brother-in-law who had long ago learned to manage without him. Seemingly blind and deaf to all else, he gave himself to canvas and paper and copperplate; he ate and drank art. With pen, crayon, burin – his tools of survival – he could blank out the world.

But if he opened his front door, the horror hit him. This morning the street surged with rage, the yells and abuse filling the air. V paused as the human wave swept past. In the doorway he was a step or two above the gesticulating arms, the glaring eyes, the brawling relish of the crowd, which swelled into a roar as a tumbril slowly forced its way through the throng like a ship breasting the seas. Huddled in the rough wooden cart were two men, and an old woman in a mud-splattered, ragged silk and lace gown. She gripped the side of the tumbril, jaw sagging. Rotting vegetables flew through the air, and an overripe tomato landed on the woman. Her throat suddenly dripped scarlet, bleeding before the blade had fallen. V gazed at her over the heads of the mob and for a moment their eyes met, but hers were blank, dazed, beyond terror. In any case, the middle-aged man staring across the crowd would have meant nothing to her. He himself recognised her only in the instant the tumbril carried her out of sight: the wheels jolted on the cobbles and something about the angle of the flung-back head, the open mouth, pressed the lever of memory. *Her hot, dark mouth, her pale fingers*; in all his dreams of bitter repayment and revenge he could never have imagined such a reunion with Angélique.

Four weeks after his night-long conversation with V, they came for Robespierre. V watched the unfolding of the drama. He saw how the Incorruptible One held himself apart, ringed with a sort of rage, like Achilles sulking in his tent, ignoring the muttering, the way the hostility of the crowd and its leaders merged. Then came the convulsion, the many-headed worm turning; the accusations, the arrest of the Tyrant (how quickly labels change!) and his tiny band of loyalists.

Paris. Murmurs of rebellion growing louder. A blazing July day; air so hot it might have blown in from the Sahara: scratchy, unsettling. Perfect weather for a coup. It is not only the revolution that dies in office, but also the revolutionaries.

The city simmered in the July heat. The figure of dread was swept from his pedestal, but for the authorities embarrassment followed: a tyrant in custody and nowhere to incarcerate him! The guard at the Tuileries, disconcertingly loyal to the fallen leader, refused to confine him. He and his little group were shunted about like unwanted baggage until, as the sun dropped low, Robespierre made a decision: he led the way, and defiantly they barricaded themselves in a chamber of the Hôtel de Ville. As for those officials outside: 'A ragbag of rebels,' Robespierre said disdainfully. Impasse. Stand-off. Stalemate.

Baptiste too knew what was going on: people talked. The price of bread, the problem of storing fresh meat in the present temperatures, the shortage of vegetables, all gave way to the question of Citizen Robespierre and who would do what next? Someone suggested there might be another uprising. Odds were given. Bets were placed. The force of cross-counter gossip set shop windows rattling.

Still, at the end of a long day, with the master at work on one of the official portraits that occupied much of his time these days – 'Boring but helpful, Baptiste' – the valet's thoughts were less on political upheaval than the need to breathe some fresh air, though 'fresh' was a description open to question as the stench of refuse and rotting food hung over the streets.

Preoccupied, his mind on Lucia and the child, so hopelessly out of reach in Venice, Baptiste walked on. It was past midnight and the stifling heat of the day had cooled to a bearable warmth. Busy with his own thoughts, he only gradually realised that something about the street was unusual. Surely there were more people about than was normal for this hour? The mood, the very air was charged with expectation. He found himself, like others, pulled towards the town hall, drawn by a muffled noise like the humming of bees.

Then, turning a corner, he was caught up among bunched groups with flaming torches; soldiers, officials calling out urgent instructions. All around, people were leaning from windows, peering through the darkness. And without any obvious source, the noise grew, rumbling from throat to throat; the shouts building to a roar, and Baptiste was almost knocked off his feet, swept to the town hall entrance, as mingled cries and shrieks floated back from within. He found himself carried along, in the wake of the soldiers surging through the entrance, to the door of a locked chamber. Ahead of him, men battered down the door and burst into the room as the sound of a pistol shot reverberated. Peering over their shoulders, glimpsing the scene in fragments, like reflections in a shattered mirror, he could see the little group, frozen into momentary stillness, and Robespierre slumped across the table, his face mangled, bloody. Among the shouts and curses Baptiste picked up half-heard words – it seemed a pistol shot had blown through the incorruptible jaw.

One of the group sprang forward to bind up the injury in a strip of linen torn from his shirt, then the soldiers lifted Robespierre and carried him out, with the gentleness of butchers shifting a carcass. His eyes were closed, face twisted in pain. As they carried him past, Baptiste saw that the fine cloth of Robespierre's coat was stained dark with blood, and spattered with fragments of bloody flesh. A particular humiliation for a man whose personal linen was always immaculate.

Like a ragged procession, everyone trailed after the soldiers and their sagging burden, out into the street, and then, suddenly, Baptiste felt nausea rising within him. Pressing his forehead to the relative coolness of the stone wall he tried to control his heaving guts, but then he saw again in his mind that gaping, bloody jaw and the vomit rose, filling his throat, to hit the pavement with a pale splash.

When he at last got home he found it difficult to find the 'right' words:

'Citizen Robespierre,' he began, 'Robespierre . . .'

V lifted the scalpel away from the copperplate on the desk. He looked up.

'Yes?'

Starting, stopping, fumbling, Baptiste described the scene: the crowd, the shot, the injury to the jaw, the coat splattered with blood –

'What colour was the coat?'

'Blue –'

'Light or dark?'

And when he heard: 'I know the one.' The coat was a special sky blue, Robespierre had ordered it for the festival to celebrate the Supreme Being. That added, somehow, to the irony.

'So you saw him do it –'

'No. I heard the shot, but we can't be sure who pulled the trigger.'

Had it, V wondered, been a botched suicide, or an ineffectual helping hand, an attempt to put the leader beyond the reach of his enemies? Whichever, it had failed.

An invitation to an execution was a new experience for V, one he was dreading. He preferred his death scenes to be operatic or allegorical, and found the squalor of Robespierre's journey to the guillotine abhorrent. Flung into the tumbril and driven through streets filled with people cursing his name, singing and dancing to celebrate the occasion, the great man seemed already lifeless. Then a woman leapt on to the cart, spat on his muddy, buckled shoes and screamed, 'Death to the tyrant!' and, shockingly, the eyes flew open, glaring, in the bandaged face.

The sun still blazed from the colourless sky as it had the day before; the heat lay on the city, heavy, enervating; and only their feverish spirits kept the crowd alert. V would have preferred to be anywhere else in the world, but he had been ordered to attend and he did what was required. Unlike Robespierre, he knew how to survive.

It was almost four o'clock when they carried Robespierre to the foot of the scaffold. His white stockings, grubby now, had fallen down, ruckled over his ankles. The executioner wrenched off the sky-blue coat and pulled away the stained strip of linen so that the shattered jaw yawned open, mangled, horrible. Robespierre looked up at the guillotine and gave his only sound: a hoarse, hideous cry. Then the blade fell.

Held aloft by the executioner, the severed head dripped crimson tears. A woman swung her scarf to soak up evidence of the tyrant's end. David would have been the man to capture the moment, but the official artist of the Revolution was not there to memorialise the latest victim of the Terror Robespierre had himself created; David had problems of his own that day. He had been a Robespierre man, after all. V was not the only one who had heard David calling out his emotional declaration of loyalty – 'I'll drink the hemlock with you!' – a promise so much easier to pronounce than carry out . . . There was a turning away from David, and someone else recorded the end of the icy Jacobin, someone with a talent for drawing, for capturing a likeness: Robespierre would live on, brought back to life on paper by citizen Denon.

On display was the head of a monster, a gorgon, held up for all to see, the executioner's fingers twined through the hair. V nerved himself to peer closely, outlining the bones of brow and nose, reconstructing the butchered jaw, and a metamorphosis took place: on paper the ferocity drained from the features as blood had flowed from the body. Eyes closed, there was a calm, a resignation about the features. In death Robespierre attained a humanity he had lacked in life.

Baptiste recognised the distraught woman demanding to speak to his master.

'If you would wait in here, Madame David . . .' Baptiste was never comfortable with the flamboyance of '*Citoyenne*' and in any case, as a royalist, Marguerite would not have thanked him for it. He had heard her declare once, interrupting her husband, 'I'm not deceived by the rhetoric.' She had seen the Terror for what it was from the beginning and said so. 'My dear Jacques-Louis, you are an idealist.' A sceptical shake of her head. 'Idealists can be duped.'

And wives who prove too uncomfortable can be divorced.

But now, Marguerite, white-faced, was at V's door. Life's see-saw had shifted: she, or rather her former husband, needed V's help.

'Marguerite –'

'He's been arrested.'

'I will do everything possible. We should discuss your best course of action –'

'I shall demand –'

'I think not. Demanding may not be the way to go about this. There are various approaches – requests, petitions, inquiries . . . manoeuvre is the word I am arriving at –'

'And while we – manoeuvre – he could be sent to the guillotine!'

'He's far too valuable, and too popular, for the Directory to let him rot in jail for long.

'You sound very optimisitic.'

'I am. He is their iconographer: through his eyes, his canvases, the Revolution will be recorded. No one can do it better. With a little encouragement they will be only too relieved to have him back at his easel. And you can provide the encouragement. We just need to work out . . .' He smiled. 'The manoeuvre.'

Appeals were made; words dropped in appropriate ears, old loyalties invoked. The artist's wife emerged from the wings to centre stage and flung her own eloquence into the plot – albeit modified, tempered, magnificent. Soon, cogs were engaged, wheels turning.

Not long afterwards, V was pouring wine for two. He raised his glass.

'Welcome home. Now we can get back to work.'

But it seemed David had been at work, in prison. 'A big subject.' A way for him to express his thanks to Marguerite for getting him released. 'I can't think how she managed it.'

V sipped his wine and nodded. He managed not to smile.

Few people would recommend prison as a means of marital reconciliation, but it worked for Jacques-Louis and Marguerite. There on the wall for all to admire hung David's *Intervention of the Sabine Women*. Flamboyant spear-flourishing men, glistening torsos, dead bodies, chaos and tumult. And at the centre, the magnificent woman holding the men apart – an eloquent tribute from the artist, a public acknowledgement, a love letter in oils.

'What do you think of it?'

V stood before the canvas in all its oversized, highly coloured turmoil.

'Spectacular.'

An accurate, if deliberately limited, description. 'What does Marguerite think?'

'She approves. It's dedicated to her, you know. We're remarrying.'

This time V did not need to control his smile.

'To be proposed to twice! What woman could resist?'

★

There is a limit to revolutionary fervour. There comes a point when grand gestures no longer quicken the blood; the human scale reasserts itself: the desire for a new pair of shoes, a jacket or dress, however modest, can no longer be denied its place in everyday life, and nor can the urge to gather together and gossip.

A member of the Directory commented disdainfully to V as he sat for his official portrait, 'The people appear to care about nothing but eating, drinking and pleasure.'

Pleasure! In his uneasy resting place Robespierre performed a revolution of a different sort . . . But Robespierre had never really been at ease with people.

On the desk of V's room on the Quai Voltaire an unfinished letter lies waiting.

'*Ma chère* Bettine . . .'

Usually he writes a few lines before retiring, to continue the following morning. But today he has written nothing, trapped here in his bed, lying like a beetle on his back, scrabbling among the sheets. Even now, at his age, he frets at a day spent without putting something down on the page – a drawing, a letter, an observation on this artist or that building.

He allows himself a brief wallow in the luxury of regret; he never created a masterpiece, no rectangle of canvas or paper that would ensure his name lived on. He had not even completed the task to which he dedicated himself so long ago. In another room, filling shelves, drawers, boxes, lies material for the great book, his History of Art. He should have finished it years ago. But there was always another discovery that needed to be noted, another artist to be considered. And the days passed, time slipping through his fingers like an endless silken cord. And suddenly, now, he wants to hold on tight to the cord, stop time, while there is still time to stop.

★

The Parisian salon had risen from the ashes of the Terror not so much like a phoenix as a bird of paradise. Excess had become the norm.

'*Ma chère* Bettine . . .'

Entertaining was back in fashion. The *ci-devant Vicomtesse* de Beauharnais was charming and physically appealing. She had lovely eyes but poor teeth. Having lost her title in the Revolution and her husband in the Terror, Marie-Joséph Rose de Beauharnais had emerged from her spell in prison with a useful best friend: Thérèsia de Barrus, who shared her cell.

'Thérèsia, now Madame Tallien, has no objection to plunging her little white hands into the political clay. She has acquired what passes these days for a salon; the gatherings are lively enough and often amusing: she has a delightful laugh and likes it to be heard.'

Meanwhile, Marie-Joséph Rose, the widow of General Beauharnais was now the mistress of General Barras of the Directory, and she too had a salon, which, with her excellent connections, drew the right crowd. Though perhaps, V commented, 'right' was not quite the word.

Nevertheless, before long V was a regular at both salons. Inevitably he compared them with Isabella's *casinò* and found them wanting: he thought of her drifting through her Venetian rooms and sighed. There was a febrile air to these gatherings, a lack of elegance, a lack of restraint . . .

And he described, for Isabella, the way Madame Tallien, in her rosy splendour, had every man in her drawing room transfixed as she confided that she liked strawberry juice squeezed into her bathwater. Among the listeners, General Barras leaned closer, gave his lazy smile. 'You almost tempt me to share the experience . . .'

V glanced round the room. Next to him, an old Academy friend growled, 'I find all this somewhat garish.'

'Aesthetically unappealing,' V agreed, 'but they have been starved of that most serious of needs: frivolity, and are making up – noisily - for lost time.'

And then they were interrupted. 'Citizen Denon, my wife insists on meeting you . . .'

Tonight, as on so many nights, at the end of the party he had work to return to: a portrait to finish, a pamphlet to read on a new engraving technique – lithography – that sounded intriguing . . . But before all that, there was a letter to be written, a reply to one from Venice.

He poured wine, left it untouched while he paced. He returned to his desk, shuffled sheets of paper. Drained the wine goblet. Brooded. Picked up his pen.

'*Ma chère* Bettine . . .'

His generosity and grace were to be tested to the full . . . or perhaps not?

When he read Isabella's letter it burned in his hands like one of the Medici poisoned parchments. She was writing to tell her 'dearest Vivente' that her marriage of convenience to Marin had finally been annulled: she was freed from the kind and elderly man who for so many years had provided the material framework for her life.

The next words danced before V's eyes like a brilliant code that says one thing and conceals another meaning: '*You will remember Giuseppe – Count Albrizzi*,' she wrote, '*you were good friends. He has asked me to become his wife.*'

The dilemma confronted her: she was fond of Albrizzi, but she did not love him – she hardly needed to tell her dearest Vivente that. '*If I do accept, the union will have to be kept secret for a while: family strains and disagreements over Giuseppe's patrimony will make it necessary to conceal the marriage for the present.*' But, she reminded her dearest Vivente, for a woman to be alone in an unstable world was not an enviable condition.

A question, unstated, hung in the air. V studied the letter with deepening despair.

What was Isabella really doing? Was she asking his advice, or was she giving him a chance to seize the moment, to fling his glove in life's face and take the consequences? Was she waiting by the window overlooking the canal for him to appear, and shout up to her, don't do it! Don't marry him! You're free, I'm free, we can spend our lives together! He could do it, there were precedents: unsuitable unions, elopement, defiance: it took a particular kind of courage to take the risk, but it could be done. Abelard and Héloïse. Francesca da Rimini and Paolo. The Portuguese prince and Inez de Castro. The leap of faith can be dared, he knew that, if love is strong enough. But Isabella was a practical woman. Perhaps she was forcing them both to face the reality of their situation, of what they were.

His eyes rested on the portrait he did of her on a happier day, hanging now on his wall, her dark hair blending into the fragile black net of her mantilla. His pencil had caught her smile, eyes affectionately observing the artist at work. They had been reading Dante together. Then, the poet's personal sorrows had seemed a merely literary affair; now, he felt a chill within himself as he tried to recapture the warmth of Isabella's smile. *'There is no greater sorrow than to recall past happiness in a time of misery.'* No greater sorrow . . .

Her question hung, awaiting a response. He picked up his pen.

'*Ma chère* Bettine . . .'

He wrote, the pen slow across the page, the words dull and stiff:

'Albrizzi is a good man and he has the means to protect you. I, alas, have not. He will do everything to make you happy. He is a good man, who loves you. You should accept his offer.' And then the words that condemned him, that released him into a hollow freedom: 'I give the marriage my blessing.'

And, realistically, what else could he do? What could their future be? He a Frenchman with a precarious income, living through a time of shifting peril. He could have sent an eloquent lament, beseeching her to wait for him. Events were moving so fast, he himself rising in the present hierarchy; he might soon be in a position to – what? Gallop across the border, climb to her window like Romeo and snatch her away from her too-safe destiny? And then? Where would they go, these two urban, elegant creatures, where could they spread their wings and shine? Would it not be selfish of him to claim her for himself?

'I would die for you,' he had said to her once. And meant it. But that was not being demanded. This was harder than dying for her; this was learning how to live without her. Priorities impose themselves, not simple ones – career first, love second – he had learned it was never that simple. Nor did he accept that he could never give himself wholly. There was no fortune-teller here to paint a picture of his future; he had no way of telling what lay ahead for him; he could only believe he was thinking of Isabella's welfare. How much more comforting it must have been for Pluto and Persephone, each time they parted, to have a season of happiness to look forward to.

'I love you,' each had whispered in Venice, meaning it. But how much? As much as life itself? As much as salt? As much as ease and laughter? Tears must follow if such a question cannot be answered. And V, twisting the knife, asked himself again, and again, how should he answer?

Not even Baptiste could know how long his master paced the room, pouring more wine, groaning, writing one letter and tearing it up to begin another; banging his fist against his head and facing a dawn as grey as his soul. Until the final answer made its way to Venice: *I give the marriage my blessing.*

When he wrote his next letter, was it to make it easy for Isabella that he told her he was managing to amuse himself? It was, after all, the truth: too many women found V attractive for him to be able to reject them all.

'I am constant, and unfaithful.' But he knew the diversions for what they were. 'In my heart I am always faithful.' There could be no real happiness without his *chère Bettine*. Write to me, he begged; his mood fragile. 'The unhappiness of lovers is like that of children, laughter close to tears.' Each occupied a privileged place in a glittering circle, and the dance went on.

It was a time of letters, of regrets and tears and, for some, a hunger for news. Baptiste wrote to Lucia, 'And how is our girl, our Isabelletta? Has she grown? Talking yet? Will she speak French too, one day? I want to teach her nursery rhymes about naughty French cats and foolish shepherds.'

One of these days, Baptiste promised her, he intended to find the right moment to talk to the master, to explain the situation. He was finding it more and more painful to conceal his state of mind, to keep his feelings secret. 'But things are changing. He is not happy in Paris. I can see a time when he might want to go home, to go back to Burgundy. Sometimes I find myself about to tell him everything, but to speak of a wife, a family! It seems impossible. Nevertheless I must speak. He is human, he would understand that I'm not just a valet but also a man.'

And in Venice the carnival continued.

Dearest Vivente,

Another theatre has opened. I thought of you as I attended the gala: once you would have been with me. Now there are many at my side, none of them a part of me. There is a feeling here that we are walking on fragile ground. Rumours spring up and die. But artists continue to paint, poets to create their own worlds. Within a wider world that is tilting this way and that, Venice holds its equilibrium, for the present . . .

The secret marriage had taken place but Albrizzi, it seemed, was as complaisant as her first husband. Isabella reigned, the First Lady of the Serenissima.

There continued to be young men who found themselves dazzled by those beckoning eyes – a sculptor, then an artist, and one balmy evening, a youth from the wrong side of town, Ugo Foscolo, penniless, drawn by chance into Isabella's orbit. And favoured.

'Ah, Vivente, how touching they are, young poets, blazing with genius and rage; thin and bony and almost certainly hungry. I told him, come again, Signor Foscolo; bring me more of your poems.'

Once she had greeted another new arrival in the city: Monsieur De Non, who quoted Virgil's tragic lines, while looking absurdly happy, singling him out and imprisoning him for ever. Was she now – it would be only human – punishing him for failing to be at her side? He lacerated himself with the thought that he had only himself to blame for his suffering.

In Venice, for a few days of spinning rapture, a young poet was privy to the inner sanctum. The most beautiful woman in Venice made him the happiest man in the world.

And then. A few weeks or months later – who could be precise at such a time? – he presented himself once more at the *palazzo* entrance. But the door was closed. The Contessa was away on her honeymoon. Shattering news for Foscolo and other young hopefuls, but for Isabella it meant the marital skeleton was out of the cupboard: family matters had been amicably taken care of. She re-entered society in a grand new role.

'*Ma chère* Bettine . . . So the secret is out. My spies in Venice keep me *au courant*. My one and only true love is officially *la contessa* Teotochi Albrizzi. I can now openly mourn my loss – but of course I would not dream of embarrassing you with rumours of my despair . . .'

Despair? As V's smile lit up the room and his eyes reflected the chandelier's brightness, an unkind Venetian acquaintance had voiced the opinion that Isabella's cavalier lacked the sense of unhappiness essential to a great artist. V himself once remarked that he found the public expression of unhappiness vulgar. He was, after all, an eighteenth-century man; he knew how to suffer elegantly.

The Coming Man

It was *Citoyenne* Beauharnais who introduced them, at one of her soirées. She was always pleased to see Denon, who made her feel more beautiful than she was, and who made her laugh. Unlike the wretched Bonaparte who, she noticed, was just arriving at the door. She moved away, in the opposite direction. Scrawny, edgy, the man was a bore, she never knew quite what to do with him. No jokes, and with his yellow skin and terrible clothes he looked like a scarecrow. She would not have bothered with him, but Paul Barras was his commanding officer and seemed to like him, and Barras paid her bills so she knew that, as an accommodating mistress, she too was expected to like him. Nevertheless, at a salon a scarecrow was a liability.

Slipping unobtrusively into the room on the lookout for his master, Baptiste noticed ahead of him a young officer who could clearly have used the services of a good valet: unkempt and unsmiling he glowered at the other guests, pushing past them to get closer to his hostess. The *Vicomtesse* de Beauharnais, as Baptiste still thought of her, was in conversation with another woman on the far side of the room. He recalled her late husband quite well, a man with a sense of *noblesse oblige*, an aristocrat and a soldier who knew not only how to live but to die with dignity. The guillotine had not diminished him, and he could see for himself that the widow was surviving cheerfully. The spell in prison had failed to rob her skin of its pearly sheen. *Citoyenne* Beauharnais in her diaphanous gown, breasts much in evidence, was making a graceful welcoming gesture to someone with her fan; Baptiste noticed her slender arms. *Lucia, her arms pale in the darkness, stepping from the gondola* . . . For a moment the noise of the salon faded and he heard again the slap of water on stone quayside . . .

V turned to his hostess and bowed with exaggerated reverence: 'Marie-Joséph Rose! The perfect, fragrant blossom; what a gardener God is!'

She breathed a sigh of relief: she was saved. The ever-delightful Denon with his wicked smile was by her side, and coming their way was the gaunt young soldier whose muddy boots, she feared, might leave marks on her precious carpets. No sense at all of how to behave in company. She seized V's arm.

'General, may I present . . .'

Bonaparte gazed at her silently, and with an intensity she found repellent, which caused her to step back a pace as though from a threat. Reluctantly he turned his head to acknowledge the man at her side.

V was skilled at the salon game: there would be a meaningless exchange, an unruffled social moment, then a routine disengagement. What followed was something very different. What should have been a nod and a bow became instead a moment of mutual questioning. Could two people have been less alike? One glowering from the other side of an invisible barrier, the other a social magnet, always the centre of a group, who knew what to say and when to say it.

But the man with an anecdote for every occasion found himself at a loss for words, drowning in a dark gaze that seemed to have sucked the ground from beneath his feet. He knew instinctively that Bonaparte had no use for drawing-room conversation; and here the General was face to face with a man known for his frivolity. Their hostess, with a sense of self-preservation, had already moved on. The silence grew.

Bonaparte muttered a clipped comment: he was thirsty. He needed a drink.

In V's hand: a glass of lemonade. 'Take mine,' he said.

He could hardly believe the sound of his own voice. Why on earth had he spoken those words? How uncouth he must seem! Why had he not simply summoned a flunkey to bring the General whatever he wanted? But the question had a curious effect on Bonaparte: he looked into V's face for a moment (they were the same height) and gave him a smile not often exercised. V felt a brief and unexpected blast of warmth, like the sun breaking through storm clouds. The glass changed hands.

And the two men began to talk.

Perhaps it helped that V was not tall – Bonaparte was accustomed to the depressing experience of other men looming over him. V by this time was no longer the slender cavalier he once had been (his jackets, while fashionably square-tailed, were cut to flatter an undeniably thickening body). But his eyes offered intelligence as well as humour. There was also the matter of the smile, of the dimple that came and went in V's left cheek. Letizia, the adored and awesome Corsican mother, had a dimple in her cheek.

What did they talk about? Did Bonaparte ask V about Italy? About Venice? Did V enthuse about the art to be admired there? And did the Corsican eyes then gleam more brightly?

Now they were talking of the movement of the stars . . . Sicily, the volcanoes of Etna and Vesuvius, the attraction of ancient civilisations and faraway places. At some point Bonaparte mentioned India: he had certain ambitions in that direction. V, too, had ideas about the East. Which of them was it who mentioned the seductive allure of danger?

Then their hostess returned, a man at her side.

'I thought you needed rescuing,' she whispered to V.

The new arrival was suggesting, with patronising graciousness, that the social round in Paris must seem very trivial to the General.

'More a waste of time really. I hate wasting time.'

A silence. Bonaparte was glowering again. V remarked cheerfully, 'Casanova once said he only wasted one day of his entire life and that was when he slept for twenty-seven hours after a ball in St Petersburg. The Russians can drink and dance all of us into the ground.'

'But what does one *do* there?' put in the new guest. 'They're barbarians!'

'Not completely,' V said mildly. 'You'll recall Voltaire sent the Empress a copy of his *Philosophy of History* —'

'Dedicated to her,' Bonaparte cut in with a disapproving frown.

'Which proved extremely useful when three thousand copies arrived by sea and sold out in a week.'

'But who could read it?' *Citoyenne* Beauharnais was growing bored.

'Well . . . everyone at the court spoke French.' V shrugged. 'And knowing Catherine, any Russians with intellectual pretensions knew they had to work their way through it without delay.'

'I mean to visit Russia one day,' the General announced, but his hostess had heard enough. Abandoning Bonaparte to the uneasy attentions of the newly introduced guest, she drew V away.

'He calls me Joséphine all the time. I said why can't you call me Marie-Rose, and he said my husband had called me Marie-Rose and he didn't want to share any part of me with my husband. I said, he's dead, for God's sake!' She fanned her glowing face impatiently. 'Don't you find the creature somewhat peculiar?'

V's own guess was that Bonaparte wanted to erase the

existence of the Rose who had unfurled her petals and bloomed for more than one man before him, but he kept this view to himself.

Her mouth was close to his cheek, her slightly sour breath filled his nostrils. A heat came off her that found its way through the velvet and linen he was wearing. V found he had difficulty breathing; there seemed to be a constriction in his lungs. He took a gulp of air.

'I think you should trust the General. The name suits you perfectly and I shall use it from now on. *Ma chère* Joséphine, you have been reborn, a new Venus rising from the revolutionary foam. Alas, there is no Botticelli to capture the moment. But Citizen David could do it justice.'

She shrugged. 'Is he any good at women? I thought he did uniforms.'

'His flesh tones are superb; you would glow like a pearl.'

She smiled and touched her cheek. Then, raising her voice to an appropriate social level, she turned back to the group. 'When you publish your great work, will you dedicate it to me, Vivant?'

Bonaparte performed his slow, silent head–turn. He studied V for a moment.

'What are you writing? A novel?'

'Nothing so exciting. A history of art.'

Joséphine tapped V's arm. 'The General wrote a novel once, he told me.'

'Did you find it difficult?'

'Easier than winning a battle. But in some ways more interesting.'

Joséphine put her small white hand on his sleeve but the General had not finished.

'So you're an authority on art.'

'Can we say I am a student? There is always more to learn.'

'Have you seen David's *Intervention of the Sabine Women*?'

'Of course.'

'It's an important subject,' Bonaparte said, like someone issuing a military order.

'Well, it's certainly a testimony to the power of love to end conflict.'

'Not at all: it's about calling an end to civil strife,' Bonaparte said.

In the lexicon of resonant phrases, 'the power of love' said more to V than 'an end to civil strife'. But he recognised that he was not a statesman; he was simply a man who felt love mattered more than power.

'He's a fine artist,' he said tactfully.

'And of course his flesh tones are superb!' Joséphine exclaimed. 'Now, General . . .'

V watched them moving away from him through the crowd. Joséphine had arranged her features into an enigmatic smile – possibly, V suspected, she was practising a smile that would conceal the increasingly fragile condition of her teeth.

The force of Bonaparte's dark gaze had rekindled a spark in V, reminded him that he had once been an explorer who found a soaring pleasure in the mystery of distant lands. The General's body that Joséphine found so unattractive in its clenched narrowness, reminded V of Robespierre, another austere soul burning with ambition. But there was a crucial difference: there was vulnerability here: the slight figure, the awkwardness, the back of the neck so thin. V was aware of a reluctant feeling of compassion for Barras's awkward protegé. Their meeting had awoken something unexpected: a protective instinct. He realised he was old enough to be the boy's father.

Baptiste, a servant, invisible in this brightly coloured throng, had been making his way round the perimeter of the room. As he came closer he caught a phrase, an intriguing word or two. Now he was at V's elbow, He coughed discreetly.

V turned at once. 'Yes? Something for me?' The valet had instructions to bring any letter from Italy to his master without delay: Isabella had been unwell, and V was aware that although a place of beauty, Venice was malodorous; in that heavy, torpid air fevers and disease flourished.

Weighing the envelope in his hand, he was impatient to read what it contained.

'Baptiste, will you call up my carriage?'

On the way home he thought over the night's entertainment.

'Did you see our hero of the hour, General Bonaparte?'

'Yes indeed.'

Baptiste had eavesdropped on a brief conversation between two elderly guests who were watching the progress of the young Corsican through the crowd.

'There goes the end of the Revolution,' one of them murmured. Baptiste had no idea what he meant, but he suspected that V would.

'Is General Bonaparte to be in the government?' he asked.

'Of course not. He's a soldier.'

'So was Julius Caesar.'

V turned and looked thoughtfully at his valet. 'What made you think of Julius Caesar?'

'I was putting away some of your books the other night; there was an engraving . . . when I saw the General tonight, I thought there was a certain resemblance.'

'He has a good profile. I'd like to do his portrait.'

He almost laughed aloud now, at his earlier fleeting thought. Absurd, for a pampered merrymaker, a part-time jobbing artist to feel protective towards a successful soldier burning with a wolfish energy. And yet, again that paternal twinge . . .

A few weeks before, the thin young man had ruthlessly opened fire on his own rioting countrymen and killed two hundred people – 'the Mob', he had called them distastefully. To feel compassion for a force of nature of this magnitude seemed a poor joke.

'He eats like a starving man, but he's not interested in food,' Baptiste said. 'I watched him at the buffet.'

'He would probably say it's a waste of time. I don't think we have a lot in common, the General and I.'

A salon was, among other things, a meat market: interwoven with the light-hearted conversation, the intellectual showing-off, the exchange of views and introduction of the needy to the useful was an erotic thread pulling this man towards that woman; signalling the beginning of something and the end of something else.

It took a little while for the reality to become apparent to Joséphine (she had resigned herself to the name after Barras himself expressed approval). The fragrant widow found that her lover was increasingly busy elsewhere, that their amorous rendezvous were tailing off. She was nearing thirty and in a strong light she could trace lines as fine as a spider's web on her skin. Barely visible, as yet, but . . .

Bonaparte was the coming man, Barras told her. As he climbed off her bed one night, he said, yawning, 'He's a genius, but an innocent. He needs a wife.'

She shrugged, uninterested. 'And must I try to find him one?'

'You might have noticed he's besotted with you.' His hand on her shoulder was paternal rather than amorous. 'You could do worse.'

Somewhere a clock chimed. She glanced in the mirror on her dressing table: time was moving on.

'You could do worse,' Barras repeated.

The next time Joséphine saw V, she dragged him into a corner, giggles and whispers intermingled, tickling his ear.

'You'll enjoy this: last week at a soirée there was an American woman who thought she could speak French. Suddenly she caught sight of Bonaparte across the room and exclaimed, 'There is my zero!' Joséphine rolled her eyes. 'Her accent was abominable. I was about to say to her, I suppose you mean hero. But then I thought: perhaps zero is, after all, quite a good description of our gloomy little General, don't you think?'

For once the smile failed to materialise; for once an anecdote missed its target.

'No, my dear Joséphine, I don't. I think he's a great man.'

She raised her eyebrows mockingly. 'Have we a case of zero-worship here?'

'He's to be made Commander-in-Chief.'

'What, the scrawny dwarf?' Clearly, the fact that V was the same height as the General did not strike Joséphine. 'Are you serious?'

'Perfectly serious. Your favourite soldier will be in charge of the army.'

A few days later she accepted the General's proposal of marriage.

Watching the ceremony Barras murmured to V that while Joséphine may have been a reluctant fiancée, as a bride she was convincingly radiant.

'And will be even more so when David does her portrait,' V agreed. 'He has a rejuvenating touch. People bloom under his brush.'

It was a slightly shifty ceremony, with both parties falsifying their age – a fact noted by Barras with some amusement: 'It is not unusual for a woman to lose a couple of years on these occasions, but it is not often that a man adds to his.' Officially, he observed, Bonaparte and Joséphine were now both twenty-eight.

The groom, watching his bride approach, exclaimed how the serenity of her expression made her look even more beautiful than usual. V, who had learned to read Joséphine's face, saw not serenity but resignation as the Corsican placed the ring on her finger. And with the signing of the register the Viscomtesse de Beauharnais lost her nobility; she was now the wife of Napoleone Buonaparte. But that name, too, would change before long, as would her status.

Next day, as Baptiste served his master a late breakfast, V mused on the future of the unlikely coupling. 'Montaigne said the ideal marriage would be between a blind wife and a deaf husband. In this case, it might help if the husband were both deaf and blind. Then he wouldn't notice the deepening wrinkles or thickening waist. Not to mention the teeth. Or the lovers.'

A few days later the bridegroom left to command the army in Italy, promising he would soon be home – 'The Austrians will collapse like straw.'

Joséphine restrained herself from telling him not to hurry back, and returned with relief to normal Parisian life. Soon everything was much as it had been – except for the letters. She had not expected her husband to burden her with constant affirmation of his devotion.

'*Tender and incomparable Joséphine . . .*'

'Read me the good bits, Vivant dear, I can't waste time on all the detail.'

Letters were brought to her almost daily, post-chaises criss-crossing the countryside, men in uniform delivering them.

'*Sweet and incomparable Joséphine . . .*'

In the breathing space between battles, where some men slept, Bonaparte dealt with dispatches, dictated his journal, and wrote to Joséphine. She passed his letters round to friends, yawning over the battles – 'Here's one telling me how he stormed the bridge over the Adda River: he says, "It's a principle of war that when you can use lightning it's better than cannon." Whatever that means.' She mocked the passionate declarations – '*Not a night passes without you filling my thoughts . . .*' She shuddered. 'The way that lank black hair hangs round his face – he looks like a street urchin!'

V's face did not betray his discomfiture: he too was not tall, he too was less than handsome. His curly hair was sparse now. But he had been lucky enough to find a woman who loved him. Who still loved him, of course, though in a more distant fashion.

Joséphine was quite enjoying her married status: at least she was left in peace to live her normal life in Paris. Her bridegroom with his sun-thinned Corsican blood, shivering in the slightest chill wind, had occupied her bed and invaded her body for no more than two nights before galloping off wrapped in his old grey military coat.

At the next soirée she admitted to V, 'I'm not sure where he is, but he's fighting the Austrians. Isn't that what he said, Paul?'

Barras, her former lover, with the strawberry-scented Mme Tallien now on his arm, confirmed that the General was indeed fighting the Austrians. In Italy. And when his ragged, hungry army won the battle of Lodi he wrote an exultant letter home. Convinced he was a man of destiny, he made the mistake of telling his wife: '*Sweet and tender Joséphine, I have a star I must follow.*' He could always amuse her when that was not his intention.

She read that letter, too, aloud to friends, mocking the General's immoderate declarations. Joséphine was behaving no worse than she had in the past but, increasingly, V felt less indulgent towards her.

Again he did not join in the laughter. And not only because he, too, had more than once poured out his own dangerously uncensored feelings and thoughts to a woman, feelings so heated that the paper risked igniting. He felt a sadness; he had a sense that something precious and fragile was being ridiculed here, and might be catastrophically damaged. And where might that lead?

★

239

Meanwhile other letters, too, went back and forth.

'*Carissima* Lucia,' Baptiste scribbled, 'No news from you . . .'

The master, he told her, had become acquainted with General Buonaparte, already the hero of the Austrian campaign. There were rumours of plans which could include the Venetian republic. 'Nothing may come of all this; rumours spring up and die, but you should be careful, perhaps you could go home to Corfu on a visit? The Contessa is a kind woman, she will understand.'

'*Mon cher* Vivente,' Isabella wrote, 'We are playing the diplomatic game rather well, and keeping our balance, I think . . .'

For a while he thought Venice might escape unharmed.

The republic had declared its neutrality and the General had nodded – with a proviso: 'Any support for Austria and everything will change.' And indeed everything was to change.

It was Joséphine who alerted V, unwittingly, to what could lie ahead.

The letter from the front was waved in the air. It seemed the General was deeply angered with the Venetians. 'The silly creatures have been helpful to the Austrians. I almost feel sorry for them. It'll be the wrath of God. He doesn't like to be crossed. Or deceived,' she added. 'I shall have to be careful when he gets home!'

V had remained convinced at first that Bonaparte's plans would not affect those he cared about most. Borders, frontiers, divisions of various sorts, it all sounded rather abstract, but he now saw it in more personal terms. Precautions should be taken. He would write a carefully worded warning. The world was spinning; would it be thrown off balance? How would the map of Europe look next year?

'*Ma chère* Bettine . . .'

He considered his words: here he was in Paris, sipping champagne in a room with velvet curtains and fine carpets and the world seemed quite normal.

'Until I hear about the General's plans for the Venetian republic . . .' His pen hovered over the page. He tore up the paper. Began again.

V finished reading the latest letter from Venice, put it aside and returned to work at his desk. Baptiste eyed the folded sheets. They would contain nothing of personal interest to his own life, the master and the Contessa moved in a different world. And for Baptiste, Isabella's letters remained unread, as he had long ago decided, outside his territory, private. Still, these were troubling times, and the letter might hold some general information.

'How is the news from Venice?'

'Everything much as usual,' V said absently.

In fact, everything was not as usual: Isabella had added a little domestic note, to tell him her maid had left: 'You will remember Lucia, with me for so many years; one grows attached to someone, even a servant. She was charming, and we were together for so long; since girlhood. She brought me your first letter . . .'

But what interest could the departure of Isabella's maid have for Baptiste? So V said nothing about Lucia.

The valet was increasingly agitated: no word, no news of the child. He should have spoken up earlier. Hurriedly clearing the table, he came to a decision: he would say something now: he would explain, ask permission to go to Venice.

As he turned towards V, preparing the words, a plate slipped from his hands and shattered noisily on the floor. V flinched.

'For the love of Christ, Baptiste, watch what you're doing!'

For both men things were not as usual. But it was V who spoke first.

'Baptiste . . .'

Trying to appear calm, the valet stood waiting.

'Two ambassadors from Venice have been here for the past week. They're about to return home and I can arrange for you to go with them. I want you to deliver a message, to the Contessa. A personal message, rather than a letter.'

Only as an afterthought did it occur to him to enquire, 'Will you do that for me? Will you go to Venice?'

He was surprised by the warmth of Baptiste's response.

On the Brink

Arriving in Venice alone was disconcerting: now and then Baptiste stopped in mid-stride, looking about, convinced there must be something he had forgotten. He had forgotten nothing, it was simply that there was less to do. No one to look after; no duties, no responsibilities, no baggage to carry except his own.

But it was not only his circumstances that were different: the city was subtly altered.

There was something in the air that was new; the careless elegance had been displaced by a sense of impending disaster. Baptiste thought of Pompeii; the way the master had described it to him in Naples, the people unaware, unsuspecting that their days were numbered. Here it was as though they knew, but waited, unable to move, as an invisible wave of fire rolled towards them, about to engulf the republic.

At first sight everything looked the same: the gentry moved from salon to gondola to gaming room; music could be heard wafting from open windows. But when he reached the *palazzo*, the servant at the door was a stranger (of course: time and servants moved on; why should he expect to find a familiar face on duty?). But when he asked for Lucia, the man stared at him, puzzled, and suspicious.

'There is no Lucia here.'

For a moment Baptiste believed him: foolishly he must have confused one house with another. He was about to apologise and turn away, but as he stood irresolute, a gondola glided to the steps and a familiar figure, swathed in black silk, was helped ashore. She passed the valet without glancing his way, but as she reached the steps he called out, more loudly than he intended:

'Contessa!'

She turned, surprised, still smiling at some witticism from her companion. She frowned, the smile fading in puzzlement. Then he saw recognition flood into her face, the frown replaced by sudden anxiety.

'Baptiste?'

She beckoned him to follow, said goodnight to her companion and led the way to her private sitting room. When her maid appeared, small, round-faced, the girl was dismissed, and Isabella hastily removed her mantilla. She tugged at her cloak and the silk caught on the embroidered decoration of her gown. She struggled for a moment, until Baptiste stepped forward and deftly freed the garment, lifting it from her shoulders and folding it tenderly over his arm. How often he had seen Lucia take the cloak and fold it, so, the silk no smoother than her own slim arms . . .

'Thank you, Baptiste.' She waited, expectantly. 'You have a letter for me?'

'No, Contessa. The censors . . . people are being stopped on the road, searched . . . Monsieur felt it would be . . . indiscreet' – he avoided using the more flamboyant word, dangerous – 'to risk a letter at this stage.'

He was himself the missive.

He should without delay pass on the various messages, advice, words he had memorised, but when he spoke, to his own chagrin, he stepped outside their circumscribed territory, blurting out his question:

'Your maid, Contessa. She's new. Where is Lucia?'

At another time such intimacy, so personal an approach, would have verged on insolence, but the times were changing.

246

'Lucia has returned to Corfu. To her family.'

She caught a sound, a half-word from Baptiste. He cleared his throat.

'And the child?'

She said, 'Ah, you knew about the child. Sadly, the little one died of a fever.'

She saw how his face crumpled. He was twisting her cloak between his hands, she could see it risked being damaged but she said nothing. She looked again at the pale, drawn face and knew all she needed to know.

'Oh, Baptiste, I'm sorry –'

'I meant to speak. When the time seemed right. But in Paris, with all that was going on . . .' He shrugged helplessly. 'Why didn't she tell me? Even a letter . . .'

But Lucia, it seemed, had herself been unwell, half out of her mind after the death of the child. Then her brother arrived and everything was swiftly arranged.

'They could have reached me!'

Treading carefully, Isabella said, 'The family did not wish Lucia to renew a relationship without a future.'

Baptiste said forcefully, 'We *had* a future! We were a family. In the eyes of God. Before I left Venice we were married.'

She was startled: servants making decisions, marrying without permission. The world was indeed changing. Kind-hearted, capable of brushing aside the powerful barriers of class and wealth, Isabella was also a woman waiting to receive news from the man she loved.

'We must talk further about this, Baptiste.' And then, 'Did your master have a message for me?'

'Yes, yes, of course.'

His head whirling, sick at heart, he tried to assemble his thoughts, to transmit V's words to Isabella now. There had been warnings: General Bonaparte was preparing to send a considerable force to blockade or attack –

'But we have remained neutral!'

'It seems not entirely.' He knew little, but he had heard exchanges; the cornered Austrian force had slipped away using Venetian territory. Bonaparte was enraged: the republic had betrayed him. The republic would pay.

'The General is an honourable man,' Baptiste said, repeating V's words, 'he is strict with the men, he forbids looting. But in the heat of battle . . . Monsieur was concerned for your welfare, he said you should consider leaving Venice. And that you might remove objects of value to a place of safety . . .'

Baptiste was aware that much of the master's own art collection had been left in Isabella's care.

'Thank you, Baptiste.'

'There was more.'

He gave her other messages he had memorised: they had followed fast, one on another, as V remembered important information that should be passed to Isabella. Finally there was the matter of a painting, *The Marriage at Cana* . . .

Weddings came in many different forms, in paintings, in Bible stories, in life. Bitterly Baptiste recalled now his own wedding, a hurried affair: a shabby church, an old priest who understood the pain of enforced parting, an exchange of rings, an embrace. Something more formal was to follow later, possibly in Burgundy, a kitchen banquet, yellow dishes piled high with fish and fowl, but a wedding of a sort there had been –

'Baptiste?' Isabella prompted him, 'You have more to tell me?'

'Yes, there was an important matter, concerning a painting. He wanted me to be sure to tell you.'

'A painting? Is it one he wants me to purchase? Or one he wants disposed of?'

'It was a question of saving it from possible harm. A Veronese –'

She laughed, but without tenderness. If you had to choose, she had asked him one day, between saving a painting and saving a person, which would you choose? And she remembered his reply.

'The master wanted you to warn the monks, advise them –'

But she broke in to say she was tired. He should call on her the following morning; they would talk further. Baptiste bowed and backed out of the room. At the door he realised he was still gripping her cloak and laid it carefully across a chair.

He made his way across the piazza, turned left, then right, over one bridge, then another, following the path home he had taken so often after delivering a letter to the contessa. Outside the house he stopped. The glass of the windows was so thick with dust that even without curtains the interior was shielded. The place was empty, and builders' materials were piled untidily against the door. Baptiste knew the way of labourers; he lifted a heavy plank that lay across the entrance and tried the door: it opened enough to allow him to slip inside.

The smell surprised him: there was nothing familiar in the air of the room; no hint of cologne and candle wax and the sharp tang of ink, just dust and damp and a sense of something stale. Underfoot, no soft warmth of rugs. How different it had been, that day, that night, when the master had been saying his long farewell to the Contessa, and Baptiste had brought his bride to what, for a few hours, they could think of as their place.

Blessed by the kindly priest, serenaded by the gondolier who by this time knew their names, Baptiste and Lucia had hurried, laughing, to the door. He took her cloak and led her to the armchair near the fire, kicking the logs into life. She sat like a lady while he brought in food, poured wine, served her. When it grew dark he lit candles so that they sat in a small pool of light, the room in shadow around them. They talked a little, embraced lazily in the firelight, relishing the ease of it all – no hurried meeting, parting. Hours lay ahead in which they could simply be together.

In the still air the candle flame was steady and Baptiste, turning his head, saw that Lucia's silhouette was thrown sharp and clear against the wall, and when he leaned towards her, their shadows kissed.

'Be still,' he said. 'Stay as you are.'

A sheet of drawing card, a stick of charcoal and a steady hand were all it took. Fixing card to wall, he followed the line of Lucia's profile with the charcoal. Holding his breath, bracing his elbow on the table he captured her – the tilt of nose, the lips, small chin, the curve of her neck.

She stared at the drawing, surprised; he was an artist, she said. He shook his head and shrugged off the compliment.

'I watch, I pick things up,' he said. 'It's poorly done, but I'll have your likeness to keep me company, always.'

Later they lay together, naked in his bed and Baptiste explored Lucia's body; in the darkness of the gondola, loving had been clumsier, the lifting of skirts and fumbling with breeches awkward as the craft rocked beneath them.

At dawn they dressed and Baptiste rolled up the charcoal profile and put it in a chest.

'It will stay with me wherever I go,' he said.

Standing in the dusty, empty room he glanced about, trying to recreate it as it had been. On the window ledge there was a rippled cone of wax from a melted candle. When he stepped closer to the walls he could see rectangles, paler than their surroundings, where framed pictures had hung. He looked at the wall next to the fireplace, where the candle had shown him Lucia's silhouette, but it was no longer blank: on the plaster a builder had scrawled calculations of the quantity of paint to be ordered.

On that final day, when they were leaving Venice, Baptiste's belongings had been dealt with somewhat hastily, left till last, and in Paris, when he unpacked, his drawing of Lucia was nowhere to be found. Perhaps the cleaning girls had swept it up and carried it away in their basket.

He left the empty house, replacing the plank of wood across the front door.

The child was dead. Lucia gone. He ordered wine and drank steadily, blindly, drowning himself in glass after dark red glass, deadening the pain. It was early morning before he staggered to his bed. When he woke the sun was high. Mouth furred, limbs slow to obey, he washed and dressed and was gulping a bowl of warm coffee when he remembered that the Contessa had said he should call on her in the morning.

At the *palazzo* entrance the young servant gave him a sceptical look: the Contessa, it seemed, was no longer at home. She had left at noon, accompanying her husband on an extended visit to friends in the country.

The city had fallen into a silence; a dazed quiet prevailed, at least within the *palazzi* of the nobility. In the squares and alleys, as Baptiste moved through the town, he was aware of muffled disturbance, confusion. The word in the bars and cafés was that Bonaparte was offering a way forward: submit and be saved; through the French could come revolution by peaceful means. Greater freedom for the downtrodden. To the downtrodden, this sounded like good news. In effect the Frenchman was demanding the abdication of the oligarchy, the abandonment of the ancient constitution, to be replaced by a democracy. Baptiste left Venice with hope: it all seemed very reasonable

But later, the General's mood changed. And he made sure that the contents of his dispatches, and his personal letters, were no longer secret: from Joséphine and Barras alike V

251

heard the message: 'The only course to be taken is to destroy this ferocious and sanguinary government and erase the Venetian name from the face of the earth.'

And what had earlier sounded to the Great Council like a polite request for them to consider the possibility of removing themselves was now replaced by the outright threat of annihilation.

Then Bonaparte sent his soldiers to the shore of the mainland. And he waited.

My dearest Vivente,

The truth is now inescapable; Venetians have a gift for ignoring unpleasant reality, but we can no longer do so: reality is facing us as palpable as the *aqua alta* you always found so amusing when it lapped at the door of your house. But this is less amusing: just as the water overflowed the canals and engulfed the city, the reality now is Bonaparte. I can feel his gaze fixed on the Doge's palace. He hates us and all we stand for. He wants our winged lions and our Corinthian horses, our precious canvases and treasures. What will become of us? What will become of Venice?

Before V could reply she had her answer: like a puff pastry castle, everything collapsed. Hail the conquering hero! Bonaparte's battalions in the streets, marching across the little bridges, fretting as the General forbade the usual military reward of anarchy and pillage. Erect the Tree of Liberty in the Piazza San Marco! Burn the Golden Book of great names! Open up the ghetto! Throw in the towel, or rather, the Doge's hat: it won't be needed any more.

From the windows of the Doge's palace the flag of the new republic floated in the breeze. And great works of art flew off walls and altarpieces into Bonaparte's hands like iron filings to a magnet.

Not everything escaped unharmed: the *Bucintoro*, the ceremonial ship representing the Venetian state, had caught the eye of the French.

My dearest Vivente,

Y ou remember the beautiful *Bucintoro* floating across the lagoon? The flags, the ribbons, the music, the entire ship glittering in the sun! The *Bucintoro* is no more; the soldiers chopped it into a thousand pieces, and then the beauty was burned: they melted down the figures and decorations that were made of gold.

'Bring me the best they have!' Bonaparte commanded, not so much to punish the Venetian Empire (though he intended to), as to embellish the empire he was building. It was a consuming lust.

The monastery of San Giorgio was on the list. With the monks locked away in one corner, the dismantling got under way. An 'agreement' between the Officer General of the Italian fleet and the Governor of Venice provided the excuse to get the wagons loaded: nearly two thousand books, rare fifteenth-century editions, more than 150 manuscripts, codices, paintings. The monks had been unprepared. Among the spoils carried away by the French was their most prized possession: a Veronese, *The Marriage at Cana*, sliced in two so that it could be more easily packed and carried off to Paris.

And the treasures wended their way across rivers, over mountain passes, by sea; wagons and carriages, horses, mules and men, loaded with the plunder from churches, public offices, palazzi: 20,000 pictures – Carpaccios, Titians, Correggios . . . sculptures in wood and stone, the winged horses of St Mark lashed securely to sturdy wooden wagons, left unwrapped, gleaming in the sunlight to astound the countryfolk. There were chests filled with candlesticks, crucifixes, works in gold and silver, pearls, diamonds and rubies. With paintings carefully rolled in wax cylinders and statues wrapped in plaster and straw, the procession jolted its way across the land, along the treelined roads and splashing through forges, villagers running from houses and fields to watch it pass; and finally, here it came, trundling over the cobblestones into Paris, a flamboyant re-enactment of the Triumphs of Caesar, Mantegna's great cycle brought to glittering life, complete with exotic beasts – camels, ostriches – as the loot circled the city and headed for the doors of the Louvre.

'The human race is governed by its imagination,' Bonaparte said to V one night in one of their hurried conversations. The General had a way of throwing out his thoughts like a man sowing seeds in a field, as he stalked through a room or down a corridor. 'I want to fire the imagination of the French people and art is one way to do it. The more great art they see, the more they will be inspired.'

It was not, V felt, the moment to point out that most of the great art they would be seeing came off the walls of churches, monasteries, ducal palaces and great houses beyond their borders. The General was ordering him to procure for France the best, the most beautiful. So while one set of people would be inspired, another would be deprived. No one, V reflected, had ever equated art with justice. To the victor the spoils, to the loser the empty plinths and blank walls. It was hard, at the beginning; he was mortified, and guilt slowed his hand. In a uniquely high-handed, non-military way, was he not looting? Then he turned to reason and logic; the notion of the greatest happiness of the greatest number. Was it not, ultimately, better for great works to be made safe; jewels displayed in their proper setting: the greatest museum of the modern world?

He began to make lists.

★

Some years later, V guided his master round the museum, soon to be renamed the Musée Napoléon. The great man strode past the paintings as though reviewing a regiment: he noted, *en passant*. At one canvas, of St Jérome, he did stop, studying it for a moment.

'I remember this one.'

'It came from the Duke of Parma's gallery.'

'Yes.' The Duke had tried to buy off the General, offered him a vast sum if he would let Parma keep it.

'What did you tell him?'

'The truth. The money would simply have been spent. The picture is a masterpiece. It will inspire everyone who sees it – you told me so once, and you should know: you're an artist.' He granted V a quick, malicious grin. 'When you find the time.'

Time was the price he paid: acting as Napoleon's procurer, creating his museum, brought V honours while the work was inevitably put to one side. But these two understood each other; they always had and always would. Trust and affection had grown out of a shared passion.

Striding ahead, Bonaparte had reached a magnificent display: a wall covered with Raphael canvases newly hung by V, and knowing how his master enjoyed these breathing spaces from politics, V trotted after him, expounding (briefly) the theme of *ars longa, vita brevis*. He threw in a mention of Seneca and Hippocrates, and as they moved on, spread his arms wide to embrace the next painting: *The Marriage at Cana*, whose luminous glow he had first seen in the convent of San Giorgio Maggiore in Venice, restored now and apparently unflawed.

'Priceless,' V murmured. 'Immortal!'

Napoleon stopped, rocked back on his heels, and stared up at the canvas. 'Immortal? Really? How long will it actually last?'

'Well . . .' V thought for a moment. 'With care, several hundred years more, certainly.'

The Corsican lip curled. He gave a shrug. 'Some immortality!'

He moved on briskly.

V lingered a moment, savouring the richness of the wedding. He recalled that there had been a time when he burned with remorse for the removal of the canvas from its convent wall; he had felt in his bones that it belonged with the monks, had even attempted to protect it from the invaders.

Had he not told Isabella once that he thought a Veronese was certainly of more value than his own life? She pointed out, later, that he had failed to save this one, but by then he had changed his views: he had come to see that there could be different ways to protect a work of art. Had it been left with the monks it would almost certainly have been looted, sold, destroyed in the chaos into which Venice had sunk.

In his own mind, at least, he had saved endangered art for posterity: the French knew how to look after priceless things. And in any case, as the Emperor had pointed out more than once, the Venetians themselves had plundered their winged horses from Constantinople.

The house on the Quai Voltaire is accustomed to visitors. Friends – and distinguished friends of friends – who arrive unannounced and are not turned away. Baptiste has instructions to show them round. They exclaim in admiration at the Memling portrait of a young man, the Dutch watercolours, the Italian primitives, the Rembrandt. Dürer and Parmagiani drawings . . . V himself, when at home, may play the guide - why not, it's no hardship to wander with congenial people through his rooms, showing them old favourites that occupy walls or shelves. What will become of it all, he wonders sleepily, his collection; masters old and new, remnants of

Egypt, and his miniature *musée*, his cabinet of curiosities? What a man collects will reveal something about him.

What will the death mask of Robespierre reveal, or a mummy's foot from Egypt; a fragment from the skull of El Cid, one of Voltaire's teeth? Marvels and fascinating oddities, they are evidence of abiding passions. But a scrap of the Emperor's shroud is something more personal. Everyone has a view of the Emperor – great General, force of nature, barbarian. For V he was a heroic figure who was also, improbably, an object of love.

En route to an official engagement, he saw the First Consul, ahead, dismissing his carriage and setting off on foot. For V this meant doing the same. Out of the carriage and trotting to catch up with his fast-moving master, V paused for breath outside an old shop in the Place du Carrousel, his eye caught by a painting propped against the wall by the door: an oddly clumsy Pierrot, moonstruck, lost. He went closer, saw that some words in thick pencil were scrawled across the grubby surface: *How happy Pierrot would be if he had the art to please you.*

Bonaparte checked his stride and turned back. He glanced at the canvas. 'Whatever it is, it's ruined,' he said.

V ran his finger gently over the scribbled lines and saw that they could be removed. He studied the face.

'I think it's a Watteau.'

The First Consul grunted. 'Not one of his best.'

But for V the canvas conjured up something achingly lost, something Italian.

'You like little "Gilles" do you?' the shopkeeper said. 'You can have him for three hundred francs.'

V bought it on the spot.

'He would have taken less,' Bonaparte called back, striding on.

V had the painting taken to his carriage. That night he propped it against the wall and studied it while he sipped his wine. The round face, undistinguished features, a sense of unease lurking behind the masquerade. Was there a hint of another bright-eyed young man, ingenuous, vulnerable, transfixed? An open-faced boy: easy prey for a beautiful, cold-hearted woman. Ah, Gilles! Ah, Pierrot! Ah, V . . .

He gazes at the picture from his bed now, through the tunnel of time. He sees it differently today; the glade more threatening: Dante's dark wood with its animals, leopard, wolf; Pierrot himself, a gleaming figure blurred into Virgil, beckoning. But it is only a boy after all, with a white, lost face, frozen, helpless. Doomed.

Ultimately, V acknowledges ruefully, all are doomed: he with his crumbling body, Baptiste, even Isabella, still smooth and bright-eyed as she was when he last saw her. They are all embarking, if not for Cythera, for a less certain destination, but some will catch an earlier boat.

A Line in the Sand

Denon's sketch of the Sphinx

Afterwards it seemed to Baptiste that his whole life had been a preparation for Egypt. The years of carrying messages and packages, watching out for problems before they arose, navigating risky social waters on behalf of his betters; in short, the years of measuring out his days in terms of other people; waiting to begin a life of his own. Was there, he had wondered sometimes, ever to be a life of his own? Happiness?

There was a certain contentment to limited ambition, to being useful, appreciated. But could happiness be found along with the ache in the heart, the heaviness of limbs and spirit, the tightness of throat and pricking of eyelids that caught a man unawares, lying in wait like shadows at the edge of everyday life?

'Baptiste!'

'Sir?'

He might never have seen Egypt. V did not order him to go.

'I want to do this more than anything else in the world. I would cling on to the tail of Bonaparte's horse, suffer a rupture or broken bones falling off a camel – I have to go . . . But you could stay in Paris, there must be people out there who can help me –'

Stay in Paris. More empty days. What would be the point of that?

V added, 'It would give you an opportunity to do things you don't normally have time for – I'm aware I am

261

demanding.' He shrugged enquiringly. 'There may be something that holds you here.'

'No,' Baptiste said, 'there is nothing that holds me here.'

So Egypt was to be the next faraway place.

'Egypt,' he said, about to ask more, but V broke in:

'I feel it, Baptiste, pulling like a magnet! Incidentally, could
you try to remember that we are not going to Egypt. No one
knows where we're going and the General wants to keep it
that way. If anyone asks you, say it could be Ireland. That
should put them off the track.'

'And why are we going?'

'Why? We're going to explore. There will be tombs!
Temples! Monuments, ruins, flora and fauna, minerals – an
ancient culture to decipher. What better reason?'

'I just thought: Bonaparte's in charge of the army. We
might be going to fight a war.'

'Well. Yes, of course. That too.'

'What, we're declaring war on Egypt?'

V corrected him: Bonaparte was going to liberate the
Egyptians from the oppressive rule of the Mamelukes. He
would bring them freedom, based on the French model.

'The people will have a voice in their own destiny –'

'As they had here, in Paris?'

V ignored the question. He saw things from a different
perspective. Regime change was the military aim. But the
Commander-in-Chief was also taking nearly two hundred
geologists, archaeologists, botanists, mathematicians, artists
and men of letters.

'Will it be dangerous?' Baptiste enquired. But the master
was back at work and the question was left unanswered.

In Paris the season spun on, but for V it had lost its savour:
social life had acquired a coarseness; the celebrations were
lavish, guests and hosts played their parts with enthusiasm, but
the actors seemed to have lost the art of performing with

elegance: the green austerity of Revolution had ripened into depravity.

The Terror was over and the guillotine lay idle. Deportation was the new execution, prisoners transported in iron cages, writers and editors silenced. Critical words could cause damage, and the Revolution must be protected. Entertainment was a safe objective: dance, drink and be merry.

'How was the evening?' Baptiste enquired, as always, while he helped his master undress.

Struggling into his nightshirt V attempted simultaneously to yawn, shrug and reply. 'Mmm . . . Energetic. The smell of over-warm bodies does not encourage the appetite . . . Madame de Beauharnais – Bonaparte, I mean – was there. And General Barras.' Joséphine's former lover had arrived looking languid and voluptuous and, as usual, remarkably pleased with himself. He had acquired a new woman, beautiful, but rather fat, in V's opinion.

'I glanced round the room: people draped all over the furniture, doing things better done in private. Someone said to Barras, "Parisian salons are beginning to look more like seraglios these days." He gave that slow smile of his and said, "I see nothing to complain of there." I think I'm getting old, Baptiste.'

He had, in truth, not enjoyed the fashionable gathering; the little dancers from the Opéra fluttering like butterflies as well-fleshed gentlemen pinned them to the wall or played leapfrog over their slender stooping shoulders and stuffed their mouths with delicacies.

Later, men and women alike, having eaten and drunk too much, tousled, dishevelled, reeled home at dawn. V had learned from Baptiste that the People in all their freedom could no longer afford meat. In the purifying fervour of the early days St Just had declared that the populace should consume 'only vegetables, fruit, bread and water'. That many of them were now doing so, V realised was not from choice, and on some days even the bread was beyond their means.

Was this really the end towards which the Revolution had raged? A weariness came over him and a sense of helplessness. The world would spin on, and for a while he would spin with it, but the dance was no longer enjoyable.

There was still the pull of a distant land, the journey, the quest. But sooner or later, you had to come home. And where *was* home? Venice had felt like home.

He got out of bed and picked up his pen:

'*Ma chère* Bettine . . . You have never, I think, been loved in Egypt. Shall I carve your name on the pyramids? . . .'

The street lights glow in the mist along the Quai Voltaire.

Baptiste, seated across the table, watches Zenobia without seeming to. He sees the way she blinks hard to hold back the tears. She has to clear her throat before speaking.

'To be here, in his house. I've imagined this moment so many times: what I would do, what I would say. I have behaved like a thief, but all I was trying to find out was the truth.' And then, like a lamentation: 'Baptiste, I want *answers!*'

Answers.

The answers she sought would provide no solution; answers were like double-edged knives, they could wound, damage.

He should have been firm, shown her to the door while she was tearful and full of apologies. He would have been safe: banished, she would not have returned. Instead, he finds himself trapped, finally, into approaching the dangerous subject of the adventure his master shared with the Emperor.

'The nuns always told us Napoleon was a monster.'

'If you examine a monster,' Baptiste says, 'from some angles, he can look like a god. Ovid talks about that —'

She breaks in: 'He sent me a copy of *Metamorphoses* once.'

'Did you read it?'

She shakes her head: 'The nuns confiscated it.'

'Well, Ovid tells us about the way things – people – change their shape. If two lovers are parted, if they cannot share their lives –' he pauses, unprepared for the pain that still washes over him, after all these years – 'would it not be a consolation if they could be changed into two streams flowing together, mingling –'

He breaks into the fleeting, transfiguring smile few people see. 'My apologies. We were not talking about Ovid, but about my master and the Emperor. I did not agree with the Baron's view of him but I could understand it. They shared a passion.'

Baptiste has known they will find their way to this point sooner or later and he no longer has the strength or guile to evade it.

The problem with Egypt, as Baptiste had suspected all along, was that nobody knew anything and the Commander-in-Chief was keeping what he knew to himself. With the French Army heading into unknown territory, the soldiers were uniformed as usual. Hot weather? Cold? Who could tell what lay ahead? So: heavy boots and standard issue jackets.

In any case, before the destination was arrived at, Baptiste anticipated the usual accompaniments to a sea voyage: sickness and storms. The possibility of death by drowning.

V waited at the rail, watching for the first glimpse of land. 'It's like a flower bud unfolding: you can never quite catch the moment the petal moves.' And with that momentary glancing away to Baptiste as he spoke, he missed the almost imperceptible break in the horizon, the shift as the sea gave way to the rising line of land. Egypt.

This landfall had a particular significance for V: if Venice had been a dream of love, a time out of time, he had a curious sense that Egypt was where everything would come together in reality. At a time when he had thought his life as good as over, when, at fifty-one, he felt he was slowing down like an old clock, here he was, caught up in Bonaparte's grey coat-tails and hurtling towards adventure. He had avoided using words like danger and hardship when discussing the journey with Baptiste, though danger there would be, but alongside all that would come discoveries he could barely visualise. He thought of the Ptolemies assembling the great library in this harbour town and, later, the fatal obsession, Rome meeting Egypt, the empire of glory sacrificed to the empire of voluptuousness.

Alexandria, with its past glories and crumbling present, stirred his imagination: the resonance of vanished splendour, the great library repeatedly destroyed, Antony bringing manuscripts to Cleopatra as a gift of love, restoring the library, though it would burn again.

Isabella once affectionately described V as a geographical Don Juan, endlessly travelling in search of the perfect place. In fact, he was a hard-headed lover of antiquity and he was on the trail of what he craved most. The past.

'*Ma chère* Bettine, Egypt awaits us. There will be temples. There will be tombs, evidence not only of death but of life. Shall we decipher their writings? What will we learn?'

Anchored offshore they were wrapped in darkness, lights flickering here and there on invisible land, the only sound the swish and slap of sea water against hull. Then, as the sky brightened, the rattle and clash and shouting of the men filled the air. For a moment, V had a sense of almost drunken euphoria: great events would take place here and he would be part of them. He would follow the Corsican star and share the fate of the men around him.

Baptiste, too, was thinking about their destination. How did they live, these people? Would they be savages wearing leaves, what did people eat here?

'Just remind me,' he said, 'Why are we invading Egypt?'

'I told you: we're going to liberate them from the Mamelukes.' The idea of the Mamelukes intrigued and baffled V; 10,000 warriors, dazzling, mysterious as centaurs, with their sleek horses, their jewellery and gold; riding to battle clad in silk, moustaches gleaming. An army of not quite mercenaries, which replenished its ranks by purchasing Caucasian boys, not quite slaves, and training them, to become in their turn, the next generation of fighters and, once trained, free men. A very oriental scheme.

Meanwhile, the French were preparing to land, and –

'I think,' Baptiste said with some apprehension, 'we are being shot at.'

After weeks at sea, the men could barely stand upright; packed into landing craft, soaked by the waves, seasick, vomiting, and fearful of being dashed against the rocks, they stumbled ashore, sinking under the weight of equipment. Terrified horses were dragged ashore, rearing and collapsing into the surf, out of control. The beach looked like the aftermath of a vast shipwreck: men, cannon, supplies, livestock and local dead littering the shore, bodies and dead horses floating in the surf.

Six frigates, thirteen gunships, various ships of the line and supply vessels heaved in the rough swell, attempting to put ashore 35,000 troops, 1,000 horses and two hundred unarmed intellectuals, all under resistance from the locals, fighting with whatever weapons they had.

The Commander-in-chief attempted to parlay and received his reply in gunshots. The result: trumpets, gunfire and infantry charge. Men bleeding. Dying. Six hours later the battle for Alexandria was over; there was no question of sacking the city: the people had little desire to be slaughtered and the Commander-in-Chief did not wish to be delayed.

Bonaparte had promised the men six acres each of the land they were liberating, but all the soldiers could see was desert. A landscape of nightmare engulfed the dusty, tired troops. They found themselves trapped in a foreign, unstable and hostile element: sand.

Sand had not been discussed. It was everywhere. Sand grated between the teeth, scraped the eyeballs, blocked nostrils and ears, infiltrated boots and breeches, scouring the dampness of groin and anus until the men were aflame, sore and itching. It blew in the wind, the very air a veil of sand, and settled on hair and eyebrows, turning the darkest Frenchman blond. Sand shifted beneath their feet like a lumpy mattress, and cut the skin like a scraping blade. What manner of place was this?

V and his drawing pad were never separated, even on the battle of the beach. He made his way further round the bay, away from the troops, and got to work, sketching, recording, making hurried notes.

Baptiste said tentatively, 'Sir. The General is moving off . . .'

V was absorbed in reproducing the carving of a shabby stone column.

'Not now, Baptiste.'

The lines spread across the page, some curved, some angular; a pattern, a section of a pattern. When he next looked up the port was deserted.

'Where is everyone?'

'They've moved on.'

Baptiste glanced about uneasily: he disliked this abandoned place. He felt the menace sunlight can lend to an empty street, a quality of waiting that can cause a man to look behind him though there has been no sound of footsteps.

'Why didn't you tell me?'

Baptiste controlled his features and his voice. 'I did, sir.'

'Did you?'

'Yes. You said you did not wish to be disturbed.'

A last detail, a curlicue, and V sprang up, pencil between his teeth, grabbed drawing pad and materials and stumbled off across the sand towards town.

He handed his bag to Baptiste and scrambled over some rocks. 'You should have been more persistent. Remember Archimedes. I don't particularly want to be killed by a lurking Arab; there must be some about the place.' Baptiste, sharing the thought, was looking closely at every side street they hurried past. V saw things differently: he noted the immobile beggar appealing for alms, his outstretched palm moving from side to side like a cobra's head; the faceless women in long, ragged garments, shrouded, mysterious as ghosts. Overhead the kite-hawks screeched and dogs snapped and snarled from the gutter.

From further off came the sound of the invading force on the move; a subdued, generalised roar – boots tramping the ground, weapons clashing, voices calling out, and soon the two stragglers had caught up with the Commander-in-Chief.

V's way of attaching himself to the group around Bonaparte was so informal, so effortlessly dégagé, that no one could object – it would be like challenging a passing cloud: he drifted up, sketch pad in hand, amiable, smiling; he was simply there, part of the scenery.

They approached the city through winding side streets so narrow that no more than two could walk abreast. The town seemed deserted, but any doorway could conceal an enemy: in such conflicts there are always some less than grateful to be liberated. Bonaparte, studying a folded map, moved at his usual steady pace, eyes on the chart, seemingly unaware of his surroundings. From his place at the rear, V saw what happened next: a man and a veiled woman, dim as shadows, materialised not in a doorway but at a low window above eye level, and began firing frenziedly with battered rifles at the passing French. The two advance guards spun round, swung their rifles up and raked the window repeatedly with a speed that left V breathless. Gobbets of crimson flesh spattered the wall. The man and woman fell forward, flopping clumsily over the window ledge like bloodstained scarecrows. There was no dignity in death here.

Bonaparte's finger remained on the folded map; his pace had neither quickened nor slowed. For a moment V wondered whether he had even been aware of the incident. Had it not been for the pair of grotesquely twisted corpses hanging out of the window, their own blood dripping from their fingertips, V himself might have wondered whether it had actually taken place.

Was there ever an invading army, Baptiste wondered, in which quite so many people were occupied in recording what they saw and heard? Bonaparte dictated his journal whenever there was a pause. His secretary Bourrienne discreetly scribbled his own diary in off-duty moments; V filled notebooks with words and pictures; Redouté was recreating birds, beasts, fish – indeed, some creatures so strange it was questionable whether they came from land or water. Baptiste watched with some amusement the scholars falling over each other, describing and measuring; analysing and delineating everything animal, vegetable or mineral that came to their attention. Anything that caught the eye, petrified or moving, must be chronicled. Meanwhile, there was a war to be fought.

When the Commander-in-Chief made the rounds of local forts, V was at his shoulder, unobtrusive, a shadow. On his pages the forts appeared, as they did before his eyes: crumbling ruins, affording no shelter. A bivouac was established here and there, and when a soldier squatted, wearily snatching a few moments' rest in the shade of an old wall, V was there, capturing a slumped body, splayed legs, the droop of a head. When a man limped past, a comrade helping him along, V's pencil was ready: a few lines, and he had caught a moment of pain or tenderness.

'I'm no Rembrandt,' he had said once, wryly, to one of his students, but with these ordinary men in their unforgiving landscape he caught something of the master's sense of humanity.

It was time to leave for Cairo, but before Cairo, the Mamelukes must be confronted. Amid the bustle and movement Bonaparte paced, withdrawn, head lowered, preparing himself. Sweating, his clothes steaming in the heat, V watched. His pencil moved across the paper.

The men had quickly realised that uniforms suitable for Italy or Austria were an affliction here. And water was hard to find; once, the city's ancient cisterns could have kept its citizens from thirst for a year; but time and neglect had damaged the system. Alexandria was an inauspicious beginning.

For V, who had acquainted himself with some knowledge of the terrain, all this was a setback of no consequence. Marvels lay waiting to be discovered; the Commander-in-Chief would be sending an advance guard ahead on horseback and he meant to be with them.

'We'll need horses, Baptiste. And a mule for the equipment.'

V was an accomplished rider; Baptiste merely adequate: as with the other accomplishments he possessed – reading, writing, fencing, an understanding of numbers and words – it came from a childhood spent jogging along behind V. He had been groomed for suitability, another word for bondage: a good servant should have some acquaintance with the furnishings of his master's mind; in this way he could anticipate problems, provide solutions. Baptiste had met some servants who knew more than the gentlemen who employed them. He himself was luckier: V's curiosity and zest had kept him on his toes for a lifetime. But he had never shared his master's love of horse riding.

The march began. Still not recovered from the sea voyage, sharing their few water canteens, the troops quickly ran out of water. They coughed incessantly, throats cracked and sore, their misery intensified by the horrors of the mirage: wherever they looked vast lakes shimmered before them, which as they advanced drained away into dry, arid ground. Villages that from the distance appeared to be ringed with water, were indeed raised on stilts to save them from inundation at flood time, but the stilts stood now on dusty earth. Sharing the men's deprivation, V was entranced by the mirages, a phenomenon he found magical.

The troops stumbled on. Flesh bleeding from insect bites, blinded with sand sickness, half mad from sunstroke, the soldiers raged with thirst. When they reached the Nile they threw themselves fully clothed into the water, to drink from every pore, their bodies steaming, no longer caring that the Mamelukes were entrenched nearby. The men, already exhausted, faced a battle they were ill-equipped to fight.

Called to attention, they stood, swaying with weariness. Dismissed, they collapsed like marionettes with cut strings, in a tangle of arms, legs, equipment.

V crouched in the sand, his back supported by a boulder, shading his eyes with one hand, pad on his knees. He drew quickly: palms, troops, horses and mules, in the distance the triangular structures of the Pharaohs. The men wrenched at tight jackets, strangled by their collars, uniforms dried out and once again soggy with sweat. The sun was not yet at its height but already the heat fell on them like a hammer.

Bonaparte prowled, a circling shadow, arms behind him, hands clenched, the dark eyes sunk deep in their sockets. The light scraped the flesh from his bones, leaving the thin face as stark as a skull. He paused behind V and examined the evolving scene.

'You've left out the camels.'

Even as Bonaparte spoke, V's pencil, with a few strokes, conjured the distant beasts on to the page – spindly legs spread wide under the weight of the load heaped on their backs.

'The camels are coming towards us, so I felt it was safe to leave them till last, General, and make sure I got the men, in case you suddenly ordered them to march on.'

'They're barely capable of standing, let alone marching on. This is Mameluke territory; the enemy is at home here.'

V could only agree. 'We're about as comfortable as cats swimming in the sea.'

'What can I tell these lads that will help?'

'You found the right words in Italy.'

'In Italy I told them the eyes of all Europe were on them. Who's watching them here? The camels?'

Invisible as usual, Baptiste stood to one side, holding bags, and V's boots, removed to allow air to dry his sore, sweating feet.

His master squinted across the sand at the pyramids and back to the page, adjusting a line. The sun had inched higher, throwing a blinding light on the paper. V's hand hovered, his pencil followed the slack reins of the camels and moved on. He paused, corrected the angle at the apex of a pyramid.

'Do the men have any idea how old these monuments are?'

V's pencil hovered over a pyramid. 'We think we have antiquities at home, but these stones were put in place more than four thousand years ago. Do you feel they could be observing us, judging us, perhaps?'

The Commander-in-Chief stared across at the pyramids through narrowed eyes, down at the drawing on the page, up again at the pyramids. He held out his brown, slender hands as though for inspection, regarding them with quiet approval. Then his head turned in an unhurried movement, taking in the cluttered scene, the men slumped in groups, the drooping horses. He nodded several times, slowly. The intent, inward-turned gaze would have been familiar to Joséphine.

She had whispered to V before he left Paris, 'You must write to me from Egypt, let me know the really important things: what are the women wearing? Do they know how to dress? Is the great man faithful to me? Tell me everything!'

That these two men could talk to each other at all astonished her. One with his social graces, the other so ill at ease with people – 'And we all know the creature has no sense of humour.'

Joséphine was incapable of grasping that once Bonaparte overcame his initial aversion to what he regarded as courtier behaviour – the gossip, the levity – he was able to relish the way V took pleasure in pleasure. Napoleon's father, Carlo, had also enjoyed life, and the boy had expressed his disapproval by ostentatiously placing himself above mere hedonism by reading – gorging on history, memoirs, law, science. With V he could talk about books: 'Bourrienne tells me I have over five hundred books here – I didn't realise I'd picked out so many, but apparently he's counted them, secretaries do that sort of thing. You might care to borrow a few.'

They talked about Rousseau, about Italy and art. About writing:

'Did you read my novel?'

'I'm looking forward to it, General.' A silence from the author. V added, 'I like to save a few treats for later. But I did read your history of Corsica.'

'A bagatelle. Hardly Gibbon.'

The soldiers waited, standing to attention, sagging at the knees, heads drooping like flowers in need of rain. The Commander-in-Chief confronted the troops, impassive, his eyes sweeping the ranks. These feeble specimens were the men he must send into battle. The sight was not encouraging.

Bonaparte was a short man, but someone commented that he seemed two feet taller when he put on his General's hat. Now, he drew himself up. He loomed. His voice floated over the massed ranks of the troops: 'Soldiers! We go forward together!' He glanced up at the pyramids. 'And remember, from the heights of these monuments forty centuries are observing us!'

The General certainly knew how to deliver a line. The drooping heads snapped upright, slumped backs straightened.

And V drew him as he stood, arms akimbo, surveying his men marching past, boots churning the sand into a choking dust. Later, when the General had become the Emperor, when his face had lost the sharp, hawk-like edge, hair thinning, the slight body grown stocky, only those who had seen him in the blazing vigour of his youth could have any idea of the dazzling creature he was.

The Generals told the men what to do. The scholars had to fend for themselves, living on lentils, watermelon when it was available, sleeping on the floor of abandoned mud huts.

Sometimes there *were* no lodgings, and they slept, wrapped in their cloaks, on the sand, Baptiste curled like a shield by V's head. Was this why we came to Egypt? he had wondered one night, before sleep rescued him. Half-starved, bruised by the travelling, throat parched, flattened by heat and thirst and sandstorms, on every side he heard the muffled voices of the troops recalling with nostalgia how easy things had been in Italy, how hard it was in Egypt. And the Commander-in-Chief had it no easier, barely sleeping, driving himself as he drove the men. Baptiste was not an admirer, and he argued with the master, later, about Bonaparte. But in Egypt he was astounding.

★

Baptiste has been out of the room for a few minutes. Now he returns, and from the doorway he sees Zenobia, the slender body crumpled, head fallen to one side, asleep in the chair, her mouth half open like a sleeping child, her face smoothed into serenity. He himself is accustomed to white nights, catching sleep for an hour or two when he can, waiting for the master's return from social engagements. Zenobia, exhausted, has escaped from turmoil into oblivion.

He stands very still, reluctant to risk disturbing her, but she twitches in her sleep and jolts awake to find him watching her.

Disconcerted, she sits up straight, brushing back her hair in the familiar gesture.

Baptiste crosses quickly to a bookcase on the far wall of the salon and opens the glass doors. He runs his finger along the spines. The same title, in French, Italian, English, Dutch, German . . .

One edition, with much gold embossing, looks different from the others. He takes it down from the shelf and places it in front of Zenobia.

'The Emperor had one edition privately printed for friends.'

She reads aloud: ' "*Travels in Upper and Lower Egypt, during the campaigns of General Bonaparte*. By Vivant Denon".'

'Egypt!' she exclaims, startled. 'Does he write about –'

'Yes,' he says, and waits.

She reads the dedication:

To Bonaparte:

To join the lustre of your name with the splendour of the monuments of Egypt, is to link the glorious triumphs of our age with the fabulous times of history; it is to rekindle the ashes of Sesostris and of Mepes, like you conquerors, like you benefactors.

Europe, in learning that, in one of your most memorable expeditions, I accompanied you, will feel an eager interest in my work. I have neglected nothing to render it worthy of the hero to whom I desire to present it.

Vivant Denon

She turns the pages, stopping when an illustration shows her a battle or a palm-ringed oasis, a group of Arabs or a minutely detailed townscape. At her shoulder, Baptiste's voice, barely audible, recites names and places grown familiar and famous: Alexandria, the sphinx –

'The Battle of the Pyramids . . .'

She studies the turbulent scene, the fallen horses and men, the guns, the smoke. 'Who are these men, with their moustaches and flashing swords and handsome faces?'

'Those are the Mamelukes.'

'He fought these . . . Mamelukes?'

'He was certainly there for the battles. Doing his best not to get killed while he got on with his drawing.'

Zenobia has been turning over the pages impatiently, searching, her eyes skimming the lines.

She picks up the book now, holding it out to Baptiste. 'And in all these pages, where am I?' she asks.

Baptiste stares down at the page and Egypt melts into a jumble of images, of charges and gunfire and screams. Time has dimmed the scene until only one thing stands out: the event that changed his life for ever.

The Transformation of Icarus

Denon drawing the ruins at Hierakonpolis, Egypt. (*British Museum*)

When V went through his jottings later, he found hastily scrawled experiences and descriptions, some almost illegible, written on the move, or between actions, as he huddled behind a boulder or in the shelter of a temple wall – 'The sun veiled by white, dry, burning vapour . . . it excites thirst, parches the skin, enflames the blood, irritates the nerves . . . we breathe at the mouth of an ardent oven, everything we touch is burning . . .' And when it was time to move on: 'How can a man be expected to take accurate notes under these conditions!' Always hoping to be granted a few more minutes before the trumpet sounded or the yells of the men signalled departure time.

Worst was the humiliation: when conflict threatened, the troops were ordered to form hollow squares – 'mules and scholars in the middle!' After a while V managed to evade this shameful protection and wormed his way to a position where he could at least observe what was going on – even, occasionally, participate. Between hardship and danger, he lived mostly in a state of elation, eyes and fingers engaged in a constant race against regimental orders.

He learned to gallop off with the advance guard so that he could reach the next temple or monument ahead of the main party. He would happily crouch in the sand, pad on his knees, squinting at a statue, or feel his way into the dark mouth of a tomb. Till the trumpet sounded, and, to his fury, the men moved out.

'That trumpet! It's the signal of doom,' he exclaimed to Baptiste as they curled up next to a rock, swathed in blankets against the chill night. 'If there's something of interest, something I want to get down on paper, we have to move off. When there's nothing but emptiness, there they stay, stuck in the sand like a line of rocks.'

He shared his frustration with the Generals, Desaix and Menou, who had become friends: 'It's intolerable! Barely a temple I've been allowed to explore thoroughly, not a tomb I've been given time enough to examine properly.'

They sympathised. But as Desaix pointed out, 'We can hardly delay a military advance to allow you to unwrap a mummy, my dear Denon!'

He flung out his arms in comical despair: 'I don't see why not! The Mamelukes have been here a mere few hundred years; the mummies four millennia. Surely they have priority!'

He became adept at lingering for a few moments longer than the last of the troops, to give him the time to finish a drawing. One morning, when he had hung back longer than was wise, he glanced up from his pad to see an Arab horseman heading his way at a gallop. The Arab swung up his gun and pulled the trigger, V ducked, and the shot skidded across his sketch pad. He fired back wildly, leapt into the saddle and fled, swerving to avoid the pursuing bullets.

Next day, V was working on the uncompleted drawing when Bonaparte paused in his prowling and looked over the artist's shoulder. About to move on, he took a closer look.

'The line of the horizon's crooked,' the Commander-in-Chief commented unhelpfully.

The line, V agreed, was indeed crooked. It was the line the bullet carved across his pad. 'Blame the Arab.'

The trumpet sounded and he cursed quietly as the troops moved out, towards the pitiless horizon line: above, the burning blue; below, the burning sand, and ever-present thirst.

An old man's body is no longer fresh: a sickly emanation infects his bed linen. He resents this, he whose body had the fragrance – so a girl once told him – of verbena and fresh wheat. There is a sour mustiness in the room. If he could reach the window, or some water . . . the sulphurous tincture Baptiste slipped between his lips has dried him out; his tongue sticks to the roof of his mouth like a snail to a wall. It is thirst that prompts the memory. His mouth is parched now as it was then. Feeling as old as Methuselah – 'You've outlived your Emperor,' a friend commented, the day the news came from St Helena – he finds himself thinking of Egypt, an adventure dim as a half-forgotten dream. Dryness was a condition of life in Egypt; nature was cruel, withholding moisture. On those desert marches brackish water was handed out in little cups, precious as brandy. There is cool water by his bedside but the carafe is out of reach. Unusual for Baptiste to miscalculate such details. Even in Egypt he usually managed to find a few drops to assuage their burning thirst. The valet had even secreted a bottle or two of the family Burgundy with their rations; holding the wine in reserve, saving it for a time of real emergency.

Egypt shimmers in V's mind like a mirage: images swirl. Soldiers so young they had no need for razors, mere boys, telling him about their lives, their hopes; dying before the sun had set. One, his leg shredded by a Mameluke bullet, lay, moaning quietly, bleeding to death because they had no instrument for amputating the shattered limb, asking V to tell his mother he made a good death.

At its most intense, the sun burned V's feet through his boots, roasting his toes; he found himself hopping from foot to foot like one dancing on coals. Halting briefly to make a sketch, he called Baptiste to stand between him and the sun so that he could work in the shade cast by the valet.

The scholars carried their own baggage, slept ten or twelve to a room, when there *was* a room, though V preferred the open air. Indoors or out they were eaten alive by mosquitoes. 'I can live with the insects,' one of the architects groaned, 'but yesterday, when those Bedouin attacked us as we were trying to measure a column, I thought: Great God, if I'd known it would be useful, I'd have studied marksmanship instead of draughtsmanship.'

But they knew that without Bonaparte the finest marksmanship would not have prevailed.

The Mamelukes were beautiful – V snatched drawings from the sidelines of the battle, admiring their boldness, their dash. Their horses were champions, their uniforms were brilliant and shiny, their moustaches luxuriant, their fighting skills awe-inspiring, their courage phenomenal. The French cavalry numbered two hundred, the Mamelukes four thousand. All they lacked was a Bonaparte to lead them.

V scribbled his account of events before the blood had dried. 'It was no longer a battle but a massacre; the enemy seemed to defile only to be shot, and to escape the fire of the battalions only to be drowned. Astonishingly, only ten French soldiers were killed, thirty wounded.'

After the battle, French soldiers bent their bayonets into hooks to fish drowned men out of the Nile, and search the sodden bodies for silver and jewels: they all knew Mamelukes carried their wealth on their persons. The bodies hung suspended in the water, drowned or shot or decapitated. The smell of decomposing flesh drifted without discrimination among the living.

In these inhospitable surroundings, skin abraded by the sharp sand, throat dry and sore, eyes smarting, V found himself completely at home. Twenty years seemed to have fallen away from him; at over fifty, he felt young, he felt invincible, and was astonished by the realisation, though he could have picked up a clue from his affinity with Ovid, a man who spoke to the exile from personal experience, whose characters changed their shape, and hence their destiny. V too, it seemed, could change his shape, his style – from courtier to soldier, scarlet heels swapped for spurs – transformed for the new role.

'Have no fear,' he assured Baptiste one night, 'we will survive.'

A lifetime later, his skin grown soft and pouched with age, V finds it hard to believe he had the speed, the force, the energy to live through the moments when he came close to death – he faced bullets, swords, a jaguar that leapt from a cave and, briefly, sank its claws into his shoulder. There were days of thirst and hunger and, later, in houses captured from the Mamelukes, the risk of poison contained in a silver dish of Arabian food offered to the French occupiers by ladies whose graceful hospitality might be far from sincere.

Egypt has a special place in his heart; it was a time when he felt every part of himself used to the utmost, muscles, sinews, eyes, fingers; feet for marching, sense of smell for detecting the presence of green things growing nearby.

Above all, the discovery of an ancient people, the records left on the walls of tombs and temples.

The first tomb was stumbled on accidentally: given an hour while the troops were resting, V found his way over a rocky outcrop to a narrow cave, guided by an elderly Arab, his faded djellaba blending into the rocks around them. Following the man, V felt his way down roughly hewn steps that widened to a lower cave. The guide handed him a small oil lamp, and moved on, to what had been a sealed entrance shattered at some earlier time by native grave robbers in search of jewellery buried with the dead. The two men stepped together through the broken door and V halted, confronted by a phantasmagoria of dazzling colours and shapes.

As the Arab moved round the tomb, the flame from his lamp lit up scenes of everyday life, celebration, embalming and worship. For V, accustomed to the art of Greece and Rome, the rosy realism of Renaissance paintings, the work at first seemed ugly, bizarre: attenuated figures drawn in stylised profile; thin, mysterious women, their brilliant almond eyes outlined in black. Priests, sinister in masks of wolf or bird. This was a way of depicting the human form that he had never encountered and he was repelled. Then, holding his lamp close to the wall, studying the images, he began to see a different kind of beauty; the delicacy and astonishing skill with which every detail was drawn – the fruit, flowers, drapery, water brimming in golden cups. The colours – turquoise and red, green and gold – shone undimmed by time, undamaged by human hands.

The flickering lamp sent shadows leaping up the painted walls so that the figures wavered and V felt for a moment that he was being scrutinised by those watchful, black-rimmed eyes. He pictured the anonymous artists, carrying out their task, all of them knowing that oblivion awaited their creations: the tomb with its delicate figures and brilliant colours would be sealed. For four thousand years this artistry had remained inviolate. Scattered at V's feet were tiny earthenware lamps, remnants of cloth, fragments of gilded furniture. A sarcophagus lay wrenched open. He felt like a robber; he too was stealing, not precious stones or golden necklets, but the privacy of the dead.

From outside the cave he heard shouts, a trumpet. The troops were moving off. Scholars and artists must move with them.

One night, V, looking for a dune behind which he might empty his bowels in some degree of privacy, came upon the Commander-in-Chief, staring at the heavens – looking perhaps for that star which was his. He spoke, as one thinking aloud, of Caesar and Louis XVI, of the power of the mob he had watched rioting against the King, the same mob who, not long afterwards, stood cheering as the blade fell on Robespierre. 'Cicero was right: nothing is more uncertain than the favour of the crowd.' He waved an arm towards the arc of the sky. 'Silence and solitude are a consolation.'

'Virgil would have agreed with you,' V said. 'He spoke of the friendly silence of the still moon.'

In the lengthening silence he began to sketch the scene before him. Why were they here, in Egypt? Bonaparte was in search of something, power obviously, though the General would probably have put it differently. As a lowly civilian camp follower, V had more modest ambitions. He concentrated on the page, on reproducing the effect of moonlight on sand and rock.

'You seem at home here,' Bonaparte said, with a touch of irritation.

'Not at home; this is alien land. But . . . with such treasures . . .'

A silence. 'Egypt is just a stepping stone,' Bonaparte said suddenly. 'India would be the real prize. To pluck that from the claws of the British . . . I can see myself wearing a turban, riding an elephant across the plains . . .' The Commander-in-Chief stared out across the moonlit sand. 'Have you ever ridden an elephant, Denon?'

'No, General, they never really caught on in Europe, despite Hannibal.'

Bonaparte did his slow turn of the head, right to left, and watched V at work.

'If your book does well it could make you famous.'

'Fame was not forecast when my palm was read. Fame and glory are *your* emblems, General.'

Bonaparte said, in the tone of one honing an aphorism, 'Glory is fleeting but obscurity is for ever.'

It was somehow easier to disagree with the Commander-in-Chief while busy on a drawing.

'Well, obscurity by its very nature, can be a lasting condition, but a man can spring from obscurity to recognition' (he wondered if he should mention the example of the General himself) 'and glory can endure. The statue bears witness to the conqueror long after he is dead. When the Emperor is dust, he lives on in medals, coins, marble.'

V had reached for the word 'emperor' without thinking, but the Commander-in-Chief fastened on the word.

'True. An emperor puts a lasting stamp on things.' He added, 'Alexander died at thirty-three, and according to Horace, the normal lifespan of a man was thirty-five, so I have six or seven good years ahead of me.'

'I, on the other hand, am fifty-one. Exactly the age Virgil was when he died, leaving the *Aeneid* unfinished. I too have a book I should have completed by now. I certainly have fewer years ahead than you, General.'

'We cannot be sure of that!'

V looked up from the page. 'Then we can both afford to live recklessly.'

He had his reward: one of the General's rare smiles. More: he actually managed an ironical, rasping laugh. Joséphine would have been astonished.

Bonaparte moved on. V closed his sketchbook. India. Did Mughal palaces and Hindu temples lie ahead? Another journey?

Meanwhile, perhaps he could get on with emptying his bowels.

When they were all back in Paris he would tell Joséphine

about these extraordinary months with her husband; perhaps it might strike a spark of admiration in the indifferent wife, quicken her interest.

But before that could happen, there were those who decided that the adoring husband could no longer be left in ignorance of certain matters concerning Joséphine.

'He has to be told.'

'He can't be told.'

He was told.

In the desert there erupted a volcano of black rage, a hurricane of despair, a flood of self-pitying tears, the shock of hurt pride and, above all, the brutal confirmation of unrequited love. Bonaparte's fury and jealousy consumed him, a fever. The great welling-up of love, the tenderness, the generosity of affection, all turned inside out, soured, blighted.

Joséphine, lifting her skirts for the latest lover in Paris, was unaware that the details were even then being laid before her husband in Egypt.

V had known a sense of trepidation in Paris, when he watched Bonaparte's face soften at the approach of the woman he adored: the obverse of such adoration could be terrible indeed. And what he feared had come to pass. 'Love does more harm than good,' the General now announced, in the decisive tone he used for ordering an advance on the enemy. His eyes were pitiless.

Bonaparte said later that he forgave her. He wiped the tears from her face as she knelt before him, and allowed her back into his bed, but things were never the same – rather, *he* was never the same. All his early harshness, suspicion, ascetic scorn for the gentler things in life returned.

But meanwhile Joséphine in Paris was too busy being unfaithful to write back to a man who had found the time to write burning love letters from the sand-swept desert camp – '*Adorable wife, you are far away . . . take great care*

*of yourself, you are worth more than all the universe to me . . .
incomparable Joséphine . . .'*

The time for tenderness was past. He fell on the Mamelukes, almost with relief.

In the cold light of the desert stars V considered his own life: perhaps a man who spent so much of his time away from where he belonged could feel at home nowhere or everywhere? And where was home? It was a question he often asked himself.

Once, perhaps, he might have said Burgundy. Later, Venice. Now he began to feel he belonged to France. The nation the young Bonaparte was impatient to bring back to life. Was this to be his path? To follow that blazing star?

Was it after Egypt that V began to change? Perhaps, like Icarus, he flew too close to the Corsican sun and lost, not his wings, but something less immediately discernible. No visible change had taken place, but V was altered.

Baptiste was no longer surprised by the way his master swung up on to horseback with the agility of a man twenty years younger. Beneath the brim of his hat, eyes reddened by the gritty wind, sparkled with expectation; looked closely at everything. He was revitalised.

The men's diet consisted of what they could tear from the unforgiving land – roots and wild fruit if they could find any. At the sight of the French on the horizon the local inhabitants gathered up harvested grain, flocks and utensils, and melted into the landscape. Passing abandoned fields the day before, a few of the men, driven by hunger, had scythed unharvested wheat with their swords, threshed it with rifle butts and ground the seeds to rough powder between stones. Without ovens there was no way to turn this flour into bread, so they boiled it in brackish water to produce a sandy gruel.

'Does it have something of the consistency of polenta?'

V asked Baptiste as he thoughtfully stirred the mess on his plate.

'No,' the valet replied very firmly.

'Remember Italy?' one of the men yelled to another, recalling not the modest looting that had been allowed, but the land of plenty they had occupied. 'The lamb they roasted for us, the fat chickens! The wine. Riches, eh?' Assiduous scraping of spoon on dish, and someone shouted hopefully, 'Any more of this filth in the pan?'

The scholars were, if anything, worse off than the troops. V noticed Redouté limping badly, and helped him to a sheltered corner out of the wind. The younger man held out a swollen, inflamed foot. 'Vivant, it's like walking on needles!'

'There's sand in the wound. Do you have any water?'

'No.' Redouté winced. 'We're not fit for this sort of thing. Too soft.'

'We won't be soft by the time it's over.'

'If we survive. My eyes are getting worse, some days I can hardly see to draw what's there. Will I see Paris again?'

V moved further off and, with Baptiste's help, hollowed out a patch of sand where he could curl up, where the subdued chorus of complaints from the intellectuals could be ignored. One of them was lamenting the lack of a mattress.

The Commander-in-Chief, who was at his best in discomfort, won golden opinions by stretching out to sleep wherever the men were encamped. Which was all very fine, Baptiste thought, except for the General's library of useless books occupying good mule space that might have carried nourishing supplies for all of them.

Once again Baptiste came to the conclusion that very brilliant people could be as witless as village idiots, and said as much to his master.

V, amused, defended the General's need for books: 'He told me he'd left out a good many favourites. I think he brought too many English novels, but on the whole it's a good selection: art, science, geography – even poetry and romance.' Though with the debacle of Joséphine's disgrace V doubted whether the romantic bundle would even be unwrapped now.

Meanwhile, as the stars burned and the temperature dropped, V made himself as comfortable as possible, using his folding stool as a pillow, his cloak as a blanket. 'How fortunate that I am no longer the thin lad I was – the extra flesh cushions me well. Baptiste, if you could tuck my cloak round my feet and pass me my sword . . . perfect.'

But Baptiste retorted that in his view hunger got in the way of perfection. Like everyone else he found himself dwelling on food remembered: in Venice, tiny clams and liver simmered with onions and served with soft fat cushions of polenta. In Naples, the tomatoes sliced with cheese. Doubtless the desert dwellers too had their specialities, but these were not available to the French. He had been hungry since they arrived.

Between marches, in odd moments, V reached for his pen and continued his usual conversation with Isabella. His words, tucked into the pouch alongside military reports, would cross desert and ocean till they rested in her hands.

'*Ma chère* Bettine . . .'

The night before, by the light of the moon, he had drawn her portrait from memory, flanked by two small obelisks, 'on one of which I wrote the words: Isabella, Queen of the Nile. And on the other –'

But before he could finish the sentence the trumpet was blowing, men were in their saddles, spurring their horses to a gallop. Was it an attack or time to move out? The letter must wait. Meanwhile, where would today take him? Within every structure, behind every monument half buried in sand, lay possible danger: an enemy poised to surprise them; Arabs,

Turks . . . villages that could conceal snipers . . . But for V the thrill of the quest continually outweighed the danger. Tomorrow he might find a mummy to unwrap, marble Canopic urns to open up, another ibis to disinter, its tiny, curled up skeleton giving it the look of an unborn babe. Or he might simply face an uncomfortable ride over the sand. Up front were officers; presumably the Generals would know what lay ahead. He spurred his horse to a gallop and Menou called over.

'Come to Rosetta! He's just made me Governor.'

Baptiste had reacted glumly to the prospect of a sea journey round the coast, though V sounded reassuring: 'It's not far, just a few miles.' But while they were still in sight of land, the ships began to heave and dip, the sea alarmingly turbulent. Baptiste cursed steadily. He hated ships, he hated Egypt with its sand and bitter winds, he hated the Mamelukes. He was convinced he would never see France again.

But this time it was the master who hung over the side coughing up thin green bile. For once, V's cheerful disregard of conditions failed to save him; he groaned his way round the coast, his mouth sour with vomit.

Rosetta – Rashid to the Arabs – was a pink city; its special rosy bricks hinted reassuringly at its Venetian past, and fountains murmured in shady courtyards. A few days after V's arrival, the men, excavating a fortification ditch, found a puzzling slab of rock, black basalt, beneath the rubble they were clearing, and V knelt to examine the rock, running his hands over the mysterious triple text incised on the dark surface, the shapes blurring in the fading light. As usual, he was interrupted.

'Come up to the tower!' Menou called to him. 'Agreeable spot, looks out over the sea.'

They climbed the old tower above the bay of Aboukir, and

the General handed V a lunette of brass and wood. 'Have a look at our ships.'

It was close to sunset, the sea a dark, metallic blue. The low rays of the sun caught the wavering surface so that it glittered indigo and crimson, like shot silk. V slowly scanned the shoreline, the limited vision of the telescope revealing new perspectives as he moved from one view to the next, one ship to another.

At his shoulder, he heard Menou say, 'See how Brueys has handled the mooring? Clever. Strong defensive position.'

V saw that the admiral had placed his ships in a long curve, their port side parallel to the land – 'The shoal protects their back, d'you see; nothing can get past – too shallow.' The starboard side, cannon at the ready, faced the open sea. A hot August wind blew from the north, whipping up sand and debris around the tower. Menou wiped his eyes, cursing the grit.

'Brueys says there'll be no engagement before tomorrow at the earliest. Nelson wouldn't risk his ships here by night. We don't even know where the damned English are.'

V had focused on the broad sweep of sea beyond the bay. A bulky shape slowly moved into his line of vision. He handed the lunette back to Menou.

'I think you'll find they're here.'

The English fleet, buoyant on the waves, took up positions. The *Bellerophon* was sending signals from ship to ship, and slowly the pattern of the fleet changed: half the ships hung back, spaced out across the bay, while the other half seemed, unexpectedly, to be heading fast for shore –

'They're coming in!' Menou exclaimed. 'The fools! They'll go aground!'

As he spoke the English ships, with their shallower draughts, were already approaching a gap in the defensive line. V held out his hand for the telescope: the two were taking it in turn.

'I thought you said the water was too shallow there?' V called out, but before Menou could reply, the English had slipped in, one after the other, floating above the reef. Suddenly the safely entrenched line of French ships looked disturbingly at risk, now vulnerable to attack from both port and starboard, caught between the open jaws of the English fleet.

The sun had sunk into the sea and V felt a chill: from where he stood, the French were now not the predators but the prey. As light was swallowed into darkness, he could no longer follow the action, even with the telescope. Only the cannons spitting fire and an occasional sheet of flame showed where the attacks were taking place. Then the *Orient* became all at once completely visible, her graceful shape outlined with flame as though for a celebration. The conflagration engulfed sails and decks, spreading fast. Dismasted, drifting, she swung dangerously close to the next French vessel.

'Dear God,' Menou groaned. 'Dear God.' V was gripping the lunette so tightly that the wood grew slippery beneath his fingers.

And under the cover of darkness the English ships came at the French, back and forth, battering, pounding. There was a pause, a dreamlike silence, the scene wrapped in smoke, and then the *Orient* went up like a giant firework as the fire reached the gunpowder magazine, the explosion splitting the vessel, hurling blazing fragments and men high into the sky.

The fire spread, the flames leapt from ship to ship, the masts crackling like flambeaux. Menou cursed steadily, V lost in despairing silence as they watched the English Admiral and his men destroy the French fleet. One by one, holed, the ships sank into the shallow water they had thought would protect them.

Only two got away, cutting free from the end of the line, fleeing clumsily. The blaze lit up the scene, and through the lens V could see men swimming away from the ships, black specks struggling in the flame-bright, burning water.

Menou said, with professional briskness, 'Must get word to the Commander-in-Chief,' and clattered down the steps.

The fires burned for hours. When it was all over and the flames had died down, V closed up the telescope and slowly descended the steps of the tower. He walked back to his quarters and wrote in his journal, 'The English have broken the fabric of the power and glory of France. We have bestowed the empire of the Mediterranean on our enemies.' Everything was changed.

How would Bonaparte receive the news? Never one to shoot the messenger, the General would tell the soldier to find somewhere to rest. Then he would pace slowly back and forth, hands behind his back, head lowered, eyes fixed in that concentrated, inward-turned black gaze that Joséphine so hated. He would be thinking, brain whirring with possible alternatives, weighing up, discarding.

V felt for him, but the feeling was subsumed in a greater pain: the sadness he felt for France. Only Bonaparte could have survived such a debacle. He rallied the near-mutinous troops and held the land. But the great hope, the dream of an empire to be established to the glory of France, had died in the flames that danced above the water.

The wretched chill is clogging his lungs and his brain, but he has rested long enough; he feels it is time to leave the unpleasant confines of the bed. To his surprise the message fails to reach his limbs. How odd, to be so helpless, like a babe. But he has come to see that life is, after all, a slow spinning back to one's first state, time's arrow circling like one of those curious antipodean wooden artifacts.

Yesterday, before this ague gripped him and the fever dried his mouth, he was browsing through his cherished

Montaigne over a glass of wine – he can see the volume now on the desk across the room. In one of the essays he came upon a passage he had marked on some earlier reading: 'I have long since grown old but not one inch wiser. "I" now and "I" then are certainly twain, but which "I" was better?' He, too, has grown old. If he asked himself the same question, what would be the answer?

The choices people make, change them. Choices. Bonaparte's eyes sharpening with interest when he mentioned St Petersburg, that night they first met. *I mean to visit Russia one day . . .'* Bonaparte trusted him from the start; and he trusted the Commander-in-Chief. Later, he might have wished some things done differently, but he had never wavered in his loyalty. He had been there, he had stayed at his post to protect the Emperor's museum, the treasures they had assembled together – (*Bring me the best!*) – held in a sacred trust.

A day of gentle spring warmth, fragrance drifting from pale flowering shrubs. Two men strolling through the Tuileries gardens, V and Bonaparte, at a pace not often associated with the First Consul. Beyond the gardens, the walls of the Palais du Louvre, grey stone soft in the sunlight. Bonaparte stopped and glanced about, at the trees, the receding perspectives of the city. He murmured, almost to himself, 'How I love this place.' A sharp breeze whipped the leaves into rustling movement and he hunched his shoulders. 'Still, there are moments when I miss that Egyptian heat . . .' They walked on.

'You've written a fine book.'

'I had a good subject.'

'I liked the story of your Cairo neighbour generously sharing the plague with her husband and her lover.'

'It was sad, later, watching all three die.'

Bonaparte said, his tone neutral, 'I've seen too many die.'

Most men would read the first few pages of a book dedicated to them, but it was clear that the First Consul had absorbed *Travels in Egypt*, and retained the details. V was aware that some people found the dedication fulsome, excessively flattering. He could have claimed, in self-defence, that he meant every word of it.

Bonaparte took his arm in a familiar gesture.

'Your life could make a novel.'

'Rather less dramatic than yours, General,' V said tactfully.

Bonaparte inclined his head. 'Well, I suppose that's true.' Pause. 'But how would you end my story?'

V was a practised courtier; he barely paused.

'There will certainly be more victories – the eyes of the world will be observing you, General.'

A grin of complicity. 'The pyramids. That was a day, wasn't it? With French soldiers there's no enemy in the world I can't vanquish. It's the bastards here that are the problem. On the battlefield at least I never had to watch my back.' They approached the edge of the gardens. 'Now. I want to have a look at the Louvre. I don't like the sound of what's going on.'

As Bonaparte disappeared through the museum entrance, V allowed himself a mischievous twinge of amusement: the visitor was in for some surprises.

The Louvre was a town within a town. The corridors were filled with domestic clutter; cots and bassinets, baskets of fruit gathered from trees growing in pots on the roof. There were dogs, cats, a chicken or two. A goat tethered outside a door.

As the two men picked their way along the corridors, they glimpsed, through half-open doors, rooms that held wood stoves and beds as well as easels. The vast building hummed with the subdued roar of wives, mistresses, children, models and artists, all going about the daily business of living. There was a simmering of pans, the smell of meat roasting and of refuse uncollected. V was familiar with it all: he himself had an apartment in a distant wing that he used as a studio. To Bonaparte it was a revelation, and not a pleasant one.

He swung his head in that familiar slow arc, eyes narrowed. 'This is supposed to be a museum. Who are these people?' V tried to think of a tactful way to explain the situation.

'Artists . . . they live here.'

'Not for much longer,' the First Consul said grimly. 'I want the buggers out by the end of the month.' He favoured V with his rare, potent smile. 'Take care of it, will you, Denon?'

He would, of course, but for a moment he felt a sinking of the spirits: failed artists subsisting on scraps; successful figures for whom this was a traditional way of life, like Fragonard, ageing and henpecked by wife and mistress but hard at work, they would all expect him to protest, to resist this change. They would be outraged when they found their old friend playing traitor.

What could he say? 'Bonaparte wants the Louvre cleansed of artists so that the art can be properly displayed.' How would the soon-to-be-homeless artists feel about that?

Should he try to explain that the proper role of a museum was to provide the best possible setting for its paintings and sculpture to be seen by the People? This too would seem outrageous: since when did the People have anything to do with it?

The most shocking aspect of the affair was that, fundamentally, he agreed with Bonaparte. A collection of art – a collection of any sort – carried obligations. The Louvre would hold the finest collection in the world. The great palace, cleaned and restored, and properly lit, would house all the paintings and statues he had loved in their original, often imperfect settings.

Not everything went smoothly: he wrote to Fontaine, the government architect:

You have dismantled, sir, both the public and the staff latrines without making alternative accommodation available. I have the honour to point out to you that the museum is unable to dispense with these conveniences, either in the case of the public or the staff. I therefore invite you urgently, sir, to reinstall them as soon as possible in order to avoid *ordure* being deposited in the courtyards, the staircases and perhaps even the exhibition rooms of the museum – a situation that will infallibly arise . . .

The dismantling of masterpieces, wrenching them from their altarpieces and monasteries, their *palazzi* and public rooms, no longer troubled him. He was convinced now that this was where they belonged, where they would be cared for, kept safe, and be put on view to the eyes of the world. The Louvre would be the museum of all Europe; the greatest museum in the world. It was a sacred trust.

'You know what you're doing, don't you?' one of the dispossessed remarked as he watched the builders move in. 'You're behaving like a vandal.'

V gave his beatific smile. 'Vandals destroy. I am preserving.' And among what he preserved was not only the plunder from Europe, but those artefacts the British had permitted them to bring back from Egypt.

For the soldiers it had been a battlefield, but Egypt had revealed herself to him, lifting one veil after another, in the course of that year: Rosetta with its courtyards, its date palms and bananas; Cairo, dirty, ugly, crowded, yet with a strange, serene beauty when the Nile in flood transformed the city into an oriental Venice. The scholars had measured and done their accurate drawings of the structures, but for him the temples, and, above all, the tombs, were peepholes into an unsuspected past, in whose underground chambers, when his torch lit up the dark, his were perhaps the first European eyes for four thousand years to see the walls brightly painted with frescos, mud floors piled with gilded furniture, statues and the jewelled, swaddled figures of dead kings.

And he had carried home, too, images of the living people; filling whole notebooks with drawings of the men, some proud, some abject; the women with dark eyes and supple hands, the children with their putti-like roundness. There was one child unlike the rest, a child screaming, in agony, who had survived and learned to smile . . . He peers into the dimness, trying, but failing, to bring the child into focus . . .

Zenobia's eyes have skimmed the pages; she has glanced at the pictures: the battles, the pretty women lounging in their filmy trousers, the changing landscape as the artist and the soldiers moved up the Nile, facing privation and danger. Now she, too, is approaching, unaware, a place of danger. She turns a page and begins to read. Baptiste, watching her face, waits with a sense of dread.

The Veil of Isis

Battle scene and the death of Brigadier Duplessis

The day began with confusion and alarm. The sight of the French was always a signal for villagers to panic, to anticipate punishment and flee. In vain, the soldiers would signal that all they wanted was to take a tract of land, not slaughter the locals. Occasionally, with the help of translators, the message was accepted, but when the troops reached the point on the Nile where the tiny island of Philae lay across the water, they failed to allay the villagers' fears. For days the French attempted to negotiate. Finally they ran out of patience. The advance guard improvised rafts, met by howls, threats and showers of spears hurled by desperate natives.

The scholars, regarded as a liability, were kept away from the action, but V slipped through the troops almost to the water's edge and sketched the Nubians on the far shore, the men naked, women wearing a small fringe of cloth and beads.

When the villagers saw the foreigners making ready to cross the river, soldiers in uniforms, buttons glittering bright as knives, shouting and waving threatening weapons, crossing with cannon and ammunition, they realised they could no longer defend their homes: escape or death were the only choices. Some jumped into the water and began swimming desperately away from the island, towards the farther shore. Parents of babies and young children carried away those they could, but some, unable or unwilling to risk the long swim, were thrust beneath the surface and drowned, to save them from what might follow if they were left behind. Or, with the sort of decision that to the onlooker seems wantonly cruel, unforgivable, to the parents a form of protection against something worse, girls who risked violation by the soldiers were stabbed or wounded by a mother or father, sometimes fatally, but usually in a way to make them less appealing to a possible rapist.

On Philae, the hostile inhabitants assumed the worst.

' "On Philae, the hostile inhabitants assumed the worst." '

Zenobia reads the words aloud, her finger moving down the page:

' ". . . men, women, children, all cast themselves into the stream, to save themselves by swimming; maintaining the ferocity of their character, mothers drowned the children they could not carry, and mutilated the girls –" ' she falters, then carries on – ' "mutilated the girls to preserve them from the violence of the conquerors . . ." ' She has stopped, head bowed.

Baptiste says, 'There is more.'

'You have always known this,' she says. 'You were there.'

'Of course. I was with him.'

V could have stayed behind, remained on the river bank, but he was intrigued by the small island; he had glimpsed a ruined temple, obelisks, and he crossed soon after the advance force, Baptiste following. Among the yelling, the shouting and the noise of the occupying troops, a screaming child would have been easy to overlook. V, however, turned back, catching a high-pitched shriek of such agony that it pierced his ears.

The child lay on the island shore, writhing and twitching on the ground, her spasms as extreme as though she were in the throes of a fit. She was like a creature made out of dust:

her legs, face, hair, thick with dust; only her pale pink mouth stretched in a grin of agony showed that she was human, not an effigy of dried mud and straw. But then, going closer, V saw that the child, a girl of seven or eight, was terribly mutilated, deeply slashed between her legs. In her agony she was threshing, twisting from side to side, her body shaken by convulsions.

Baptiste, slowed down by all the gear he was carrying, was unaware at first why the master, ahead of him, had stopped and dropped to his knees. When he came closer he caught sight of the child, the dark clotted mess at her groin, her legs thin as twigs drenched with the blood from the genital wounding. She was screaming, eyes squeezed shut in terror. He had a momentary flash of the night in the town hall – the Paris heat then had been as intense as this, and Robespierre's jaw had gaped dark and bloody below his closed eyes. Baptiste felt the sour bile rising in his throat again, but there was no time for weakness. The master had wrapped the small body in his own coat, swaddled like an infant, holding her still. He was telling Baptiste to find the army doctor – 'Bring him here now, now!' He seemed to have lost control of his voice; he was shouting.

Baptiste stood for a moment as though dazed, then turned, and ran.

Kneeling over the child, cradling her, V found himself making the sort of soothing, calming sounds that his wet nurse used to croon to him, creating by force of will a sort of hush above which the crash and clatter and shouts of the army became a muted roar. He had forgotten those lilting, murmured half-words that could lull childish fears, ease pain, though his grazed knees or bruises had been gnat bites compared to the horror of this child's suffering. He realised that the small, helpless creature could be dying even as he held her.

★

The surgeon had blinked and stepped back a pace when V unwrapped the bloodstained coat to reveal the child. The doctor was accustomed to blood. Men sustained injuries, limbs were shattered, guts spilled, heads broken. That happened in war. This was something else. The mangled remains of innocents caught up in attack, retreat, invasion, these he was not generally called on to witness, and certainly not to attend to.

'Can you do something?'

There were more urgent demands on the doctor's time, and at first he resisted.

'Prolonging the child's agony might be more cruel than allowing her a swift release.'

'But she might be saved? Can we try?'

'We can try. You'll have to hold her down.'

Baptiste had brought water and clean strips of linen; the wound was cleansed and then – the worst part – the surgeon performed what he termed a counter-operation, using the scalpel, needle and thread to repair the genital wounding.

By evening the island was calm. From across the shore, hidden among the boulders, there might be natives watching the invaders making themselves at home, cooking what small provisions they had, creating a bleak camp. More likely, the villagers would be miles away, fleeing a force from which in fact they had nothing to fear, an army that had quite other aims.

Next day, in the shade of a temple wall Baptiste and V kept watch in turn over the child, fanning her with a palm leaf, to cool her and to keep off the swarms of flies. For the valet this was a duty that brought back to him an old, buried anguish: he was protecting a child, helping her back to life. His own child, his Isabelletta, had died with no paternal hand to ease her pain.

★

Zenobia's dark face is closed, a mask of grief. She carries a memory of pain as though through a veil, its cause, its location lost to her, a mysterious torment, for which she has somehow always blamed herself. Surely she must have been guilty of some terrible misdeed to merit such punishment?

There is no adequate description for that pain. Agony, she learned later from books, has been equated with the pangs of death, but she knows from witnessing it that death can be calm. This pain picked her up in its jaws and shook her like a rat. Agony – she found the word in another of her books; one early lexicographer defined agony as extreme bodily suffering with throes or writhing. And yes, that came close. She remembers the writhing, trying to escape the pain. She screamed, but screaming was no help. At her centre there was blood and mangled flesh. She had been torn apart. The pain achieved a level that was almost dreamlike; she floated on the pain. Until it eased. Her body cooled with water, she gulped liquid that burned her throat but comforted her.

They carried water from the river to wash the child, and the surgeon advised immersion in tepid water to bring down the fever. Later, Baptiste spooned fresh water into her mouth, mixed with some of the master's good Burgundy, which (even travelling light) always accompanied them. Gently he took her small, brown hand and held it, his white fingers curved protectively round her roughened skin.

Finally she slept. In her sleep she moaned and whimpered. Occasionally she cried out, but she no longer threshed convulsively.

V, too, watched over her and took his turn at fanning the child, but between those duties he studied the architecture of the temples that crowded the little island, the small, graceful buildings, the avenue of columns and the finely etched hieroglyphs that covered the high walls. With quick, sure strokes he captured the ancient slabs of stone, the delicate decorations and the surrounding desert landscape.

One small edifice, the temple of Isis, he found so perfect in its modest scale that he stood before it enthralled. If he could carry off, transport, one monument, this would be it. He called to Baptiste. 'No grandeur here, no massive scale, but this little temple touches the heart. This is truly impressive!'

Baptiste observed his master gazing up at the temple wall: the small figure, the dumpy body, legs spread wide, hands on hips. Lost in contemplation, he glowed with passion; in the sunlight his greying curls were bright silver. It would never have occurred to V that he could be impressive.

One of the scientists had told him Philae stood at twenty-four degrees north and thirty-three degrees east, almost at the tropic of Cancer, where the sun reached its zenith at the summer solstice, and turned in its course to go southwards again. It was, in that sense, a furthermost point. This was also his furthermost point so far, and who could know how far he had yet to go? A Mameluke bullet, an Arab sword, a poisonous snake, a crocodile, a fever, could spell the end.

In the blinding white light of midday, while the troops prepared to move on, with the island safely secured – sub-dued, emptied of its inhabitants and scoured free of communal life – V raced to complete his drawings: when the last soldiers were ready to leave the island, he knew he must leave with them.

He stood at the western entrance to the little temple of Isis, studying for one last time the painted, water-damaged walls, two slender obelisks, one still standing. How hard it was to convey the brilliance of it all – the depth of blue in the sky, the pinkish stone, the glowing frescos – in the limited medium of black and white.

He had stood before a temple of Isis at Pompeii years ago, its crumbling steps leading to a ruined courtyard, talking to a pale girl with freckles strewn across her cheekbones, a young woman about to abandon the world. 'Shall I pray for you?' she had asked. And perhaps she had, in her cloister.

Isis was a healer, a giver of life, and once this courtyard, this temple would have been thronged with worshippers, pilgrims, stonemasons, temple workers. Now there was just Baptiste in a shady corner, watching over the child. Life had been restored to her, and it was oddly appropriate that it should have happened here, where the old horror story of the Egyptian gods concluded, with the finding of a buried heart and the beginning of a new life. Isis seeking her husband, the murdered Osiris, lovingly reassembling his dismembered body for one final act of creation, of procreation: Horus, their son. In a sense the story had been repeated now: a wrecked body put together, reborn.

In one of the myths Isis had turned herself into a sparrow-hawk to hover over the body of her murdered husband, fanning life back into him with her long wings. He saw Baptiste was fanning the small creature reclaimed from the dead, waving a palm leaf back and forth to keep away the flies, an unexpected new responsibility for the valet.

V looked down at the child, clean and clad in a shift Baptiste had fashioned out of a scrap of linen. She was able to sit up now, on the blanket, watching them with her golden eyes. To amuse her Baptiste had twined together a wreath of leaves and mimosa blossom and had placed the circlet on her head.

'I see our little one has been crowned,' V said, smiling. He knelt and took her small, bony hand. 'I shall call you after a Nubian queen.' He touched her brow with his fingertips.

'You are Zenobia.'

In the sky above the Seine there is a murmur of thunder; a light pattering of rain in the street. A shawl drawn round her shoulders, Zenobia has stopped reading. The tears slide down her cheeks, drip on to the page. Baptiste, unable to prevent his instinct for protecting the master's property, moves the book out of danger and gently dabs the page dry, taking care not to smudge the print.

She rests a hand on the book, as though drawing strength from it.

'Why was I never told?'

'We – he thought it might confuse you, cause you suffering.'

'Truth is truth. I should not have been deceived.'

Now he feels that familiar ache in his guts, spreading to take possession of his body. Truth? Deception? Was it possible to deceive someone and for the deception to become a sort of truth?

They left the island in the darkness, torches flaring, the light catching the gleam of metal and men's eyes. The sun always surprised them, dropping out of sight too quickly, a velvety black sweeping across the orange and crimson sky with the speed of a theatrical curtain.

V was no longer travelling light: from Philae, loaded on to mules, he had taken terracotta temple lamps, urns, fragments of carved stone. And Zenobia. Wrapped in a blanket against the chill of the desert night, she went with them, a burden, an inconvenience, an unplanned appendage.

He had attempted disengagement, seating her on a prominent rock earlier in the day, hoping a family member might venture near enough to snatch her back. She remained unsnatched.

'The officers recommend we leave her on the island, with food and water to sustain her until the villagers return,' Baptiste reported to V.

'Will they return? And what will become of her? If no one returns, she will starve.'

They talked over her head and she seemed to listen, looking up at them, turning first to one, then the other, her eyes glinting in the darkness.

She had kept her wreath, clutched tight in her hand. Now she replaced it on her head, her eyes fixed on V as if she willed him to take notice of her. And he did, glancing down at the withered circlet. The small, dark, upturned face, the circle of leaves . . . there had been a small stone bust topped by a vine wreath long ago, he had delivered it to La Pompadour, an errand where one thing led to another, to one of his many lives. He squatted, smiling, more with resignation than amusement, and adjusted the wreath on her brow.

'What's to become of her, Baptiste? Do we abandon her, now that she's better? Do we simply leave her to her fate?'

They both knew the answer. She joined the books and the booty, the wine and water supply and rode, clinging to a mule, behind the army as the march began. V called across to Baptiste.

'The sheikh of Elephantina is well disposed towards us. We can leave her with him until they hear news of her family. Then she can be restored to her parents.'

Zenobia reads the words aloud, incredulity in her voice: '"Restored her to her parents"?'

Baptiste gives the vestige of a shrug, a helpless movement. 'That was the idea.'

His long, thin face is drawn with exhaustion; she sits slumped, leaning on her elbows. The room has grown chill; a hint of dawn is inching into the sky, and Zenobia, shivering, repeats, '"Leave her with the sheikh"! As you would offload a sack of vegetables or a parcel of clothing. That was how I was perceived, of course. As an inconvenience. And what happened? I assume the sheikh refused to accept this . . . inconvenience?'

Baptiste's hands are clenched in his lap, his whole body tense. He gets up and makes a show of replenishing the fire, encouraging it to a small blaze. Turns and looks down at Zenobia seated at the desk, her fingers repeatedly touching the book. He is aware that, for different reasons, both are in the grip of intolerable agitation.

He recalls the sheikh's evasive eyes, his unspecific phrases of reassurance, offered along with glasses of mint tea. *Of course Monsieur Denon could assuredly leave the child with his household, there would be no problem. A solution would be found . . .* V had cut through the circumlocution:

'Might one enquire, what solution?'

The sheikh was an elegant man, and he sympathised with these foreigners and their awkwardness: they seemed incapable of entering into the subtle rhythm and cadences of Egyptian life, like a camel attempting to manoeuvre its way through a narrow archway in the kasbah. Clumsy. But he was becoming a little impatient.

V, the born survivor with the gift of sensing the unspoken, picked up the truth of the matter: the sheikh would bow and wave them on their way with his effortless Arab charm and grace. And the child would become irrelevant. Passed on to the servants, who might or might not decide to feed her. Who might or might not be kind. By now V had accepted that the parents would not be claiming the girl: she was tainted goods.

By saving her life, he had done no more than extend her misery. But he could not shrug off the responsibility.

'He picked me up and took me with him, part of the booty: pieces of carved stone, some painted vases, one child —'

'He saved you.'

'I know that.' She sounds drained. Leaning back in the big chair she seems smaller than when she arrived. 'And I am grateful to him. My whole life has been spent thinking how to repay that debt.'

She pushes her fingers through her hair, distracted. 'But there was also the other thing, later. He abandoned me like an unwanted pet dog.'

In her closed face Baptiste sees the hurt she has nursed all these years for the way she was rejected. Now would be the time for truth; now he could explain to her that her life has not been the rejection she thinks. But his nerve fails him. Instead, he reaches for an old story told to him by his mother a lifetime ago, on a night when, aged seven, he was ordered to sleep alone on the floor outside a bedroom door to calm the fears of a pampered young master; a night when, shivering with fear himself, he felt abandoned and unloved.

'There is an old story of a little bird whose mother tried to protect it against the winter frost by wrapping the tiny thing in comforting shawls. The shawls were so tight that the bird could neither sing nor fly . . .' Baptiste gives her a quick look to see how she is taking it. 'In a choice between over-protectiveness and being forced to rely on yourself, I think the latter is preferable. To attempt to protect someone from all harm is not to protect them from harm but to protect them from life.'

She simply looks at him, her eyes as eloquent as words.

'No, it doesn't help, does it?' He sighs. There was, after all, another side to the story.

Colloquy in a Cloister

Arriving at the convent of Santa Chiara in Naples Baptiste was by no means sure he was at the right place. Not much to guide him: a name, the master's recollection of a meeting years before with a freckled girl who might not even be here. Might no longer be alive. He knocked on the door with muted expectations and asked for Sister Angelina.

The nun who appeared was clearly the wrong person. Baptiste had been expecting someone elderly, wrinkled, a wise woman with bad teeth, particularly as he gathered she was now the Mother Superior. Sister Angelina seemed radiant with youth. Her hair was hidden, though he assumed it had been chopped off; but across her pale cheekbones he saw the freckles the master had described, a sprinkling of dark gold dust.

She received Baptiste politely but heard what he had to say with bewilderment: the *signore* wished to leave a child at the convent? But it was not an orphanage, they had no funds for such purposes. At which it had been for Baptiste to explain that his employer wished to place the child with them to be cared for. Regular payments would be made, to cover the cost.

Bewilderment hardened into something less friendly: a gentleman, whose name meant nothing to her, proposed to burden the convent with a child little better than a savage, not to be taken in as a poor orphan of charity, but to be given an education!

'We are not a school, Monsieur. This curious request must be unequivocally refused. Life in the convent is delicately balanced: prayer, a frugal existence. We cannot accept –'

Baptiste cut through her words: 'I recognised you at once, from his description.'

She frowned, narrowing her eyes in disbelief, not pleased. 'How can that be? Who is this gentleman?'

'You met him once, many years ago, in the ruins of Pompeii. He was much impressed by your piety.'

The nun's face remained blank. Casting about for something more to offer her, he remembered an additional detail: 'It was at the temple of Isis.'

He watched the slow blink of recollection, the change seep into her face: a memory of a distant, sunlit day amid ruins, a conversation long forgotten.

'Ah,' she said. 'The Frenchman who talked about the goddess, the giver of life. He had a singular smile.'

'He has it still.'

'He asked me to pray for him.'

'Evidently your prayers were answered.'

'He is well, then?'

'Very well.'

'I am glad to hear it. But in this matter, I cannot help him.'

'I shall explain your position. He will know you would have helped had it been possible.' He gave a small, helpless shrug. 'If you could have seen the child, that day. Mutilated, bleeding, left for dead. He saved her life. To have abandoned her in Egypt would have been leaving her to die a second death.

'Now it is a question of what sort of life she will lead. We rough men,' he said, choosing his words carefully, 'are at a loss in such a situation. He wants to give her a chance to make a good life for herself. Well, we shall have to look elsewhere. And hope . . .'

From the courtyard outside a small sound of woe

320

penetrated the room: the wail of a frightened child. Sister Angelina's fingers reached for her rosary and she moved towards the door. The small, pinched creature stood on the threshold, staring up at them. Baptiste had tried to teach the girl a few words of Italian in preparation for the event, but they remained unspoken. She backed away and sank to the ground, mewing like a frightened cat. Everything about her was clenched, even her toes.

Sister Angelina shook her head. 'What you ask is impossible,' she said firmly.

'I understand. But perhaps you could advise . . .' Baptiste was playing for time.

For a while they walked in the cloister, past the yellow majolica columns with their brilliantly coloured flowers and birds. A fountain glittered at one end, and as they talked, the splashing water covered the sound of their voices, sealing them into a hushed conversational intimacy. Baptiste was discovering unsuspected ingenuity within himself: describing the appalling conditions in which he and his master had existed in the desert. Conjuring up the landscape and monuments of Egypt, he captured her attention, drew questions from her, prolonged the interview, finding to his surprise that he had learned to love antiquity, as he created pictures in words, describing the sphinx buried in sand, the statues, the stone lions, the Nile. And, finally, the tiny temple of Isis, so like the one she had admired at Pompeii, which rose from the rocks of Philae, the little island where the panic-driven natives had hacked and drowned their own children, 'to save them'. Tears came to her eyes but she remained adamant: she feared the child would be too much for them, unteachable, resistant to taming.

They turned and looked at the small, dark figure trailing behind them. She had paused by a column, looking closely at the gleaming surface, the dark yellow background, the blues and greens of the flowers. She touched a ceramic petal, cautiously, caught Baptiste's eye and smiled at them both, sharing her pleasure and surprise. He glanced at the nun and saw the way she watched the child. He prepared himself for a lengthy discussion. But he knew the cause was won.

Sister Angelina suggested that Baptiste should not delay leaving: extending the farewell could prove unhelpful. He embraced the child but when he released her she clung to him, wailing, clutching his legs, his feet. Then she shrank to the ground. As he left the room and was shown out to the office where the practicalities would be discussed, he could hear a soft keening from along the corridor. Just once he looked back. She had wrapped her thin arms round her knees and was moaning quietly, rocking to and fro. Deep within him, a pain began to grow.

Zenobia's hands are on the book; she draws it towards her, pressing down, as if she fears it might fly off the desk and out of her reach. 'Is there more? About the child? After leaving Philae?'

'A few lines. It was, after all —'

'A journal of his travels in Egypt. An account of an adventure he shared with Bonaparte. Yes.'

'If you knew how much he left out! So much precious research, so many observations, drawings, discoveries. The Institute later produced a huge official tome. You were —'

'A detail. An anecdote along the way.'

'I would say he was — for once — discreet. Would you have wished to be the subject of salon gossip?'

She shakes her head, mouth downturned. 'Yet, at the convent, later, they could have told me. Even he, in one of his letters . . .' A silence. She sees he is distracted, and she lifts her head as though she, too, now is listening for a sound from another room. She frowns.

She asks, 'How long has he been unwell?'

'He was in perfect health until yesterday. It was the icy rain . . . a chill. I shall take up his coffee, later.'

He gets up a little stiffly from the chair. 'He may be awake.' At the door he hesitates. 'I have to see if he needs anything.'

The door closes behind him. She presses her hands to her face, rocking to and fro in the chair, unknowing that this is a gesture she learned as a child. After a few moments she turns again to the leather and fine paper, the printed words. "Mothers mutilated the girls to preserve them from the violence of the conquerors . . . A little girl of seven or eight . . . a cut, inflicted with brutality and cruelty . . . "

And: "I departed at dark night, loaded with my booty, and my little girl . . ."

The troops had battled on, but faced with hostile forces and plague, the heart had gone out of them; it was simply a matter of time. Bonaparte left the army to do what it could – 'We have beaten the Turks!' he announced encouragingly, as he slipped past the British blockade and sailed back to France ahead of the bad news.

V left with him, feelings in turmoil. Later, others recreated what they thought went on in Egypt. He was there, drawing from life and death. Here and there, in every room of the house on the Quai Voltaire, in drawers, tucked between the pages of books, there are images of Bonaparte, when V caught the General on the wing, against a desert horizon, at a military briefing, even on horseback; sketches, etchings, drawings. Nobody wants them any more. Once they were icons: Bonaparte in Egypt, a heaven-sent theme.

When they sailed home, they stopped at Corsica en route to France and anchored in the bay at Ajaccio. By sheer force of oratory and a magnificent disregard for the facts, Bonaparte converted humiliation into its opposite. The Egyptian campaign was – officially – a triumph. From local hero he became a god: the flags, the welcoming cannon boomed, the cheering populace surrounded their vessel in little boats packed so tight the harbour became land. Hail the returning conqueror! Nobody realised till much later that it had been a defeat. When V got back to Paris, Gros asked if he could borrow some of his sketches, to make a painting of the General visiting the plague-ridden in the convent outside Jaffa. And then Gros got it all wrong, or rather, made it up. Never trust an artist. And there was Thiebault's confection: Bonaparte, Christlike, touching the plague victims. V had been grimly amused by the romantic idealisation: in fact, the General strode through the hospital without pausing; no laying-on of hands took place. But then, V recalled, he did something astonishing: he refused to leave the sick men behind to be butchered by the enemy, as expediency would have dictated. He insisted on waiting, so that the mortally sick and wounded could die surrounded by their comrades, a delay that could have proved fatal for the regiment – and for the Commander-in-Chief. No wonder the men loved him.

How adept the great man had been at self-presentation. As skilled as La Pompadour. Canvases glowed from walls as proof. The battlefield! The glory! The coronation! V finds it hard now, to pick out a favourite; the muck in the medicine bottle must be fogging his mind, but he'll settle for David's romantic warrior riding a fiery Arab steed across the Alps – in reality it had been a mule, with Bonaparte in his usual plain grey greatcoat, not the swirl of crimson silk in the portrait, but Jacques-Louis had never been a man to let a fact get in the way of an emblematic image.

Best not to dwell on the darker days, the fall, the sadness of exile, the great man mewed up on that godforsaken island. V had wept, the last time he saw the Emperor. His hero was much changed: fat, bloated, his back stooped. It was all over.

★

Looking back, which is the most frequently adopted view he has of life these days, he has always been aware that a man can skim through life and with agility, ducking and weaving, stay afloat. On with the ball, the *divertissement*. The word means both an entertainment and a distraction, and there have been many distractions; too many. It irks him that the History of Art, worked on for so many years, remains unfinished, but what pleasure there has been along the way.

He had known only briefly the shared happiness of life with the one person he truly loved, but maybe a life with people he loved in various ways was to be his consolation, a life filled with beauty and the warmth of friends, laughter, the generosity of women.

Dying is confirmed as a fact of life with the passing of time. People are inconsiderate, they fall away: the Emperor, sad Joséphine, parted from her roses, Prud'hon, Byron and his fellow Englishman, William Hamilton, who quoted Shakespeare to V as they listened to a faraway mandolin in the ruins of Pompeii. All in their boxes now. And David mortally sick.

He must turn his mind to something more cheerful, and the future does not inspire confidence. But before he can summon up a moment of long-ago laughter, of *jouissance*, Baptiste has slipped through the door and is clucking disapprovingly like a mother hen.

No doubt the valet plans to increase his discomfort with another dose of devil's linctus. 'Not now, Baptiste!' he would say sharply, under normal circumstances. But, like his limbs, his voice is not obeying him today. As his bedclothes are rearranged, he decides to lie still, mouth and eyes clamped shut.

'Look at you! You have thrown off your coverings.'

Is this the way to address a man who burned in the Egyptian sun with Bonaparte?

Hortus Inclusus

From the beginning there had been specific instructions about the child's education: Italian was a beautiful language of course, the language of Dante, but it appeared Monsieur thought French should also be acquired – in addition to the Latin that would presumably be part of convent routine. Now a letter arrived that made mention of mathematics and geography. Consternation in the convent: the distant benefactor was generous and Sister Angelina did her best to follow his wishes, but this was a new problem.

Apprehension swirled like mist: mathematics and geography? These were not skills to be found among nuns. Nor should they be. God was not served by daily recitations of latitude and longitude, by multiplication and division, but by prayer. In other circumstances the child could have found herself ejected from the convent, or the benefactor's instructions might have been quietly disregarded while the little heathen was saved for the Lord, taught humility and competence with needle and embroidery thread. But Sister Angelina found herself fired with an ardour that was almost improper, an urge to try and assist the transformation of the small, wild creature. A child close to death had been brought back to life; a lost soul had been put into her hands. She was aware that her own path to God had not been the usual one: the convent had been a place of safety, her sequestration an escape from the conjugal forced labour and secret tears of an arranged marriage. She found herself wondering what sort of mind could be awakened in this dumb, frightened creature? How far could the transformation go?

From time to time a nun fell ill – there were diseases that could penetrate the convent walls. On these occasions Sister Angelina sent for the doctor. While one of the sisters chaperoned proceedings, the physician made his examination, prescribed medication or treatment – did what was necessary. And when the sick woman had been attended to, the Mother Superior and the medical visitor found their way to a quiet corner not altogether on a direct route to the entrance.

Today, as they circled the cloister, he asked, as usual, 'And how are you yourself, Sister?'

And she replied, as usual, that she was well.

She noted that the lines around his eyes had grown deeper; his hair was less luxuriant than it used to be. But his eyes were bright. She touched his hand, briefly.

'What news?' she asked, not something a nun should wish to know, and studied him while he talked: often his face gave her as much as his words. The pale skin shone with vitality, the freckles dark against his cheekbones. Her older brother was her conduit to the outside world.

But today Sister Angelina had questions, questions concerning mathematics and geography and the ethics of directing a life in one course rather than another, akin to changing the course of a river. Did one have the moral right? And then, pre-empting his reply: 'Is not an open mind preferable to a closed one?'

Her brother's eyebrows rose sharply. 'I suspect that would be regarded as a heretical question by your masters! The Church dislikes questions.' He turned to practicalities: the child had, it seemed, learned to speak, to read, to count. 'Now,' he suggested, 'you must teach her to think. After that, it will be for her to choose.'

In the normal way a convent child was instructed in

obedience; restricted in experience and taught to fear and mistrust the outside world. All part of the maintaining of innocence (independence of mind being a sure route to ruin). In another convent any sign of spirit in Zenobia might have been punished, stamped out. So she was lucky: her own emerging character, a stubborn and implacable constitution, would help to drive her through barriers and discouragement, but the benediction was the presence of Sister Angelina. The child was given a good Catholic name for official purposes, but Angelina permitted opinions others would have considered unacceptable, encouraged questions.

Only one avenue remained closed: when Zenobia asked about her beginnings, and how she came to be at the convent, Sister Angelina had little to offer her: a country called Egypt across the sea filled largely with sand. Her family, she was told, had perished. She owed her life to a distant philanthropist who provided for her.

In time, on those occasions when the doctor was sent for, when treatment was required, it became accepted for Zenobia to assist him with tasks that could be unpleasant: she learned to lance trapped putrefaction, cleanse a wound, to cool and calm a convulsive fever; even to diagnose the possible cause of this or that condition. She was learning to read the body, to draw conclusions and suggest action. One day, when the visitor had left, she asked Sister Angelina how a person might become a doctor and Sister Angelina replied that one became a doctor by attending medical school and studying for many years. As Zenobia's eyes brightened it then became necessary to explain that to become a doctor one also had to be a man – which might have put an end to the barely formed ambition. But Zenobia's curiosity unexpectedly led to a different conclusion. For this she had to thank Sister Angelina's brother, though he was unaware of his part in her plans. Helping him change a dressing on one of his visits, she asked about his own training to be a doctor: Where had he studied medicine? In some faraway big city, she supposed.

'No. I studied in Salerno.'

He had been fortunate. The ancient medical school at Salerno just down the coast had admitted him; a place unique for its enlightened attitudes, a place where married students were allowed to study. Also Jews. And Women.

'Women?'

'Yes, Salerno has always accepted women.'

He was too busy applying the dressing to notice her expression.

When Zenobia decided to run away, her first thought had been to get as far from the convent as possible. But thanks to Angelina's brother she saw that she might find a hiding place nearer to what she had learned to call home.

Now she was grateful for those little regular sums that arrived year after year, folded within a sealed letter beginning always, 'My dear Zenobia', and ending, 'With affection'. Until the day communication ceased, abruptly, without explanation, cutting her off from a conversation that brought colour and adventure and the thrill of the wide world into her tiny white-walled cell. The letters had been a lifeline and it had snapped.

As she wrapped the envelopes carefully in a square of silk and placed them at the bottom of her bag, she called up words from memory, and mentally navigated her way from page to page, from city to city,

'*My dear Zenobia, I have mentioned St Petersburg before . . .*'

'*My dear Zenobia, in Florence there is a statue . . .*'

'*In Mantua, in the palace of the Duke there is a chamber . . .*'

'*In Rome, the fountains . . .*'

Centres of delight, clearly, but the city that more than any other had taken root in her mind and heart, the city described in the letters with such vivid nostalgia, such an ache of loss, was Venice. She read and reread the descriptions of this magical, floating necklace of islands linked by gondolas and bridges, its masked balls and music, its brilliance, and vowed that she would see it one day. But Venice was a distant goal, one that must wait.

When she packed her bag and escaped, she knew where she wanted to go. But first she must find her way through Naples, a place she had barely seen. The nuns were kindly, and thanks to Sister Angelina she had enjoyed unusual privileges, books, lessons, freedoms, but the freedom did not extend beyond the cloister and the *hortus inclusus*: the garden was beautiful, and she had helped to maintain its scented richness, but the wall that surrounded it was high and the gates were locked.

Slipping away from the convent, unseen, early in the morning as supplies were delivered from the market, she found herself in a place of teeming, pullulating crowds, of noise, of brusque voices and pungent smells. Each new experience was like a blow. Narrow, twisting streets lined with tall, flat houses went steeply downhill, slippery underfoot with running water and filth. Unaccustomed to weaving her way through busy streets she was buffeted, thrust aside by hurrying people. So tall were the houses that the street itself lay in the shade, only a narrow strip of brilliant blue glimpsed high overhead.

There was a moment, that first day, when she almost lost her resolve; when she contemplated turning back, knocking at the convent door and falling back gratefully into the calm and isolation. Then, reaching into her bulky bag for a coin to buy bread, she touched a silk-wrapped package: the letters.

She bought the bread and walked on. Salerno was, after all, not so far away, and her determination had been building for a long time.

★

In the salon on the Quai Voltaire Baptiste listens while Zenobia describes her escape from the convent.

'Were you aware of the pain you caused? They feared for your safety; a girl alone. Sister Angelina was distraught. We were all anxious.'

'Surely,' she says, 'for him it simply meant that an inconvenient responsibility had been removed.'

She had in truth given no thought to their anxiety. 'And in any case Sister Angelina knew I was capable of survival.'

'She blamed herself. The fault was clearly hers in allowing you too much freedom. She saw your flight as her punishment.'

Zenobia knows she should feel mortified; express remorse. But she can only recall her leaping elation, the sense of wonder she experienced, when she reached Salerno: a new world lay before her, boundless. A world of learning. Her first lesson, shockingly, had been to find that her savings would pay for little more than her food. Again, tenacity saved her: she sought out mothers with small children; women who needed help of one sort and another; widowers, the old – no one was overlooked, and before long Zenobia had found people to teach her, in return for hours worked.

'It seemed like a dream and, alas, it proved to be so: one day we were studying, tranquil; the next, officials arrived, with soldiers, and broke down the doors – in fact there was no need for force, they were not locked. We kept asking: what have we done wrong? In the end someone told us Napoleon's brother-in-law, Murat, had been made King of Naples and was penalising us for some past political misdemeanour.

'They closed down the school but they could not close down our minds. We continued, in rooms, here and there, in one house and another, anywhere a few students could be crowded in. I was allowed to go on studying.'

★

334

She had letters of recommendation from Salerno, one to a physician in Bologna, another to a professor in Padua. The professor was kind, and allowed her to extend her studies, but he felt he must point out to her that even were she to complete her medical education and gain a degree, she faced an insuperable problem: 'You are a woman. You would not be allowed to practise.'

Nevertheless she persevered; like a thirsty plant she sucked up knowledge, she made herself useful, equipped herself with skills and understanding she would never be allowed to employ.

'I was lucky,' she says now to Baptiste, 'to find myself in Padua; perhaps nowhere else could I have learned so much that I needed to know.' Padua, where they told her how the Englishman Harvey had followed the trail into the mystery of blood and its movement; Padua, which had a clinical medical ward based on the blasphemous notion that disease was physical, and not the result of sins or random bad humours. She dared to hope for the first time that her pain might not be her own fault.

She met with kindness, first at Salerno, later from strangers, some who understood her need to be of help to the sick, to ease their suffering. They sympathised, but they also knew that what she sought was impossible. 'A woman cannot practise medicine. The law is clear.' But there were unstated exceptions.

'For the poor,' she tells Baptiste, 'for the old, the hopeless, the lines of the law were blurred. I was permitted to ease the last days of the dying in a hospice, to care for orphans, widows, drunkards, the deranged. Those I could help. And women giving birth without the benefit of husband or family.'

Here, above all, she felt her skills most needed. Women died often, and puzzlingly, in childbirth. And she sensed a curious familiarity about this suffering: blood and mangled female flesh, agony and writhing, so like what she had known. Reluctant to reach into the womb as physicians so often did, straight from the dissecting room to the delivery bed, with their casual, wrenching hands, she held back from invading the woman's body, encouraging, easing, participating in pain that culminated in the delivery of a precious gift. One that survived.

'To bring a life into the world . . .'

Her hands bloody, she held the child, cradling the most fragile of objects. She saw a movement beneath the tiny skull like the beating of a bird's heart. She handed the small bundle to the mother. And for a moment she forgot herself, she was at ease.

There were occasions when one of the legally sanctioned practitioners of the trade, sympathetic, drawn by her polished dark beauty, offered affection, attempted physical closeness. But for Zenobia that was *terra incognita*, and one she had no wish to explore. She could not imagine a man knowing her body, with its misshapen, cobbled-together parts. She functioned as a woman only so far as everyday biological needs dictated. Sometimes she wept, when she read about love between a man and a woman, as a prisoner might weep to hear about mountain tops, open fields, a fair wind in a traveller's face. She knew she should be grateful – she *was* grateful – for the gift of life. It was simply that, just now and then, she wanted more.

Now and then she studied a globe and traced the outlines of a place called Egypt, she followed the course of the great river which cut through the sand that covered the land, as fields and streets did in Italy. If she should find the means to cross the sea, where would she go? Who could she ask, a lost soul without a family, without a birthplace she could search for?

Instead, one day, she decided it was time to see the floating city of the letters.

★

But when Zenobia got to Venice it was a place much changed. Her Venice was bleak. On a January morning it was rimed with frost; later, rain gleamed on the paving stones and speckled the canals which lay sullen, a dull grey, not the jade green of her expectations.

She found the streets filthy, the rooms shabby, the people poor. On every side, the *palazzi* of pink and red and ivory she knew from the letters had fallen into decrepitude. Washing hung, dripping, from balconies. The city seemed forsaken; only foreign visitors, mostly from England, wrapped in wool and fur, braved the sad prospect.

Zenobia saw the city as in a double image: how it was and how she had dreamed of it. She was not an ideal visitor: she experienced Florian's and Quadri's from afar; the price of one coffee in a tiny china cup would have kept her from hunger for days. She had a proxy relationship with luxury, watching the waiters swirl and bow, close enough to sniff the fragrance of the Venetian kitchen.

Walking the narrow passageways she glimpsed interiors where lamps shone on gilded mirrors and painted ceilings; chandeliers glimmered on velvet hangings and vast dark canvases, and the sound of music drifted from open windows. For an inner circle the dance went on, but the city was forlorn; its glow had faded; the gaiety described in the letters, subdued. The true *dolcezza di vita* was gone and she was swept with a stab of loss for the swirl and glitter of the great days. This was a Venice pocked and raddled; bad times had put a mark on the fair features, and the mask was no longer in place.

Caught between what had been and what was to come, Zenobia mourned the death of a Venice she had never known, the silencing of the old music. Poets would lament the sadness, but Venice defied destruction and drowning. Venice, like Lazarus, would find new life – like Lazarus would be raised from the dead. Repeatedly.

There would come a day when Zenobia saw Venice from a hotel with damask silk walls and a roof terrace where she would stand and watch the blue sky purpling into dusk. She never did have coffee at Florian's, being a serious-minded woman, but she went back, always finding something new, something undiscovered . . . She went to Venice weary and felt life rekindled within her. The Lazarus moment.

The Sorcerer's Apprentice

When the child was put into the care of the nuns, Baptiste had made it clear that while his master would provide for her, he wished to remain anonymous. He explained that it was the French who had destroyed her village, who were the cause of the horror and her homelessness. It would be less of a burden on the child if she knew none of that; she would not feel pulled between hatred and gratitude.

Baptiste communicated regularly with Sister Angelina on his master's behalf, sending funds, checking that all was well with the child. It had early on been explained to Zenobia that she owed her life to a faraway philanthropist. To an enquiring spirit this was the beginning, not the end of a statement: questions tumbled out, but Sister Angelina, for once implacable, refused to say more. The deviousness of children should never be underestimated, however: Zenobia simply waited, and watched. Before long, with the help of judicious eavesdropping and a glance at letters left accidentally on Sister Angelina's desk, she had learned at least a name.

One day, a few months later, Zenobia handed a folded sheet of paper to Sister Angelina. 'Please send this to the gentleman in Paris. I want to thank him.'

When a letter from the convent arrived for V, Baptiste, as usual, opened the envelope. He read Sister Angelina's apologetic explanation. Then he turned to Zenobia's letter, a touchingly eager note designed to show that she could now both read and write in French, to show, as she put it, that her life had been worth saving. He studied it, smoothing the page, noting the childish, uneven writing, and found himself suddenly in tears. He intended to carry it, with the rest of the day's mail, into V's study, but paused for a moment, contemplating the letter as it lay on the table. A decision hung in the balance.

The scales were evenly weighted: on one side, loyalty to a master who had never knowingly been less than kind and his own dislike of deception. On the other, an awareness that throughout his life he had put his master's needs before his own; that loyalty and caution had robbed him of a life. Had he acted differently, long ago, he now asked, would his own daughter be alive?

The death of a child is an event apprehensive parents rehearse constantly: accidental drowning, infection, a fall from a swing – small flies are so easily swatted by the hand of fate. Most parents manage to live with the terror which lies just below the surface of everyday family life like a shark on a shallow reef.

Composers and artists have an enviable means of release on such occasions, laying out personal anguish on manuscript paper, scoring a sonata in the key of grief – even with unconscious prescience mourning a loss yet to be experienced; an artist who is also a parent can paint a portrait luminous with a sense of what is to come. An awareness of the shark.

Pulled between grieving as a parent, and marking the event as a poet, an artist is faced with a destructive conflict: as a father he can weep, but as a poet he is complicit with death, using the loss of a child as he would use anything else. For a parent, death can offer no consolation. For an artist a work can live on.

But Baptiste was not an artist. His secret daughter died of a fever. He could mourn her only in secret.

After troubled nights, he had known false dawns when, for

a moment, memory failed to catch up: a new day could be welcomed. Then, like a blow on a bruise, came consciousness: the desolation, the dullness of pain that must be lived with.

Moreover, V was increasingly occupied; the Egyptian book had brought him fame; it was difficult to find the right time to put any question to him – 'Not now, Baptiste!' – there was a lecture to give, a reception to attend . . .

And, increasingly, the First Consul required his presence. There were enemies who said his master was the First Consul's poodle, but Baptiste saw it differently: for V, Bonaparte was the apotheosis of a hero: no longer a man like other men.

The valet saw how the master's affection for a thin young Corsican general had grown into an unquestioning devotion that robbed him of the power to demur or criticise. Once, this or that situation, this or that problem would have been discussed informally while Baptiste was shaving V, or helping him dress for a ball or a banquet. But there was no time, these days, for their old conversations. No time to raise the matter of replying to the girl in the convent.

It was not a happy time for Baptiste. He had imagination. He recognised himself in an unflattering role: a poor creature concerned with cravats and the cut of a coat who spent his time in readying others for activity while he remained invisible. Perhaps it had always been so, but now he saw it for himself.

He removed Zenobia's letter from the silver salver and placed it in a drawer. The remaining letters, invitations, visiting cards and official communications he carried in to his master. Later, when his duties had been completed, he sat before a blank sheet of paper and thought for a while. He picked up his pen, expecting it to scald his fingers, it was, after all, an instrument of trickery. If he used it, he would be stepping off the highway of propriety on to a shadier track; one of deceit, lies, and possibly danger.

With a deep breath he put pen to paper:

'My dear Zenobia . . .'

It was a double betrayal: he had not told his master about the child's letter and he was about to steal his identity – even his language. Now he was grateful for those painful nights in Sicily when he became, for a while, his master's hand, resentfully writing down the words dictated, seeing how a sentence could be shaped to a purpose, even disciplining his scrawl into a script more appropriate to a man of letters.

Learning Italian in Naples, urged by V to persevere when he flagged, he had exclaimed one day that he could manage well enough with simple sentences, but more complex verbs he found difficult: 'I can cope with the present tense. I don't have much confidence in the future.'

'How pessimistic of you, Baptiste!' He was aware that the master was teasing him, but for once Baptiste remained grim, pouring coffee without responding. Still, he had persevered at the language, without which he would never have found a way, later, to talk to Lucia. Reading the master's letters had taught him how to use words. Nothing in life was wasted, he now realised.

'Was anyone so often revived as Lazarus?' V asked Baptiste, in one of those questions that needed no answer. 'I mean to put some of them in the book. A long list, and here I am, adding to the number with one of my own.' He laid down the scalpel, flexed tired fingers and took a mouthful of wine. 'A miracle, the way a dead man comes to life, on canvas, on plaster, on copper, in wood – there's a Giotto in Padua, one in Assisi, a Duccio in Siena. Caravaggio, of course, and Rembrandt, some studies by Veronese. Florence, Rome - in Venice they're all over the place.'

Baptiste did not feel qualified to offer an opinion on a work of art: he was a servant, not a gentleman, but he thought he understood about Lazarus. It was the possibility of a second chance, the 'if only' dream made real: touch me, bring me back to life. Not that he said so to his master.

Later, he justified his act of betrayal to himself: the master had always been concerned not to become known to the child; a relationship could only add to her confusion about her past. But the truth was that, for Baptiste, writing to Zenobia was a way of bringing his own dead child back to life. When he wrote 'My dear Zenobia', he lived a Lazarus moment: he cooled the Venetian fever, he bathed the burning flesh, healed his daughter: Isabelletta lived.

He slipped into deception as a man steps into the sea: first a toe, then a foot, wading a little further, not too deep, finally out of his depth. He intended only a brief response: congratulations on her achievements, encouragement in her studies, good wishes. But of course she wrote again, she told him of her day, what flowers grew in the *hortus inclusus*, how reading was teaching her about the world. Soon his parrying responses were abandoned: his caution seemed merely cold. And he saw that whereas in life he could never occupy a central role – he could only hold the coat, brush the hat, guard the bedroom door – in his lies he was freed into an alternative truth. He was drawn into description, story-telling, jokes. Trapped by her innocent questions, he recalled a past for her that both was, and was not, his own: the yellow palaces of Petersburg, the canals of Venice, the black velvet of a gondola against the jade water, the *palazzi* with their marble filigree and painted mooring posts; the way lights would quiver in the opera house as though wavering in the wind of music. He would write just one more letter, he told himself each time. But she would ask about Venice, or about volcanic fire because from the upper floor of the convent she could see Vesuvius, and she could picture him, she said, climbing up through the still-smoking ash.

What had it been like? she asked. How did it compare with Etna?

How could he not write back?

One day he told her about the many paintings in Venice of St Jerome with the lion, the tenderness of that story, of a wild creature tamed and loved, the danger and the beginning of trust. And she wrote, asking: 'What became of the lion? What is the end of the story?'

It was too late to disengage: she delighted in the flow of thoughts and information. And he had her letters, her questions, her admiration, perhaps her love; the delight of knowing that just this once he was not the onlooker with his nose pressed to the window.

'My dear Zenobia . . .' And the years passed.

An Old Lion

Denon working in the Diana Room at the Louvre. Allegorical portrait
by Heinrich Reinhold, after Benjamin Zix. (*Bibliothèque nationale de
France, departèment des Estampes et de la Photographie, collection Hennin*)

The silence in the salon is broken by clocks in room after room – chiming, striking, high and low, some clear as bells, some booming.

Here it is, the moment he hoped never to encounter; the deception, the old guilt, buried deep with the passing of the years, confronting him as he opened the door, when she stood there on the threshold yesterday and said: 'I am Zenobia.'

At first she is bewildered.

'It was you who wrote the letters?'

'Yes.'

'All of them?'

'Yes.'

'So . . .' Words elude her; she shakes her head, incredulous. 'So . . . he had forgotten about me. I had ceased to exist!'

She has risen from the chair and stands, arms crossed tight across her chest, staring at him, her face blank with shock.

'Did he read my letters? Any of them?' His hesitation gives her the clue. 'Did he even *see* them?'

Another silence. Then: 'The fault is mine. Had he known of your letters he would have written to you.'

Baptiste pushes to the back of his mind those occasions when he had begun to speak of the child, to be cut short: 'Take care of it, Baptiste.' A valet took care of details.

'I never told him. He saw no letters.'

'But you allowed me to believe . . . So my whole life was

built on a lie.' Her voice is colourless, drained of force. 'Why did you do it? I don't understand.'

'I never meant it to harm you. I wanted to make you happy —'

'But you cast me off, abandoned me . . .'

'It was an act of panic, to give me time, to think what to do.'

'And what *did* you do?'

'Nothing. I could think of nothing. But I never forgave myself. I ordered the convent to search for you —'

'And had they found me, what then?'

'I dreamed of how it might be, seeing you —'

'Dreaming is easy!'

His shame, her anger fill the room.

She picks up the bag, holds it away from her as though fearing contamination. 'All lies.'

'They were the truth for me. When I wrote them, I *became* that person.'

'You were pretending! It was just a game.'

'Never. What I described as happening, did happen. I handed the experience on. I was . . . a sort of guide. As to the rest, the questions, your welfare, the . . . feelings. They were entirely my own. I cared about you.'

She paces the room, agitated, squeezing the bulky bag between her hands.

'You remember St Jerome and the lion?' he says, 'Well, suppose St Jerome had saved a poor dying bird one day, bound up its broken wing and put it in a place of safety. And suppose the lion had taken to dropping a worm or two beside the bird, to keep it happy. It would not diminish the saint's original act of kindness. And would it be wrong of the lion to befriend the bird? He too has feelings.'

It had been so easy, at the beginning: he reported that he heard from the convent how well the child was doing, how grateful she was to her unknown benefactor. He was suggesting that a present might be appropriate for her saint's day, when V, overworked and abstracted, broke in: 'Take care of it, Baptiste, would you?' And Baptiste nodded, aware that his master had not even heard what 'it' was.

The valet chose and dispatched the gift – a turquoise set in a silver ring. Already he had made a small decision of his own: swept a little further out on his sea of deception he had begun, at regular intervals, to enclose modest sums of money from his savings – 'to be kept safe for when it might be useful to you'.

Other presents followed: an alabaster box, a shawl, a volume of Ovid. He who had sneered at the fanciful Roman, inwardly heaving sighs of boredom, sometimes of incomprehension, as he listened to yet another story of yet another nymph or god changing shape, now found himself borrowing not only the words of his master, but his passions. At what stage did it cease to be disguise, at what stage did he too change his shape and become another person, neither V nor his valet, but the letter writer, the father figure, the source of comfort and wisdom?

She had in an early letter asked about her beginnings, about the place left behind, and Baptiste found ways to explain and to obscure the detail of the event. He remembered Egypt for her, the hard white light, the heat, the sand – sand that could be soft and yielding, or hard beneath the feet like steel, and driven by the wind, sting sharp as a knife-cut on the skin. But always at a certain point, between the reality of the place and the leaving of it, there was a blur. No mention of the war, or of the horrors that went with it. No mention of her people, whoever they might be. The child was found, the child was saved. 'And how are you progressing with your mathematics?'

The danger signal came in a letter thanking him for a gift – a ring and a piece of silk he felt appropriate for a girl who must be approaching sixteen. The silk was beautiful, she wrote. Though of course the nuns would never countenance the wearing of something so luxurious! Then came the words he had somehow failed to anticipate:

'I hope, before long, to make the journey to Paris, to see you, so that I can thank you in person.'

Had he remained calm, Baptiste could have told Zenobia he was about to leave on a long journey; corresponding would be difficult. He could have warned her that letters might be mislaid. He might have provided himself with an excuse that would also have provided her with some comfort. Instead, on behalf of his master, to Sister Angelina he sent a brief explanation that for the present she would not be able to reach them. Funds would arrive as usual. In an emergency, he could be reached via the bank. This information she should regard as confidential.

And after a night of dark thoughts and too many glasses of wine, he scrawled on the dangerous envelope a note in an untidy hand to inform the sender that Monsieur had moved from this address and his whereabouts were not known. He returned Zenobia's letter apparently unopened.

The silence came as a shock. A pain. The letters, both the receiving and replying, had over the years become central to Baptiste's well-being. He had been given a reason for existing beyond that of being the good servant. Now it was gone.

V was aware of a change; he saw that Baptiste's face had grown more gaunt. The sceptical humour he had relished in his valet was quenched. He meant to have a talk but the publication of *Travels in Upper and Lower Egypt* increased his celebrity. He had become, to his surprise, a luminary, high priest of *le style outre-Egypte* – the art of the Pharaohs was the talk of every salon, he the most sought-after guest.

And Bonaparte was a demanding master. The talk with Baptiste would have to be left for a less busy time. But there was not to be a less busy time.

When the First Consul decided the nation's stock of art needed replenishing, he turned to a man whose taste and eye he had learned to trust. The bond had been forged long ago, one night before the Egyptian adventure, before the Italian triumph, when Bonaparte revealed his view of art: 'Art,' he pronounced, 'is just an imitation of nature.' V stared at the young General, for a moment deprived of words. He rubbed his head, the curls springing up, wiry, as he thought his way to an argument that might convert an unbeliever.

'Study art,' V began, 'and you will learn about everything else; about Athens and Rome, about emperors and slaves, the passing of ancient gods and the birth of Christ, the geography of the world, the discovery of perspective, the development of architecture, the way men and women dress and decorate themselves, the life of plants, the significance of the stars, myths and the way bread sits on a dish. The rise and fall of heroes. The power of love. The truth of seeing . . .'

Bonaparte had always been a good listener. And when the time was right, 'Bring me the best,' he ordered.

The First Consul read his way through V's list – Mantegna, Benozzo Gozzoli, Correggio, Masaccio, Giorgione, Dürer, Uccello . . . at some less familiar names he paused: a female miniaturist, a monk, an obscure Venetian –

'Guardi?'

'A genius,' V assured him. Bonaparte looked unconvinced. V said, 'When Van Eyck finished his portrait of the Arnolfini betrothal, he added a note after his name, to testify he was there. Guardi is doing that, we all –' A momentary, rueful hesitation: 'All true artists are doing that, they're sending us a message. Their work says "I was there".'

'If you say so,' the General conceded, grudgingly. He returned to the names, glanced up at V with an ironical lift of the brows: 'No Corsicans?'

★

'*Ma chère* Bettine . . . I read your letter again, late last night . . .'

As always, while he followed her words, he pictured her, left arm resting on the table, the pen privileged to be held in her hand – ah, to be that pen!

'My dear Zenobia,' Baptiste sometimes found himself scribbling in the margin of a shopping list. And then? What words could he reach for, when he himself had cut off the flow?

Bringing wine or clearing away an empty glass he might glimpse the master's latest letter to Venice, before it was abandoned when a summons came from on high:

'Some news: I am to be made Director, placed in charge of museums – nothing will escape my searching eye! Paintings, sculpture, porcelain, tapestries . . . I feel like a child in a nursery filled with wonderful toys. Can something so pleasurable be called "work"?'

Had Baptiste not cut the link with his eager correspondent, he might have been slipping away to his room, to fill his own blank sheet of paper. Instead, he sank himself in his quotidian duties and grew paler, more silent. He had now lost not one, but two daughters.

Zenobia was introduced early to the inevitable tragedy in the relationship between parent and child, the fragile thread that binds them. The young climb towards the source of comfort, conquering the foothills, the slopes. They reach a brief, elating plateau where parent and child appear to be at the same point – equals. This is an illusion: one is on the way up, the other down; implicit in the meeting is the parting to come. The thread is tightening; one day it will snap. In the fullness of time, parents die, properly lamented or waved off with relief. But how does a child feel, abandoned prematurely by those who should provide security, love? By the untimely death or disappearance of parents?

Zenobia lost her parents. Then came the day when, it seemed, she lost a second father. *No longer at this address . . .* Rejection, less obviously lethal, can bring about a death in the heart.

She was not fooled by the scrawled note; she knew she had been cast off. It was a blow; a wound in which bitterness grew and festered.

V flung himself into his assigned task with fervour. He might have been uneasy, at the beginning, about where a work of art really belonged, but his views had changed. One thing alone had not changed: the paper chain that linked France and Venice.

When Isabella described the opening of a charming new theatre, V teased her with questions about the latest young poet – were his poems worthwhile? did he make her laugh? 'Merely thinking of you I smile, then feel like weeping. So many miles between us, our words travel overland like pilgrims, but thoughts can fly through space, unimpeded. I think of you and you are here.'

He longed to be with her in Venice, but Bonaparte took up ever more of his time, demanding monuments for what was becoming, increasingly, 'his' city: the First Consul had a weakness for obelisks, triumphal arches and fountains. 'I provide them. And we need more paintings, always more. We will have the finest temple of art in Europe. The world will applaud what they see, Paris will be the world's museum!'

Baptiste had no such distractions to occupy him. Now he would have been grateful for faraway places. Danger. Distraction. Anything to break up the emptiness of the day. Of life without Zenobia.

The delicate task had been achieved: out with the artists, in with the art. *Voilà la Musée Napoléon*, as V had renamed it.

As one step follows another, the *gentilhomme du roi*, the youth who catalogued a royal collection of marble, the young man who offered the monarch Greek vases from Italy, had become the bailiff, then the procurer, the official plunderer – some said the thief – the eye of Napoleon, ever at his heels, like a shadow. And here he was with his *Légion d'honneur*, greeting the man whose dream he shared, embarking on a tour of the premises: no messy artists cluttering up the place; new, spacious galleries, new windows. And of course, the art, displayed in a new way.

The wall of Raphaels, *The Marriage at Cana* . . . Immortal! A few hundred years? A dismissive Corsican glance: 'Some immortality!' On to the next room.

Baptiste, helping V out of his coat, noted a downward turn to the muscles of his master's increasingly wrinkled face. 'Well? Was he pleased?'

'He approved of the hanging.' V's voice was flat. 'It didn't take long: he appraises a gallery like a battle terrain.' But the battles were over and the spoils of victory now hung in the General's *musée*.

They had walked through room after room, the walls filled with treasures brought from elsewhere. And slowly, like surf insistently eroding a shoreline, a question nagged at V concerning his part in all this: had his love of art, his own passion for collecting, led him into transgression?

He glanced round his own room now, troubled. 'All these objects, Baptiste. How did we acquire so much?'

We? Baptiste echoed silently. His acquisitions were few indeed. Once he had possessed a wife. A child. Not objects, but treasures. Then he lost them. Later, living a dream, he had been given a second chance. That too was lost.

V was rearranging his cabinet of curiosities to make room for a new addition. In the ancient Egyptian Book of the Dead, the priests weighed the heart of a man against the feather of righteousness in the scales of justice. How would he fare in such an assessment? Was his heart weighed down by sin? Which way would the scales tip?

Soon he had other preoccupations. The next letter to his *chère* Bettine gave her some unexpected news: the revolution, it seemed, had been well named; there was a circularity to its progress: '*Vive l'Empereur!*'

Once more there was a court, and where there is a court, there will be courtiers: *jouissance* was back, and royal portraits. Citizen David, who had captured the tincture of mortality in the features of a murdered Jacobin, was filling vast canvases with the glitter and pomp of a coronation, smoothing out the lines on the Empress's face and catching the Roman hauteur in the imperial profile. Celebrations were in order, at home and abroad.

Over the Grand Canal loomed a curiosity: a newly built Arc de Triomphe. Boats, flags, finery were brilliant against the grey of a cold, wet day; Venice was welcoming the Emperor. But V sensed an uneasy note to the festivities: true, the Emperor was reclaiming the Venetians from the hated Austrians. But it was Napoleon who had handed them over to the enemy in the first place; destroyed their republic; denuded them of their treasures. Seeing Venice *sans* lions, *sans* winged horses, V was stung with regret. But. Again he asked himself, if left here, how much would have survived? His beloved Veronese might have been been lost in the chaos or rotted on the damp wall of the monastery. Restored, it enjoyed a new lease of life in Paris. He had to believe that.

Venetian bitterness simmered. Put out the flags, decorate the boats; but there was ambivalence in the lavish welcome: the Arc de Triomphe that spanned the Grand Canal was, after all, built of wood, hollow.

'*Ma chère* Bettine . . . My impatience to see you is giving me a fever . . . When, when, when can we meet? Send me word.'

The Emperor inspected work in progress: the *Ala Napoleonica*, the Napoleonic wing of the Piazza San Marco, was nearing completion. The architects hovered.

'You've made a good beginning,' Majesty conceded.

V, by his side, was aware that to build the wing with its ballroom and great halls, the Emperor's architects had razed Sansovino's pretty little church of San Geminiano.

'A pity the church had to go,' V commented incautiously, 'it was charming.'

'There's too much charm already in this place. That's the problem. Outside the *charming palazzi*, there's poverty. Inefficiency. The whole *charming* place is sinking into the lagoon, there isn't even a decent burial ground – we need to talk about that. And I intend to fill in the canals: better for trade and communications.'

The argument was logical. But V glanced from the window and worked out an extremely efficient use of canals: one, leading to another, turning a corner, under a bridge, would take him straight to Isabella's window . . . He hoped that the Emperor would find more important things to occupy him.

Still no word from Bettine. V wrote again; frantic to see her: when could they meet? The visit was going disastrously, he added. The Emperor disliked the rain; he huddled inside his greatcoat, shivered and sulked. He tore through dinner in his usual twenty minutes, and leapt up from the table while his entourage was still eating, forcing them to abandon their unfinished food.

'If I hear nothing from you I shall present myself at your door tonight. Be warned!'

A letter from Isabella arrived that afternoon: her husband had not wished to take part in the farce of a welcoming ceremony; he had therefore become diplomatically unwell, in need of fresh air, and was resting at their country house. Isabella was with him.

V wrote back at once: when did they plan to return? Was it possible his reunion with Bettine would suffer the painful hypocrisy of a formal presentation at some official function, he bowing, she inclining her head as they were introduced: 'The Contessa and I are acquainted, Your Majesty. I drew her portrait . . .'

The Emperor liked to have his men about him at all times; there were no off-duty hours. When he himself discreetly retired to a private room for an *intervallo amoroso* with a chosen lady summoned for the occasion, it was swiftly over – the Emperor's carnal pleasures took little longer than his meals – while the courtiers waited in the ante-room.

During one rushed supper he paused in mid-mouthful and announced that he wished to inspect the *Bucintoro*. There was a moment of appalled silence: someone would now have the disagreeable task of reminding him of an awkward fact: his own occupying troops had burned the Doge's glittering barge to ash and melted down its golden filigree decorations for the French exchequer. Who could present him with the unwelcome news that there *was* no *Bucintoro*?

'Ask Denon,' someone suggested. 'He'll find the way to do it.'

But for once V was not at hand.

On the cobbles of the Quai Voltaire there is a pattering of rain that an old man's ears have failed to pick up. The droplets quicken and the wind drives them noisily against the window and now he hears the sound. He finds it soothing. No longer feverish, V feels a gradual chill and shrinks gratefully into the warmth of the comforting sheets. He listens to the rain.

Venice, on that appalling visit with the Emperor, had been rainswept, the deluge continuous, hostile, unwelcoming – or so the Emperor found it, despite the flags and pageantry.

For V it had been . . . how had it been? He tries to concentrate: one Venetian scene can blend into another and there are, after all, so many to choose from.

Then, faintly at first, growing stronger, as a sketch becomes a study that deepens into a finished portrait, Venice returns to him. Not its rich, carnival colours, but a wet, grey day, a man, a narrow bridge, a window.

Isabella's letter had been brief – 'We are back.' A meeting had still to be arranged. He made the familiar journey to the tiny canal, then up the steps to the bridge. He stood in the *piazzetta* at the end of the canal and gazed up at the tall house wavering as if melting in the heavy rain. It had been the custom, in his day, when a private concert was given, to fling open the windows even in cold weather, so that those less privileged could share the music. Sometimes he and Isabella would find themselves by the window and, shielded by the curtain, snatch a moment of intimacy, a kiss as light as the touch of a moth's wing, his hand on her smooth throat, her breast, the nape of her neck.

He looked up at those three windows, a swathe of dark curtain just visible, lights glittering beyond, and listened as music drifted down through open shutters. The old custom survived: the Albrizzis were entertaining this evening.

He could see her in his mind, seated to one side of the salon, her head tilted, the lips curled in that smile she had: a sweet *volupté*. There would be friends, acquaintances, a young man or two hovering nearby, drowning in her dark eyes.

Leaning on the parapet of the bridge he followed the melody: the strings supple, the rhythm sprightly. He caught the eye of a passing local who nodded appreciatively, the rain bouncing off the rim of his hat.

'*Bellissima.*'

He looked back at the window; his gaze pierced the walls and he found her in the gilt and brocade chair, one delicate shoe peeping from beneath her hem. Once, he would have led her to their private boudoir, removed the shoe and kissed her arched foot, her knees, her thighs, breathing in the honeyed smell of her flesh. He could go now, cross the little bridge, present himself at the door, follow the footman through the *palazzo* and see her smile, rise from her chair and come towards him with that swaying walk –

But he would find it impossible to maintain the poise, the appropriate social attitude demanded by a public encounter. He turned away to where his gondola waited. A step down and he sank back into the sheltered velvet cushions. For a moment or two he and Isabella were linked by the music, then as the gondola moved off, Vivaldi grew fainter, and was swallowed into the listening air and the hissing of rain on water.

And on that grim, rainswept evening he was made aware once again of the futility of planning, of dreaming, when a greater power holds the reins. They were to meet the following day: letters had been exchanged, the place, the time arranged. But the Emperor decided Venice had charmed him for long enough. Official protests were swept aside:

'We return to Paris. Immediately.'

'*Ma chère* Bettine, by the time you read this I shall be en route for France, my spirits in desolation . . .'

There were consolations: the work, the journey, the woman of the moment – he was never long without the presence of a charming companion, the warmth of an *amitié amoureuse*. But the woman for all time had always been, would always be, Isabella. This was the fundamental gulf between him and the Emperor, who had learned to live without love, its sweetness turned to ashes. He had watched it happen, witnessed the sad absurdity of a great man in thrall to a woman who could not even appreciate his greatness until it was too late.

The rain is heavier now, washing the cobblestones of the Quai Voltaire and V wonders, *What if?* picking at the scabs of memory as old men do.

What if Joséphine had been generous of spirit and had given her heart to her thin, desperate, lovesick general? Might he have decided Moscow was a journey too far, and found some other route to the future? Might he have spent more time in his museums? Cultivated his garden? Dictated his memoirs at Malmaison, not St Helena. *What if . . .*

And Monsieur Denon, the Chevalier De Non, the Baron, the Emperor's Minister for Art. What if, V asks himself drowsily, instead of choosing the path he did, he had responded differently to Isabella's letter? What if he had made the daring leap?

On one of their drifting, dreaming gondola rides, rereading Virgil, when it seemed the dream would last for ever, Isabella had returned to the story of Dido and Aeneas. Had she perhaps known, already, what the end of their own story would be?

'You realise, don't you,' she had observed, 'that Dido is a threat to the gods. She offers Aeneas the chance of love, of a life both could live if they defy those who pull the strings.'

And when the moment came for him, those who pulled the strings won the day. The choices people make change them, and he was changed.

If there was a military campaign to be fought, he was there, recording the event, assessing the treasure. At Austerlitz he waded in mud till the fungus seeped through his boots and grew into his skin. In Danzig, at almost sixty, he found himself scrambling over the trenches, elated, dodging the bullets, because the Emperor had asked for a progress report on the siege. In Spain, the streets still spattered with blood, the horrors hanging from trees or piled up by the roadside, he moved through the nightmare, searching out hidden works of art like a water diviner. Looting for Napoleon.

It seemed the war dance could go on for ever, the brilliant manoeuvres, the use of men and arms, the building of an empire. But the music faded, the drums died and on a bitter day the great man, broken, finally surrendered – this time to the captain of the *Bellerophon*, the ship that sank the flagship of the French fleet at the battle of Aboukir bay as V watched through a telescope. Here there were no flames, no men crying out, struggling and burning in the water. But there had been death in plenty over the years. V's unswerving devotion to the Emperor had been tested to breaking when he heard how many died in Russia.

It was a strange parting, V in tears, the Emperor remote, except for one brief phrase: 'Look after my museum. *Our* museum.'

And he had, using reason, guile, passion, fighting to hold on to paintings, sculptures, frescos, delaying, disputing, insisting that the Louvre, as it was once again named, was a world museum, the works belonged there. He defended to the last, but he was never going to win the battle.

The terrible day came when the Allies lost patience, and sent in the troops. Helplessly, V watched them plunder – albeit respectfully – his beautiful collection, to 'reclaim their property', in the justifying phrase which he refused to accept. It was as though he had a thousand limbs, and they were amputating them one by one; the treasures were being dispersed, hauled away. Everything so assiduously assembled, so carefully restored, so lovingly displayed, wrenched off the walls, loaded on to carts and bundled off back to where it 'belonged'. He warned the intruders that no one would ever display the works to greater advantage; no city could be better placed to keep them safe, to be their home. Ownership of art is a troubled condition, he can acknowledge that in the counterfeit wisdom of old age, but the stewardship is tested by its success, and he had been an immaculate steward.

The dismantling went on as he watched in distress. Carried away, back to lesser cities, inferior museums, how would they fare, his children – the vulnerable marble, the fragile canvases? At least he had held on to more than a hundred. His best trick: 'You can't touch *The Marriage at Cana*! The fabric is already weakened, the paint fragile; move it again, and I cannot speak for its survival.'

No one had the confidence to disregard his words. He had saved the Veronese. It stayed where it belonged, in the Louvre. *His* Louvre. He could have struggled on, the newly restored monarchy was cordial, but V let it be known at court that he had had enough. Ultimately, the time comes to bow out, does it not?

Raising his head from the damp pillow, V is dimly aware that an unfinished letter lies on a table top almost within his reach. There is still so much to tell his *chère* Bettine. He can picture her smiling, raising the page to her lips when she reaches his farewell, as always: 'I embrace you with all my heart.'

The last time they met was on her long awaited trip to Paris, she a widow, arriving with a strapping young son already taller than her dearest Vivente, there to act as chaperone. He folded her in his arms, shaky with emotion and a twinge of rheumatism.

He had rented a villa for her close to the Louvre. She walked with him along the banks of the Seine whose muddy waters aspired to Venetian green in the sunlight, and it was as though their parting had been for no more than a day. Only with their first exchange did they acknowledge the passing of time:

'You haven't changed,' he said.

'You still have your smile,' she said, tactfully, 'your wicked smile. Dearest Vivente . . .'

'Ah, Bettine . . .'

A sadness, a sense of what might have been, that old, unspoken question: *What if?* threw a shadow over that visit filled with laughter and memories; the poignancy of a love remembered with greater force than it now was capable of. Isabella, gently touched by the years, was still beautiful, still the woman in his portrait. He himself, no longer the *cavalier-servant* blazing with passion but an old man with an impressive belly and a bald pate, only the tenderness undiminished. They walked between the Louvre and the Quai Voltaire. And the conversation resumed as though it had never been interrupted. After all, they had been talking, one way and another, for nearly thirty years.

Baptiste has been called away – a tap on the door, a whispered word or two from a maid and he has slipped through the door, vanishing like a shadow, leaving Zenobia pacing the room. She stares out at the dawn sky, like pearl over the Seine, at the paintings on the walls, some she now knows are masterpieces, part of a personal collection that has filled a man's lifetime.

She reaches into her bag and turns over the letters, the grubby, much folded limpness testifying to their age. One she opens up, hardly needing to read lines which she knows by heart: 'In Egypt, one day, we came upon a tomb with a sarcophagus broken open, and one of the guides held up the foot of a mummy: tiny, delicate; the foot surely of a princess, so perfectly formed we knew no shoe had ever constricted its natural shape . . .' She folded the paper, knowing what followed: the letter had recalled Zenobia's tiny feet, unshod when she was found, 'as perfectly formed as that of the Pharoah princess'. Did the nuns provide her with comfortable sandals? the writer wondered. Footwear too rough could misshape her small feet . . .

And now, reluctantly letting go of anger, she sees the words differently: not as the impersonal kindness of a busy gentleman but the tender questioning of a lonely man.

From beyond the salon Zenobia hears murmured voices, hurrying footsteps and the thud of the front door. Then Baptiste comes in. The flesh of his face seems to have fallen in and his eyes are red.

'His condition has changed.'

'Let me examine him!' she says, urgently.

'No.'

'But I could be of help –'

'No.'

She knows what he is leaving unsaid.

'He's dying.' She speaks calmly, to mask more turbulent feelings.

'I have asked the doctor to return immediately.'

'Will you allow me to see him?'

Baptiste is shaking his head again when she adds, 'To say goodbye.'

He stands, motionless, for a moment. Then he gestures towards the door and leads the way. On the walls she sees landscapes of placid cattle and quiet river banks, portraits in which light falls from mysterious sources, brown ink drawings of old men and young warriors. In an embrasure is a marble bust. A table holds a group of tiny Egyptian figurines, pebbles, ancient coins, the skull of a bird.

The mahogany banister is like silk beneath her fingers, the stair treads creak under her feet. Her lungs feel constricted and her heart pounds as though she were running. And now Baptiste has paused, turned back. He ushers her into his master's room.

She looks down at the man in the bed. How often she has pictured this meeting; waiting to confront him, but nothing is as she imagined. In one sense, it is an anticlimax: the secret hope that the father figure would open his arms, enfold her, that has gone. And the anger too. She has no need now, for explanations from this famous old gentleman to whom she is a stranger.

How small he is: his rounded shape barely disturbs the bedcovers. His eyes are closed. She knows that once, long ago, he stood beside an old philosopher's bed, studying the wizened face, and she thinks how much he has grown to resemble his own portrait of the sage of Ferney. Now *he* is the little old man in a nightcap, and hers the young pair of eyes, though more forgiving.

She leans over the bed, her mouth close to his ear. 'Do you remember Zenobia? She thanks you for saving her life.'

Can he hear her? He gives no sign – or does he? Is there a trace of a dimple in the soft pouch of his cheek, or is it just the shadow of a wrinkle? Blinded by tears that take her by surprise, she moves towards the door, guided by Baptiste. She does not see a wide-eyed boy in silk, staring out of the frame into the room.

She makes her way back through the house, past the pictures on the walls, the objects on table tops, shelves and chiffoniers, his cabinet of curiosities, and there she sees it, tiny and delicate: the foot of a mummy, surely an Egyptian princess . . .

All around her is evidence of long-ago and lifelong passions. Everything here speaks of love, of one sort and another. Those lies, the letters, told her so much, after all.

Baptiste, aware of her distress, helps her into her coat, hands her the bag filled with the letters that were so precious to her, and which now, he is sure, she sees as meaningless.

She takes the bag, holds it against her breast, for a moment unable to speak. The room is brightening as the sky grows lighter.

'What will you do now?' Baptiste asks.

'Oh, I shall manage.'

'But in a strange city –'

'I have learned to look after myself.'

He could say to her: there are a few years yet, for the old lion; he glimpses a possibility, a future moment, sees himself curled up in a corner of a study, where a serious young woman looking a little like the Virgin in an Annunciation, though with dark, wiry curls, works at her desk. But a lifetime of diffidence is hard to shake off. He remains silent, and they stand, uncertain how to disengage. She is looking up at him with her alert, questioning eyes.

'You and he between you saved me. He saved me on the island. But then, later . . . I wanted to be worthy of the letters. Your letters. Those lies.'

He says, 'I hope, one day, you will be able to forgive me.'

She reaches out, takes Baptiste's hand in both hers, and raises it briefly to her lips. Astonished, moved almost to tears, he stands with his fingers protecting the hand that has been kissed.

She opens the door, steps out on to the Quai Voltaire and walks quickly away without looking back. He makes for the staircase, and realises, too late, that he does not know how to find her again. Then, at the door of the salon, he pauses, his eye caught by an unfamiliar object occupying one of the chairs.

Zenobia has left behind her fur hat.

V feels a vast weariness pressing down on him, so that even the action of opening his eyes requires an effort. Breathing has become curiously burdensome.

Just a couple of weeks ago he wrote:

'*Ma chère* Bettine, your last letter was so full of youthful elation and life that, reading it, I felt we were both twenty!'

Baptiste must have drawn back the curtains because in the early-morning light he can just see the tops of the trees. Still wet from the rain they sparkle almost silver, like a Tuscan olive grove. Thoughts drift through his mind like ghosts, hard to pin down. The smell of olives . . . leaves . . . Goethe told him once that the colour green was the symbol of hope and of heaven. This should be comforting: he is, after all, an optimist. His head cloudy, he drifts across the canvas of his life touching patches of green: the ribbon of the Nile against the dun sweep of the sand. The jade of the Grand Canal. The gloom of Persephone's glade. His father's Burgundy orchards, the plums weighing down the branches, the long grass smelling of greenness, tasting of greenness; and now he begins to cough, the effort racking his body, breath eluding him. He feels a glass against his lips, the cool blessing of water in his mouth. As ever, Baptiste is with him.

Author's Note

I first came upon Vivant Denon in the pages of Alan Moorehead's *The Blue Nile*, a brief mention of an artist who took part in Bonaparte's Egyptian campaign – 'a civilian, a queer fish', a minor aristocrat who became a trusted friend of the General, later the Emperor. Intrigued, I embarked on a trail that would last for years. I followed in his footsteps wherever possible to see what he saw, not only in Egypt but across Europe. Increasingly drawn in, like all who knew him I was captivated. I read my way through virtually everything written by or about a man who was both a charmer and an enigma. The most outgoing and generous of friends, he withheld a part of himself. *A Conversation on the Quai Voltaire* looks at the life of one who was, it seemed, a happy man.

I have remained faithful to the known facts: born in Chalon-sur-Saône in 1747, De Non (the family name) arrived at the court of Louis XV as a youth. He wrote a play – his sole, disastrous attempt – which ran (briefly) at the Comédie-Française. As a diplomat in St Petersburg he was presented to Catherine the Great, but after an embarrassing episode involving the botched rescue of a French actress incarcerated for spying, he was recalled in disgrace.

On a diplomatic tour of Switzerland he made a detour to meet Voltaire at Ferney and drew a less than flattering picture of the revered philosopher. The letters quoted in the novel are my translations of the barbed correspondence that followed.

Point de Lendemain, his small, erotic masterpiece, was first published – without the author's name – in 1777, the year Denon travelled to Italy, where he remained until 1785, exploring Sicily and the south, before serving at the French Embassy in Naples. The publisher claimed that the novella, with its ambiguous seductress, was based on a true event.

Denon was adored by women and liked by men – even those whose wives were in love with him. By no means conventionally handsome, he had a charm and gift for gossip that made him a salon favourite – though Marie-Antoinette and her sister, the Queen of Naples, were not among his admirers. In 1788 he arrived in Venice and met the Contessa Isabella Teotochi, who remained the love of his life to the end. He was in Venice when the French Revolution erupted, and returned to Paris only after being expelled by the Inquisition under suspicion of being a French spy – an irony, since he himself was on the blacklist of émigré aristocrats.

Returning home, De Non, or rather Denon (the name expediently democratised) was saved from the guillotine after an intervention by the official artist of the Revolution, Jacques-Louis David, and a midnight interview with Robespierre. Denon's drawing of Robespierre's severed head is now in the Metropolitan Museum, New York. Viewable by appointment.

The fateful, serendipitous meeting with Bonaparte in 1797 led him to Egypt, his participation in the campaign, and the book, *Travels in Upper and Lower Egypt*, which set off Egyptomania throughout Europe and brought him immediate world fame.

In 1802 Bonaparte made Denon Director of Museums, and entrusted him with complete responsibility for the Louvre. Later, Napoleon made him a baron of the empire.

He was an artist and engraver, an intrepid traveller, a keen-eyed writer, an obsessive collector with a voracious curiosity. His was a life filled with *objets d'art*: paintings, obelisks, statues. Under his guidance Paris became a treasure house of art taken from France's defeated enemies. He virtually created the modern Louvre; the French collection is housed in the Denon wing, and his name can be seen today, carved in stone on the façade of the museum. After Napoleon's final defeat, Denon retired to the house on the Quai Voltaire filled with his personal art collection, his days enlivened by the friends who continued to seek him out. He was a man of many talents but his masterpiece was his life.

He died in 1825 after catching a chill, his last, unfinished letter to Isabella on his desk. The relationship, concealed even from his close friends, lasted to the end of his life; they had written to one another for nearly thirty years, meeting just a few times after he left Venice. Only in 1987 was a cache of hundreds of letters from Denon to his '*chère* Bettine' discovered and published in France. I have quoted briefly from a few of these, and from the correspondence with Voltaire. In other communications I have imagined what might have been said. The quotes from letters and Denon's other writings are my own translations.

In looking at any life one leaves some doors unopened, there are paths not taken, and this applies to Denon: he was on good terms with his nephew, who helped complete the unfinished History of Art after his uncle's death, and the last years of Denon's life were cheered by the presence of a charming woman – the last of his *amitiés amoureuses*.

Those are the facts, but a novel does not confine itself to the facts. I have not changed what is known of Denon's public life and I send him nowhere he didn't go, but in sifting through his writings, I became aware that behind the hedonist, the art-lover and the adventurer, something lay hidden. Perhaps the incorrigible gossip had taken to heart Voltaire's comment that words are a good way of concealing thoughts. Feelings too, perhaps. There are chinks: hints here and there, from which another picture can be constructed.

Alongside what is known, I could imagine intriguing possibilities, unrecorded companions.

Into the rooms, the gardens, the scorching desert and faraway cities I have introduced imaginary characters, the most important of all, Baptiste, a valet who must in various manifestations have existed, but who for me is embodied in one man.

As for Zenobia, Denon himself, in his Egypt book, described the rescue of a child: his action saved her life. But what became of her? She was a mystery, a figure frozen in a childhood horror. I have given her a name and a destiny.

Author's Acknowledgements

Pitfalls await the author of a biographical fiction like a minefield. For helping me avoid at least some of them, I would like to acknowledge the authors of the publications, historical and contemporary, listed below, and the keen eyes and/or expert knowledge of a number of people. I would like to thank, in France, Marie-Anne Dupuy-Vachey, formerly of the Louvre; Josselyne Michel; Sylvie Taj of the Musée Denon; in Venice, Barone Ernesto Rubin and the Biblioteca Nazionale Marciana; in New York, Eileen Sullivan of the Metropolitan Museum. The London Library was unfailingly helpful.

Friends and family read, criticised and questioned fruitfully, among them Prudence Fay, Harvey Mitchell, Deborah Moggach, Simon Richmond, my agent Clare Alexander, my long-time editor at Chatto, Penelope Hoare, and above all, my husband Theo Richmond, without whose help I might still be staring at an unfinished manuscript.

Among the books I read:

by Vivant Denon:
Voyage dans la Basse et la Haute Egypte pendant les campagnes du général Bonaparte, Vols 1 & 2, 1802
Voyage en Sicile, 1788
Point de Lendemain, 1777
Monuments des arts du dessin chez les peuples tant anciens que modernes, décrits et expliqués par Duval, dit Amaury-Duval, Paris (Brunet-Denon, 1829)

Lettres à Bettine, édition preparée par Piergiorgio Brigliadori, Elena Del Panta, Anna Lia Franchetti, Anne-Marie Pizzorusso, Anne Schoysman, sous la direction de Fausta Garavini (Actes Sud, 1999)

by other authors:
Quand les artistes logeaient au Louvre, Yvonne Singer-Lecocq (Perrin, 1986)
'Vivant Denon' Homme de Lumières 'Ministre des Arts' de Napoléon, Pierre Lelièvre (Picard, 1993)
Vivant Denon ou La Conquête du bonheur, Ibrahim Amin Ghali (Institut Français d'Archeologie Orientale du Caire, 1986)
Vivant Denon: un roman, Claude Lougnot (Editions de L'Armançon; this is a biography, not a novel), 1995
William Beckford, James Lees-Milne
The Memoirs of Mme Elisabeth Louise Vigée-Le Brun (John Hamilton, 1837)
Passages from my Autobiography, Sydney, Lady Morgan (Richard Bentley, 1859)
Memoirs, Sydney, Lady Morgan, 2 vols, W.H. Allen, 1862
France, Sydney, Lady Morgan, 2 vols. (Colburn 1817; Saunders & Ottley 1830)
The Blue Nile, Alan Moorehead (Hamish Hamilton, 1962)
Inventing the Louvre: Art, politics and the origins of the modern museum in eighteenth-century Paris, Andrew McClellan (University of California Press, 1994)
Trophy of Conquest: the Musée Napoléon and the creation of the Louvre, Cecil Gould (Faber, 1965)
Le Cavalier du Louvre, Philippe Sollers (Gallimard, 1995)
Dominique-Vivant Denon, L'oeil de Napoléon, catalogue, musée du Louvre (1999)
'Les Années Italiennes de Dominique Vivant de Non, 1777–1793', Josselyne Michel (*unpublished thesis*)
Description de l'Egypte publié sous les ordres de Napoléon Bonaparte 1808–1822